The Rebel's Daughter

The Woulfes of Loxsbeare – Book 1

By Anita Davison

Amazon Print ISBN 9781772995206

BWL
Books We Love
A quality publisher of genre fiction.
Airdrie Alberta

Cover art by Michelle Lee

Dedication

To the Historical Fiction Critique Group for their invaluable help in telling Helena's story.

Preface

In 1675, a private Whig society met at rooms in the King's Head Inn, Chancery Lane. They called themselves the Green Ribbon Club. On special days their votaries wore ribbons in their hats, of "Leveller Green". Their patron, James Scott, 1st Duke of Monmouth, the eldest illegitimate son of King Charles II, was a regular visitor. He wore "*the green*", and they honoured him by tilting their hats and brims over one eye in the "*Monmouth Cock*", toasting him openly as Prince of Wales.

The members swaggered across the cobblestones of Whitehall, talking of the days when "Jemmy" travelled through the West of England, *"dancing the green"* and *"carrying of the Plate"*.

Toasts were drunk to *"Bless his Majesty and confound the Duke of York"*, with little fear of the pillory or Newgate prison. Monmouth's popularity was high, particularly in the West Country, with its mines and rich woollen trade, owned by non-conformists who had been severely punished for their dissent.

June 11, 1685 was known as the first of the Duking Days, called so because that was the day Monmouth sailed into Lyme Bay, accompanied by eighty-one hopeful men.

His aim was to wrest the British crown from his uncle, James II, the newly crowned king, and within days, six thousand West Countrymen had rallied to his cause. Monmouth was declared "King" in Taunton market place in front of an enthusiastic crowd. But his army was poorly armed and badly disciplined, and many of the promised gentry did not arrive to support him.

In retaliation, James II sent his troops to the West under Lord Feversham, with John Churchill as Second-in-Command.

On the night of July 5, Monmouth launched a surprise attack on the royal army, on marshland outside Bridgwater, in Somerset.

The Battle of Sedgemoor was the last encounter ever fought on English soil.

Chapter 1

Loxsbeare, Exeter, June 1685

Helena clung to the hanging strap of the bulky wooden carriage as it clattered down St David's Hill and took a stomach-lurching turn into Northgate Street.

"Make way there!" the haughty footmen clinging to the rear yelled at a driver of a slow-moving cart who rounded the corner into their path. The journeyman's face, twisted into a snarl, flashed by the window as he hauled his barrow onto the verge, narrowly avoiding a collision.

Helena flinched at the man's distorted features, though she doubted his bad temper was directed at her. However, recent events had sharpened her perception of disrespect, and she expected less than perfect manners from strangers these days. Bayle sat opposite beside her mother, dwarfing her younger brother Henry, who would have surely fidgeted more had there been room.

Their manservant did not usually attend church with the family, though that morning his insistence was accepted by her mother without comment.

Nathan Bayle had been part of Helena's life forever. "Ask Bayle" was the watchword at Loxsbeare, where house servants and estate staff alike called him Master Bayle, whether he was within earshot or not. Only her father ever called him Nathan.

Despite his imposing size, he was a gentle soul, with wavy brown hair slicked back from a high, flat forehead, and expressive brown eyes. His mention of their needing protection puzzled Helena. Or did the entire city know Sir Jonathan Woulfe had gone to join the Duke of Monmouth? Even so, surely there were those among them who would applaud him.

The aromas of hot leather and horses, sunbaked grass and starched linen within that confined space made Helena queasy. Her mother sat, silent and upright, her delicate features turned toward the window. She kept her face averted, but Helena sensed her unease as she tugged repeatedly at a lace lappet dangling from her headdress.

Exeter sported few private carriages; therefore the knot of curious onlookers who watched them roll to a halt on the cobbles outside St Mary Arches Church was little cause for concern.

Bayle did not wait for the footman to let down the wooden step, but leapt onto the ground in one fluid movement. His hand reached back to help the other occupants down.

Helena nodded in greeting to several of their acquaintances at the lytch gate, though, unusually, no one acknowledged her. Instead, self-conscious or scornful eyes raked her as they entered through the church door. A woman started forward, a hand raised in greeting, but at her husband's shake of his head, she hesitated and returned to his side.

Others made no pretense of their revulsion, and hurried inside, hushing children who chattered and pointed.

Seated in the family pew at the front, her mother sat stoically, her gaze fixed on the altar, feigning unawareness of curious eyes, or low murmurings from adjacent pews.

"Let them whisper and gossip," Helena muttered under her breath. She was proud that her menfolk had stood up for their principles and joined the Duke's cause, although she had not slept a full night since they had left for Lyme two weeks before.

Before the service began, the Minister, a humourless man with a weak chin, paused before the altar. "I have been instructed," he said, swallowing, "to read a pronouncement issued by his Majesty." His myopic eyes flicked to the figure of the magistrate who hovered in the transept.

"Didn't he read a declaration last week?" Henry asked, sotto voce.

"That one was Monmouth's," Helena said out of the

corner of her mouth. "The one he read at Taunton saying he was the rightful king."

"I don't understand," he said, louder. "Father said Monmouth didn't seek the throne."

"Hush!" Helena nudged him, deflecting a scowl from their mother.

Triske coughed, and began reading from a rolled parchment. "*His Majesty King James decrees that his nephew, James Scott, Duke of Monmouth, and all his, adherents, abettors and advisers are traitors and rebels*."

As the words reverberated round the church, rage swept through Helena's veins. Traitors? How dare this insipid cleric call Sir Jonathan Woulfe such a thing? Rebels indeed! Didn't he realize Monmouth protected the very church where Triske condemned his loyalty?

The minister reached the end of his short speech. After a nod from the magistrate, he commanded the congregation kneel in prayer. There was the shuffle of feet and the odd self-conscious cough.

Only self-righteous anger sustained Helena through the rest of the interminable service, aware as she was of the whispers and hard looks thrown their way.

Before the last notes of the choristers trailed away, her mother rose abruptly and swept back down the aisle.

Staying close to her skirts. Helena followed, looking neither right nor left, drawn by the shaft of sunlight thrown onto the flagstones by the open church door.

A young friend of Henry's started forward from the last pew, his face alight with greeting. A male hand clamped down on the boy's shoulder and after a brief, fierce exchange, his father guided him away.

Helena narrowed her eyes at the man, angry for Henry, who had harmed no one. Was this what they were to expect from townsfolk who relied on the wool trade provided by Sir Jonathan Woulfe? Were it not for him, where would they find the food for their families, and the clothes on their backs?

Her mother paused to acknowledge Master Triske at the church door, but did not linger to chatter with friends, as was her usual custom. Instead, she walked rapidly back along the path, past a glowering Lord Blanden and his sneering wife, Lady Maude.

The Blandens owned an ancient manor at the top of St David's Hill, and though it had been built before that of the Woulfes, possessed a less noble heritage. According to Helena's father, the respect of the city's citizens had so far eluded the Blandens, a fact which still rankled.

On her seventeenth birthday, Helena had made no objection when her family announced she would be betrothed to their son. She liked Martyn well enough, though she had hoped to feel something other than brotherly affection for the man destined to be her husband.

That her father granted her a generous portion, commensurate with the Woulfe name, went some way to igniting her enthusiasm. Dazzled by his generosity, she had moved through a haze of over-indulgence, exhilarated to be the centre of so much attention.

Despite the heat of the churchyard, Helena shivered at the memory of the morning, in the previous December, when Martyn fell ill during a visit to Loxsbeare. His manservant had carried him to his horse and bore him away before Helena could bid a proper farewell.

In the days that followed, her enquiries as to his well-being were deflected with vague responses, until a messenger arrived from Blanden Manor to tell them Martyn was dead.

Relieved the marriage would not go ahead, guilt made Helena exaggerate her tears.

Lord Blanden had appeared more frustrated than grief-stricken, an observation made by her mother, who claimed he had instigated the betrothal so he might bask in the reflected glory of the Woulfes' reputation.

Recalling her mother's scorn, Helena hurried through the sun-filled churchyard, conscious of Blanden's sharp eyes boring into her back, all the way to the carriage.

"What do you suppose he wants?" Henry cocked his chin at the black-garbed City Magistrate, who strode grim-faced down the path in their direction, a hand raised to command their attention.

Bayle rapped the roof smartly and the vehicle lurched into Fore Street, leaving the Magistrate standing in the middle of the road, scowling.

"His duty can wait a little longer," Bayle muttered.

Helena gave him a thin smile, unable to bring herself to ask what that duty might be.

The carriage rumbled beneath the stone gatehouse over the north gate and climbed the steep Longbrook, the precarious sway forcing Helena to hang on to the strap over the door, to prevent colliding with her brother.

Henry remained silent during the short but oppressive journey home, his chin propped in one hand, his elbow on the sill. He would never complain of his treatment at the church, though Helena knew he felt the rejection keenly. She pouted and blew air upwards creating a breeze that lifted the "favorites" at her temples. She would be glad to get out of this stifling coach, albeit suspecting the rest of their Sunday would be no more restful.

* * *

Helena strolled the lawn in the garden, tearing off leaves from the thick hedge, only to drop them at her feet as she walked. Her mother relaxed on a bench piled with cushions set against the garden wall, while their steward Lumm played a game of ring taw with Henry.

"Shouldn't that game be played on a hard surface, and standing up, Henry?" Helena asked, irritated by Lumm's attitude. Their steward would never have lounged on the grass so casually in her father's company. His shirt lay open at the neck and he had removed his cravat. Even the buttons on his jerkin were undone.

"It's too hot to go racing about," Henry answered. "Besides, I'm winning." His marble hit Lumm with a crack and sent it out of the makeshift circle of stones they had arranged on the grass.

Defeated, Helena turned away, waving her feather fan lazily in front of her face, the fronds catching on her damp skin. The heavy fragrance from the overblown eglantine blooms clinging to the wall threatened to give her a headache. A dribble of sweat trickled between her shoulders, and her skirt clung to the back of her legs. A housemaid appeared from the rear kitchen door carrying a pewter tray on which were a jug and goblets. She crossed the lawn and set it down on the stone table between the three curved stone benches like a miniature amphitheatre.

"Thank you, Milly," Helena said, eying the tray. "I thought my tongue would shrivel up in this heat."

"Pity you can't sweeten it a little too." Henry laughed at his own joke. Lumm punched his arm playfully.

Helena swallowed her sharp retort, suddenly aware she had been brittle, and maybe snappish, lately. Who could blame her? With nothing to do but household chores best fit for servants, and waiting for news, no wonder she was bad-tempered.

A window on the floor above opened. A hand appeared, waved a white cloth, then pulled the window shut again with a bang.

"I wonder where Father is now." Helena asked no one in particular.

"Seeing off King James' men, I expect," Henry said. Teeth gritted, he spun his marble as he threw, sending Lumm into the longer grass. The steward groaned, and Lady Elizabeth clapped politely.

Helena caught her brother's set jaw, something no one else appeared to notice. He was almost sixteen, hardly a child any more. Yet their father had almost laughed when Henry asked to go with him to Lyme.

For weeks beforehand, Father and Uncle Ned had shut themselves up for hours with a succession of anonymous visitors he forbade anyone to see, much less ask about.

Helena had tried to listen at the door once, but heard only a low murmur of male voices, the chink of glass on glass, and an occasional short laugh. When the distinctive sound of a chair being scraped back had threatened discovery, she had turned on her heels to flee, barging straight into Lumm.

Strong hands had closed on her upper arms, and his eyes had danced with amusement. "I beg your pardon, Mistress."

Her thoughts raced in search of a credible reason for her being crouched outside the door. She squirmed from his grasp.

Lumm's smile remained when he dropped his hands, as if what he held had no more effect on him than a sack of flour. "May I assist you, Mistress?" he had said with a smile, reaching past her for the handle.

Mumbling that she had changed her mind, Helena retreated. With a mocking bow, he disappeared into the room, blocking her view of the occupants.

His triumphant laugh, followed by Henry's yell of protest, brought her back to the present with a jolt. She studied the steward from the corner of her eye, resentful of his easy smiles and the way his thick brown hair hung loose on his broad shoulders. Aaron should be here, laughing and playing marbles with Henry, not him.

As if he sensed her thoughts, Lumm's gaze slid toward her, and he gave a slow wink.

Annoyed he had caught her looking at him, Helena turned away, just as Bayle hurried across the grass. His frantic face and the papers clutched in one hand confirmed her suspicion that his return to the city that day had little to do with obtaining supplies, as he had said. On a Sunday? Did he think her so easily fooled?

Her mother's face tensed at his fixed expression. "What news, Bayle?" she asked, pointing to the bench opposite her.

He sketched a bow as he sat, then removed his wide-brimmed felt hat, leaving a ridge in his hair. "Well, don't keep us in suspense!" Henry demanded, his tone reminiscent of their brother Aaron. "What does the newssheet say?"

Bayle swiped a hand across his brow, smudging a white streak in the dust there.

He offered Lady Elizabeth the newssheet, but she waved it away. "You may as well read it to us," she said, sighing.

"According to this, Lord Feversham and the King's men have reached Somerset, my lady." He waved the page instead, showing he knew the contents by heart.

"Feversham is in command?" Lumm looked up in surprise. "Hah! John Churchill will feel slighted by that." He handed Bayle a cup of elderflower water from the tray. "Being overlooked in favour of a Huguenot is a blatant insult."

Helena brought her cup to her lips, then grimaced, lowering it again and picking flecks of petals from the surface. Bands of Huguenots arrived in Exeter each day with stories of families in France being dragged apart, with children of Protestant parents forced to accept the Roman faith. She and her mother distributed alms to them sometimes at St Olive's, these days referred to as the French Church.

"If King James is a Catholic." Henry shielded his eyes with the newssheet Bayle handed him. "Does that mean we all have to be Papists?" He had discarded the peruke and tied his sandy hair back into a queue. Helena liked him better that way.

"I fear, Master, that if he isn't stopped." Lumm rolled into a crouch, his arms wrapped round his knees. "What is happening in France may affect us here, too."

Helena closed her eyes briefly, the sun glowing red behind her eyelids. Isn't that why her father had gone to join Monmouth? To stop King James turning everyone into Papists?

"Perhaps not that," Bayle said, his voice soft. "From what I hear, he was more in favour of removing the restrictions on Papists. Give them equal status to Anglicans."

"Huh!" Henry snorted. "How can they have equal status? This is a Protestant country." Henry quoted their father word for word. Did he even fully understand what he was saying?

Helena opened her eyes and caught the look of understanding that passed between the steward and manservant. Circumstances had wrought a change between them these last weeks, where Bayle deferred to Lumm on duties he had performed since he was a boy, and Lumm, for his part, often sought the older man's advice. Lumm might wear more velvet and fine linen than any steward she had seen, but despite her misgivings, their combined presence was reassuring.

"Monmouth and Churchill used to be such good friends," Mother said, her voice low and distracted. "I met him once, such a handsome man." Mother gave a sigh, her eyes empty. Helena was surprised she had been listening. Since her father had left, Mother's concentration had suffered. Her conversation had become discordant and rambling at times, or she panicked so badly she had to be given sleeping draughts by her maid Ruth.

"Says here," Henry read from the newssheet, "that Monmouth and his rebels have gained possession of Axminster, and saw off Albemarle's militia outside the town." He pushed strands of damp sandy hair away from his forehead.

"Don't call them rebels, Henry," Helena snapped, nibbling at a thumbnail. "I hate that expression."

"When they reached Taunton," Henry continued, ignoring her, "the townsfolk lined the streets to welcome the duke. A party of schoolgirls presented him with a pennant." He slapped the page, grinning. "You see, Mother? They love Monmouth."

"It's not all good news, Master Henry." Bayle batted away a persistent fly with a hand the size of a small shovel. "There was that skirmish at Ashill."

Helena jerked up her head and stared at him. "What skirmish?"

"A party of Lord Oxford's Horse tried to roust the rebel outposts." A rivulet of sweat worked its way down Bayle's forehead. "Monmouth lost four of his men, and many were wounded." Lumm offered him a lace kerchief, but at Bayle's dismissive snort, returned it to his pocket with a flourish. Lumm's cavalier ways had always been a source of amusement between them.

“Did the rebels kill any troopers?” Henry asked, tugging a wide leaf from a nearby shrub and chewing the stem.

Helena winced but chose not to reprimand him again. Bayle already knew she was a trial to her parents and suspected Lumm was fast coming to the same conclusion. “Not subservient enough for an unmarried girl,” she had heard Bayle say once.

“They lost three men.” Lumm leaned back on one elbow. “Churchill’s Lieutenant Monoux got a pistol shot through the head for his trouble.”

Henry raised a fist, and gave a loud whoop, which was greeted by amused laughter from the two men.

“There wasn’t supposed to be any fighting.” Helena slumped down on the nearest bench, replacing her empty cup on the tray. “Father said Monmouth was to take a contingent of men to London and demand King James establish the supremacy of the Anglican Church. Now all the talk is of armies marching and who has claimed which town…it’s as if we are at war.”

“Mistress Helena,” Lumm said gently. “The king was hardly going to sit back and let his nephew usurp his throne.”

“That wasn’t the plan.” Helena brought her fist down on her thigh. She recalled the day a messenger who came to tell them Monmouth had landed at Lyme with eighty men. No dark, brooding stranger riding a sweating horse into the courtyard under cover of night, but a nondescript labourer on an old carthorse.

How delighted her father had been to receive his summons to Lyme. Uncle Edmund and Aaron could hardly wait long enough to saddle their horses before they were gone.

The snap-snap-snap of a startled pigeon crashed through the canopy above brought back her thoughts to the present.

“Helena’s right,” her mother’s voice held tears. “They should never have challenged the king. He’ll crush them.”

“Monmouth’s cause might still prevail, my lady. The

people still want him," Bayle said

"Don't try to humour me!" Mother snapped, her eyes flashing now where they had been lifeless a second before. "King James has declared Monmouth a traitor. His own nephew—and he wants him dead! What will he do to my husband for the same offence?"

She grabbed the newssheet from Henry and thrust it under the manservant's chin. "Monmouth has accused King James of killing his father and appropriating his crown while the rightful heir was out of the country." She jabbed the sheet with a fingernail, reading aloud. "And here, it says that his nephew must be, *'seized and apprehended, together with all his, adherents, abettors, and advisers.'"* She flung the pages onto the grass. "They're signing their own death warrants."

"But Monmouth says…." Henry began, but she cut him off with a snort.

"Monmouth says," she mimicked. "James the Second is our crowned King, and Catholic or not, anyone who says otherwise is putting themselves on the side of the devil."

"Mother!" Helena's stomach lurched. How could she talk of Father in that way?

"What are we to do?" Mother muttered, her eyes darting round as if on the lookout for eavesdroppers. "We'll lose everything, and I'll never see my husband again. We're doomed."

Henry's face blanched and he eased away from her reaching hand, clawing at his sleeve.

"Bayle!" Helena rose, a hand flapping toward him. "Do something!"

However, it was Lumm who scrambled to his feet, calling to a passing servant. "Fetch Lady Elizabeth's maid."

Tense moments passed until Ruth arrived at what passed for a run on her tree-trunk legs. She swept the occupants of the garden with accusing eyes, then ushered the distraught woman through the rear doors into the house, slamming them shut.

Helena stared at her lap, dismayed at how Mother's outbursts had become more frequent in their vehemence, though what she said made awful sense. To the world outside Loxsbeare, Sir Jonathan Woulfe was a traitor. Traitors were executed in the most horrible way; their heads displayed on pikes on London Bridge, their possessions seized by the crown, and their families disgraced.

Her throat felt dry and tears threatened. She palmed them away, unwilling to let Henry see her cry. What would happen to her father and Uncle Ned? Aaron was only twenty; his life had hardly begun. What sort of future could any of them have with their father disgraced and their name sullied?

Then her fears turned inward, and her selfish bone intruded. Would any respectable man want to marry his son to a traitor's daughter?

Chapter 2

In the space of a few days, the weather changed from blistering heat that dried up ponds and cracked the earth to relentless rain that battered the standing corn to the ground. Damp crept into every crevice of the house, tracing patches of green slime on north facing walls, dragging Helena's spirits even lower.

During a brief lull in a summer storm, a visitor trotted his sorrel Percheron through the manor gates, and dismounted. Familiar with its surroundings, the sturdy horse stood passive, and would likely remain so until he was led away.

"Good Morrow, Master Ffoyle." Helena strode forward in greeting. "And how is this soft old boy today?" She cupped the horse's wide muzzle in both hands, and was rewarded with a gentle whicker.

As tall as Bayle, though he carried less bulk, Samuel Ffoyle's smiles were infrequent, the sound of his raised voice even more so. He always dressed in unadorned earth colors, which Helena's father always said was less a religious display inherited from his Puritan parents than his aversion to wasting time visiting tailors. The changing times of Charles Stuart's reign had fostered a close relationship between Samuel Ffoyle, sheep-farmer-turned-merchant, and Sir Jonathan Woulfe, landed gentry and courtier.

"A good man in a crisis," her father always said of him.

"Mistress Helena." Samuel Ffoyle inclined his head, though did not slow his stride toward the front door.

Helena hurried to keep pace with him.

The footman bowed the visitor into the great hall but refused Helena's offer to sit.

"You are an honest Anglican, are you not, Master

Ffoyle?" Helena asked, drawing his attention away from a painting of a long dead Woulfe wearing a ruff he must have seen a hundred times before.

Instead of an answer, Samuel's eyes swiveled to her face and remained there, waiting.

"I know you are, of course," she said, aware of having already stepped beyond the boundaries of propriety. "Yet you chose not to go to Somerset and uphold that faith?"

His eyes widened fractionally, then with sigh, he placed his hat on a table. "I have a wife and six children to protect, and a large farm to run. Indeed, my eldest sons would have taken themselves off to Somerset by now, had I not reminded them of their duty."

"You forbade them to go?" Helena pictured the faces of Elias, who was Aaron's age, and Seth, a year older than Henry.

"When they have households of their own to manage, they will be free to abandon them as they choose."

About to voice a disrespectful retort, Helena clamped her lips together, resentful of the fact the Ffoyle offspring were safe at home while her menfolk were not. It didn't seem fair. Before she could voice her feelings, the rustle of heavy silk heralded the arrival of her mother. With a flick of her hand, she indicated Helena should withdraw.

She was about to obey, but at the last second took the window seat, telling herself she would accept whatever punishment Mother would mete out later.

Samuel perched awkwardly on a spindle-legged chair, his knees angled outward from the narrow squab.

"Lady Elizabeth," he began slowly, as if unsure how to approach the subject, "King James has demanded Prince William of Orange return the Scots Brigade from Holland to add to the forces against Monmouth."

"Prince William did not acquiesce, surely?" she said, her manner calmer than she had been lately. "He supports Monmouth, who was brought up with the Princess Mary. They are cousins, and very close."

"The prince can hardly refuse." Samuel sighed. "Those troops were on loan only in his fight with the French. They are King James' men after all."

Lady Elizabeth's delicate hands fluttered to her throat. "Do you think Monmouth knows?"

"If we know, then we must assume he does too." Samuel shrugged his shoulders resignedly.

"Also…the news from Scotland is…disappointing." Samuel rubbed his hands along his thighs. "A strong militia presence ensured the few men who dared turn out in support of the Earl of Argyll. He managed to elude the militia for a couple of weeks, but few gathered to his standard, for fear of reprisals. He's been arrested and taken to Edinburgh." He closed his eyes and exhaled.

"Argyll made Monmouth promise not to declare himself King," Mother said, demonstrating a rare moment of lucidity.

"He was, my lady. However," Samuel paused. "In Cheshire too, the number who arrived in support of the duke fell short of that anticipated."

"I see." Lady Elizabeth stared blankly, the colour draining from her already pale face.

"The rebels are having a rough time in Somerset," Samuel went on. "Their supplies are nearly gone, and rumour has it that they have resorted to pilfering and free quartering on the locals."

"I doubt that made them very popular," Lady Elizabeth gave a snort. "Is it true King James has pardoned those rebels who have agreed to return to their homes?" She rocked back and forth in her seat.

It was a bad sign. Samuel saw it too, and winced.

"How many have left the rebel army?" Helena demanded.

Samuel swung his head in Helena's direction, his eyes sad. "Hundreds maybe. Possibly a thousand."

Lady Elizabeth's delicate fingers picked at the lace on her cuffs until it tore, and for long seconds no one spoke.

Helena's glanced out of the window. How much bad news could there be? Beyond the leaded panes, slate clouds gathered their skirts to bustle away and deluge another part of the Devon hills. The silence stretched, broken by

Samuel's cough as he rose and bowed. "I must take my leave."

"So soon?" Lady Elizabeth looked distraught. "I hoped you would dine with us."

"Forgive me, my lady, but the roads will be quiet at this time of day, and the fewer who know I am here, the better for you."

Helena followed him out, and loitered beside the open front door, as a groom brought Samuel's horse to the mounting block.

She frowned, wondering why the lad was not Parry, then remembered with a pang that the cheerful boy with the permanent grin had gone to join the rebels.

Helena retreated, then paused as Lumm appeared from the stables and engaged Samuel in conversation.

Helena watched, bemused by the intensity of their exchange. She would have given half her dowry to know what they were talking about.

If she still had a dowry.

* * *

"You didn't show Lady Elizabeth the other newssheet then, Tobias?" Samuel nodded to the folded pages that peeked from the steward's jerkin, signalling to the boy who held his horse to wait.

"What good would it have served?" Tobias glanced down, but didn't remove the paper from his coat. "Monmouth has marched toward Bath."

"Bath, eh? Samuel stroked his chin. "A brave move, since the Royalist troops are there."

Tobias shrugged. "They were attacked at Norton Saint Philip by the Duke of Grafton's troops."

"Grafton fighting his half-brother," Samuel mused, nodding. "I expect he's eager to prove disloyalty doesn't run in the family. What happened?"

"A disaster for both sides." Tobias's gaze raked the courtyard. "The report says they were penned in by the hedges, and that blood ran like a river down the lane where they fought."

Samuel winced. "I suppose there's no way of knowing the names of those killed?"

Tobias shook his head.

The lad holding his horse shuffled and the animal whickered, stamping his massive hooves.

"Trust you to use a working horse as a personal mount," Tobias reached to stroke the horse's soft muzzle.

"I like him, he's slow, steady, and nothing will topple him. He suits. Now what else do you have to tell me?"

"Monmouth cut his losses and retreated to Frome," Tobias went on. "They got as far as Trowbridge, but the royal troops men cut off their escape route."

"Where's Monmouth now?" Samuel asked, frowning.

"The report ends before that." Tobias tapped his pocket. "Though gossip in the city says he reached Wells two days ago. The rebels damaged the west front of the cathedral. They tore lead from the roof and smelted it into bullets."

"The fools!" Samuel mounted the block and slipped into the saddle. "Monmouth won't get to Bristol now, let alone London."

"Gets worse," Tobias added. "They broke the windows and smashed the organ and the furnishings. They even stabled their horses in the nave." He squinted up at the mounted man, shielding his eyes from the sun with one hand.

Samuel adjusted his hat before replying. "You're right not to upset Lady Elizabeth further, Tobias." He turned the horse toward the gate. "However, if I were you, I'd keep that newssheet away from Mistress Helena. She'll be asking awkward questions soon enough."

"She distrusts me, that one." Tobias pulled a face.

"She doesn't know you, Tobias."

"Doesn't know who I am, you mean?" His voice held bitterness.

Samuel turned his horse away, not prepared to discuss the subject further. Not at the present moment.

Tobias rushed forward and grabbed the reins, halting

the horse who champed noisily at the bit. “I would never have raised the subject in Sir Jonathan’s presence. But now?”

“It’s a bad time.” Samuel grimaced, urging his horse forward. He had reached the gates before he heard Tobias’s angry shout.

“It’s always a bad time!”

At the top of South Street, Samuel slowed his horse to a canter, his thoughts dwelling on recent events. Two hundred Whigs had been arrested in London, among them prominent cloth workers and members of Samuel’s guild. He had written letters of protest on their behalf, while reassuring the City Magistrates of his own loyalty to the king despite his own Whig leanings.

Unsurprisingly, Samuel had come under scrutiny since the Duke’s landing, although he chose not to mention that to Lady Elizabeth. His father had been a Puritan, but disinclined to martyrdom, Samuel had furrowed a less controversial path. Although he still had to watch out for accusing fingers.

There would always be those willing to throw suspicion on others, to further their own ambitions.

With a nod to the porter at the West gate, Samuel urged the plodding horse on the Exe Bridge. Entering St Thomas, he pulled his cloak tighter against a gust of damp wind, and peered beneath the rim of his hat at the darkening sky. Leaning forward, he patted the animal’s steaming neck, murmuring reassurances.

The big old horse didn’t like the rain.

An image of Tobias’s discontented face floated unbidden into his head. Samuel sighed, recalling a year before when he had come across him lounging on the cobbles outside the *Ship Inn* in St Martins Lane; a restless air and an eye for mischief.

Over a jug of fine ale, Samuel had struck up a conversation with the landlord.

“Tell me, Jim,” he lifted his jug towards Tobias, who stood with his arm round a serving girl, making her blush. “Why’s your Tobias hanging about with nothing to do but annoy the wenches?"

Jim's eyes slid sideways resignedly. "Aye, he's a puzzle that." He poured a jug of ale and served another customer, then balanced an elbow on the back of the chair opposite Samuel. "Too proud fer this place, and restless. And him all o' three and twenty. Dunno what's to become o' him."

Samuel nodded, thoughtful, just as Emily Lumm sashayed into his line of sight.

"Master Ffoyle." She bobbed a slow curtsey, which for all its simplicity held a solicitation. She impaled him with her brown-eyed stare in a look Samuel recalled from her childhood. As if she knew something, but had promised not to tell. The years had given Tobias's mother a more voluptuous body, but she still possessed the bearing of a girl.

And that look.

After a brief word with Sir Jonathan, Tobias had been installed at Loxsbeare in the post of steward.

His new employer found the young man entertaining and intelligent, with ideas of his own to improve the estate. Even Bayle accepted him as an asset without resentment, and Henry certainly liked him.

The older son, Aaron, didn't seem to take much notice. His position as crown prince of Loxsbeare was secure, giving him no reason to be on the lookout for usurpers.

Helena, on the other hand, cast suspicious eyes in the direction of Tobias. Headstrong young man that he was, Tobias teased the girl without a thought for how she, or the other servants, might view such forward behavior.

What did his future hold, should Sir Jonathan not return?

Fat drops of rain drummed onto Samuel's cloak. His horse nickered and shook his mane, sending an arching spray of water into the air.

Samuel sighed again, too weary to tackle that particular problem today, and gave himself up to the old horse's canter until he turned into his own gate.

* * *

Jonathan's boots scuffed the well-worn steps, an occasional clang of a sword against stone followed by a muffled curse, audible from below. Evidently, he was not the only one who found St Mary's church tower a hard climb.

Below the tower, the River Parret snaked like molten silver through the centre of Bridgwater, toward the flat expanse of marshland. Jonathan bowed to the man in head-to-toe black at the parapet, the garter star emblazoned on his breast. He stood taller than most men, with the air of someone used to the subservience of others. In his case, though, his status had been achieved later than most.

The wind lifted his black periwig from his shoulders, threatening to tear his wide brimmed hat from his head and launching it into Cornhill, below.

On any other day this would have amused him. Yet today, his handsome features twisted into an expression of irritation. James, Duke of Monmouth was a troubled man in no mood for levity.

Lord Grey handed the Duke a spyglass, as Captain Hucker and Major Wade emerged through the low door onto the roof.

"Would you say they are about three miles away?" Jonathan asked, his spyglass trained onto the rows of white tents dotted with red coated figures spread on the moor; men Monmouth once commanded to defeat the Scots Covenanters at Bothwell Bridge in seventy-nine. Friends who were now his mortal enemies.

"More like four," Lord Grey said. "Our plan might work."

"What might work?" Jonathan folded his arms across his chest and regarded Grey with suspicion, his normal stance since he had learned how manipulative the man could be.

"Attack under cover of darkness." Gray's unctuous voice made Jonathan squirm. "If we surprise them, we have a good chance at victory."

"Better, maybe, but not good," Jonathan muttered. "What about the original plan to blockade the town?" This, too, seemed an equally bad move, as the townsfolk were unlikely to commit their cattle and grain to what they must by now consider a lost cause.

"A ploy only, Jon." Grey waved a dismissive hand. "Attack is our best option."

Jonathan fell silent, resigned to the fact that Grey always spoiled for a fight. With flattery and false assurances, he had swayed Monmouth to his way of thinking. The Duke still believed they could reach London, where, Grey had convinced him, the Capital would welcome him as their king.

"Feversham's men are well-trained, many with battle experience," Jonathan said. "Churchill is a good soldier, and then there are Percy Karce's men." Those infamous 'Lambs'; men who wouldn't be cowed by a bunch of farmers wielding nothing more threatening than sharpened scythes attached to pitchforks, though Jonathan forbore to say so aloud.

"They look to have no more men than I." Monmouth swung his spyglass over the horizon "However, I know those men. They will fight."

"Tell His Majesty what you told me." Lord Grey beckoned to a nervous-looking young man in shabby clothes who hung back by the tower door. He had given his name as Godfrey, and claimed he possessed useful intelligence.

Jonathan flicked Grey a glance of distaste. He wished the man wouldn't insist on calling Monmouth that. Wasn't the duke already full enough of his own importance as it was? He had even started retelling the story of Lucy Walter having married King Charles when a prince in exile, a claim dismissed as lies by his father, King Charles, years before.

Godfrey crept forward, kneading his felt hat in both hands. "There be two thousand on the moor, sir—Your Majesty. 'Bout a thousand in Middlezoy and the same in Otherey. But they don't know the ditches like I does." He sidled closer to the Duke. "If you makes for 'ere, sir." Godfrey dragged a grubby finger across a hand drawn map pulled from inside his coat, "…go along the old Bristol road towards Bawdrip, and then turn south along Bradney Lane and Marsh Lane. It's the longer route, but your chances of being seen are low." His dirty-nailed finger stabbed at the page. "Here be the Black Ditch, which is marked by a large rock. I could get you the other side of the Bussex Rhine and right into their camp before they know what's happenin'."

Monmouth lowered his spyglass and stared at the man down his nose, then raised the glass again. "The horses are set far apart from the foot. If we can infiltrate their lines and keep them apart, we may have the advantage. Our spies tell us their discipline is not good."

"Indeed not," Captain Hucker gasped, still winded from the climb. "They drink themselves into a stupor on local cider every night."

"No guards have been posted," Nathaniel Wade added. "Though they have guns laid out on the town road."

"We could avoid those by making a detour north of Chedzoy." Grey arched a brow at each of them, looking more sly than reassuring. "Our chances of victory are doubled."

"The Cavalry could lead, your Majesty." Gray's lip curled into a leering half-smile.

Besides, by now the whole countryside knew what they were about. Perhaps anything was better than dodging Ogelthorpe and his troop through the countryside, until they ended up back at Lyme where they started, or being captured and hanged by Feversham's men.

Nothing had gone the way he had thought it would. They should have been in London by now, cheered on by an enthusiastic crowd, not still being harried across Somerset by the King's troops. Besides, his lodgings were squalid, and the landlord sour-tempered, although more civil since being assured his guest intended paying his bill.

Most of their men were camped out in peoples' houses, or in fields sodden by days of rain, with no shelter at all, ransacking the local farms for horse feed. No wonder Bridgwater had been less than happy to receive them.

Their march into Taunton had been the high point of the expedition. The celebration that followed at Captain Hacker's house was reminiscent of those heady days of the *Green Ribbon Club*, when they would drink the night away at the Kings Head, speculating on a world under Monmouth's kingship.

Those days were an illusion, Jonathan realised now, and King Charles, aware of his bastard son's involvement in a traitorous society, had protected him, and in doing so, his friends too.

It was one thing drinking to Monmouth's health and damning the Duke of York when King Charles was still alive. Now, King James had the perfect opportunity to exact his revenge on the nephew he hated.

Jonathan glanced across at Monmouth, whose head was bent over Geoffrey's plans, a frown on his handsome face. Was his resolve still strong? Jonathan's brother, Edmund, seemed to think so, but then for years Edmund had been straining against his domestic tethers in search of adventure.

Now, they were cornered, unable to get to Bristol, let alone London, with that Frenchman out on the moor biding his time.

"We shall do it." Monmouth snapped the spyglass shut for the third time in as many minutes. "That Huguenot would never expect it." He handed the spyglass over his shoulder without looking to see who took it.

"We march tonight at midnight, with strict orders to maintain total silence. Every man is charged with dispatching the man beside him with a knife, should he utter a sound to betray our presence." He looked into each of their faces in turn, gave a curt nod, then clattered down the tower steps, the others following.

"How many of the men do even have knives?" Jonathan muttered. Sighing, he pushed himself away from the wall and set off back to the inn and his flea-ridden bed in the hope of a few hours' sleep.

Chapter 3

Henry leaned against a wooden stall and watched his sister through a crack in the half-closed door, as she stomped over clumps of wet hay scattered across the yard.

"She doesn't know I'm here, does she?" Bayle said from behind him.

Henry jumped and swung round, having thought himself alone. "No, she's going toward the kitchens."

Bayle half rose in a stance that preceded a bow, halted by Henry's impatient gesture that sent him back down again. Henry sported more manure on his clothes than a cowshed, and had hay sticking out of his shirt. This was hardly a time for formalities.

"I suppose I cannot avoid her forever." Bayle hooked his foot round a stool and dragged it toward him, gesturing Henry to sit.

"What does she want?" Henry asked, straddling the stool.

"She read something about Colonel Percy Kirke in the *Gazette*. When asked, Lumm said he knew nothing about the man, so he warned me she would search me out instead."

"Who is he? This Kirke, and what do you know about him?"

Bayle picked up a small tool and applied it to a piece of leather.

"The Queen Dowager brought Tangier as part of her dowry when she married King Charles."

"I know. Father told me about Tangier, though I don't recall much. It's a far-off place he said, very hot, and with savage people."

"No more than our own," Bayle said under his breath, then continued, louder. "Kirke maintained the garrison there, in command of the regiment. Their emblem was a Paschal Lamb, which earned them the nickname "Karce's Lambs".

"A strange emblem for fighting men," Henry mused, frowning.

"I believe the Lamb is from the house of Braganza, and signifies Christian men against the Infidels."

"Don't the Moroccans and Berbers call us infidels too?" Henry asked, aware he was being provoking. However, at least his present audience wouldn't threaten him with a whipping for insolence.

"I believe so, Master, though if you don't mind, I won't argue the point with you just now." He twisted the softened leather round his fingers, snapping it gently. "As I was saying, Kirke has a fearsome reputation. His men are brutal, taking pride in their savagery."

"How do you know that?" he whispered, wishing now he had not asked.

"I grew up with a man who served with 'im. He's been dead these two years." He shrugged, as if this fact made a difference. "Karce's a drunken brute, in charge of a drunken regiment, who would kill a man merely to test the edge of his weapon." Henry's horrified gasp was smothered too late. "Don't listen to me, Master," he rushed on. "Who knows the truth of it? When a man's belly is full of cider he'll say anything."

"And these Tangier soldiers? They are to fight against Monmouth?" Henry fought to keep his voice calm.

"Aye," Bayle exhaled slowly, muttering, "and may God protect those poor boys."

The smell of manure clogged Henry's throat, and the need for fresh, untainted air became suddenly urgent.

He leapt to his feet, sending the stool over behind him and headed for the house, ignoring Bayle's voice calling after him.

He slammed the heavy oak door behind him, and took the stairs two at a time, startling a maid on her way down.

In the comparative safety of his room, he wrenched off his filthy work clothes and hurled them into a corner for a maid to rescue. The words, "*a drunken brute, in charge of a drunken regiment*" kept repeating in his head as he struggled into a clean shirt and wrestled with the drawstrings.

Father may be able to fight Karce's men, and perhaps Uncle Edmund could handle himself against soldiers, though neither had ever been in a real fight before. What of Aaron? His big brother's only experience with a sword had been played out on the grass on the Weare Cliffs. Surely in a proper battle he would be killed.

His panic for his family was slowly replaced by burning shame that Bayle's talk of the Tangiers brought such overpowering relief for himself. How he had argued and ranted with both his father and uncle against being left at home, insisting he could fight as well as any of them.

"There'll be no fighting," his father had laughed. "This isn't a battle. It's more of a protest under arms."

Father had been wrong. They all had been. King James wasn't sending veteran fighters to meet a protest.

* * *

On his way downstairs again, Henry paused on the half-landing. His mother would be with Ruth at this time of day, and the Great Hall was a lonely place on one's own.

Instead, he retreated to the window seat, one leg bent and his arms wrapped around his knee.

A heavy rainstorm had moved west, changing to cloudless heat in the space of an hour, the stillness disturbed by an occasional call of a bird or bleat of a sheep from the fields beyond the courtyard walls.

Henry came to a decision. He would keep his cowardice to himself in front of Mother and Helena. How else could he describe the giddy relief he felt at not being expected to wield a sword against another Englishman?

The sound of Helena's familiar footsteps as she climbed the stairs brought a smile to his lips. "I'm convinced Bayle is hiding from me." She threw herself onto the seat beside him, forcing him to budge to make room. "They treat me like a child still, when I am quite old enough to be an adult. I mean, I was betrothed this time last year, I—Henry, are you listening to me?" She nudged him roughly.

Her voice droned on beside him like a demented bee. She jutted her chin close to his face. "I said, have you noticed how bad-tempered Mother is lately?"

"She misses Father." Henry sighed, not looking at her. "All this talk of fighting makes it worse."

"I'm aware of that. I'm not dense," Helena complained. "Even Lumm is making himself scarce."

"Tobias is busy. He doesn't have time for idle chat."

"Why do you always call him by his given name?" Helena asked, her head tilted to one side.

Henry shrugged. "He calls me Henry, so I pay him the same compliment."

"Exactly. As if it's necessary to compliment a servant." She sniffed. "It's not as if you need a friend, you have plenty of those, with your sunny nature."

Henry was about to ask whether she had noticed any of these 'friends' coming to call, of late, but restrained himself. The only visitor they had had in the previous month was Samuel Ffoyle.

"To refer to your first question," he began. "I *have* noticed Mother's bad temper. She's either raging round the house, or in her chamber, sunk in apathy. I don't know what to make of her. She ordered me to my room earlier, for no reason at all."

"Is that where you're supposed to be now?" Helena slanted a look at him through long lashes, her pigeon-wing eyes flecked with yellow.

Her chestnut hair was wet and hung down her back in waves. Then he remembered she had had to wash it after an incident in the dairy with a cow that had a particularly good aim. The memory made him smile, though he had more sense than to refer to it. "She won't care where I am," he snapped. "She spends all her time with Ruth these days."

He continued watching Helena from the corner of his eye, surprised at how he had forgotten how good-looking she was—for a sister.

She didn't walk; she glided. She had a unique smile that began slowly, like a flower opening up. Then as you watched, it spread over her face, until you realised you were smiling too.

"You miss her don't you?" Helena's voice dropped to a near whisper.

He shrugged. "How can I miss her, when she's still here?"

"Because I do, too." Her startling grey eyes looked suspiciously moist, and she kept sniffing. He suppressed an impulse to wrap his free arm round her, afraid he might open the floodgates for them both. Instead, he leaned back against the cushions with a sigh.

Mother had been so unpredictable since their father left. She had abandoned her elaborate gowns, and went around déshabillé in a loose manteau over a plain linen shift. Her physical change upset him every bit as her mental one, though he had no idea what to do about it. She met any display of affection with copious tears and clasping hands, so he tended to avoid her.

"She'll be better when Father gets back," Henry said, with forced lightness.

"When Father gets back," Helena echoed, but even less conviction.

The sun slipped behind a cloud, and the temperature on the landing dropped. A crow on a nearby tree set up a high-pitched screech.

Henry shivered.

"What's going to happen, Helena?" he murmured, his chin on his bent knees.

"I don't know." Helena chewed at a cuticle on her thumb, something she used to do when she was little, though she had taken to the habit again this past month.

"Then tell me about Great-grandfather Julius, and how he built Loxsbeare for his child- bride." At his groan, she nudged him again. "Go on, you're much better at storytelling than I am."

The pleading look on her face made him laugh aloud,

shattering the tension.

"It was the year sixteen hundred and thirty two...."

* * *

Jonathan's bay Iberian mount grew restless as he and his commanding officer, Nathaniel Wade, led their infantry onto the moor. They had been marching for almost an hour in blanketing darkness, the smell of peat marsh strong in their nostrils. Keeping the men quiet proved an added burden, as an occasional muffled retching indicated some still suffered the effects of the rough cider they had drunk the night before.

They had managed to negotiate the Black Ditch without mishap. By Jonathan's calculations, they ought to be close to the Langmoor Rhine, though he could not be sure they had yet passed the rock Godfrey said marked the edge of the ditch. In this clinging mist, they could just as easily have passed it without noticing.

Cursing the infernal Godfrey beneath his breath, Jonathan suspected they were going the wrong way. Briefly, the mist parted, giving a clear view of the cavalry ahead, now bunched close together, the snorts of startled animals colliding in the dark as they struggled through knee deep mud.

"Why are they stopping?" Jonathan whispered, forced to halt.

"They cannot find the pludgeon," Wade said sotto voice. "The planking Godfrey said was set across the ditch."

The moon was full, but the fog lay so thick, his troop broke ranks and wandered about in the gloom. He dared not issue an order to re-assemble, as they were still under a strict order of silence. Johnathan cursed. Without knowing how deep the water was, he daren't order his men across, and risk them drowning.

A murmur confirming that the pludgeon had been located moved backward among the ranks, and Jonathan saw Wade urging the men ahead.

“Thank goodness for tha—!” A flash and a shot split the night. Jonathan released a low groan, in the ensuing silence, hoping the discharged weapon was a fluke and meant nothing. Maybe the sleeping troopers had not heard.

Shouts and a rumble of drums started up in the distance.

The enemy was awake.

A ripple of fear ran through him and his thighs tightened on the saddle. Feversham’s men would be upon them in minutes.

A command to charge went up from the cavalry ahead, followed by thundering hooves heading away from them at speed.

Jonathan cursed again, this time in frustration. Grey had taken his cavalry forward too soon. They had no infantry support—and Aaron was among them.

“May God go with you, my son,” Jonathan murmured under his breath. He had no idea where his brother was, but thrust thoughts of him away. Edmund would survive, he always had.

“The royal troopers have been alerted!” A voice to his left brought Jonathan’s head round to Major Wade, who had pulled up beside him. His face was little more than a grey blur, but he was recognisable by the huge outline of his horse.

“That’s obvious, man!” Jonathan snarled. “We’re too far behind. We must get the men across the next ditch to back up Gray’s cavalry.”

“We cannot find a safe place to cross!” Wade jerked his panicked horse round.

“We’ll have to fire from this side of the ditch!” Jonathan yelled back. “Battle orders! Start firing!”

There was the click and slide of muskets being loaded, followed by volley after volley as their shots sailed across the moor, making no impression.

“Too low!” Jonathan yelled. “Fire higher!”

The men obeyed, and this time their shots found their mark. On the other side of the ditch, men screamed and fell. But there was no time for Jonathan to feel triumphant, for just then a massive flash and boom rent the air.

The royal cannon! Jonathan watched in horror as the weapon carved swathes through the ranks of his men. Bodies flew into the air or were cut to pieces, falling into the mud to be trampled by others who filled the gaps.

"Keep firing." Fist raised, Jonathan rode up and down the line, shouting orders and rounding up stragglers, his eyes growing accustomed to the dim light.

Instead of breaching the ditch, Gray's cavalry had split into two columns; one group had swung to the right, moving steadily towards the distant glow of hundreds of tiny lights coming from the direction of the town.

Jonathan frowned, peering ahead at those lights. Then he gave a loud, colourful curse, his guts cramping as it occurred to him what he was really looking at.

"Runner!" he screamed, rewarded by a swift-footed boy who hove into view.

"Get over to my Lord Grey," he ordered the breathless boy. "Tell him those lights aren't the town. They're the matchlocks being made ready to fire. Tell Wade and the others to train their muskets on those lights."

The runner sped away and Jonathan prayed he was in time. If the troopers fired first, they would cut the cavalry to pieces and scatter them over the field.

The distant boom of cannon fire made Jonathan smile, partly because it wasn't in his direction. From the shrieks that rose from the king's troops, it was clear that Monmouth's Dutch gunners were wreaking havoc among the Dumbarton's Infantry; the indignant yelling of their officer to return fire confirmed it.

Gunfire screeched toward him, followed by a thick plume of bitter smoke that drifted across the field. The smoke stung his nostrils, engulfing the horses' heads as they wheeled in fright, plunging backward into the upcoming infantry.

Jonathan urged Buchan to one side, out of the way of the terrified horses, hoping Aaron had kept his seat and his mount, Strider, on course.

Most of Gray's cavalry had fled the field. A blow, but

there was nothing Jonathan could do. He hoped the handlers of the ammunition carts left at Peasey Farm would stand fast, as the horsemen were headed that way.

"Turnabout and line up by the ditch. Keep to the ditch, men!" Jonathan's throat burned with shouting, though his message had the desired effect as the infantry formed a ragged line along the edge of what must be the Bussex Rhine.

Jonathan slashed and cut, grunted and flailed, fighting to keep his seat on Buchan, who reared and screamed in terror. It took all his strength to keep the animal from bolting. His head ached from the roar of the cannon, his voice hoarse from shouting for more ammunition from men too dazed to hear him, or too terrified to obey—for none came.

From the corner of his eye, Jonathan saw Monmouth, his half pike in his hand, waving his men onto the edge of the ditch, ordering them to fire, while in the distance Feversham's officers ordered the cavalry brought up for an attack.

Wiping sweat from his eyes with one hand, Jonathan looked up. No longer black as pitch, the sky showed purple and blue in the distance. Fingers of light crawled across the horizon, harbingers of a summer day so many would not see. Dawn was coming. How could the night have gone so soon?

The dragoons had formed into an imposing barrier behind the ditch. Musket fire continued off to the left, though all around him silence fell and horses pawed the ground, some whickering in fright. No one moved forward.

What are they waiting for?

Then it came to him. Of course. Feversham was holding off until daybreak so he could order a full charge in better light. Still nothing moved.

Well, come, if you are coming, you bastards.

As if in response to Jonathan's silent scream, a wave of horses and men flooded across the ditch across a waterlogged field, and the royal troopers fell on his men.

Jonathan's chest swelled with pride at the sight of his

ill-equipped troops, running full pelt at the royal horse, keeping up a constant fire on the foot battalions. There was the repeated wet whoosh of steel slicing into flesh, and the primal cries of men in agony, doomed to be trampled by horses—'friends or foes'.

Dawn showed that the first enthusiastic wave of rebels had been forced back, the stalwarts who fought on being steadily shot or slashed without mercy.

Most of Jonathan's men had been scattered, and even those still able to hear his orders were most likely dead, or too injured to obey. He urged Buchan on, between and over fallen men of both sides, his ears closed to the shrieks of the wounded, until his mount's flanks shook with exertion.

"I have more to ask of you, boy." Jonathan reached forward and patted the clammy neck. "I have to find the Duke."

Their options were few, but the next decision was not Jonathan's to make. He found Lord Grey and Monmouth beside a massive tree at the edge of the field, their armour piled at their feet.

Buyse and Anton stood nearby, their faces haggard.

Jonathan halted beside them. "What now, my Lord? Our men are all but slaughtered."

"We have no choice, Woulfe." Lord Grey stepped in front of Monmouth, who seemed unable to look at Jonathan. "We must get away as best we can."

"You're leaving us?" Jonathan's anger made him reckless. "Look at them!" He waved an arm at the devastation on the field. "They're being massacred. You cannot abandon them."

Grey winced and made to step nearer, but Buchan gave a half-rear. Holding up a hand to fend the massive horse off, he raised his voice. "If the Duke is no longer here, the troopers may show some mercy."

"You coward, Grey," Jonathan growled, his head bent to inches from the man's ear. "I'll see you pay for this treachery!"

Grey started as if he had been slapped in the face, then his eyes narrowed and he stepped back, his place replaced by Monmouth, now mounted.

"You've been one of my best and most loyal, Jonathan." The duke held out a hand toward him. "Come with us."

Temptation pulled at Jonathan, and he looked into the distance to where the Polden Hills, and possible freedom, stood. He sighed and turned back to Monmouth, though neither man spoke.

Monmouth nodded, dropped his hand and kicked his horse into a canter.

Jonathan watched them crest the hill, wondering if James Scott, Duke of Monmouth, could still hear the sound of the faithful men he had left behind as they fought to their death in the mud. For him.

He knew with certainty that he would never hear anything else.

Chapter 4

With over half the stable lads gone to join Monmouth, everyone had to pitch in with the outside chores.

Helena was unused to outdoor work. After an hour spent feeding horses and sweeping stables, she took out her temper on her hapless brother, who trailed behind her across the courtyard, muttering the odd complaint.

Glancing up, she saw Bayle and hastily smoothed down her stained skirt in embarrassment, keenly aware of her dirty apron and dishevelled appearance. She realised he must have heard her shouting at Henry, and uttered imprecations under her breath while warmth crept up her neck.

No one at Loxsbeare would take her for a lady if she couldn't control her temper in front of the servants.

She took in Bayle's drawn face and the way he stared back at her with lifeless eyes, and she froze.

"Helena," Henry protested from behind her. "Watch what you are doing, I nearly tripped…." Cold, muddy water had splashed onto her feet, but she paid no heed.

"What's happened?" Helena demanded of Bayle, her voice strangled by dread.

"There was a battle," Bayle began. "A terrible battle. Hundreds are dead."

"Who's dead?" Henry split a look of horror between them.

"Where?" Helena gasped. The yard swayed around her, and Bayle's face blurred and receded. His hand came down upon her shoulder, as if he sensed her fight to stay upright.

"Somewhere near Bridgwater," he said, his voice low. "They attacked the king's men last night."

Helena tried to scream that he was wrong, but her

throat constricted.

"The rebels fought bravely but the king's men drove them off the field," Bayle went on. "Those not killed have most likely been captured by now."

"Captured?" Henry's bucket hit the cobbles with a thud. "They cannot be! Father said they were going to London. Bridgwater isn't anywhere near…."

"Master Henry." Bayle gripped his arm with his other hand, drawing them into a tight triangle. "Bridgwater is now full of troopers searching for escaped rebels. It's all I know. We may hear more later."

Henry clutched at Bayle's arm. "What of the Duke?"

Helena glared at him. How could he mention that man's name when his first thoughts should be of their family? Although tempted to harangue him for his lack of feeling, she asked instead, "How do you know all this, Bayle?"

"News has been filtering into *The Ship Inn* all morning. One of the tap boys came up to tell us."

Nodding, Helena swiped a hand across her face that came away wet, aware that several house servants had drifted out into the courtyard, watching curiously from a distance.

"Don't let them see you upset." Bayle leaned closer, apparently having seen them too. "If they believe all is lost, they'll likely desert Loxsbeare."

"Is Monmouth dead?" Henry murmured, his head down.

Bayle closed his eyes briefly. "He left the battlefield. That is what I have been told."

"He fled?" Henry's eyes rounded and Bayle shook him gently. "Stay strong, Master. The stories are wild. No one knows the truth yet."

Helena's eyes filled with tears. "What about Father? And Uncle? Where's Aaron?"

Her panic transferred itself to Henry, who gaped. "Will the King's men come and arrest us?"

Bayle wrapped a protective arm around him. "I think not," he whispered.

"Why not?" Helena snapped, scornful. "Everyone must know Father joined the rebels."

"Hush!" Bayle flicked another glance at the servants. Their numbers had doubled and they stared back with no more expression than a flock of sheep.

"I don't care!" she snapped. Appearances were the last thing on her mind. After today, the Woulfe name would be used in the same breath as *traitor*.

Not that it mattered, not to her. She wanted Father home again, to feel his laughter rolling in his chest as he held her against him, the scratch of his rough coat on her cheek, and the smell of his skin in her senses.

"Mother was right." Panic rose in her chest, but she couldn't think, or even move. "We are all doomed!"

"Which is why you must leave here." Bayle's voice remained calm.

"That makes no sense." Henry rubbed has face with a dirty hand. "If we are not to be arrested, why must we leave?"

"Because, Master," Bayle said softly, "condemned traitors forfeit their property to the Crown."

"They will take Loxsbeare?" Helena gasped on an exhaled breath.

Henry's face paled and he groped for her arm.

Bayle's face twisted in anguish. "They will expropriate everything Sir Jonathan owns."

Grief vied with rage in Helena's head. What value did their father's high principals for the Anglican Church have, now they would be driven from their home? Where would they go, and how? Panic built up inside her until she wanted to scream. Her breathing quickened and just when she thought she might give way to her horror, she made a decision.

"I must go and find them."

"Go where, Helena?" Henry asked, his misery replaced by abject horror.

"To Bridgwater, or wherever the battle was." She shrugged away from Bayle's grip, lifted her skirts, and pounded towards the house, calling for her maid Chloe as she ran.

"A battlefield is no place for a gentlewoman," Bayle said when he caught up with her on the upper landing.

"It's not a battlefield any more is it?" Helena waved him away. "From what you said, everyone is dead or captured." She was being unreasonable, and she knew it. She couldn't spend another day waiting anxiously in the house for the worst to happen while her mother grew more self-absorbed by the hour.

If she could find them and bring them all back, perhaps it might rekindle some of the spirit which had deserted Mother these last weeks. With Aaron restored to her, she might forgive their father for taking him away from her in the first place.

Propelled by anger, she opened chests and drawers, hurling items of clothing onto the coverlet.

"You cannot go!" Henry followed her round the room. "You have no idea where they are!"

"I'll find them." Her oldest shifts and two plain, worn gowns joined the pile heaped on the bed. She glanced down at her muddy skirt, where bits of straw still clung to it. At least she looked the part. "Chloe," Helena addressed the confused maid who limped on her damaged leg into the chaos. "Fetch one of Father's traveling bags." When the girl hesitated, her snapped "This instant!" sent her back into the hall at a run.

Into the commotion strolled Betty Humbold, their housekeeper, a tall, gaunt woman with large bones. "What's sent that lass Chloe running like demons was after her?" she demanded.

Bayle gave her a brief explanation, then issued instructions for provisions to several housemaids who crowded the hall. The girls repeated their orders to others in the hall, together with Helena's name, their voices echoing through the house in a mixture of alarm and excitement.

Into the noisy mêlée stepped the elegant figure of Lady Elizabeth, an enquiring expression on her face.

Helena's heart lurched and she turned away, murmuring under her breath, "*Not me, please don't let me be the one who tells her.*"

Bayle gently detached Lady Elizabeth from the crowd, drawing her out of Helena's line of vision. When they returned a moment later, she was deathly pale, her blue eyes clouded with pain.

Helena's shoulders slumped, angry with herself for even thinking of leaving her. "Mother I…."

Her mother held up a quivering hand to silence her. "Go. It may be possible for you to travel where others cannot. We must know what has happened to them."

"Mother!" Henry glared first at his mother then at Bayle. "You cannot allow her to go!"

Mother wrapped an arm round his shoulder, shushing him.

"I will go with her, my lady," Bayle said. "We can take the heavy cart and two of the moor ponies."

His words lifted Helena's heart. "You would really come with me?"

He nodded. "If we travel under the guise of a wool merchant and his…" Helena imagined he was about to say *daughter*, but he changed it to *niece*, "…we may be able to get past the troopers without arousing interest." His hand reached into the bag where Helena's journal lay in plain sight atop her plainest gowns.

"You cannot take this." He held up the brown book she had bought in Taunton Market, its leather strings trailing like an appeal. "We're traveling merchants who know nothing of the rebellion." He thrust it at her. "This would give us away in an instant." He strode to the door and shouted for Lumm to pack a few things for him and meet him in the courtyard.

Helena handed the journal to Henry, who clasped it to his chest. "Put it somewhere safe, would you?" she asked.

He nodded, blinking back tears. Then he lunged forward and wrapped his arms around her waist, whispering. "Why cannot I come with you?"

Helena's glance went to her mother, though even before she saw the rapid shake of her head and the fist she pressed to her mouth, Helena knew she had to refuse him.

“I cannot, Henry.” She grasped his upper arms and held him away from her. “If the troopers assume you are a rebel and decide to take you, I would have no means to prevent it.”

“What if they should take you, Helena?” he murmured, too low for their mother to hear. “Do you think they wouldn’t hang a woman?”

Helena stiffened. The thought hadn’t occurred to her. Yet she couldn’t weaken.

Bayle hoisted Helena’s bag onto his shoulder and barged through the muttering servants who crowded the door. “We’ll concoct our story together on the way.” He led the way down the stairs and out onto the sunny courtyard.

Helena’s sweeping glance took in their mode of travel with resignation. No fine horses and best garments for Nathan Bayle and his young *niece*, simply two of the hardiest horses the Woulfes owned, hitched into the traces of the provisions cart.

Helena eyed them uncertainly. “Must we take these?” she asked dismayed. “They’re not even proper horses. We could move faster on the bay and the chestnut.”

“No doubt.” Bayle offered with a cynical smile. “Or shall we take the carriage? The one with the Woulfe crest on the door?”

His sarcasm cut into her, and a burning flush crept up her neck, though she couldn’t help muttering that the carriage would have been faster than these scrawny ponies.

Ignoring her, Bayle handed her into a seat that sported a loosely-packed sack of hay. Helena could swear her back already ached.

“No doubt it would be.” Bayle had evidently heard her. ‘And what would you do if a trooper tried to take them from you because they are finer than his own?” He threw her a hard look as he arranged the cart and issued orders that sent maids and grooms off in all directions.

Helena groaned at her own stupidity, though she offered no response. For the first time she realized that being left with two women, a boy, and a houseful of the weaker and less able servants must have been hard on

Bayle these last weeks.

He might live under their roof, but she had no idea if he agreed with her father's choice to join Monmouth.

She was asking herself the same questions about Lumm, when he caught her sideways glance and bent in a slow, courteous half-bow, halted mid-way and winked.

Helena sighed, saved from a sharp rebuke as the cart surged forward onto the road. Her last sight was of her mother with both arms wrapped round Henry, who was leaning against her as they watched from the front steps.

* * *

"Don't look so terrified, Mistress," Bayle said good-naturedly as the cart rumbled down the Honiton Road. "At least the sun is out, which may even dry out after the flash floods of these last weeks."

Helena smiled, her face lifted to the sun. He was right. It felt good to be in the countryside after being cooped up at Loxsbeare for so long, though she couldn't help looking toward the horizon in search of mounted soldiers.

"They won't have reached Devon this soon," Bayle said as if reading her thoughts. "They'll be tied up in Somerset for a day or so yet."

"I suppose so." She forced herself to relax, her gaze falling on the loaded flatbed behind them. "Why so many sacks?" she asked.

"To sleep on, Mistress." Seeing her startled expression, he added, "There are inns along the way, but we might have to keep off the main roads."

Her mouth formed a silent *O*, as another thought occurred to her. "Do we have any coin for innkeepers?"

He smiled, arching an eyebrow. "And for horse feed, if we can find any."

She fell silent, aware of Bayle's indulgent smile on her profile. How could she possibly even have contemplated making this journey alone?

Above the steady clip-clop of the horses' hooves came a rustling from the hedgerows. A deer crossed in front of the cart, its soft eyes regarding them steadily before disappearing into the woods beyond the hedge. Helen followed the flight of a bird over her shoulder, shielding her eyes with a hand against the high noon sun.

Beyond shoulder-high dry-stone walls on either side of the road, bent-backed workers sliced rhythmically with scythes, heaped wheat stalks into piles, and tied them together heads uppermost to dry out.

"It's early for the harvest," Helena murmured.

"Heavy rain has flattened the corn." Bayle nodded toward the fields off to their left, where exhausted workmen paused to watch their progress. "It's back-breaking, dirty work. They are saving what they can." He sighed. "I anticipate a hard winter this year."

Helena wondered if, besides reaping an almost ruined harvest, the workers also scanned the horizon for royal patrols.

"Bayle?" Helena asked when they had covered another mile. "Does the *Green Ribbon Club* still exist?"

He glanced briefly at her. "Not as it once did, Mistress. Many of its most prominent members are dead, though plenty in these parts uphold their beliefs. Why do you ask?" He left her father's name unspoken, but the inference was clear.

"Is John Trenchard one of them?"

"The member of Parliament from Wolverton way?" he asked. "Aye, I believe so. He ran a Rebel club out of the *Red Lion Inn* in Taunton."

"Ran?"

"Aye. A warrant went out for him when all this started. He was an exclusionist. A thorn in the King's side. I gather his Majesty included him in the Whig Arrests."

"Exclusionist?"

"Those who tried to have King James excluded from the line of succession, because he's a Papist."

"Was my father an Exclusionist?"

"This uprising wasn't as much of a secret as some hoped," Bayle said, ignoring her question. "Trenchard was—is—a conspirator. He fled abroad to avoid being arrested."

"He helped purchase weapons, didn't he?" Helena asked slowly.

"How did you know that?" Bayle turned and stared at her.

"Last winter, Father took me to Taunton. When we reached *The Red Lion*, Master Trenchard was waiting for us. Father tried to tell me it was a chance meeting, but I'm not as gullible as he supposed." At Bayle's wry smile she continued. "They talked about buying muskets. It was the ribbons that made Father angry."

"Ribbons?" Distracted, Bayle loosened the reins, allowing the cart to slow a little.

Helena nodded. "Father gave me some coin and sent me to look round Taunton Market. I bought that leather-bound journal you insisted I leave behind. I also bought some ribbons in a shade of emerald green that the stallholder said would suit me. I returned to the inn and showed them to Father before dinner."

"What did he say?" Bayle asked carefully.

"It was what Mr Trenchard said that I remember. 'Green ribbons, eh? How appropriate,' he said it in this loud, braying voice like a private joke and pounded Father on the shoulder. Father was furious. He didn't say so, but I could see it in his face."

"Did anything else happen on this journey?" Bayle asked, giving her the impression he knew more about this man than he had revealed.

"When we left the next day, Master Trenchard bowed over my hand, and when I said I hoped we would meet again, which wasn't entirely truthful as I didn't much take to him." She caught Bayle's wry grin and shrugged. "Anyway," he punched the air with his fist and said, "most assuredly, for we have fellows in scarlet to take off, do we not Jonathan?' He didn't even lower his voice. An expectant hush spread over the inn yard as everyone stopped to listen."

"I doubt Sir Jonathan would have been pleased about that."

"He wasn't." Helena snorted at the memory. "He was livid. His face was just an inch away from Master Trenchard's when he snarled at him, something like, 'Hush man, you don't know who may be listening!'" She swallowed and released a long breath. "I didn't understand what it all meant. Not then."

"Does it all make more sense now?"

She nodded. "Father had been planning this for months, hadn't he? All those night visitors he didn't want us to see. Do you know who they were?"

"Some of them, perhaps, though it's best I don't mention any names."

"Suppose the soldiers come to Loxsbeare when we are gone?"

He didn't reply, his attention ostensibly on guiding the horses around a hay cart blocking the road.

"What will Mother and Henry do if that happens? They can't fight the king's army." Awful possibilities crowded her head, the least of which was their being dragged away in chains. She bit her bottom lip, hard enough to draw blood, horrified for not having considered this eventuality before. She had left her home without a thought, in search of her father, but the parent for whom she should have been caring was now alone. Lumm was there…if she could trust him.

"Don't fret, Miss Helena." Bayle took one hand from the reins and briefly squeezed hers. "They'll be gone by tonight, your mother and Henry."

"Gone? Gone where?"

"To the Ffoyles. That is the arrangement."

"Father knew this would happen?" Suddenly, everything fell into place. Samuel's visits to Loxsbeare, his private talks with Lumm, and probably Bayle too.

"Sir Jonathan was always committed to the Duke of Monmouth's cause, never doubt that." Bayle flicked the reins to hurry the lethargic horses along

"But he thought the cause might fail?" Anger bloomed and grew inside her chest. *If so, how could he have left us like he did?* "Is that why Samuel Ffoyle didn't go to Lyme when Monmouth landed? Because he didn't believe in it? Why didn't he try to persuade Father not to go?"

"Master Ffoyle is not a Monmouth man, but that doesn't mean he could turn your father from his own beliefs."

She twisted in her seat to face him. "He should have tried harder!" her anger made her unreasonable. "He told me himself he had forbidden his sons to join the rebels. A decision he must be grateful for now."

"Not Monmouth's, perhaps." He arched an eyebrow at her. "But he *is* Jonathan Wolfe's man. Master Ffoyle doesn't deserve your anger, Mistress."

"I know." She folded her arms tightly across her chest, as if to keep her fury inside. "Father's the one I'm angry with, for leaving us. For making Mother so distressed she has made herself ill. For taking Aaron away from her when everyone knows he's her darling."

The rhythmic clop of hooves continued along the dirt road, and the birds sang in the trees above them. Bayle did not react to her bitter tirade, as if he knew she needed to say aloud the words that she had kept pent up. He simply kept the reins loose across one bent knee, his foot on the guard, and his gaze straight ahead.

"Do you think we'll find them?" Helena asked at last, her voice small.

"Whether we do or not," he replied slowly, "Loxsbeare Manor is no longer your home."

"What are you saying?" She clasped her hands tightly in her lap. *How could this be happening?*

Her great-grandfather, Julius Woulfe, had built the house for his fifteen-year-old bride when the first King Charles occupied the throne some sixty years before. In an effort to make the nervous girl's transition to married life easier, and the prospect of her twenty-four-year-old groom less terrifying, he named their new home after the village near Tiverton, where she was born.

His son, Thomas, Helena's grandfather, possessed a more artistic nature than his Puritan father. He had the interior white plasterwork painted with swathes of leaves and flowers that trailed up the staircase and across the tops of doorways.

"Now the Duke has been defeated, the soldiers will come, Mistress."

The thought of soldiers trampling through her home made her grip the rough wood of the cart so hard that splinters cut into her hand.

Her rage subsided, and her breathing slowed down somewhat, as her rational side took over. Everything had changed, and harping back to the past would not help them now. The thick branches above them swayed and collided in the wind, throwing off the remains of the last storm to sprinkle the cart with droplets of cool water.

Helena took a deep breath. "Then you had better stop calling me Mistress."

Chapter 5

The sound of steady hoof beats approaching brought Henry's gaze to the wrought iron gates that separated the courtyard from St David's Hill. He leaned on his broom, grateful for a break in the hot and arduous task of sweeping the cobbles, watching as Samuel Ffoyle rode into the courtyard and summoned a groom.

The youth moved with insolent slowness until Samuel reprimanded him for being kept waiting.

The groom had come into his elevated position since the departure of the original incumbent for Monmouth's army. However hard he tried, Henry couldn't like Benjamin.

Henry propped his broom against the nearest wall and fell into step beside Samuel. "Is something wrong, Master Ffoyle?" he asked as they mounted the steps side by side.

"Not here," Samuel barked, ushering him to where his mother, clothed in a cream gown from neck to toe and bathed in a shaft of light, waited in the entrance hall like a nervous wraith.

On catching sight of them, her face closed, as if in anticipation of more bad news.

Samuel bowed over her hand, though he wasted no time on preliminaries. "Lady Elizabeth. Monmouth's army has been routed, and the king will show no mercy to known rebels. You must leave here at once."

"My husband could return at any time, Master Ffoyle." She withdrew her hand from his, and lifted her chin, defiant. "I cannot possibly leave."

"Somerset is swarming with troopers." Samuel persisted. "Devon will be too, in a day or so. My lady, if you don't depart of your own volition, you may find yourself taking flight with only the clothes on your back."

"We must listen to Master Ffoyle, Mother." Henry placed a hand on her shoulder. "He would never give us bad advice."

She stared about wildly. "Where would we go? We have no family, and no friends who aren't part of this…?" She broke off, her true feelings about the rebellion suppressed even now, though Henry knew what she had been about to say.

"Master Ffoyle will help us." Henry took in Samuel's calm yet determined expression, adding. "My father asked you to do this?"

Samuel nodded. "There's no time to explain, but I promise we'll talk later. You must pack up everything you need. Hide your valuables, or send them away with someone you trust."

"You are the only one we can trust, Master Ffoyle," Henry said, aware he sounded bitter, but he couldn't stop himself. He felt redundant, inadequate, with his father, uncle and brother off fighting for a cause of which he too could have been a part. Even Helena had followed her own impulses; and where was he? Caretaking an empty house occupied by a distraught woman who scorned his care.

While Henry reassured his mother, Samuel had taken command of the servants. Handing his hat and cloak to a footman, his gaze swept the lofty entrance hall as if marshalling his thoughts. "Three of my carts are on their way to take your goods to my home. Bring anything you don't wish the king's men to plunder or destroy to this hall, and I'll organise the servants to begin packing."

Plunder or destroy? The words made Henry's bowels cramp, but he kept silent. He must not show weakness now.

"Henry," Samuel looked down at him from his massive height. "You and Helena must dress yourselves in simple clothes, no silks or taffetas. You must pass for local farming people and…."

"Helena is not here," Henry interrupted, flushing. "She left for Somerset just this morning."

Shame rushed through him at the memory of having thrown his arms around Helena and begged to go with her.

He had meant it at the time. But when the watching servants had dispersed and he was alone again with Lady Elizabeth, he realised it had been an empty wish. The thought of meeting armed soldiers eager for blood turned his stomach.

Samuel dropped his arms and stepped closer, frowning. "Somerset? Alone? Why?"

"Nathan Bayle is with her," Mother said, as if that made it acceptable.

"They've gone to find Father and the others," Henry said, his voice flat.

"I see." Samuel pursed his lips in a silent whistle. "Well, Bayle knows the plan, so when they return," he paused, the word *if* hanging in the air between them, "he knows where to come."

A shadow passed the window. There was the sound of multiple cartwheels rumbling into the courtyard.

"Ah. My men are here." Samuel hauled on the front door and addressed someone Henry couldn't see. "When the carts are loaded, cover them and conceal them in the stables. Don't leave them in the yard, as they would be seen from the road." With a curt nod to Henry he bounded down the front steps.

"Master Ffoyle, what about Helena?" Henry called after him.

Samuel halted at the bottom and turned back. "Pray for her."

His mother recoiled with a sharp cry, then hurried away into the house, calling frantically for Betty and Ruth.

Henry found himself alone in the hall, unsure of what to do next. He had taken an oath to take care of Loxsbeare and his mother, and yet they were about to abandon their home. Would his father ever forgive him?

As he stood there arguing with himself, two servants emerged from the steward's room, struggling with a heavy oak chest they manhandled out of the front door. Samuel followed behind, his arms laden with ledgers and two gold candlesticks. The estate accounts were almost as valuable as the contents of the chest.

Henry's stomach knotted again. The Woulfes were really leaving Loxsbeare. For how long? Until the panic had died down—or forever?

A maid came running into the hall, only to halt in front of him when she caught sight of his face.

He straightened and brushed past her, taking the stairs two at a time.

* * *

At a small village called Staplegrove, Bayle stopped to buy small beer and allow the horses some rest. There, as in every village they passed through since entering Somerset, news of Monmouth's defeat was on everyone's lips. Small groups of villagers huddled round the public pump and crowded the inn, repeating what they had heard to anyone who would listen.

Helena climbed down to stretch her legs, while Bayle removed wheat stalks entangled in the cartwheels. Some locals struck up a conversation with him.

Others, less eager to talk, tried to ascertain whether they were strangers who might either threaten their existence or bring more news. Once Bayle had convinced them that he and Helena were of the second category, they clustered around him to demand what they knew.

"Troopers 'ave been through 'ere already today." An elderly man with wrinkled, sunbaked skin told them.

"Where's the patrol now?" Bayle asked.

"They took off through those fields over there, after a couple o' poor wretches on t'other side of that wall." He pointed a dirty finger down Fore Street, back where they had come. "But I don't think they woz rebels. They had 'orses with 'em."

Thanking him, Bayle jerked his chin at Helena, who scrambled reluctantly back into the cart. Her back was stiff from being bumped against the unyielding wooden seat. Her jaw was so sore, she could swear her teeth had worked themselves loose. "Are all Somerset roads so narrow and bumpy?"

Bayle gave a wry smile. "I'm afraid so."

Helena kept further complaints to herself as they passed through villages with names like Cheddon Fitzpane, West Monkton, Adsborough and Thurloxton—a route with which Bayle appeared familiar, since he did not stop to ask for directions.

Helena scanned the fields with narrowed eyes, half expecting to see ragged and blood-splattered figures crawling through the undergrowth, or peering out from behind trees.

She saw no one.

The landscape remained quiet and still, the empty fields basking in the afterglow of the early evening. When hunger intruded, she picked at her package of bread and sliced meat, handing morsels to Bayle.

Daylight faded into a pink and yellow evening. The road ahead was a wide, flat plain with empty fields on either side; a few low trees scattered in the distance.

The sun sank behind the horizon, and the temperature dropped swiftly.

She was about to ask if they would spend the entire night traveling, when a cluster of buildings materialised out of the gloom on the road ahead.

A squat church with a thin spire rose behind a row of houses. A range of hills shrouded in mist loomed in the distance. But the village, if that's what it was, contained little else.

The rumbling cart entered a deserted main street. Bayle pulled to a halt below a sign that sported a white bird in flight, the bottom half obscured by dirt and grime.

An upper storey overhung the ground floor in which small, square windows with bottle glass panes and deep sills dotted the façade at various heights. Soft yellow light streamed out of the lower windows onto the road, while the sounds of chattering voices within mingled with the clatter of pots and plates.

"Where are we?" Helena whispered, her hunger awoken by enticing cooking smells that hung in the air.

"Weston is about five miles on the other side of that

marshland." Bayle pointed toward flatlands outlined by clumps of trees. "We'll stay here tonight. There'll be soldiers all over the roads into Bridgwater by tomorrow."

"Would they bother with us, do you think?"

"Whatever their intentions, we are at their mercy. Remember not to show any interest in the rebels. Churchill's men will be well-organized after the initial chaos of today, and every soldier in the county will be searching for fugitives."

"Do you regret coming with me?" she asked, hauling her pain-filled body onto the road.

"We're here now," he said, without looking at her. "By tomorrow or the next day, pray God, we may be home again, but I fear the countryside has seen nothing of the King James' vengeance yet."

* * *

Astride a hay bale inside the stable door, Henry stretched his arms above his head and tried not to groan as his muscles protested.

The third cart had left a half hour before, and with the last one almost ready to go, he had taken an opportunity in a lull in the activity to take a rest.

Two grooms idled outside in the courtyard, pitching horseshoes at a stake in the ground, an occasional clang the only sound above intermittent birdsong.

By midafternoon, three carts and four horses from the Loxsbeare stables had left for Ideswell, although their hard labour appeared to have made little impression on the contents of the manor. Henry had never worked so hard in his life; who thought piles of clothes and pewter plates could be so heavy?

He had enjoyed the sense of purpose the task gave him. He didn't even mind when Samuel stepped in to call a halt because he had allowed the servants to stack the goods too high.

"Not only would it slow the horses down," he explained, "but they are too obviously the possessions of a wealthy family in flight, and bound to attract attention."

The stable door was flung wide, and Samuel strode inside. "No long now, Henry."

Henry jerked awake from his light snooze, unwilling to let Master Ffoyle think he was slacking. He liked the Guild Master of Clothworkers, a man who had always been kind to him. As a child, while his older brother practiced swordsmanship on the Weare Cliffs behind the house, Henry had begged to accompany his father and Master Ffoyle into Exeter.

When Henry grew bored with merchants' talk in the Customs House, or the pipe smoke in the *Bishops Blaize* inn irritated his chest, Samuel always came to his rescue. He would take him to Tuckers Hall to gossip with the wool men, or among the drying racks in the Crulditch outside the city walls, where the lengths of serge were hung to dry. He always thought they looked like sails flapping in the wind. With a pang of sadness, Henry wondered if he would ever spend days like that again.

A shadow blocked the entrance and Henry looked up, startled. It was only the groom, Benjamin.

Samuel rolled his eyes and Henry gave a nervous laugh as the man sidled through the doorway and paused, his hands in his pockets, morosely silent.

Benjamin had elected to remain behind at Loxsbeare, whether from cowardice or loyalty, Henry could not decide. While everyone else worked to clear the house, the groom had been neither help nor a hindrance. He was little more than an irritant, so Samuel had sent him to keep watch for approaching soldiers.

"Well?" Samuel demanded, his brow furrowed.

"Dragoons," Benjamin muttered under his breath. "Man on an 'orse passed by, said they came up Shepcote Hill s'morning," the sullen groom mumbled.

"Where are they at this moment, man? Never mind this morning?" Samuel cuffed him round the head in frustration.

"Prob'ly near North Gate b'now," Benjamin staggered and rubbed his ear.

"God's Blood!" Samuel ran outside with Henry at his heels.

"You!" Samuel turned back to point at the indolent groom, then changed his mind and called to another boy instead, "No, you, man. Move this cart into the rear stable out of sight." Samuel yelled, not stopping to see if the man obeyed.

"Will they search the house?" Henry cast a fearful look at the upper windows, just as Lumm came running from the rear. "I've just heard troopers are on their way up St David's Hill, Samuel. How much time do we have?"

"I've no idea," Samuel called back. "It's too soon for the trained bands to begin systematic searches. We'll have to bluff it out and hope they don't look too closely."

Nodding, Lumm leaned his weight into the shoulder of a stocky pony in an attempt to force the animal to budge.

Indecision left Henry stranded in the middle of the courtyard while grooms, kitchen maids and footmen rushed between the house and the outbuildings, their arms full.

"Churchill's men won't have got this far west so soon." Lumm leaned his shoulder further into the reluctant animal's side. "Like as not, they'll be militia patrols. Surly, tough men, but none too bright."

Henry's first instinct was to run back into the stable and hide in the hay-loft, but rejected the idea as cowardly. He had no idea where his mother was, or even if she knew the soldiers were on their way. Would she hide or face the soldiers?

The clink of bridles and the rhythmic pounding of hooves told Henry he had left his decision too late. The soldiers were here.

* * *

"Welcome to *The Dove*." The barrel-chested landlord greeted Helena and Bayle at the entrance, before leading them through a low-ceilinged hall, its uneven walls covered with mottled yellow lime-wash.

A narrow, uneven staircase stood at one end, curving

to the upper storey like a series of elbows at odd angles.

Bayle negotiated their accommodation while Helena stood fidgeting under the suspicious stare of the landlord's wife, a brown-faced woman with mousey hair peeking out from under a grubby white cap.

"Do they have rooms for us?" she asked, when Bayle rejoined her.

"For you, certainly." He guided her to a table in the corner of the room, amongst a motley collection of tradesmen and merchants. "The one he offered me is at the front." He kept his voice so low, she had to bend forward to hear him. "I cannot see the horses from there, so I'll sleep in the stable. We don't want anyone depriving us of them in the night."

They had arrived too late to avail themselves of the evening meal; instead they were served a supper of soup, sliced ham and potatoes fried in bacon fat, coarse bread and strong ale. The food was hot and appetizing; the soup reminiscent of a meaty stew and the bread was still warm.

"Are you sure about spending the night in the stable?" Helena asked, her voice reduced to a croak by the smoke from tallow and lard candles on the table in front of them.

"I'll be happier there." Bayle spooned food hungrily into his mouth. "The hay there will probably be fresher than the mattress you'll be sleeping on." He glanced over his shoulder at a florid man with stained teeth who appeared to be holding court.

"I can guess what he's talking about." Bayle tore a chunk of bread off a loaf and chewed. "Everyone I've spoken to claims to have seen king's men rounding up rebels."

"Did you believe them?" Helena nibbled the heavy bread, picturing her mother and Henry at home in the dining hall eating roast leg of lamb and potatoes. Then she remembered. *They will have left Loxsbeare by now*.

The man kicked his stool aside and advanced toward their table.

"He's coming over," Helena gasped, ducking her head to avoid his gaze.

"Heard about them rebels have ye?" He rolled his eyes toward the front windows. "They're being hanged by the roadside wherever they're caught. The royal army has run out of wood to build the scaffolds." He wiped a dirty hand across his dirtier mouth and fixed Bayle with a penetrating gaze through bloodshot eyes.

"Can't a body eat his dinner in peace!" Bayle swung his head in the stranger's direction and made what Helena deduced was an obscene gesture with one arm. "I've been on the road all day with a whining lass. I don't need you prattling on about rebels who should have known better."

The man backed away rapidly, muttering to himself.

When she was sure they weren't being observed, Helena widened her eyes, and mouthed *Whining lass*?

Bayle's lop-sided grin appeared but instead of a response, he speared a chunk of bacon with his knife and popped it into his mouth, masticating noisily.

They finished the rest of their meal in peace. Then a maid in a food-stained apron escorted Helena to her room under the eaves with a crooked door that hung askew from the frame.

The bed bore thin, rough sheets and a coarse blanket; set lower to the floor than Helena was used to, it brought images of scurrying rats to mind. At least the bed looked clean.

Helena peeled the bodice of her gown away from her itching skin, letting the skirt fall to the floor. She was more weary than she could ever remember and yet proud of how far she and Bayle had come since morning. Dressed in only her shift, she crossed to the low window where grimy, diamond-paned glass at waist level gave onto the road.

She leaned her hands on the cracked sill and squinted at the shadowy outline of Bridgwater off to her left. The smell of grass and wildflowers drifted on the air, combined with the sharp tang of the stable. She thought of Bayle, bedded down amongst the hay, hoping he would not be too uncomfortable sharing it with the horses.

Her smile faded. *Where was Father sleeping tonight*? Beneath a hedgerow somewhere, or in the Taunton gaol house? That he may even lay dead on the battlefield was also a possibility. The thought made her shiver, though the night was warm. And where were Aaron and Edmund? Were they together, running from the troopers? Or had they split up and taken off across the countryside alone, and could they be on their way home at that very moment?

The image of them as chained prisoners was something she didn't want to contemplate. She pushed the notion into the back of her mind. The man downstairs had said captured rebels were being hanged on the roadsides.

Helena scanned the horizon, where a cloud of dust grew larger, then separated into riders, approaching from the direction of Bridgwater.

The soldiers sat on their mounts with an arrogant air, leaning over their saddles to stare into windows and scattering the villagers, who ran ahead into houses and slammed shut their doors.

Helena stepped back, her back pressed against the wall, her breath held until she heard the thump of her own heartbeat.

Loud voices called from the landing outside her room, followed by the slamming of doors from the floor below. Shouts and the sound of running feet on wooden boards reverberated through the building.

What should she do? Run and fetch Bayle, or stay where she was?

The seconds stretched and the sound changed pitch, then receded until she could hear nothing at all. She exhaled slowly, dizzy with relief. She crept back to the window and saw they had ridden past.

Weak with relief, she climbed into the creaky bed. Despite her exhaustion, she lay awake for what seemed like hours, until the tiny patch of sky beyond the window darkened to black.

As she teetered on the edge of consciousness at last, her father's face swam into her mind, seeming so real, she mumbled into her lumpy pillow, *Stay alive until I get there, Father.*

Chapter 6

Henry peered round the stable door as the patrol of twelve soldiers cantered double file through Loxsbeare's gates, their hooves clattering to a halt on the cobbles.

The officer's glare raked the empty courtyard, fixing on Samuel, who strolled forward, a puzzled frown on his face, as if their appearance were a mystery.

The officer dismounted while Samuel drew himself up to his considerable height and returned his arrogant stare.

Henry sensed Tobias's presence behind him, and whispered, "Master Ffoyle is not easily intimidated, is he?"

"Nay, Henry. Let's hope they believe his story."

Henry was about to ask what story, when a black-coated figure dismounted beside the officer. Henry glowered at the sight of the magistrate who had tried to waylay them outside the church three Sundays ago.

"What can I do for you, Master Prendergast?" Samuel said, his voice carrying across the yard. He folded his hands in front of him, a half-smile of enquiry on his face.

"I apologize for our unannounced presence, Master Ffoyle." The magistrate avoided Samuel's gaze, as if he were reluctant to be there. "This officer has business with Sir Jonathan Woulfe."

A grimace of distaste passed across the officer's face, one already marred by a livid scar that ran from beneath his right eye to the corner of his mouth. "I have orders here for the arrest of Sir Jonathan Woulfe." His voice was a snarl as he withdrew a parchment from his coat. "On the charge of treason against His Majesty King James the Second, and the seizure of all his goods and property."

Henry groaned. "How had they arrived so quickly,

Tobias? They must have captured Father."

"Quiet, Master Henry!" Tobias silenced him with a painful grip on his shoulder.

Samuel took his time to read the document through. His ploy did not work, for the other soldiers had dismounted and stormed the house. The thump of booted feet on floorboards drifted across the yard, accompanied by a man's shout and a shrill female protest.

Samuel held his hands out in surrender, the paper held aloft as if its contents confused him. "What is the meaning of this? Sir Jonathan is in London, sir, on Court business."

The officer narrowed his eyes and said something Henry couldn't hear above the sound of a crash from inside the house. At a shouted order, the remainder of the troop fanned out through the grounds.

"Henry," Tobias said, his voice low and urgent. "Find somewhere to hide. I think there's going to be trouble."

Henry gave a brisk nod, then scampered round the side of the stable toward the dairy and kitchen garden. Both appeared empty, but he had no intention of hiding—not with Mother still in the house. He had to protect her. Listening for the crunch of booted feet, he crept around the fruit bushes in the kitchen garden. Having reached a side door, he had already dragged it half-open when a rough hand grabbed him by the collar.

"And where might you be goin'?" a rough voice snarled close to his ear.

A fist struck Henry in his lower back, cutting off his response. His lungs emptied, the momentum of the blow sending him barrelling into the wall. He bounced off the stonework and he slid to the ground.

"Hopin' to grab some of the valu'bles, wuz we, lad?" The soldier, in a stained leather jerkin and battered hat, stood over him, grinning.

Dazed, Henry staggered to his feet, but the soldier cuffed him again, sending him sprawling. This time, he stayed put, his cheek pressed into the gravel.

The soldier gave an obscene oath Henry only half-understood, and with a throaty laugh, moved away.

When he was certain he had gone, Henry wobbled to his feet, heart thumping. He gave silent thanks to Samuel for insisting he wear groom's clothes that morning. Had that soldier known who he was, the treatment would have been far worse.

Henry staggered into a rear corridor, where two soldiers had found the meat locker and were tussling over a joint of cooked ham.

Sara, the kitchen maid, stood with her hands on her hips, glaring at them as if they were naughty children.

A third soldier with greasy hair hanging in rats-tails raked Henry with speculative eyes, which dulled when he saw nothing to interest him. With a contemptuous snarl, he gestured Henry away.

Henry turned and fled before the man changed his mind. Jumping at every sound, he crept along the corridor, peering into each room as he passed. They all stood empty, the floors strewn with items emptied from drawers and chests.

When he reached the main hall, a sound from above brought his gaze up to where a soldier descended the stairs. His arms were full of linens and what appeared to be a tapestry that used to be hanging in one of the bedrooms.

Betty Humbold followed behind. Showing no more fear than Sara had, she hurled insults and muttered curses, all of which the soldier ignored.

He grinned evilly over his shoulder as he gained the front door, leaving Betty to hurl frustrated abuse from the newel post.

Where was Mother?

Hearing the stable door flung back hard on its hinges, Henry made for the front door, only to be dragged backward by his collar.

"What are you doing here, Master?" Lumm snarled.

"The horses!" Henry waved in the direction of the yard.

"It's too late. There's nothing you can do." Lumm tightened his grip on Henry's coat.

Soldiers led the last of the Loxsbeare stable away,

trotting three chestnut geldings toward the gates on leading reins.

The sight of the fourth made Henry's heart contract.

Verity was hauled out into the sunlight, ears flattened and eyes rolling in fear at the unfamiliar hands.

"Don't pull her, she has a soft mouth," Henry moaned.

Behind him, Lumm made sympathetic murmurings, but his hold on Henry's collar stayed firm.

"One of those geldings was to be mine," Henry said, the closest he had come to rage since the soldiers had invaded the house.

Two uniformed men in the courtyard fought over a turkey rug on the ground. One drew his sword, but a third soldier intervened and separated them, ordering the pair away.

Henry cursed them under his breath, and Lumm leaned down to whisper. "A pile of fine bed linens, a silver candlestick, and a whole ham are real treasures to them. In all their lives they would never own such luxuries." He reached into a pocket and brought out a kerchief.

Henry stared at it, uncomprehending.

"You're bleeding." Lumm pressed the kerchief into his hand, pointing at Henry's forehead.

Henry dabbed at his temple, frowning at the unexpectedly large red stain left on the kerchief.

The officer with the scar was nowhere in sight. His second-in-command and the magistrate remained in the courtyard, idly watching the rest of the troops carry more portable goods out of the house. Then a curt order came from somewhere, and the troopers re-mounted their horses, with bulkier packs than when they arrived.

Samuel came through the front door, flinging his head back toward the courtyard. "They have my ponies." He looked accusingly at Lumm, who shrugged.

"They must have found the cart."

Henry's gaze lifted to the landing, where the officer with the scar stood, his arms full of plate and a bed hanging flung over one shoulder.

Lady Elizabeth followed closely behind, her face a

mask of anger. “Stop at once, you ill-bred thief!” she demanded, following him onto the half-landing, her eyes ablaze with ire. Heedless of any threat, she placed herself in front of the officer, who sneered and shouldered her away.

She lurched against a post and swayed, but remained on her feet. The officer turned and halted, as if noticing her for the first time. His chin jutted forward, like a fox spotting its prey. He dropped the bed hanging, and with his free hand, groped for her throat.

She gave a gasp as her sapphire pendant came away, reached out a hand to reclaim it, one foot hovering above the top step. Her position was already precarious, and with her equilibrium gone, she lurched forward and toppled down the flight of stairs with a startled cry.

As she fell, her head struck the wall and her body slammed headlong onto the floor at the bottom of the stairs.

“Mother!” Henry froze for long seconds, then galvanised into movement, yanked out of Lumm’s grasp and threw himself forward. He ran full pelt across the hall, sliding the last few feet on his knees.

She lay eerily still, her pale curls fanned out around her head, her face serene, as if in sleep.

Henry lifted her head onto his knees with shaking hands, stroked her hair. “Mother! Mother? Can you hear me?”

A trickle of viscous, almost-black blood slid from her ear down her jaw. Alarmed, Henry stared at it, his stomach churning.

“Fetch a chirurgeon!” he screamed, stroking the pale curls away from her face. “I need a cloth and water too.” *Mother wouldn’t like to get blood in her hair.*

Tobias reached past Samuel and pressed his fingers gently against Lady Elizabeth’s throat.

Henry stared at him, uncomprehending. “She’s hurt, Master Ffoyle,” he sobbed. When Samuel remained still, his gaze shifted to Tobias. He would know what to do.

Tobias glanced up at the older man and gave a slow shake of his head.

The soldier halted on the stairs above them. Watching.

Samuel gave a muttered oath, then made to climb the stairs, but Lumm wrapped both arms around him and held on. "No, Master Ffoyle," he said, grunting with the effort. "They'll hang you."

Samuel continued to glare at the soldier, fists clenched and his mouth working, but he did not move. Then he heaved a long sigh, and relaxed against Lumm, who stepped back and returned to Henry's side.

The soldier's smirk slid off his face, and his boots slammed into each step on the way down, the sapphire necklace dangling loosely from his fingers. His back to the wall, he skirted the body, then loped through the door.

"Come away, Master Henry." Lumm tugged at Henry's arm.

"What do you mean?" Henry split a look between them. "Help me get her to her chamber. Someone has to fetch the chirurgeon!"

Henry held Lumm's gaze for long seconds until he understood. "No!" he whispered, then more fiercely. "No!"

Betty Humbold appeared from the kitchens, her thick brows pulled together in a deep frown. She dropped to her knees beside her mistress, her hands pressed to her mouth and, keened in a monotone, as fat tears poured down her face.

Lumm encircled Henry with both arms and hauled him upright.

"Let go of me, Tobias." Henry struggled, but he was no match for the older man. "I want to stay with her."

"Henry, Listen," Samuel murmured. "We cannot leave her here."

Henry stopped fighting and allowed Tobias to guide him to the bottom of the staircase. He slumped onto the bottom step, his hands held limp between his knees and head down. Tobias bound Lady Elizabeth's body in the discarded hanging, and between them, they carried her outside.

Betty tried to wrap an arm round him, but Henry jerked away. The last thing he wanted now was comfort. He had let them kill his mother.

How had it happened so quickly? What was he going to say to his father when he came home?

Bile rose into Henry's throat. His stomach heaved and tears dripped onto his clasped hands as he murmured over and over in the empty hall, "Mother. Helena."

* * *

Helena bolted upright in the narrow bed, startled at the sight of the landlady's pudgy face leaning over her, thick lips curled in a mocking grin.

"Your ladyship's bath awaits." She dumped a bucket of hot water unceremoniously on the floor.

Helena rolled her eyes as the door clicked shut. At least now she could rinse her hair and scrub road dust from her gritty skin. The water cooled quickly, but at least it was enough. However, being accustomed to having Chloe standing by to deal with unreachable fastenings, the effort required to dress herself was more complicated.

Pulling the draw cords on her shift was easy enough, but attaching the bodice to her skirt proved frustratingly difficult. She gave her discarded gown a shake, bundled it into her pack, and went downstairs.

She found Bayle in the dining hall, a large breakfast spread before him.

"The woman who brought the water was positively insulting," Helena complained, sliding onto the bench beside him. She helped herself to eggs and pork from a platter on the table. "She barged into the room without knocking and—what are you grinning at?" She frowned, a chunk of buttered bread halfway to her mouth.

Bayle shook his head once and turned back to his plate, smiling.

Their host made a show of hospitality, sauntering over to their table to enquire if they had spent a comfortable night. Helena suppressed a shudder, repelled by the falsely ingratiating set of his bloated features and his enormous black-nailed hands.

"Aye," the man said. "We've 'ad troopers in and out of this place since yest'dy morning." He wiped his nose on his sleeve. "Pretty angry they are too, with all them rebels loose hereabouts."

Maybe Helena imagined it, but he spoke the word "rebel" with contempt.

Bayle forked food steadily into his mouth, saying nothing.

"Caught plenty of the poor devils too." Undeterred the landlord chattered on. "Hanged some of 'em on the road."

Then he asked the question Helena expected since she had approached their table. "Where does your journey take you when you leave us this fine morning, good sir?"

"We're bound for Bristol." Bayle lowered his tankard. "Though we have no wish to cross paths with angry soldiers or rebels. Perhaps you could you offer me some advice?"

The landlord shrugged. "There be soldiers on all roads leading east. There's no avoiding 'em." He narrowed his eyes at Bayle, then uttered a surly *good day* and moved on.

"We'd better be on our way," Bayle murmured. "Get your things and meet me outside in a few moments."

Her appetite gone, Helena scampered up to her room where she jammed her meagre belongings into her bag and clattered down again, hoping she wouldn't meet the landlord on her way out. Thankfully, she reached the road outside unseen, where she shuffled her feet in impatience, willing Bayle to appear.

When the cart rounded the corner and came to a halt beside her, she exhaled in a relieved sigh and clambered into her seat.

"Do you think the landlord suspected why we are here?" she asked once they were out on the road again.

"It cost me more than the price of our breakfast to ensure he did not." Bayle cocked his head at the receding inn. "He's making a tidy profit keeping his guests' business private."

"What do you mean?"

"Our host is duty bound to report the names of all

strangers and suspicious persons staying at *The Dove* to the militia. He would only refrain from this if sufficiently recompensed beforehand."

Helena's jaw slackened in shock.

Grinning, he gave a dismissive shrug. "He might be a rogue, but his lax morals served us well. There are those who suffer and die in times like these, and those like our landlord who use them to line their pockets. "'Tis the way of the world."

Helena was about to voice her outrage at injustice in all its forms, when he waved her off. "Keep a look out for troopers. There'll be patrols on all the roads soon."

Outside Middlezoy, Bayle's warning proved accurate. Troopers hammered on doors and pounded through houses, thrusting aside anyone brave enough to disobey.

For no greater sin than not responding fast enough to a shouted command, men and boys alike were forced to endure cuffs and insults. Those who dared answer back received hefty whacks across shoulders with the flats of swords.

A soldier insulted a local girl with rough handling, ripping her clothes. A man, Helena presumed to be the girl's father, rushed forward to defend her and received a lash of the soldier's whip across his face. The man fell to the ground, bleeding, and his persecutor delivered a vicious kick to his face.

Helena stood up in the cart about to protest, when Bayle's hand clamped onto her arm, hauling her down again. "Don't react," he whispered, flicking the reins to urge the horses on past.

"What's happening, Bayle?" Helena's voice dropped to a sob. "These people aren't rebels, they're villagers. They offer no threat."

"They hate us, they hate us all, Helena," he said. "In their eyes, the West Country must pay for its betrayal. Few armies are merciful in victory. It is often too hard won. They're savage because they can be. There's no fairness to it."

Helena had never measured her courage before,

ashamed at the cowardice that burned in her. She may not condone those soldier's actions, but she didn't accept them, either.

She had left Loxsbeare full of arrogance, determined to find her father and brother at all costs. Now she was laying herself open to possible arrest, perhaps even a beating, or worse. Bayle would be helpless if they turned their attentions to her. Enlightenment had come too late. Turning back was almost as dangerous as pressing on.

* * *

The horses plodded through rutted roads rapidly drying out from the recent heavy rains into flat, open countryside.

"Where are we?" Helena asked, impatient, though they had only gone a couple of miles.

"Up the road there is Weston Zoyland, where my aunt and uncle live." Bayle indicated a clump of trees about a mile ahead, beyond which stood a cluster of rooftops on a rise.

"What are they like?" Surprised, Helena studied his profile. It had never occurred to her Bayle had a family.

"That's a strange question."

"Yes, I suppose it is." She smiled. "Would they be able to tell us anything?"

"I know no more than you do." He sounded weary. "But it's somewhere to begin, and the best lie to tell is one wrapped in truth."

Confused by this gem she did not understand, Helena fell silent as they entered the well-kept village, its substantial stone houses clustered round a church with a square spire and a pleasant green.

"St Mary's," Bayle cocked his chin at the church. Before Helena could turn her head to look, he hauled the hood of her cloak over her head, pulling her into his side and held her there, her protest muffled in the stifling fabric.

The horses snorted and struggled between the traces, their swaying rears all she could see through the tiny gap left round her eyes.

"Get on there, go." Bayle cracked the reins, shouting. The horses whickered and sprang forward.

After a short but jolting sprint, he released her.

Helena emerged spluttering. "Why did you do that?" she demanded. "I almost suffocated under there. And what is that dreadful smell?" She twisted round to look behind her.

"Don't look," Bayle snapped. Too late.

At first sight, she thought four men sat in a tree, then reality became clear. Metal chains were looped about their necks and torsos, their hands tied behind their backs, faces frozen in grotesque parodies of human expression, which showed their deaths had been neither quick nor easy.

Helena choked back a scream, clamping her eyes tight shut to block out the terrible sight, but the image was seared behind her eyelids. "Is it? Are they…?"

"No," Bayle's low whisper reassured her. "It isn't them."

Hot tears of relief trickled down her cheeks, which turned to pity for the poor wretches who had died so horribly. She kept her gaze fixed on the churchyard, its beauty marred by groups of unkempt soldiers languishing against gravestones, while others trampled the grass.

"Don't stare," Bayle warned, halting the cart beside an oak door that showed evidence of violent treatment—dents gouged in the wood at eye level, and splinters.

In response to his knock, the door swung inward, revealing a diminutive woman in a brown dress, over which she wore a white apron; a housewife cap framed her face. Her eyes widened and wordlessly, she ushered them inside, casting a fearful look behind them before closing the door.

"Nathan!" Her hand went to her throat and the years drained from her face, giving a glimpse of the lovely woman she had once been. "I had not thought to see you here, and at such a time."

The old stone-built house had low ceilings and lime-washed walls with flat, mullioned windows under a thatched roof. The ground floor consisted of two large adjoining rooms with a narrow corridor leading into what

Helena supposed were the rear offices. An aroma of wood smoke and wildflowers overlaid by the tang of vinegar and heady beeswax, combined with a cloying, sickly smell she did not recognize.

"Mistress Fellowes is my father's youngest sister," Bayle said, taking a settle by the fireplace, drawing Helena down beside him.

"I thank you for your hospitality, Mistress." Helena inclined her head.

"So this is Mistress Woulfe?" Her intelligent eyes took in Helena's face, before she turned to gaze lovingly at her nephew. "You shouldn't have come, Nathan. These are dark days."

"I know, but we had little choice." He threw Helena a meaningful look.

On closer inspection, Helena saw that Jane Fellowes's delicate features, with a trace of worry lines etched around her deep brown eyes, were identical to Bayle's.

She disappeared through a door, returning with a female servant. Deferential but plainly anxious, the woman set down a tray of ale and small cakes before shuffling away.

"I gather then, that Sir Jonathan joined the Duke's men?" Mistress Fellows poured ale into pewter jugs and handed them out.

Helena nodded, the sound of her father's name on the lips of this kindly stranger eliciting instant tears.

"Edmund Woulfe and Sir Jonathan's son, Aaron are also amongst them." Bayle took a sip of his drink. "What happened here, Aunt Jane?"

"When Monmouth returned to Bridgwater last week, the Mayor begged him not to lay siege to the town, but he was hemmed in by Feversham, so he had little choice."

Bayle waved his jug at the window. "And here? I take it none of the rebels got this far?"

Helena sipped the cool yeasty ale slowly as she listened, surprised at how delicious it tasted.

Jane shook her head. She laid down her own jug of ale and folded her hands together, her eyes darkening in dismay.

"When Lord Feversham arrived and set up camp, he billeted troopers in every house in the village." Jane's mouth twisted in recollection. "Talk in the village said he thought Monmouth was preparing to lay siege to Bridgwater. Whether they were waiting for reinforcements or just going to starve them out, we never knew."

"How were you spared?" Bayle glanced around as if searching for signs of hostile occupation.

"We weren't. The three soldiers who were quartered here are dead. The rebels weren't the only ones to die last night." She gave a dismissive wave to signify that was another story. "Dragoons occupied the rectory and Weston Court, the manor close to here." She nodded toward the front window. "They were so arrogant and sure of themselves. They spent their evenings drinking, and singing coarse songs. We have barely slept for days...." She broke off, as if embarrassed to mention this inconvenience in the midst of such tragedy.

"Were you ever in danger, Aunt Jane?" Bayle asked.

Helena studied the woman's face. Jane, the name suited her, simple but strong and handsome too.

"Colonel Wyndham insisted the whole village pledge loyalty to King James. But that was nothing. Our guests," she stumbled over the word, "showed us no disrespect, and we aren't grand enough for the officers." She gave a bitter laugh.

"What about the battle?" Bayle consumed three tiny cakes in quick succession. Helena frowned and he grinned. "My aunt is a good cook."

"No one in Weston knew about the attack, not until we heard the gunfire in the middle of the night. All we could do was sit here and listen. It stopped soon after dawn and we watched them bring in the dead, and herd the prisoners into the church."

"How many are in there?" Bayle exchanged a look with Helena.

"Hundreds." Her voice rose in anguish. "I feel I betrayed those poor men. We offered to tend the wounded,

Gil and I, out of Christian charity, but the officers said the rebels did not deserve help and their suffering was God's judgment on them for their treachery against the king."

"Where is Gil?" Bayle asked.

Helena assumed he referred to the lady's husband.

"At Langmoor Drove." Her voice dropped to a whisper. "He's helping cover the pit where they laid the dead."

"King's men or rebels?" Helena spoke for the first time, her voice strangely calm, though her hands tightened on her jug of ale.

"Rebels, my dear. About a hundred and seventy of them. Five King's men were given Christian burials yesterday at the church, but the men they captured…." She licked her lips. "Colonel Kirke complained to his superiors about the state of the graves. He ordered a gang of workmen build a mound over them." She smoothed nervous hands down her skirt.

"Kirke did not strike me as a humanitarian." Bayle said, his voice bitter.

"He is not." His aunt's eyes clouded. "The mass grave is a pitiful sight. They did not dig it deep enough and—well, the stench has already encouraged scavenging animals."

Helena made a choked sound and Jane pressed her hand. "I'm sorry, my dear. These are dreadful things to speak of, especially in front of you."

"I appreciate your concern, Mistress," Helena said. She had not come this far to be treated like a genteel child who should be shielded from the truth. "There is no need to keep the facts from me."

Jane Fellows inclined her head, admiration in her eyes.

"What is happening now?" Bayle plucked another cake from the plate, chewing thoughtfully.

"Most of the soldiers have returned to Axbridge to collect their cannon and thence to London to report to the king." She turned sad eyes on her nephew. "Lord Feversham took his men to Wells yesterday, and Churchill and his troops rampaged through Bridgwater, scaring the townsfolk. They found some poor wretches, but not so many as they hoped." She blew her nose on her kerchief. "The Tangier regiment is staying to guard the prisoners and take them for trial at Taunton." Her eyes flashed. "They are less than men, Nathan. Yesterday, without benefit of a trial, they hanged six rebels. One of them was Monmouth's Dutch gunner, and a deserter from the Hampshire Militia. We've no idea who the others were."

"We saw some of them," Helena mumbled. "I can still smell that sweet, fetid stench." She halted at the look Jane exchanged with Bayle.

"The smell is here all the time, my dear," Jane Fellowes explained. "Those men in the church, their wounds are festering in the heat. They are what you can smell."

Helena went rigid with horror, her breathing quickened and she gulped her ale, hoping to remove the taste from her throat. It didn't help.

"They're being taken to their home towns for trial," Jane spoke again. "Either tonight, or in the morning. The parson says they'll have to fumigate the building when they are gone. The churchwarden is already complaining about the expense to the parish."

Bayle rose to his feet and adjusted his hat. "I will see if I can find Gil. He might be able to help us get inside that church."

"Be careful," Jane warned.

Helena rose to her feet on wobbly legs. "I'm coming with you."

Bayle held out a hand as if to restrain her. "It's no place for a woman, Mistress Helena. Besides, the guards would never let you in."

"They might." Helena looked from Bayle to his aunt and back again, their aghast faces doing nothing to diminish her resolve.

She didn't need to ask why Bayle wanted to see inside the church. He was going to find out if her family were among the wounded. Well, she had come all this way for the purpose, and wasn't going to be deterred now.

“No place, Bayle?” She cocked her head. “How much worse can it be than what we saw in that tree on our way here?”

Bayle sighed, glanced at his aunt and shrugged. “As you wish.” Without waiting to see if she followed, he ducked beneath the lintel and through the door.

Chapter 7

The soldier who kept watch at the door of St Mary's church barred their way with an upheld musket. "What do you want?" he snarled, raking each of them with a withering glare.

"I'm Gill Fellowes's nephew," Bayle said. "The churchwarden said my uncle was here."

Helena held her breath. They had not seen anyone on the short walk across the green, much less a churchwarden. She focused on the musket the fellow held loosely at his shoulder; but he made no threatening moves.

"He was here an hour or so ago. I dunno if he's still inside." He glanced down at his forearm, a grubby bandage visible beneath a ragged tear in his sleeve. "Master Fellowes bound this fer me. The pain is almost gone, thanks to 'im."

"I'm so glad," Bayle sounded anything but. "We brought water for the prisoners." He indicated the bucket in his hand.

"Both of ya?" The soldier frowned at Helena. "Won't be much fun fer 'er."

"This is my sister. She'll be fine if she stays with me and does as she's told." Bayle's glare held all the instruction Helena needed.

"Aye. Well, I has orders not to let anyone in."

Helena held her breath. He must let them in. This was the only way of finding out for sure if any of her family were inside.

"Perhaps you won't see us." Bayle kept his face bland.

"Them poor wretches haven't had any water all day." He licked his lips, his gaze darting nervously over his shoulder. "I need the privy, I'll be gone a while." He gave them a curt nod and left them standing in the empty porch.

The nauseating stench of unwashed bodies, blood, and decaying flesh assailed Helena's senses like brume as they entered the airless building. She fumbled in a pocket for a kerchief and held it to her face, willing herself not to be sick. All Jane's warnings had not been enough to prepare her for this.

St Mary's was not a small church; it had a high timbered roof and stone arches that ran down both sides of the central aisle. The pews had been shoved aside to make room for the prisoners, who sat or lounged on the dusty flagstones. Sunlight streamed through the arched windows, sending beams of white light onto piles of rags that covered the floor—rags that moved. A short, burly man with sandy hair approached them, his hands filled with soiled strips of cloth he must have been using as bandages. He frowned at Helena as he drew closer, but on seeing Bayle, his face cleared. "Nathan? Is that you?"

Bayle set down the bucket and the newcomer discarded his own burden so they could clasp hands. "I'm surprised to see you in this place, boy."

Boy! Helena frowned at Bayle, who had always been an adult to her. Brief introductions followed, during which Helena ignored Gil Fellowes's disapproving looks as Bayle explained their purpose.

She imagined Bayle would most likely receive a lecture from his Uncle Gil later.

"There are so many," Helena whispered, easing along the wall. "Not all of them are wounded, surely?" Some sported open wounds she tried not to see, while others appeared unharmed, though every face showed signs of exhaustion, or despair, while some were mud-covered. "About seventy out of the five hundred," Gil whispered. "Though they all look done in."

Dull, uncaring eyes sharpened with urgency when Bayle offered them water. The fittest slurped greedily, and once fortified, handed round the ladles to others, helping prop up the heads of the more badly injured who needed assistance.

"We'll need more water," Bayle said when they were

still only about ten feet inside the door.

"There's a pump out back," Gil said. "The guard there owes me, so I'll fetch some."

"Perhaps you should go, Helena?" Bayle held out the bucket.

"Keep going. I haven't found anything yet, and that other soldier will be back soon."

Gil exchanged an astonished look with Bayle, who shrugged. Helena would have liked to have gone with him, but forced herself to remain inside the stifling church, though none of the men took any notice of her as she picked her way through patches of floor space, searching for familiar features. Hair of a certain colour, or a boot she had seen before.

Helena edged round a stone pillar, where a huddle of men lay between the altar and the back wall. Helena crept closer, her skirt hitched away from blood-soaked bodies and a pool of vomit on the floor, peering into dirty faces and unfocussed eyes. A sudden jolt went through her as her gaze locked with a young face, one side caked with blood from a head-wound. He lay on his back staring at the ceiling with glazed, unseeing eyes.

"You know him?" Gil asked, moving to her side.

"Yes." Helena released a long breath, guilty at the rush of relief that had flooded through her.

"It's Parry, the stable lad." Bayle dipped a cup into the bucket and brought it to the boy's dry lips, but he had no strength to swallow, and the water dribbled down the side of his face.

"He's barely conscious," Gil whispered.

"What can we do?" Helena swallowed. Parry was barely sixteen, little older than Henry. He looked so out of place here, filthy and battered. So unlike the cheerful lad who drew Bayle's wrath for whistling in the yard.

"Nothing. He'll not last another night." Bayle straightened and approached a prone form that lay a few feet away. An older man lay on his side, one arm flung over his head. He wore a brown plush coat with a row of silver buttons that caught her eyes as Bayle rolled him onto his back.

Helena's gaze shifted to his face and she froze.

A roaring began inside her head and her breath caught in her throat as he stared down at a familiar face now devoid of animation and life. "Who is he?" Gil asked, his voice flat.

"Was," Bayle emphasized. "He was Edmund Woulfe."

Gil bent and moved the stained cravat to one side. "Slashed across the neck," he murmured. "Must have bled heavily on the field, for there is little blood here apart from what is on his clothes. Had he died there they would have left him."

Helena couldn't move, her welling tears threatening to choke her when Bayle's hand came down on her shoulder in silent comfort.

Gil held out a cup of water to an uninjured man leaning against a stone pillar, watching them.

"Almost dead when they brought 'im in," the man whispered through parched lips as he reached for the cup trembling hands. "Never woke up."

At a signal from Bayle, Gil lifted Edmund's body into his arms as if it weighed no more than a child, and headed toward an arched doorway off to one side of the church.

Numb with shock, Helena followed behind into a small lobby that held two doors.

Gil pushed through the one on the left with an elbow, his burden not slowing him down at all, only to be brought up short.

Helena looked over his shoulder to where a man sat at a table in the middle of the room, the remains of a scratch meal in front of him—a half-eaten heel of cheese, some coarse bread, and a jug of ale.

The three regarded each other in pregnant silence as the man at the table rose slowly to his feet. He wore a long cassock and Helena noticed that his hands were white and soft. A cleric.

At Bayle's questioning look Gil muttered, "Churchwarden."

"Master Fellowes." The churchwarden's gaze flicked

to the body in Gils arms. "Are you mad? You're risking arrest for all of us!"

"We must hide this man." Gil's voice held no trace of either urgency or fear.

The churchwarden cast a swift glance toward the window, and then seemed to make up his mind. "This way." He took them through an even lower arch where a flight of stone stairs dropped away into blackness. "The crypt. No one will think to look there."

"I'm grateful," Helena whispered as she passed him, though he avoided her eye.

At the last second the churchwarden looked into the face of Edmund Woulfe. He gave a shocked gasp and took a step back that brought him up against the wall. "He's dead!"

"He's my Uncle." Helena jutted her chin close to the cleric's face. "I'll not leave him here to be consigned to a death pit. I'm taking him home."

The churchwarden cast a terrified look at the door, then back at the two men. "T-transporting a body through the roadblocks won't be easy." He twisted his hands in front of him.

"Leave us to worry about that." Bayle impaled him with an unyielding stare. The churchwarden looked away. His shoulders slumped and, pushing past them back into the church, he left them to their task.

Helena doubted he would finish his bread and cheese.

* * *

Their slow walk back across the village green enabled Helena to study Gil properly. Shorter than Bayle, strong and stocky like many West Country men, he had a kind, open face.

Once back at the house, Jane sent the maid to fetch them a cooling drink, those first minutes spent on introductions and polite enquiries, like ordinary visitors making a call on a summer day.

Helena squeezed her eyes shut in an attempt to banish

all the horrible things she had seen in that church, first and foremost her Uncle Edmund, lying so still and broken on the flagstones.

In the crypt they laid him on a bench, covering his face with a sack. Helena had wanted to sit with him awhile, but Bayle wouldn't let her, and insisted she come back with him to the house.

When she opened her eyes again, Jane was looking at her. She bowed her head, mortified. Why did her feelings always show so clearly on her face? Had Mistress Fellowes seen it too? Her mother always said she must learn more…what was the word? *Composure.*

"We took some water into the church for the prisoners." Bayle blew air between his lips.

"Those soldiers showed some Christian charity at last, did they?" Jane shook her head. "I couldn't get near them yesterday."

Helena didn't like to tell her that Gill and Bayle had had to bribe the soldiers to be allowed in.

"Near five hundred of them in St Mary's now, Jane," Gil said. "It looks and smells like Hell itself." His knapsack landed on the scrubbed table with a thud.

"Weston has become a dreadful place." Jane turned soulful eyes on Helena. "I wish you could have seen it before all this death and misery came, my dear."

Gil leaned closer to his wife and whispered something. Jane blanched and looked away, a hand to her mouth, as if words were inadequate.

"I think we know someone who could help you." Gil's gruff voice rumbled from somewhere deep in his chest. "He's one of Churchill's captains. He's less eager to torture the sick and dying, unlike some."

"Who is he?" Bayle asked.

"Doesn't matter. He's been charged with listing the names of all those brought in, so he may be able to omit a name or two from the lists."

"Where do we take him?" Helena asked, dully, her head spinning. "You said we cannot go home. Not to Loxsbeare."

"Perhaps not. We'll take him to Ideswell, to Samuel Ffoyle's. Your mother and brother will be there by now."

Helena nodded, though she barely heard him. Those dreadful words kept repeating inside her head. Edmund is dead. He has not gone to the city for a day to return with Fuller's earth on his clothes, and ale on his breath. There would be no more teasing, no more secret winks behind her mother's back, no one to sneak food to her room when she was banished without supper for disrespect. He would never open his arms to enfold her in his strong hug while she laughed in protest that he was crushing her.

He was gone.

Her throat felt scratchy, and hot tears trickled down her cheeks. She palmed them away with trembling hands.

"Gil says neither Sir Jonathan nor Aaron is on the lists of prisoners, so they haven't been captured." The word *yet* hung between them. "However, there is no way of knowing whether they have been killed in battle, or escaped. Perhaps we'll find someone who can tell us something."

Helena jerked up her chin and stared at them. "No!"

Three faces stared back.

"You've been very kind to us, Master Fellowes, Mistress. However, I—we—have no right to endanger you further."

Gil inclined his head with a sad grin. "This is a dangerous place, my dear, whether you are here or not."

Jane nodded silently beside him.

"You have to live here when we are gone," Helena persisted, "where so many are being arrested on the flimsiest of excuses."

"Do you have a plan?" Bayle asked, sceptical. "The roads are going to be filled with soldiers within the next few hours. Our journey here was relatively easy. I doubt we'll get home again completely unmolested. Especially when…." He left the words unsaid, but Helena was aware they would have been *taking a body through hostile countryside*. She wasn't sure what to do next. As for a plan…she didn't have one.

"I asked some of the men if they had heard of the

Woulfes," Bayle said. "Most knew the name, but not what had happened to them during the battle, or even afterwards."

"That's hardly surprising. It must have been chaos out there," Gil said.

"It's hopeless isn't it?" Helena sniffed.

"No one we spoke to saw him fall, so that can only be good news," Bayle said. "Maybe he— they—got away."

"Or one or both of them have already been hanged on the roads…like…those…." Her welling tears blurred their faces.

Bayle's hand came down on her shoulder again. "I doubt that, Helena. That soldier at the inn told me Feversham has had orders to return all the prisoners to their home towns to stand trial. Someone like Sir Jonathan would be a good trophy for them."

"What do you mean, trophy?" Helena blew her nose on the kerchief Jane handed her.

Bayle exchanged a loaded look with Gil.

"They would want everyone who knew him to know of his…humiliation," Gil said.

Helena nodded, resigned. Everything they said made sense. If her father and brother had been captured, there was no chance of helping them escape. They would most likely reach Exeter before she did. Her best chance would be to go home and wait for them to be brought in by the militia. If they had got away, they would hardly tell everyone where they were, so again, she would have no option but to wait and see.

"By asking around as to their whereabouts, we not only put their names on the list of rebels, but we put them in greater danger by those who decide it's worth their while handing them in for a reward."

"I didn't think of that," Helena said. "But couldn't we...." A shout, followed by the sound of scuffling feet, drew them all to the window.

"They're marching the prisoners out," Bayle said.

Helena gripped the sill, staring at the men in their distinctive knee-length scarlet coats with turned-back cuffs faced with sea-green, unfastened due to the hot day. Broad brimmed black hats with green bands worn over sweaty faces, their leather baldrics and swords, and knapsacks completed their get-up.

"Karce's men," Gil growled at her side.

The church door opened, and the rebels emerged, squinting against the sudden light. Chained and fettered, the prisoners were manacled in pairs. Some walked and others shuffled unsteadily. The more badly wounded, dragging bound limbs encrusted with dried blood, needed support from those beside them.

Soldiers on either side of the column shoved and jostled them to move faster. When one or two lost their footing, they were forced back in line with the butts of muskets.

A crowd of silent villagers gathered at the edge of the green. Those getting too close or staring too hard were pushed back roughly.

Helena could not see their faces. She bit her lip so hard, she tasted blood. Even at that distance, their despair was palpable.

The column set off down the road whence she and Bayle had arrived on that morning, with two carts at the rear carrying the more severely wounded.

Helena turned away. Never had she felt more wretched in her life.

"Poor beggars," Gil murmured at her shoulder.

* * *

Helena spent a restless night in the room under the eaves, her dreams filled with scenes of her childhood, all of which included her Uncle Edmund. He had always been more like an older brother than an uncle, spoiling her with trinkets and making excuses for the boys when they got into scrapes.

He had left Exeter for London when he was eighteen to work for Master Samuel Pepys in the Navy Office administration. With a promising career ahead of him,

Edmund purchased a house in Greenwich and married Catherine Jenkins, a London merchant's daughter. Within two years they had two sons, and life held promise.

However, as philosophers and the dispossessed will testify, when men make plans, God laughs. The plague that struck to London that year killed thousands, and although Edmund escaped contagion, his young wife and their infant boys died within days. Father had told her many times of his frantic ride to London, where he found Edmund standing silent guard over their wrapped corpses, waiting for the death cart to take them to the lime pits.

As a child, Helena would often find her uncle standing morosely on the Weare Cliffs, a faraway look in his eyes, as if he were imagining a happier time; she accepted his need for solitude as a matter of course.

Helena woke as the first fingers of dawn crept across the sky, a smile on her lips as the images of her dream lingered. Then reality hit, and she moaned aloud in grief. She turned puffy eyes into the pillow, her chest constricted with dread that she would have to tell her mother, and when—if—they came home, Aaron and Father too.

Jane and Gil awaited her in the scullery, their drawn faces showing their night had been no more restful than her own. Refusing their offer of food, she sipped some milk.

"Nathan is waiting for you in the back lane with the cart." Gil hooked a thumb at the rear door. "The soldier helped us load it earlier."

Helena nodded, knowing full well what the load he referred to was, dreading the moment when she would have to see for herself.

Jane shed a tear and Gil bowed self-consciously as they took their farewells.

Unable to bear their compassionate kindness a moment longer, Helena hurried out into the lane.

Bayle stood talking to the soldier who had let them into the church the day before. A short plug bayonet hung from a leather baldric, heavily stained with a blackish crust. The ponies nickered at her approach and the soldier's eyes widened for a second, then he turned away. He gave a sharp nod and disappeared in the direction of the church.

"Can we trust him?" Helena whispered, taking the soldier's place. "He looked alarmed when he saw me."

"He has as much to lose as we do." Bayle circled the cart, checking the traces. "He would rather not have seen you."

She climbed onto the wooden bench and glanced into the flatbed. Her eyes instantly clouded with tears.

A length of black cloth hung down over the upright sides of the cart, secured at the corners with a white ribbon fashioned in the shape of a cross. Looped around the sides were roses and sprigs of wildflowers, their subtle scent drifting into the morning air.

This simple and touching display of respect left Helena speechless. Bayle busied himself with their bags, as if to allow her a moment of private grief.

"Shrouding a lie in a truth," she whispered in a choked voice.

Heaving himself onto the platform, Bayle stared straight ahead and flicked the reins. As the cart lurched forward, Helena turned and waved at the two figures who stood in the shadows at the rear of their house. Would she ever see them again?

The cart rolled through the silent village. A row of gibbets had appeared on the Bridgwater Road overnight, from which swung the corpses of summarily hanged rebels dragged from their hiding places, their captors eager for blood.

Repelled yet fascinated, Helena looked into rows of distorted faces, all frozen in their last attempts to draw breath. Like the corpses hanging from the trees, they followed Bayle and Helena with sightless eyes. She bit her lip, aware the bodies would shortly to turn to a decay the villagers would be forced to endure.

The horses threw up their heads at the swaying limbs and the stench of blood, only settling again when Bayle clicked his tongue and encouraged them gently to keep going.

"Where did you go last night?" Helena asked. "I heard

the door catch. I wasn't asleep."

He gathered the reins in one hand. "The churchwarden has furnished me with a letter that states we are transporting a Weston man who died of smallpox two days ago."

Helena nodded, inwardly congratulating him for the foresight she knew was completely beyond her. What would she have done without him?

Chapter 8

Helena spotted the patrol as they topped a small rise. Her heart hammered and she began to feel nauseous, but when she saw there were only two soldiers, she relaxed. "Not much of a patrol," she sniffed, though her hands felt clammy.

"Don't be deceived, one musket can kill as well as six," Bayle mumbled out of the corner of his mouth. The soldiers looked hot and tired, their coats flung open and hats tilted on the back of their heads. Two horses had been tethered to a tree at the side of the road, tails lazily flicking away flies, their heads down as if they had been there for a while.

Helena swallowed. These two were professional soldiers. Their long-coats had faded across the shoulders, now reddish-brown from marching long distances in all weathers. Patched in places, the turned-back cuffs were no longer crisp. The younger one had a front tooth missing, while the other sported a cropped ear and two hacked-off fingers.

"Where are ye bound?" the officer snarled.

The soldier raked Helena from head to toe with bloodshot eyes, then moved out of her line of sight to the back of the cart. Her breath hitched as he laid his musket on the ground, then flipped the corner of the covering back.

Beside her, Bayle tensed but his face remained calm. The cart creaked and a bird called from a nearby tree as the first soldier approached Bayle's side.

"What ye carrying?" the man at the rear asked, flicking a contemptuous hand at the arranged flowers.

Bayle took the churchwardens' letter from his waistcoat, handing it over.

The soldier gave the parchment a contemptuous look,

but ignored it.

"He can't read," Helena whispered, gripping Bayle's forearm.

"Whatever it is, we'll take it," the officer said, laughing. "The cart and horses too." He raised his musket slowly, but before he could take aim, Bayle lunged for the soldier, both hands clamped round the man's throat.

Helena gasped as together, they tumbled onto the road, with Bayle's full weight on top of the soldier, who had no chance to cry out.

In the instant it took for his companion to register what was happening, without thinking, Helena leapt down from the cart and swept the second musket from the ground.

The soldier froze, both hands held up in surrender, his eyes going from her face to the gun and back again.

Aware she could never work out how to fire the weapon in time, even if it was loaded, anger and desperation gave her strength as she swung it in a wide arc, catching the butt on the side of his head.

The soldier hit the ground with a dull thump, and stayed there.

With no hand on the rein, the startled horses crabbed sideways, the rear wheels threatening to crush Bayle and the soldier beneath him.

Dropping the musket, Helena ran to the front of the cart and grabbed the reins, stilling the horses.

Bayle's superior weight pinned the officer to the road, though he flailed uselessly with both arms. Bayle scrambled to his knees, pulled his arm back and punched the man squarely in the face. The flailing stopped as the man lost consciousness.

Torn between trying to help and keeping the cart still, Helena could only watch with growing horror as the soldier she had hit stumbled to his feet and pulled a knife from his belt. He must have still been stunned as he swayed, and staggered towards Helena.

She opened her mouth to shout, but just then Bayle yelled, "Helena, move!"

Instinctively, she threw herself sideways away from

the cart, hit the ground and lay still just as a shot echoed across the fields, sending up a flock of crows in a nearby tree, dying away quickly into the afternoon quiet.

She rolled over in time to see the soldier's eyes widen in shock. He crumpled to his knees as a crimson bloom spread over the front of his shirt. The knife fell from his hand and, with a final grunt, he fell forwards onto the road.

Shaking, Helena scrambled to her feet and staggered toward the cart, grabbing at the reins just as the wheels began to turn again. A groan came from the man on the ground behind them. Helena was about to call out in warning, but in two strides, Bayle raised the musket he had just fired and brought the wooden butt down on the man's temple with a sickening crack.

Helena thrust her fist into her mouth to muffle a scream, transfixed by the unnatural dent in the man's skull. She looked down at her skirt, where spots of blood soaked into the fabric.

The metallic tang of blood filled the air. The horses snorted in panic and strained against the reins, taking all of Helena's strength to keep them from bolting. When she could bring herself to look, Bayle was dragging the shot soldier toward a deep ditch at the side of the road.

"There should have been six of them," Bayle grunted as, with a final heave, the body rolled into the ditch, flattening the long grass on the incline.

"Help me," Bayle instructed, indicating the second man.

Her chest heaved and she widened her eyes in shock, but bracing herself, she gripped the end of the soldier's long buff coat and, with Bayle bearing most of the weight, they inched toward the ditch.

Helena closed her eyes as the body disappeared over the side, though it made no sound.

"They are visible if one stands here," Bayle said, "Though I doubt they can be spotted by a casual observer from the road.

"How long before they find them, do you think?" Helena asked.

"The others, if there are any, could be back at any time." Bayle jerked his head toward the road ahead. "They are always in packs, like dogs." He collected the other musket and threw both guns in after them.

"What about their horses?" Helena nodded toward the docile animals grazing a few feet away.

"We'll get rid of anything which marks them out as soldiers' mounts, then turn them out in that field over there." Bayle nodded to a meadow beyond the hedge.

While Bayle removed the saddles, Helena grabbed the trooper's hats, knapsacks and cooking utensils, which joined the bodies in the ditch.

By the time she had finished, her chest burned with the effort and the emotional toll of what they had done. What *she* had done.

The soldier's knife lay where he had dropped it, but she couldn't bring herself to return to the ditch, and instead, tucked it into the pocket of her skirt. A skirt with blood on it, which she intended to burn at her first opportunity.

The cart no longer resembled a funeral wagon. The cross and the flowers had been ripped away, leaving the black cloth draped untidily over the body.

She stood transfixed by the shape wrapped tightly in linen, the head, torso and legs clearly defined, like a large doll with no face.

At first, she could not reconcile the lifeless object in the flatbed with the dynamic man she had loved. Then common sense took over, and she knew this was indeed her Uncle Edmund. Her throat closed and tears spilled down her face, leaving her breathless and shaking.

Bayle gave a muttered curse, then flipped the cover back into place, painstakingly securing the sides. He then helped her back onto her seat and climbed in beside her.

"Let's get Master Edmund home and give him a proper burial." Helena nodded, her bottom lip gripped between her teeth.

Alert for the sound of pounding hooves, she kept a careful eye on the horizon, holding fast to the seat as the cart bumped over ruts recently dried out after days of heavy rain.

When they had gone another mile, the tremor in Helena's hands turned to uncontrollable shaking, as she could not get the image of the dead soldier's battered skull out of her head.

"We-we killed two men, Bayle."

He flicked the reins against the flank of the nearest horse, his gaze straight ahead. "Forget them, and tell no one what happened today. Ever."

* * *

Helena awoke nestled between clean sheets in a bedroom she didn't recognize. Bleary-eyed from sleep, she pushed aside the coverlet and stumbled across bare floorboards to the window, from where she could see undulating green fields lying beneath the early morning heat-haze.

A scattering of sheep grazed on a hillside, where the figures of field workers were framed against a clear blue sky.

She wrinkled her brow in an effort to think. Reality returned, and with a groan, she turned away. Last night she and Bayle had come home, but not to her home. Not Loxsbeare.

Tears stung her eyes. Would she ever live there again? She had left for Somerset days before with a determination to find her family: battered and weary perhaps, but whole and alive. To have returned with a corpse and no news of either her father or brother was an ignominious defeat.

Harsh realism she felt ill-equipped to handle had thrust away her innocent and happy childhood. How she longed for her mother's smile and Henry's laughter, but would anything be the same after what she had seen?

It was very late when they arrived, and the household had retired for the night. Exhausted, Bayle had steadied himself against the cart, one fist pressed to the small of his back. Close to collapse herself, Helena berated herself for drawing him into her misguided folly. Would he forgive her impetuosity someday? Or had he done so already?

She offered neither resistance nor co-operation as Meghan, roused from her bed and still sleepy, had peeled away Helena's dirt-caked gown.

Born in the damp hills of Wales, Meghan Ffoyle was the same age as Helena's mother, but looked older. Her broad cheekbones and near-black eyes betrayed her foreign origins. When the solitary bachelor Samuel Ffoyle visited Caernarvon in search of Welsh sheep for his farm more than twenty years before, he had surprised everyone by bringing more than thirty healthy ewes back to Devon with him.

Clad in her grubby linen shift, a garment Helena resolved to burn at the first opportunity, she had collapsed onto the bed where sleep instantly claimed her.

The room, with its low ceilings with black oak beams and sparkling white walls, seemed too large for one person. A massive four-poster oak bed stood at one end, and there was a dresser polished to a rich glow on the other side of the room.

With a start of surprise, she spotted some of her own belongings. A wooden chest that had once occupied her own chamber sat beneath the window. Her prayer book and tortoiseshell combs lay on a table by the bed beside a familiar carved wooden box containing her unimpressive collection of jewels.

With a sudden urgency, Helena rummaged through the chest. Her search came up empty. She tried the smaller box next, expelling a sigh of relief when her hands closed on her brown leather book. Henry had kept his promise, and her journal was safe.

She bit her lip, frowning. Mother must have left Loxsbeare in a hurry, even with all their things here. *Is this where they were to stay, at the Ffoyles'? And if so, for how long?*

The sound of approaching footsteps in the corridor sent Helena flying in search of something to wear over her shift. Before she could locate any of her clothes, the door swung inwards with a sharp click; it was Susannah, Samuel and

Meghan's eldest daughter. She carried a pitcher from which rose wisps of steam, and one of Helena's own gowns draped over one arm. Susannah's looks were similar to her father's: tall and spare, with an oval face and high cheekbones, her nut-brown eyes identical to all the Ffoyle children. She was nineteen years old.

"Good morrow Helena," she greeted her shyly, closing the door with a swift backward kick.

"And to you," Helena murmured, unsure of what was expected of her. Should she ask all the questions circling in her head, or wait? Deciding on practicalities first, Helena discarded the gritty shift that chafed her skin, and washed luxuriously in the hot water.

Susannah also shared her father's tact; for apart from asking Helena if she slept well, she made no mention of how she had passed the previous two days.

"I shall never take cleanliness for granted again." Helena's voice was muffled by folds of the gown Susannah pulled over her head. "I was so tired last night, I could barely stand. Is my mother awake yet?"

Susannah's hands stilled on the fastenings, but she did not reply.

Helena smoothed the gown over her hips, adjusting the bodice, frowning. "Susannah?"

"Master Henry is here." Susannah avoided her eyes as she collected pitchers and discarded linens. "Your maid, too."

"Chloe?" Helena gasped in surprise. "Why did she not come and help me dress?"

Susannah turned for the door, her back stiff. "I will send Father to you." Before Helena could question her further, she hurried out.

Puzzled, Helena sat on the bed, listening with growing unease to a murmur of voices in the corridor outside. The words were indistinct, but the timbre indicated there was something wrong. When Samuel finally appeared, Helena jerked to her feet, though her greeting froze on her lips at the sight of his distraught face.

"How are you this morning, my dear?" He strode to the

window and then the fireplace, where he ran a hand along the mantel, but after that first swift glance when he entered, he avoided her eyes.

A flutter of dread opened like wings in her stomach, threatened to fly into her throat and choke her. "I-I am well, Master Ffoyle. I must thank you for allowing us to seek refuge in your home. Mother and I are—" she broke off when he flinched.

"There's something, I have to tell you." He coughed into a fist, opened his mouth and then shut it again.

Helena waited. The silenced stretched between them, until her fear overcame her good manners. "Master Ffoyle, I beg you, tell me what has happened. Apart from us being thrown out of our own home I mean." Her harsh laugh fell flat in the face of his deadpan expression.

He closed his eyes and took a deep breath. "Lady Elizabeth…your mother…is dead."

"What are you saying?"

What cruel trick was this? It couldn't be true; Mother had been alive only three days before. Bayle said the plan was to go to Ideswell, so she would be safe. How could she be dead?

He made no attempt to reassure her, but merely stared at the floor.

Incensed, Helena flew at him, clutching at his coat. Anger gave her strength and she hauled on the heavy serge and gave him a firm shake that made his eyes widen in shock. "How could you have let such a thing happen?"

Samuel's large hands closed on her upper arms and held her still, his gaze holding hers. "I cannot tell you how distressed I am."

"How can she be dead?" Helena's hands slid down his lapels and she kept repeating the words in her head. *How can she be dead*?

"Soldiers came and seized Loxsbeare," Samuel said, his voice, calm. "Trained bands, I imagine. They were an unruly bunch." His reasonable tone started to grate, though his eyes pleaded for understanding. "There was a scuffle. Your mother—she fell."

You were there?" She dropped her hands from his coat and backed away when he nodded.

Blindly she clutched the bedpost to keep from crumpling to the floor; her grip so hard, the carvings cut into her hand, though the pain kept her from fainting, while Samuel's voice came to her as if from far away.

Her mind could barely take in what he was saying, though when he recounted the part about her mother's sapphire necklace, she thumped a clenched fist against the bedrail. "Why didn't you do something? Where were Lumm, and Henry?" A dreadful thought slammed into her. "Dear God, Henry! Where is he? Did the soldiers hurt him? Is he alive?"

"Henry is distraught, but he is quite well. He is here, waiting to see you."

Relief surged in her chest to hear her brother was alive, only to be replaced by a red mist that appeared before her eyes. "Father did this to us," she spat. "He left us all alone at the militia's mercy, and for what?" She paced the room, ignoring the pounding in her temples. "Uncle Edmund too with his obsessive hatred of Catholics. Aaron blindly followed Monmouth's men simply to impress Father." All her pent-up emotions of the last few days flooded out until, spent, she sank down on the bed. "And now Mother has been taken from me too."

Samuel reached for her arm to help her stand up. "They had to follow their consciences, my dear. Your father truly believed he was doing right."

She recoiled from his touch. "I care nothing for who rules the country! Kings, bishops or cloth workers, it doesn't matter. I want my home and my life back as it was."

Meghan appeared at the doorway, her handsome face dulled by pity. She touched Samuel's shoulder and mouthed something Helena didn't hear. He nodded and with his head down, retreated from the room.

Helena curled herself into the covers on the unmade bed, her knees drawn into her chest, the coverlet gripped beneath her chin. "It was because I didn't bring Aaron back," she whispered. "Mother's dead, because I couldn't do the one thing she wanted. And now I never can."

Her eyes burned, her face becoming sticky from tears and mucus as she wailed like a child. "She could have waited for me," she cried, knowing her words made no sense.

Her storm of emotion abated slowly, while Meghan's strong arms massaged her shoulders and stroked her hair, whispering endearments that leached through Helena's skin and into her heart.

Helena was too exhausted to cry any more, and her sobs turned to hiccoughing and moans. Susannah appeared, a bowl and damp linen cloth in hand. She sat on the side of the bed, and bathed Helena's face, alleviating the heat and removing the stickiness from her skin. At last, Helena grew calmer, and pulled away from Susannah's touch, avoiding Meghan's knowing gaze. "Where is Henry? I want to see Henry."

Her brother must have been waiting outside in the hall, for as the women withdrew, Henry dashed past them, halting self-consciously in front of her. He looked so young in a pair of too-large breeches he must have borrowed from one of the Ffoyle boys, his hair all tangled and his eyes red from crying. He held his hands away from his sides, and then dropped them again in a gesture of helplessness, his bottom lip quivering.

Helena opened her arms and he threw himself into her embrace.

"I would have killed him had I a weapon," he said between muffled gasps, his chin pressed into her shoulder. "Samuel would have too, but Lumm said the men would have shot us." He pulled back an arm's length and stared into her eyes. "Ellie, Mama did not even have the Passing Bell."

"I know." She nodded, her hands sliding to either side of his face, her gaze shifting to the bandage wrapped round his forehead. "You're injured?"

"It doesn't hurt much anymore."

"I shouldn't have left her." Helena gently stroked the

white cloth round his head. “I shouldn’t have left you.”

He straightened, his hands grasped her shoulders so tightly, she winced, his gaze locked with hers, no longer distraught but determined. “I couldn’t save Mother any more than you could have saved Uncle Ned.”

“Oh Henry, I didn’t mean…it’s just….” Weariness and misery overcame her. She would have been every bit as helpless when the soldiers came. Henry was no more responsible than Samuel, or Tobias. The troopers killed Mother, despite Samuel’s insistence that it was an accident.

She wrapped both arms round him. “I must go and apologize to Master Ffoyle.”

“He’ll understand.” Henry blew his nose nosily on the kerchief she handed him. “Those troopers could have killed me, you know, had Samuel not been there.”

“I realize that.” Shame heated her face as she recalled her outburst earlier. “Let’s go and find him.”

Chapter 9

Daylight faded as the Ffoyle carriage rolled through Exeter city's the West Gate and up Fore Street. Turning left at the top, they rolled into Mary Arches Lane, halting outside the church. The windows of the square tower glowered above them like blackened eyes.

Helena climbed down from the carriage and approached the door, her hand clasped firmly in Henry's.

Somehow, the news had spread, and the road outside was lined with curious onlookers, some of whom Helena recognised. Her gaze flicked over their faces; the Blandens were not there. Before they reached the church door, a clutter of hooves thundered into the street, and all eyes turned to stare at a troop of soldiers who halted in the road.

Helena fought to calm her rapid breathing, but the troopers did not dismount, watching with surly expressions as the party milled around the parvis.

"I don't recognise any of them," Henry whispered. "They weren't the ones who came to the house."

Helena narrowed her eyes. "Let them do as they please, they cannot hurt us anymore." She shoved Henry before her through the church door, where the musty air made Helena cough, the sound echoing into the cavernous roof.

The tiny congregation consisted of Samuel and Meghan with their four eldest children, as well as Henry, Lumm and Nathan Bayle, all seated in the front pews of the nearly empty church.

Helena's confident tone of earlier had been sheer bravado. She spent the ceremony darting furtive glances at the door, half-expecting the soldiers to burst in and stop the proceedings.

Master Triske appeared equally unsettled as he

hastened through the service, not once saying her Uncle's name aloud. He referred to him only as "our brother".

It struck Helena as a sad thing to be committed to one's grave without a name. Her gaze remained fixed on the two coffins that lay side by side on makeshift biers in front of the altar. How was it possible that her dynamic uncle and her tall, beautiful mother be contained in such small wooden boxes?

Six slow tolls of the Passing Bell sounded to signify the death of a woman, followed by one ring for each year of her age. Edmund Woulfe went to his final rest in silence.

"Mother has had the Passing Bell, Henry," Helena whispered to the silent figure at her side.

He nodded, his gaze fixed on the floor, and at intervals swiped a hand across his eyes.

When the service ended, the churchwarden helped Bayle, Samuel, and the elder Ffoyle boys carry the coffins inside the vault below the altar. When they emerged, the iron door clanged shut, the hollow sound resonating in Helena's head. Blinking back tears, she stumbled from the gloomy building into the summer night.

Master Triske caught up with her outside the church, his face a grey blur in the low light. "I trust you won't neglect your devotions, my dear. It is times such as these that your faith is tested. Even in your sorrow, you must not fail your Savior."

Helena fixed him with a contemptuous stare, then stepped closer until her gaze locked with his. "Take your platitudes and expend them on someone who wants to hear them. God has taken more from me than you could ever imagine. I have not failed Him. He has failed me."

The minister stepped back, his eyes widening at the affront, his mouth opening and closing soundlessly.

Samuel started to offer apologies, but the minister waved the Master of Clothworkers away and fled back to the vestry, his gown flapping.

Helena watched him go, taking the last vestiges of her resentment with him, the vengeful grief that had twisted her insides all day reduced to no more than a quiet sadness.

Mother and Uncle Ned were both safe now; nothing could ever hurt them again.

"The soldiers have gone," she whispered, though Susannah must have heard her, as she muttered, "Thank the Lord" at her shoulder.

Helena tilted her head back as pinpoints of light appeared in the deep blue canopy of sky above her. An owl hooted from a tree in the deserted Bartholomew Street, where a lone carriage horse whickered in impatience.

She linked her arm through Susannah's as they made their way back to the carriage. "When my time comes," Helena said. "I think I should like to be buried by moonlight."

"There is no moon," Henry muttered flatly from behind them.

* * *

During the coming days, troopers came to the village and searched houses, questioned villagers, bullied women, and struck out at young boys and old men alike for imagined insolence.

Helena watched fearfully from an upstairs window, as uniformed men hovered by the gate to the farm. Had someone told the magistrate she and Henry had sought refuge with the Ffoyles? If so, would they have to face punishment for protecting the family of a known rebel?

She jumped at the clack of the door latch, releasing a pent-up breath at the sight of Rebekah's smiling face. "Mother asks if you'll come and join us in the kitchen."

"Yes, of course. I'll be there in a moment."

Rebekah's head disappeared and Helena checked the road for soldiers again, relieved to see they appeared to have left. She picked up her piece of sewing to examine with a critical eye. Her work wasn't anywhere as skilled as Meghan's, but in her efforts to be useful and not simply an idle guest, Helena had insisted she give the task a try.

On her way to the kitchen, she hoped Deb would forgive her for the sub-standard garment when the time came.

"Wherever the duke is now, he stands little chance of being king," Helena heard Bayle say as she entered the room. He looked up and their gazes met for a long second before he turned away. The combined guilt of her mother's death still hung between them like a specter neither could face. When Bayle was told about her mother's death, he had shut himself in the stable for two days, refusing to speak to anyone.

Helena had tried to approach him, but he must have guessed her intentions, and whenever she entered a room where she was told he would be, he always made an excuse to leave.

"A Captain Morton stopped by yesterday," Samuel said. "He thinks any rebels who managed to get this far will have gone to ground by now. The militia will be disbanded soon."

"Thank the Lord for that," Meghan muttered. "No more gibbets on the roads."

Helena flinched as an image of corpses twisting slowly from a tree in Weston Zoyland floated back into her head.

"Would you fetch some ale, Chloe?" Susannah instructed, handing pewter cups around the table.

"I'm a lady's maid, not a scullery girl," Chloe snapped, throwing Helena a pleading look.

"This is a working farm," Susannah scoffed. "There are no ladies here." The cup she set before Chloe landed with a thump. "I'll get the milk, as our visitor seems too proud to soil her hands." Susannah sniffed as she left the room.

"Do as she asks, Chloe," Helena said, pretending not to see the maid's sullen expression face as she complied, her limp somewhat more exaggerated as she moved away.

Helena might lack the confidence to stand up for Chloe, but knew exactly how she felt. Helena didn't belong here, either. But then where did she belong? For the first time in her life, she had no idea what would happen to her tomorrow. Or the next day.

She and Henry couldn't stay with the Ffoyles

indefinitely. But what were they meant to do until her father and Aaron returned? *If they returned.*

Meghan reached across the space between them and, wordlessly, pressed Helena's hand before rising from her chair with a sharp clap of her hands. "Girls, come and help me lay the table for supper."

"May I help you as well?" Helena asked, half-rising.

Meghan waved her away. "I have strapping girls enough to help me here, and a kitchen full of servants who need no excuses to avoid work." She turned away with a groan. "Deb! Not three jugs at once, you'll be bound to break one."

The sound of the outer door opening announced the arrival of Elias, who had been absent most of the day. His clothes sported a layer of dust, and he looked sweaty and uncomfortable, a grim expression on his handsome face.

"Exeter busy?" His father asked, a casual question Elias didn't answer straight away. Instead, he eased out of his coat with an expressive sigh. He hung his hat on a hook by the door, then turned to face the room. "The militia found Monmouth."

An expectant hush fell on the usually noisy kitchen, hands stilled in mid-task and conversations ceased.

"It's all here in the newssheet." He slapped a page onto the kitchen table, which was instantly tussled over by two of his siblings.

He slid onto the wooden bench beside Helena, his gaze holding hers. "He was found in a ditch, somewhere near Cranbourne Chase."

"Was anyone with him?" Helena asked, her fists clenched in her lap as she awaited his answer.

"A man named Oliver Buyse, but no one else."

"I see." She summoned a weak smile, not knowing whether to feel relieved or sad.

Elias placed a gentle hand on her arm. "Helena, Monmouth's been executed. Beheaded. At Westminster Hall three days ago."

Her breath caught in her throat. "Without a trial?"

Elias shrugged. "He didn't need one. The king issued

an Act of Attainder against him. He was doomed."

Doomed. The word her mother used when she last spoke of her father. Who would tell Henry? He still thought Monmouth was a hero. When he knew he was dead, would he lose all hope for their father too? Would she lose hope herself?

"So it is over?" Seth asked, his face pale.

"It was over after the battle at Weston." Samuel silenced him with a look. "It says here, the king granted Monmouth a final audience," he read aloud from the newssheet he had wrestled from Seth. "I assume he did so to torment Monmouth, for it's a privilege usually extended to those about to be pardoned."

"How cruel," Meghan muttered from a stool where she mended a torn petticoat. Her deft fingers pleated the edges so the tear could not be seen.

Helena gripped the much creased petticoat in her lap. Suddenly her fingers wouldn't co-operate, so she abandoned it with a sigh.

"Cruel indeed," Samuel said, nodding. "It seems Monmouth pleaded for his life and even offered to convert to Catholicism."

"Oh. He shouldn't have done that." Meghan tutted. "King James would despise him for such weakness."

The door latch clacked again, and Henry burst inside from the yard, Robbie and Deb close behind. His face, if not carefree and happy, at least looked healthy from good food and time spent in the sun. His wound had healed well, a yellowish bruise above his eye the only remaining evidence, which Meghan assured him would not leave a scar.

Rebekah removed a basket of eggs from Deb's unsteady hands, handing it to her mother. She bent and whispered something to her sister, at which Deb's brown eyes slid to Helena and away again.

Robbie straddled a stool, one leg bent across the other as he struggled to remove his boots. "Two troopers offered Henry and me five shillings for turning in fugitive rebels."

Meghan transferred eggs from Deb's basket into an

earthenware bowl, pausing only to throw her exuberant son a reproachful look.

Helena tried to catch Henry's eye, but he had already spotted the newssheet.

"May I see the Gazette, sir?" Henry asked, his hand already reaching for the paper in Samuel's hand.

"Samuel." Meghan's voice held a warning, while she continued transferring eggs into a bowl.

"It will do more harm to keep things from him," Samuel said, handing it over.

Elias uttered a low groan, and Helena held her breath.

Henry's gaze slid across the page, his enquiring look changing to raw anguish. His mouth worked in silence and he staggered backwards, turned and fled the room, almost colliding with a returning Susannah, a full bucket in her hands.

"Henry?" Helena called after him, retrieving the newssheet from where he had dropped it, her gaze on the closed door through which he had disappeared.

"What's upset Henry?" Susannah asked, her eyes wide.

"That the duke is dead, of course. What did you think?" Seth snapped at his sister.

"Oh no," Susannah slumped onto the bench opposite. "Why didn't anyone tell me?"

While she and Seth squabbled, chided by Meghan, Helena stared at the door through which Henry had disappeared.

When it was evident he wouldn't be coming back, she turned back to the newssheet. Turning it over, she gasped as the words jumped off the page, turning her insides to water.

Jack Ketch had taken several blows at the duke's head before throwing down his axe. Forced by an angry crowd to end Monmouth's misery, he had finished the job with a knife.

* * *

Samuel strolled through the stone archway in

Broadgate that led to Cathedral Yard, and turned into the entrance to Tom Molds, Exeter's answer to a coffee house. "Bad morning, Master Ffoyle?" the proprietor asked, setting the cup of the thick, almost black brew in front of him.

"An unpleasant business altogether, Tom." Samuel thanked the man with a nod.

Thirty men had been brought before Judge Jeffreys that morning at the Guildhall, each of the wretched creatures huddled in the dock harangued as if the judge harboured a personal hated for each one.

Samuel had chosen a seat at the back of the hall, hoping his presence would go unnoticed. The heat and stench of the press of unwashed bodies in the airless building had made the atmosphere almost unbearable. Bending his nose to his sleeve, he gave a quick sniff and grimaced.

"All condemned?" Tom asked, applying a damp cloth to a nearby table.

"Aye." Samuel said, acknowledging Tom's resigned nod.

Samuel had not joined the crowd who accompanied the prisoners to the gallows at the Heavitree. He had never regarded the spectacle of dying men the culmination of an entertaining day. Instead, he had made his way to the Guildhall with the intention of slipping into Gandy Street unseen. What happened next was something he didn't intend to reveal to the gossiping landlord of Tom Moll's.

Before Samuel had reached the door, a warden stepped out of a room in front of him, barring his way. "His Lordship asks if you would spare him a word, Master Ffoyle." His voice held a sneer, as if he was in possession of superior knowledge he had no intention of sharing.

Samuel froze, hoping his fear did not show on his face. What would Judge Jeffreys want with him? Did he know the whereabouts of Sir Jonathan Woulfe and his son?

Beckoned by bright sunshine from the half open door, Samuel considered making a run for it. A tempting thought, but one he rejected immediately. He was too well-known.

Then there were the fates of his own large brood, not to mention Helena and Henry Woulfe.

"As his Lordship wishes," Samuel inclined his head, and followed the clerk inside.

In Moll's upper room, Samuel sipped the bitter-sweet brew, reliving that strange interview in every detail.

His thoughts were still far away, when a booming voice announced the entrance of two men. Lord Miles Blanden and a companion scraped back chairs at the table beyond a wooden screen beside Samuel.

In order to acknowledge the newcomers, Samuel would have to stand up and move into their line of vision. He decided the effort required more energy than he was willing to expend and instead, reminisced further about his recent talk with Judge Jeffreys.

Lord Blanden ordered a jug of ale in his coarse, aggressive voice before resuming his conversation. Apparently overwhelmed, the serving boy spilled ale on the table and received a stream of abuse for his clumsiness.

Samuel's mind drifted, until the word "Loxsbeare" came clearly through the screen.

Alert, Samuel leaned toward the screen to listen.

"That greedy blackguard Jeffreys has ordered an examination of the property." Blanden banged his jug on the table in a display of temper.

"You think he has his eye on it for himself?" his companion suggested.

"I doubt it. He has a fine manor in Taunton. He sees this only as a profitable exercise."

"Your loyalty to the king should be rewarded." The other man whined, in an obvious effort to be ingratiating.

"I shall be, with the house and the land," Blanden said, not bothering to keep his voice down. "Though it will cost me twice what I originally offered." He gave the harsh, grating laugh of a man unused to controlling his baser instincts in polite company. "And I'll wager our esteemed judge keeps part of the money himself when it's all settled."

"Even at that price, it's still a bargain." The second

man sounded envious.

"Aye, I know, and soon Loxsbeare will be mine."

"Have you heard that the younger Woulfes are still in the district?"

"I heard." Blanden gave a derisive snort. "I haven't seen for myself. I thought they left Exeter when their mother died."

"There have been rumors about that too."

"What sort of rumors?"

"That she was murdered by the militia for her jewels."

The hairs on Samuel's neck stood up, and he had to force himself not to burst from behind the screen and confront them.

Blanden sniggered. "Makes no difference to me how it happened. Though they would do well to be out of the district before I take possession of the manor."

The men drained the last of their ale and left.

When Samuel emerged onto the cobbles outside Moll's, there was no sign of either Blanden or his unknown companion. Tipping an idle link boy with a coin to watch his horse, Samuel retraced his steps and returned to the Guildhall.

The crowds had dispersed, and the judges long gone when he located the clerk he had spoken to earlier. This time the man showed more respect and answered his questions without curiosity, even presented a few documents for Samuel to riffle through.

What he found there gave him pause for thought on his ride home to Ideswell.

Chapter 10

Helena watched as Samuel took a clay pipe from a box on the mantelpiece, then rolled it between his fingers without lighting it. She had waited for his return all day, but now he was here, she dreaded hearing what he had to say.

The family knew where Samuel had gone, and why. As soon as his horse was spotted on the road, they had crowded into the parlour in anticipation.

"The sentences were harsh," Samuel began without preamble. "But no less than expected."

"Which was…?" Elias asked. Having been refused permission to accompany Samuel to the Guildhall, resentment was visible in his set jaw and narrowed eyes.

"Sir Jonathan and Aaron Woulfe were on the list of those ordered to account for themselves during the uprising, though they did not appear in court."

Helena expelled a breath she hadn't realised she had been holding.

"Which means they're still wanted fugitives?" Henry said.

"Or dead," Seth blurted, blushing furiously at his father's hard glare.

"Over thirty men were tried at Exeter this morning," Samuel went on. "Ten received whippings, and seven will be transported. The others…." he broke off and stared at the pipe in his hand, brows knitted.

"So much misery meted out in one day." Meghan stabbed her needle into the hem of a gown Deb had torn on a nail.

"Hundreds of rebels died in an hour and one half on Sedgemoor," Henry said, his voice hard. "Hundreds more cut down by bullets and plug bayonets as they ran or—"

"Henry!" Helena snapped, her chin cocked at Deb and Robin, who both stared at him wide-eyed.

Henry fell silent, fidgeting with the buttons on his vest.

"What does transported mean, Father?" Rebekah asked, shyly.

"The condemned," Samuel began slowly, "become the property of Queen Mary Beatrice. The master who buys them as indentured labor pays her a price for each man."

"What does this master do with them?" Deb asked, frowning.

"He's a slave-master, Deb." Henry pulled hard on a button, which came off in his hand. "He'll ship them to the plantations in Jamaica and Barbados."

Helena gripped her journal in both hands. How had her kind, sweet brother become so bitter? This was so unlike him. He didn't even seem to care that Deb was near to tears and had to be comforted by Rebekah.

"How long do they have to stay there?" Susannah asked, looking up as Bayle entered the room. Smiling, she slid along the bench to make room for him.

Helena gave him an acknowledging nod, which he returned. Aware he had ridden over to Loxsbeare that morning to see Lumm, she resolved not to ask what was happening there. It would hurt too much.

"At least ten years," Samuel replied to Susannah's question. "If they can buy their passage back to England after that time, they can return home."

"…although few survive the journey," Bayle said, looking at Helena.

"What will happen to the Taunton schoolgirls?" Helena asked. "The ones who presented the duke with the banner?"

"They're to be ransomed back to their parents." Samuel fiddled with the clay pipe, making no attempt to light a taper or even fill the bowl.

Meghan sighed. "Not one of them was above ten years old."

A tremor of unease stiffened her spine. "Did something else happen in Exeter, Master Ffoyle?"

Samuel sighed. He laid down the pipe and then picked it up again filled it with tobacco. Finally he met her eye. "Benjamin Hobbs was at the Guildhall."

"Hobbs?" Henry scowled. "Our groom Hobbs? What was he doing there?"

"He sought a private audience with Judge Jeffreys when the trials were done." He plucked a taper from a box by the fire and lit it. "I was called as a witness." An expectant silence filled the room as he held the flame against the dry leaves until a wisp of smoke curled upwards from the bowl.

"What did he want, Master Ffoyle?" Henry eased forward, his chin jutted.

Helena crumpled her sewing in both hands, wincing as the needle speared her thumb.

Rebekah handed her a kerchief, and Helena dabbed at the bead of blood that appeared below her thumbnail.

Samuel flung the taper into the fire and leaned back. "I was asked to bear witness to the fact Hobbs worked for Sir Jonathan Woulfe and was in a position to swear that his Master had joined the rebels."

"He betrayed us?" Henry spat through gritted teeth, then gasped. "Benjamin saw you at Loxsbeare that day the soldiers came." Henry's voice rose "He knew you helped us!"

"What did Hobbs want in return for his — information?" Helena asked, her voice icy calm.

"He demanded a reward, what else?" Samuel shrugged. Henry leapt from his seat and Samuel stilled him with a hand. "Sit down, Henry. The man got nothing. Jeffreys had him thrown out of the Guildhall."

"Serve him right. The traitor." Henry folded his arms, his lips clamped into a thin line.

Samuel tapped the pipe stem against his lower lip, nodding. "A man like Jeffreys would never grant favours to the Benjamin Hobbs of this world. Knowing that, I refused to give credence to any of his claims, much to Hobbs fury. I advised Jeffreys do the same."

"Did he heed you, Father?" Susannah asked. She kept

glancing at Bayle, and when he turned to look at her, she turned away, her face flushed.

"Jeffreys said Hobbs had done no more than the duty his sovereign required of him. He had him thrown out of the Guildhall."

Helena silently congratulated the dreadful judge on his good sense, though it changed nothing.

They could not go back to Loxsbeare. Maybe they never would.

* * *

"There's something else," Samuel said gently. Despite having taken only a few puffs of the clay pipe, he turned it upside down and tapped it against the hearth, dislodging the smoldering contents before he continued speaking. "In May, the city wardens received a letter that laid out Sir Jonathan Wolfe's involvement in the rebellion." He paused as a ripple of low groans circled the room. "The letter quoted dates and times of clandestine meetings held at Loxsbeare in the weeks before Monmouth's landing, naming Grey, Younge, Speke and the others."

"They knew everything from the beginning?" Helena whispered, horrified.

"Who sent the letter?" Henry clenched both fists on his knees.

Samuel paused before answering. "Lord Miles Blanden."

Bayle blew out a long breath. Helena gasped.

"That cannot be! He's Father's friend." Henry thumped the arm of his chair with a fist. "It couldn't have been him!" He gestured toward Helena. "Ellie was going to marry his son."

Samuel held up his hands. "The letter carries his signature and his seal, Henry. I saw it myself."

"What did he hope to gain by betraying us?" Henry's lower lip quivered.

"Everything," Samuel replied. "Lord Blanden has petitioned the Court for possession of the house and lands of Loxsbeare."

Blood roared in Helena's ears as guilt slammed into her like a blow. If she had welcomed her betrothal to Martyn more willingly, this might not have happened. Lord Blanden would have had the links with the family he craved. Blanden had cast covetous eyes at Loxsbeare for years. His plans had been ruined by Martyn's death. The rising was the opportunity he needed. She glanced at Henry for sympathy, but he sat rigid, staring the empty grate, his mouth working silently.

Distracted by the turmoil inside her head, Helena caught only part of what Bayle was now saying to Samuel.

"...magistrate came to Loxsbeare this morning. He was angry the manor has been stripped bare and told Lumm the house was to be made ready for a new owner."

Henry gave a triumphant snort. "Serves Blanden right, I hope the soldiers pulled it to pieces."

Helena frowned, thoughtful. That made no sense. Where were her family's possessions? The two carts that stood beneath tarpaulins in the rear stables were only part of what Loxsbeare held. Is that what Benjamin had been doing, emptying the house of valuables left behind?

Did Lumm discover his stealing and throw him out? Or...were they in league together? The conversation had moved on, and she had missed her chance to ask questions, leaving her frustrated and annoyed.

Bayle withdrew without ceremony, which Helena attributed to his sense of responsibility for Hobbs's actions, although he could not have known of the man's treachery. She resolved to speak to him about it later.

"Enough talk now," Meghan said, gathering her skirts and ushering her youngest daughter out. "There are chores to be done. You boys go and fetch some firewood."

Muttering in mild protest, the Ffoyle children filed out of the room. "Are you coming, Helena?" Henry murmured when she lingered by the window.

"No, Henry, please stay." Samuel laid down the clay pipe. "You both have a decision to make."

"What kind of decision?" Helena asked warily.

"Whether or not you wish to remain in Ideswell, or leave the city altogether."

She exchanged a look with her brother, her shock mirrored in his eyes. "Leave Exeter?" they asked together.

"You may both prefer to go somewhere Sir Jonathan Wolfe's disgrace is not so well-known."

"You are sending us away?" Helena said, panicked. "Because of Father's bad judgement? Or because we are now a traitor's children, whose father abandoned us to chase his precious duke?"

"Helena!" Henry exclaimed, aghast.

Still reeling, she turned on him. "He abandoned us for his religion. How can you support his choice now?"

"Helena," Samuel's stern tone sobered her a little. "You were the most important thing in his life. One day you'll understand."

"I don't want to understand." Her voice rose in anguish "I want him back! I want them both back. Mother and Uncle Edmund are dead. What are Henry and I to do now?" As if speaking her worst fears aloud made them real, her defiance crumbled, and she knuckled hot tears away with a shaking hand. "What did he think would happen to us if Monmouth failed?"

"He never believed the rising would fail," Henry insisted bitterly.

"I think he did, or why else would he have signed certain properties over to me, to be held for you?"

"What properties?" Henry demanded, his practical nature surfacing.

"Apart from the sheep, which have been grazing on Ffoyle land since May," Samuel began, "there are the houses in Magdalen Road, the warehouse at the Quay, and your mother's jewels."

"You have mother's jewels?" Helena stared at him, incredulous. "We thought — I thought — Father sold them to buy guns for Monmouth."

"No. They are yours. Yours and Henry's, and Aaron's if…." He let the thought hang in the air.

"Not her sapphire necklace." Henry's eyes turned to

flint. “That soldier will have sold it by now.”

Samuel blew air out from between his lips. “No, not that. However, you will both have an income from the wool manufacturing and rents from the houses. There will even be sufficient money for a dowry for Helena.”

“We won’t be rich.” Henry gave an accepting shrug.

“Without the Loxsbeare lands? No.”

Helena swiped her sleeve across her eyes. What Samuel was offering was more than she could have imagined. She smoothed the folds of her skirt with trembling fingers. “Where do you suggest we go?”

Henry turned horrified eyes on her. “You want to leave Exeter? Helena, we were born here. We don’t know anywhere else.”

She lifted her chin. “You heard Master Ffoyle. We have some means. Do you want to see Lord Blanden in residence at Loxsbeare? Lording it over us in our home with our money? Riding in our carriage? Stay then, because I won’t.”

Henry opened his mouth and then shut it again with a snap.

“Have you considered London?” Samuel said, leaning back in his chair.

Helena’s stomach lurched. *London? Would that be possible*? “Father had friends in Frome and Winchester, even Taunton, but I’ve not heard of….”

“He had acquaintances in London too, Helena,” Henry said, obviously excited by the prospect. Helena hesitated. She loved Exeter, although she ventured into the city infrequently since coming to Ideswell, and when she did, she kept a shawl handy to hide behind in case she was recognised. The familiar streets felt hostile, as if she had no place there anymore. *Why not go to London*?

Samuel held up a hand. “Do not decide tonight. I’ll write a few letters to associates of mine. Between us, we may have something to offer you.”

As they took their leave, Samuel’s discreet cough made Helena pause at the door. “Don’t give up on your father just yet.”

"Why? Do you think he's still alive?" Helena was still bitter.

"I cannot know, but to my mind, the numbers don't add up."

Henry stepped back into the room. "What numbers?"

Samuel gave a slow nod, his expressive hands steepled beneath his chin. "At Sedgemoor, Monmouth had roughly four thousand men. Thirteen hundred rebel bodies were collected after the battle. Some eight hundred or so have since been captured and convicted. Say, five hundred deserted, although reports claim that figure is high. That accounts for two thirds. Where are the others?"

Henry stared at him, his lips moving. "That would mean almost fourteen hundred men are unaccounted for."

"Exactly, Henry." Samuel nodded in admiration. "Which suggests more must have escaped Sedgemoor than originally believed. As I said, don't give up hope on your father yet."

Outside in the corridor, Henry avoided his sister's goodnight kiss, and announced he would find Bayle and suggest Samuel's theory to him. "Samuel could be right, Helena. They could both be alive somewhere."

Helena nodded, but said nothing. She didn't want him to hold on to false hopes. If either of them still lived, wouldn't they have sent word by now?

She watched Henry walk away. His shoulders had broadened and his stride seemed slower, less boyish.

Helena turned in the other direction and emerged into an empty yard bathed in watery sunlight.

Susannah sat on a low wall throwing handfuls of grain to six fat geese, which nudged her and scrabbled at her feet.

Untying the cords of her cap, Helena pulled it free, and lifted her face to the sky and let the wind take her hair, blowing it around her head. She pretended to chase the indignant geese as they flapped and squawked in panic, while Susannah laughed in delight.

Coming to a breathless halt, she turned her gaze to the soft green hills around them beneath a clear sky. For the first time in weeks, she felt her future held hope.

As for finding happiness, she would have to wait and see.

* * *

A week after the assizes, Samuel settled into his customary chair at Moll's.

"The whole city must know of Blanden's betrayal by now." Samuel addressed his companion. "I doubt he'll keep the few friends he has here."

"He's taking occupation of Loxsbeare in a few days," Tobias said from his chair opposite. "And before you ask, I left last night."

Samuel nodded. "Have all the servants gone?"

"Most of them. I'm staying with my parents at *The Ship*."

"You surprise me. I did not imagine inn-keeping was to your taste."

Tobias ran a finger between his collar and his neck. "My thinking as to what suits me and what doesn't has changed of late, Master Ffoyle."

Samuel watched as first anger and then resignation crossed Tobias's handsome features. "I sought to improve your life, Tobias. Not make you dissatisfied." Samuel sighed. "For that I apologise."

"I don't blame you for Sir Jonathan's political loyalties." Tobias lifted his coffee cup, downing half the contents with a grimace.

"Why don't you order ale if you hate coffee that much?" Samuel smiled.

"I've attempted to develop more refined tastes of late." Tobias sniffed. "It seems they're somewhat redundant now."

"Sir Jonathan was proud of you."

"Not proud enough to ask me to go with him." Tobias's eyes flashed fire, hurt twisting his face.

"Had he done so, would you have gone?" Samuel peered at the younger man over the rim of his cup.

"I don't know." Tobias folded his arms and stared out

of the wide leaded window that looked onto the cathedral. "He entrusted me with his women instead." He released a harsh laugh. "And I allowed one to run off to Somerset and the other…."

"I am more to blame than you." Samuel gave a dismissive wave, unwilling to discuss such a raw subject.

"Still, at least he managed to preserve some of his assets for his remaining children. I hear Helena and Henry will be going to London." Tobias's voice held no bitterness.

"There are still arrangements to be made, but that is a possibility. Tell me, Tobias, what would you like to do?"

"With my position as steward terminated?" He arched a well-shaped eyebrow. "What I want is not the issue. But I'll never tolerate Blanden as Master."

"Your father would applaud your loyalty."

"My father is most probably dead." Tobias's tone held regret. "My foster father, on the other hand, has asked me to take over the inn." At Samuel's surprised look, he went on. "My brothers are too young yet to be of much use."

"Will you take up his offer?"

Tobias sat back in his chair. "He brought me up. I owe it to him, now that he is no longer healthy enough."

"He's ailing?" Samuel was surprised. Jim Lumm had seemed the same as ever when they last met. Some illnesses, he knew, could creep up on a body and drain the lifeblood. He resolved to call on Master Lumm soon.

"Aye. And then there's Mother." Tobias cocked a brow to indicate she was yet another problem, but one about whom he had no illusions.

Tobias had always been ambivalent about his step-father, but he adored his mother. Pretty, wanton, fickle Emily of the sensual walk and inviting smile. She had made no secret of the fact that the kindly Jim Lumm was not her eldest son's father.

Samuel reached into his coat, removed a folded parchment and held it out.

"What do you have there?" Tobias looked at it with no more than mild interest.

"Your inheritance."

Tobias took it, turning it over in his hands before unfolding the document.

"This is the deed to the house by the East Gate. Sir Jonathan's house."

"It's yours now." Samuel summoned the server to bring more coffee. The boy took his time replenishing their cups, while Tobias fidgeted, eager for him to leave.

The boy finally moved away "How could you give this to me?" Tobias asked. "It should be Henry's, or Helena's."

"I'm not the one giving it to you. Sir Jonathan is." He raised his porcelain bowl of coffee and took a slow, appreciative sip. "He came to me before the rising, and asked me to look after his children if anything happened to him. You were included."

"He had an inkling something might happen?"

Samuel pursed his lips. "I think he had doubts about Lord Grey." He shook his head as if trying to dislodge the thought. "Sir Jonathan knew if things went wrong, he would lose everything. Thus he put some of his property in my name for his wife and children. He wasn't to know Lady Elizabeth would live no longer than he did."

"You think he's dead then?"

"Helena asked me that. And in truth, how can any of us know?"

"Are you sure he wanted me to have this?" Tobias held up the parchment. "Did he actually say so?"

"Look at that document. He put it in your name before he left. He always meant you to have it." Samuel dropped his voice as the room began to fill with patrons. "I won't pretend he ever loved your mother. It was a youthful liaison and she was a—"

Tobias held up a hand. "I know what she was…is, Master Ffoyle. Sir Jonathan could not acknowledge me publicly, but he gave me a good position at Loxsbeare."

"You don't feel he showed you a way of life you could never have?"

Tobias studied the decorated ceiling for a moment before replying. "Who knows what I might have had? Had he lived, he might have furthered my career in other ways. Thank you, Master Ffoyle. I'm grateful." Tobias slid the document into his coat, resting his hand on it for a moment. When he spoke again there was no softness in his voice. "About Benjamin Hobbs...."

Samuel tensed, wary. "What about him?"

"I caught him loading a bag with some items of plate left behind. When I challenged him, he said it was his due. Is it true Jeffreys refused to reward him for betraying Sir Jonathan?"

"It is." Samuel snorted. "Blanden pre-empted him there. Did he know about you?"

"He didn't taunt me with it, so I am certain he did not. We had an—altercation." Tobias propped his elbows on the table. "Needless to say he won't be returning to Exeter. Not in my lifetime."

Samuel held up a hand. "I would rather not know the details, but thank you for telling me."

Tobias pulled himself to his feet, looking down on Samuel with a sad smile. "Master Ffoyle, would you do something for me?"

"Name it." Samuel smiled.

"Would you wish Helena and Henry happiness in their new life? And tell them that I hope to see them again, one day?" He adjusted his hat, turned and left, his boots echoing on the stairs.

Samuel watched him go, saddened. Tobias Lumm was a fine young man, a son and a brother of whom anyone would be proud.

Chapter 11

Startled, Helena jerked upright into watery sunlight that flooded the bedroom. She was in an unfamiliar wide bed, the covers rumpled and hanging off the mattress. Memory flooded back, and she recalled they had stopped at Kingston the previous night, at an ancient inn. Its upper windows hung precariously over a narrow dirty river that ran beneath a humped bridge.

"That's the Hogs Mill," Samuel answered in response to Henry's enquiry. It runs into the Thames, while that untidy little bridge is called Clattern."

She had lain awake half the night listening to the watch, who called out every hour, until exhaustion dragged her into a dreamless oblivion.

Gingerly, she eased into a sitting position, wincing at stiff muscles caused by four days of travelling in a carriage over bad roads.

She cast a swift look at the truckle bed in the corner, where Chloe snuffled in her sleep, and smiled, nostalgia dragging her thoughts back to the day they had left Ideswell.

Her most abiding memory of that day was Bayle as he stood beneath the overhanging porch, his hands clasped behind his back and head bent toward Henry. Her brother nodded occasionally in response to whatever wisdom Bayle imparted.

Then with a final, curt bow, Henry turned abruptly away, left the porch and stomped past her into the carriage, his eyes bright with tears.

Bayle followed more slowly to where the Ffoyle coach stood, the vehicle sporting a new coat of brown paint, its faded leather curtains replaced with stiff new hide and the Clothmakers' coat of arms recreated in bright new colours on the doors. Two heavy carts piled high with the possessions Lady Elizabeth had rescued from Loxsbeare Manor were positioned behind the carriage, each with a brace of armed servants aboard for protection.

"Are you sure you won't come with us, Bayle?" Helena asked, knowing his answer would be the same as it had for over a week.

"To a London chophouse?" He arched a brow. "I don't think so, Mistress. I'm a country soul, not a city rat. I'm surprised Master Ffoyle is sending you there."

"Lambtons is an exceptional Inn, Bayle, not a chophouse." Helena feigned affront. After all hadn't she asked the same outraged questions several times since Samuel's announcement? "He says the Devereuxs are wealthy people and I will never have to enter the alehouse if I do not so wish. More importantly, they are sympathetic to the late duke, so Henry and I will not suffer at their hands from our unfortunate situation."

She owed Bayle more gratitude than she could ever repay, and although she would miss him, she welcomed this new life, free of all past complications.

"As long as you are content, Mistress," Bayle said, though his smile was not reflected in his eyes.

"And you, Bayle? Are you content?" she asked. A foolish question, for since taking up Samuel's offer of employment, he looked more the prosperous wool man than a manservant. He wore a dun-colored long coat nipped at the waist over soft cambric shirt, cravat, and polished leather shoes.

She had had a speech prepared for their moment of parting, but the words never reached her lips. When he had held his hands toward her, palms upwards, her composure broke and she threw herself into his arms in an embrace that was over almost before it began, pulling away to enter the coach where Henry waited, huddled in the corner.

Saddened that Bayle's concern would be for others in future, and not for her, Helena had been about to ask Susannah to watch out for him on her behalf. However when she turned to speak, Susannah and Bayle stood close together, their gazes locked and with soft, almost longing expressions on their faces.

Helena had looked away, smiling. Perhaps Bayle would not be so lonely without them after all.

Once Somerset was behind them, together with Helena's less than happy memories of her recent visit, the roads became more crowded. Their timing was not ideal either, for wet weather and cold winds made their progress slower, and the horses needed changing more often.

Samuel's authoritative manner had worked like sorcery on indolent maids at inns to procure the best rooms, obtain abundant hot water, and the best food available.

Now, no more than a morning's drive away from their destination, excitement replaced Helena's discomfort. She rushed to the window to take in the view. "We're almost in London, Chloe," she addressed the bundle in the corner. "Get up and help me dress. I want my breakfast."

* * *

Helena hurried down the inn stairs; almost colliding with Samuel in the entrance hall, she stepped back in surprise at his bright blue long coat embroidered in silver and a long black periwig, items Helena had no idea he possessed.

All through breakfast, while Henry sniggered, Samuel haggled with the innkeeper in threatening terms, declaring their bill was extortionate and the food barely adequate.

"Master Ffoyle," Helena said in a fierce whisper out of the landlord's earshot. "The fare was exceptionally good." She exchanged an incredulous look with Henry who shrugged.

"Doesn't hurt to keep them attentive," Samuel declared as he ushered them onto the busy Street near the Market Square. "Now where's that blackguard of a coachman?"

Their progress out of Kingston was hampered by carts and pack ponies, which prompted Samuel to bellow at slow moving traffic, cuffing traders who sprang onto the backboard in an attempt to sell them trinkets from trays.

"Life in London is harsher for servant and master alike," Samuel said when Helena challenged this uncharacteristic aggression, "and far less forgiving."

As if to validate his comments, he shrieked at link boys who clung precariously to the sides of the carriage, offering their services as guides for a penny.

"If we are set on by footpads, I'll strangle you first," Samuel said, tossing a coin to one pox-scarred lad, then turned and winked in response to Helena's shocked expression. "All street hawkers are in league with ambushing villains."

When the carriage slowed in traffic, Samuel hollered at their driver, "Use your whip, man. We'll never get anywhere in this throng, else!"

"Master Ffoyle, you're frightening Chloe." Helena scolded.

His response was simply to glare at the maid, who cowered in her seat.

Helena gave up, convinced that for all his ferocity, Samuel enjoyed the faster pace. He certainly appeared more alive in the Capital than in Exeter.

"London has more new buildings than anywhere else in the country," Samuel told a clearly impressed Henry, as the carriage swayed along cobbled streets. "The Great Fire of sixty-six destroyed many of the old wooden houses and churches."

Helena tried to imagine the magnificent city in flames, but the image eluded her. "How did the fire start?"

Samuel gave a shrug. "Some say it was the Catholics, though I warrant it was simply a dry summer and a fire not extinguished properly in a city baker's shop. Whichever the cause, thousands were made homeless. Some left London, never to return. Thank the Lord only a handful of people lost their lives." He shuddered as if dispelling bad memories. "Christopher Wren drew up new plans based on an Italian piazza with streets radiating from a central point like a wheel."

"Such a scheme would have served far better than all these crooked alleyways and courts," Henry said.

Samuel crossed his hands on the top of his cane held upright between his knees. "When your house is a charred mass on the ground, my boy, you cannot wait for the ambitious schemes of kings. Londoners had to put roofs over their families' heads, and businesses to run. They simply re-built them in the same places, though the new building regulations should ensure such a tragedy never happens again."

"I still think the Italian piazzas style would have looked wonderful," Henry said, craning so far forward, he was in danger of losing his hat and had to be hauled back inside by Samuel.

The winter afternoon had faded into a colorless dusk by the time they entered a wide cobbled street, lined with half-timbered black and white houses with uneven leaded windows.

"This area is called Holborn." Samuel pointed with his cane. "The fire did not reach this end of the street, so most of the buildings here are much older."

"Are these all shops?" Helena asked, motioning toward the bow windows with leaded panes, as they passed.

"Mostly, and with living quarters on the floors above."

They drew up before a timbered building with wooden balconies along the length of the upper floor. A row of wide, squat windows ran along the lower façade. A painted wooden sign in green and gold lettering on the front declared it to be *"Lambtons Inn"*.

"It looks like several houses joined together," Henry observed when they drew to a halt.

"It's enormous," Helena whispered, in awe.

Shadows moved behind the curtains. There came the sounds of laughter and loud chatter, together with the enticing smell of cooking.

Helena's mouth began to water, despite her hearty breakfast.

Samuel handed Helena down from the coach just as a portly man clacked toward them on high-heeled shoes.

Helena gaze levelled and remained on a black patch the size of a half-laurel covering his left eye.

"I am Lubbock," he said, tiny black eye skimming over Chloe and stopping to settle admiringly on Helena. "Master Devereux's manservant. Welcome to Lambtons."

A brace of grooms in a livery of buff jackets over black breeches directed the carts and the Ffoyle carriage into the stable yard.

"I thought he was Master Devereux," Henry whispered as the dainty little man skipped around them as if he were herding sheep.

"I thought so too," Helena whispered back. "Look at his clothes. I've never seen a manservant dress so fine."

Helena found herself in a double-height entrance hall decorated in shades of red and gold. Gilt-framed mirrors on the walls reflected light from candles clustered into a vast chandelier attached by a chain to the ceiling.

"I wonder whose job it is to change all those candles." Henry asked.

Helena shrugged, rubbing the points of her shoes into the impossibly thick, patterned carpet, spread like a colorful sea at their feet.

"Is this what all the alehouses in London look like?" Henry asked, his mouth open in amazement.

"This is Lambtons. The best Inn and Chophouse in Holborn, maybe even in London itself," Samuel replied.

* * *

A wide staircase at the far end of the hall rose into a galleried landing that split off into either side.

As Lubbock led them toward three ladies and a man who waited there, Helena paused at the closed doors on the side of the entrance hall from behind which animated laughter, the clinking glasses and loud conversation could be heard.

"Devereux, my dear man," Samuel greeted the man at the stairs. "As you can see, we have journeyed safely through dangerous countryside."

"Is that so, Master Ffoyle? And there I was, imagining you came from Devon."

So this was the real Robert Devereux. He wore a patterned brocade garment of palest blue and gold, gathered on one hip over a shirt with flounces that peeked out at the front. This strange garment reached to his knees, decorated with birds and flowers. Spindly legs clad in white hose ended in what looked like gold silk slippers completed the picture.

In place of a heavy periwig, a fur turban covered his head, a strange appearance that might have discouraged her, had he not possessed an oval, friendly face and blue eyes that twinkled as if constantly amused.

"Welcome to Lambtons, my dear Mistress Woulfe." He took Helena's hand in both of his, the touch warm, dry and comforting. "I do hope you will both be happy here." He indicated a lady beside him. "Allow me to acquaint you with my dear wife, Alyce."

Helena had imagined a London version of Meghan Ffoyle, in more fashionable clothes, but this magnificent creature who enveloped her in perfumed, satin-clad arms, was almost girlish.

She wore a silver-colored manteau that shimmered in the candlelight, pleated and fastened to reveal the top of an elaborate corset holding in her tiny waist, with an ample décolleté.

The split skirt pulled back and up was a new fashion to Helena. It was fastened on the woman's still slender hips, and draped to reveal a blue underskirt. Her glossy mahogany hair was piled in large curls on top of her head. With looped ribbons and feathers in creamy pinks and greys, it made her appear taller than her husband.

The lady stepped back a pace to appraise Helena, who could see that close up, the lady was older than she first appeared, her advancing years hidden under a careful veneer of face paint, with a crescent moon taffeta patch set next to her carmined lips.

"I'm delighted such an attractive young couple has come to live with us," she whispered huskily, making Helena wonder what she would have said had they been less so. When Henry's turn came for her embrace, she appeared reluctant release him, caressing his shoulder with one hand.

Helena tried to catch his eye, but Henry appeared bewitched by her.

"This is my elder daughter, Celia." Robert waved a hand toward a plump, pretty girl of Helena's own age in an aquamarine bodice worn open over a visible corset that made Helena stare. Her generous décolleté, cut straight across in the current fashion, only made respectable by a bertha of exquisite cream lace.

"Welcome to Lambtons," Celia's voice was high-pitched. "I hope London is all you wish it to be."

A younger girl in buttercup yellow silk who possessed all the daring, self-confident look of her mother, greeted Henry with a girlish giggle and a tap of her closed fan on his shoulder. She then turned a penetrating gaze on Helena with a narrowing of her eyes.

After a long silence, Alyce nudged her, hard. "Phebe, offer your respects to Mistress Woulfe." Alyce forced a laugh. "Please forgive my younger daughter, Helena dear, she can be rather shy on occasion."

Celia gave a derisive snort and flapped her fan.

"Mistress," Phebe murmured, her curtsey barely discernible, before she turned pleading eyes on her father. "You promised I could go to the 'Change this afternoon, Papa. I have waited all morning." She turned her back to Helena in an obvious snub.

"So you will, my love," Master Devereux, apparently oblivious of her lack of manners, slung a silk-clad arm around his youngest daughter "Though first, we have a nuncheon laid out for our guests."

Helena frowned, perturbed by Phoebe's hostility, dropped back to Samuel's side. "What is that extraordinary garment Master Devereux is wearing, Master Ffoyle?"

"It's called a banyan," he replied grinning. "A robe of silk brocade from India. Many gentlemen here have adopted them as indoor attire."

Helena found this hard to believe.

What Master Devereux had described as a nuncheon

seemed to Helena more like a feast.

The meal was served in the French style, with an array of dishes being placed on the table. Robert launched into a recital of each dish as it appeared. "Here we have venison pasties and *sallets*, carrots mulched in vinegar, a cow's tongue garnished with capers and *spinnage*, rabbit in butter, and some plump radishes."

At her hesitation, Samuel helped identify the other meats and pastries, piling her plate high as he regaled the company with their crossing of Blackheath.

"We had to wait for other coaches to join us, so we could cross in a convoy," Henry ventured between mouthfuls, his eyes round at the memory.

"Well, I think you were all very brave to venture into such inhospitable country." Alyce fluttered her eyelashes. "One dare not even imagine the consequences, had you been attacked."

Helena's nervousness disappeared at their friendliness, marveling as even more dishes were carried in and set on the table.

"What is that?" Henry pointed to an oval dish that gave off a savory aroma that made Helena's mouth water.

"I think it might be *Boeuf à la Mode*, but I cannot be sure."

"Indeed it is, my dear Helena," Robert said, forking several thick slices onto Henry's plate. "The finest English buttock beef, larded with bacon and stewed in claret, cinnamon cloves, mace, and pepper."

"The dish is a favorite of my William's." Alyce sighed, stroking Henry's cheek with undue familiarity. Helena stared, but Henry didn't seem to mind.

"William is my son." Alyce twirled her spoon in the air, answering Helena's unspoken question. Despite encouraging them all to eat, Alyce herself pushed her food round her plate after the first few mouthfuls. "He's not in London just now, but you'll meet him one day."

Celia spent the entire meal with her arm looped through Helena's, as if she had decided they were to be inseparable. Phebe imitated her mother in both lack of appetite and flirtatiousness, fluttering between the men like a bright butterfly, gazing at them from under her lashes or from behind a coyly held fan. She issued any servant moving into her field of vision with pointed, but needless instructions, establishing her position as daughter of the house.

Helena found the talk lively, if superficial, each testing the experience and opinions of the others.

Alyce probed for details of their family life at Loxsbeare. "I've never been so far west." Her inflection intimated it was a foolhardy thing to do.

"Why should you wish to, Mama?" Phebe made a moue of disgust.

"Have you ever visited the theatre?" Celia asked.

Helena shook her head. "The only plays I have seen were private performances at friend's houses."

"In that case, I shall personally correct that omission in your education. Until one has seen the magnificent Anne Bracegirdle, one simply hasn't lived, my dear."

Master Devereux quizzed Henry, probing for details of what kind of life he saw for himself in the city. Their father had planned that Henry would enter the army, but lately, Henry refused to discuss soldiering; so Helena was curious as to how he would answer Robert's question.

Alyce's husky voice distracted her. "I am determined you shall see the New Exchange shops and stalls, my dear, and there is of course Covent Garden and the Hungerford Market to visit. I guarantee you'll have seen nothing like them in the provinces. You are in for a treat."

When she turned back to her brother's conversation, Helena discovered they had moved on to horses and dogs. Disappointed, she listened to Samuel telling Celia he planned to stay in London for a week or so in order to oversee his warehouse in Freemans Yard, before returning home to Exeter.

Grateful he was not leaving too soon, Helena suppressed a yawn. The warmth of the room and the good food conspired to remind her she was exhausted.

"I feel it is time you retired for a rest, my dears,"

Samuel clapped his hands to summon Lubbock. "He will show you your rooms and we'll gather here again later this afternoon."

At the top of the staircase, a footman led Henry off down a hallway.

Helena followed Lubbock along a sumptuous upper floor with wide corridors and walls covered with richly-patterned wallpaper. One storey away from the lower rooms, the mirrors and gilt paint diminished and the candles stabbed into dark corners.

"Your chamber, Mistress," he said, showing her into a cosy panelled room that contained a four-poster bed with green and gold hangings draped on either side. A thick piled rug in the same colours covered most of the boarded floor. Helena braced her arms on the black wooden sill of the leaded window that covered one side of the room. "They have a garden!" she called to Chloe, who limped in awkwardly behind her, red-faced, and her arms full of bundles.

In a walled courtyard below, neat flowerbeds arranged in geometrical patterns crisscrossed with pathways bordered by dwarf shrubs, so different from the semi-wild expanse of lawn bordered by tall, ancient trees at Loxsbeare.

While Chloe combed out Helena's hair, she propped her elbows on top of a spindly-legged bureau, her chin in her hands, and stared into her reflection.

I'm really here at last. I'm in London.

Chapter 12

"Mistress Devero' 'as sent your breakfast, Mistress," Chloe declared the next morning, limping to the bed where she balanced a tray on the coverlet.

Helena propped herself onto one elbow, smiling as she examined her breakfast tray of tiny pastries, a beautifully crafted silver pot containing hot chocolate, and a plate of thinly sliced bread and butter.

"They sleeps late in this 'ouse." Chloe tutted disapprovingly, and opened a door to the left of the bed. "Look at this, Mistress." She revealed a closet containing Helena's clothes chest and bureau, the heavy craftsmanship incongruous in the neat space, but achingly familiar.

Helena slid from beneath the covers, plucked a pastry from the tray and sipped the cup of hot chocolate Chloe had poured out. For the first time since crossing the city boundaries, Helena could not hear ironclad wheels or rough voices, clattering buckets, braying animals, or noisy peddlers. She assumed this was because her room stood at the back of the house, the walled garden acting as a buffer from the street.

A light knock came at the door, but before Chloe could respond, two maids entered bearing steaming buckets of hot water in each hand. A third dragged in a hipbath and set it in front of the fireplace while her companion set to laying the fire, which bloomed into life and warmth with surprising speed.

While Helena observed from the sidelines, the maids lined the bath with linen sheets that gave off a fragrance of lavender and chamomile as they poured in the water.

"Do all Londoners bathe in the mornings?" Helena asked no one in particular.

The maid who stood closest concealed a snigger as if

the idea was monstrous. “Not every day, Mistress.”

“Mistress Devereux’s instructions,” the maid kneeling on the hearth responded.

The maids stepped back, two on either end of the hip bath, waiting.

With a small shock, Helena realized they expected her to disrobe while they were still in the room. Unwilling to appear unworldly, she allowed her shift to fall to the floor, though they barely glanced at her.

While Chloe stood sulkily to one side, watching with resentful eyes, Helena climbed into the hot water and slid beneath the surface. She trailed her hands under the water as the fragrant heat worked instant miracles on her sore back and stiff muscles. The water had begun to go cold before she stepped reluctantly from its caress, into a towel warmed by the fire one of the maids wrapped round her.

Another attempted to arrange Helena’s clothes for the day, but Chloe nudged her sharply aside and tended to the task herself.

Their jostling made Helena smile, and at that moment, she knew this was how she wanted to live—how she ought to live—with the entire magical city of London spread out on the other side of her window. Removing the hipbath took a deal of effort and some muffled cursing from the maids, but once they had gone, Chloe helped Helena dress in a russet silk brocade gown. The plain cut skirt, split down the front to reveal a cream silk underskirt, accentuated her slender figure. Deep lace ruffles fell from the sleeves, the bodice lined at the neck with an almost transparent lace bertha. Satisfied she would not disgrace herself in front of her hosts, Helena twirled before a long glass.

“I remember when Sir Jonathan brought this cloth, from right here in London.” Chloe fingered the heavy material lovingly.

“Do you?” Helena’s voice was nonchalant, but at the same time she felt an uncomfortable warmth creep up her neck.

“He intended it for your mother.” Chloe’s voice grew

wistful.

Helena remained silent. Of course she remembered. The instant she had seen it lying on the carriage seat, she was fully aware the silk was not for her. Determined to have it, she had thrown herself into her father's arms gabbling her gratitude for his generous gift. The resigned smile on her mother's face in response to his dismayed shrug had confirmed she had won.

Having to listen patiently while he recounted the fate of the Huguenot silk makers from whom he had obtained it had been a small price to pay.

French-made silk was very expensive and heavily taxed, and its importation restricted. However, since the arrival of the Huguenot émigrés, there was an abundance of reasonably-priced silk available in London.

Her mother had taken her to the seamstress on the morrow to have the gown made up, but despite her tantrums, Helena had rarely worn it. Now as she looked down at herself that morning, shame spread through her once again. Lady Elizabeth would have looked beautiful in this colour.

My selfish bone again.

"What's that you said, Mistress?" Chloe asked.

Her mother used to tell her she possessed a tiny, misplaced bone that only surfaced when she made a choice based entirely on self-interest. Helena's "selfish bone" became a family joke, and frequently got get her into trouble when she was younger.

"Nothing."

Celia erupted into the room without knocking.

"How was your first night at Lambtons Helena? Not too noisy I hope? London must be so different for you than the wilds of Devon."

"Devon isn't so wild, Celia," Helena said, protective of her childhood home. "It's a beautiful place." A sudden nostalgia for the sea-tinged wind and the call of seagulls over green wide open spaces made her suddenly homesick.

Busy peering into Helena's jewel case, Celia didn't seem to notice, then jumped up again and trailed plump fingers through the open trunk at the end of Helena's bed.

Helena suddenly felt her entire wardrobe was drab beside the pastel silk Celia was wearing, but when she said so, Celia was complimentary. "That colour suits your dramatic coloring perfectly," she said, from her supine position on the unmade bed. Then she leapt to her feet, grabbing Helena's hand. "I must show you the inn."

Helena looked toward the door. "Where's Phebe?"

Celia rolled her eyes. "Sulking. Ignore her. She always wants to be the pretty one, and your arrival was something of a shock."

Helena acknowledged the compliment, recalling Phoebe's reaction to her arrival. However, she had no time to give it another thought, as Celia was pulling her down the wide staircase for a tour of the inn.

"We serve the best wines here," Celia called over her shoulder as she led the way through the dining areas of the inn, each one more luxurious than the last, their arched and curtained doorways decorated with rich hangings in red and gold. One had booths for diners, sectioned off with wood and glass partitions. Candles sat in pewter and glass holders on walls and on tables, and as Samuel had promised, rows of silver tankards were lined up in the taproom where serving girls swept the floors and scrubbed the furniture to shining brilliance.

"The duty on imported wine is ruinously high, which makes it expensive, but our ale is also the best, and we steep fruit and herbs in it for flavour."

"Is the ale brewed here?" Helena asked, as was the custom in Exeter.

"Oh no." Celia's bright curls bounced on her shoulders. "We buy it from brewers in Norfolk. Father says it is a messy, smelly process, and not worth the space required."

The kitchens, located behind the rear staircase, were the largest and busiest Helena had ever seen. Rows of massive wooden dressers lined the walls, loaded with platters and trays, pitchers and trenchers with silverware, jugs and bowls, all ready for the diners who would fill the public rooms.

A long, low hallway led away from the main kitchen—with storerooms, dairy, meat lockers and storage areas on both sides—opening out on a backyard, where the stables and coach house were located. The main cooking area was a steamy, airless space, where shouted instructions were hurled across the room. Everyone seemed frantically occupied and the atmosphere was strained, but it all fascinated Helena, and the smell of onions, herbs and cooked meat was compelling.

Henry had apparently been up for some time. He chatted comfortably with the serving men, complimenting the girls who bobbed curtseys to the handsome young gentleman, welcoming him to Lambtons with shy smiles and blushes.

"You shan't have much to do with the customers. And you'll never find Mama in the kitchens. Carstairs manages the staff."

Carstairs turned out to be a jovial but strict, middle-aged housekeeper, whose role was to marshal the serving girls into their various duties. A skill she performed, Celia told her, laughing, like a mother hen.

The woman eyed Helena with mild suspicion. "Our taproom girls are from good families," she said, defending them. "Not ignorant slatterns like those in *The Sunn*, or even *Thompsons*."

These names meant nothing to Helena, who accepted Mistress Carstairs's judgment in polite silence.

"Our servers are all men, naturally," Celia announced, with all the authority of a chatelaine. "Lubbock trains them to keep everyone's personal orders in their head." She bent closer Helena, whispering, "They are more discreet than the girls when it comes to the private dining rooms."

Helena frowned, confused, though confident that, given time, everything would make sense.

On the second floor, they discovered Phebe loitering by the stairs. Helena was convinced she had been waiting for them, but when Celia invited her to join them, she looked disinterested. "I have little else to do this morning, I may think about it." When neither girl attempted to persuade her, she trailed behind them at a distance.

The ceilings were lower on this floor, and the windows smaller. Each of the rooms was furnished with a table and two chairs in an alcove; others contained elaborate canopied beds as well.

"These are our private dining rooms." Celia waved a hand. "Exclusively for the use of our married guests."

"How do you know which of the guests are married?" Helena exchanged a sly smile with Phebe.

Celia raised an innocent eyebrow. "Of course they are. Only respectable people come to Lambtons."

Helena felt a small thrill of excitement, wondering what her father would think. Then it struck her; this was her new life. A life he was not part of. *Until he returns*, a small voice in her head reminded her.

Their tour of the vast inn ended in Celia's bedchamber, where the noise of the street intruded; though when Helena commented on this fact, she was brushed aside.

"I could not bear the silence of the country. I love the clamour of city streets." Phebe shuddered, apparently having overcome what her mother called her "shyness". She produced a box of "mouches", holding up a sheet of Spanish paper with a flourish. "I use it to colour my cheeks," she explained unnecessarily.

"It can barely be seen when you do use it, Phebe." Celia rolled her eyes. "You already possess such high colour." Her pained look told Helena they had had this conversation several times before.

Helena perched on Celia's bed, her high-spirited chatter flowing over her as she cast her mind back to the summer in Ideswell. The Ffoyle girls were kind hearted, loving creatures, but she had soon outgrown their homespun kindness. To have the sophisticated, colorful city of London laid out before her was more than she could have hoped for. She could not wait to be a part of it.

Helena moved to the window and looked onto the street, where hackney coaches clattered on the cobbles and sedan chairs disgorged their occupants onto the swarming street.

It was not yet noon and Lambtons already bustled with activity. Despite the cold, the inn doors were thrown open, and from where she stood, Helena could hear the enthusiastic welcomes of Lubbock, combined with muffled greetings and chattering of the diners as they entered the halls.

Helena stared, fascinated at the swaying headdresses and billowing skirts of the ladies, the ornamented coats and impossibly full wigs of the men strutting through the doors with their oversized muffs and silver-topped canes.

Celia came to stand beside her, pointing to a black vehicle pulled by four bay horses in the street. "Oh look, there's Lord Marlborough's carriage."

Helena strained forward to see, exhilarated at being so close to the famous John Churchill. Yet shouldn't she have felt more resentment than curiosity? This was, after all, the man who had led the king's forces against her family at Sedgemoor.

Celia nodded. "He's very handsome, and his wife, Lady Sarah, has the loveliest golden hair. They have been married for seven years, and he is still madly in love with her."

"Hmm," Phebe muttered from her position at her sister's bureau. "She is proud, that one, and thinks she is more important than the Princess Anne."

Helena pressed her nose against the glass. The street was so crowded, he was out of sight before she saw his face. Mildly disappointed, she turned to lean against the sill. "I had no idea an alehouse keeper could be so—" She paused, aware she was about to be insulting.

"Father isn't just an innkeeper, Helena. He's also a goldsmith-banker." Phebe beamed with pride.

"Master Ffoyle often uses his services." Celia turned her gaze on Helena. "And I believe Sir Jonathan Woulfe, too, when he came to the city to trade wool."

"Master Devereux knew my father?" Helena's heart lurched at his name on Celia's lips.

"We saw him but twice."

Helena detected triumph in Phoebe's face, aware Helena had not known this but ignored it. If only she could make Phebe less hostile. She would need all the friends she could find in this vast city.

A worry had nagged at Helena all the way there from Devon. If their father lived, and she dared not believe otherwise, how would he find them now they had left Devon? The fact he knew about Lambtons, and had been here, made her less troubled.

She could not wait to tell Henry.

* * *

Eager to make a good impression to his hosts, Henry rose early and dressed carefully that morning, his first in London. He wandered into the main hall, only to be told by the inscrutable Lubbock than no one else was up yet. "I doubt you'll see any of the ladies much before ten of the clock, Master," the manservant said with a wry smile.

Thanking him, Henry turned to leave, though with no idea where to go or what to do next. Preoccupied, he collided with Master Devereux.

"I do apologise, sir. I didn't see you there." Henry scooped up his host's muff and cane, both of which had clattered onto the tiled floor in the collision.

"No harm done, young man." He dusted off the muff and tucked the silver topped cane beneath his arm. "What plans have you for the morning?"

"Plans, sir?" Henry shrugged.

"Well." Master Devereux turned to a gilt-framed mirror in which he adjusted his curly black wig. "Why don't you take a carriage ride with me? I have some business this morning, but the City being new to you, I imagine you'll find something of interest. What do you say?"

Henry accepted with enthusiasm, eager to see this vast city which he was now his home. Robert Devereux proved an entertaining guide, and kept up a stream of chatter all the way along Fleet Street, where he pointed out the old houses that had survived the Great Fire, comparing them with ones constructed during the last twenty years.

When they halted on Ludgate Hill, Master Devereux gathered up his muff and walking stick. "I imagine you might like to take a look at Wren's cathedral while we are here, Henry. More entertaining for you than my booksellers, at any rate." He pointed his cane at a fence opposite. "Building work has started again, and Wren has employed an army of stonemasons. The cathedral site is busy these days, and worth a look." He chattered amiably as he alighted from the carriage.

"The new cathedral, sir?" Henry asked, fascinated, jumping down behind him.

Henry's grandfather had told him all about the terrible fire that had destroyed the old cathedral of his childhood, and that nearly all the City had been destroyed by the terrible blaze.

"Was there anything left of the old one?" Henry asked.

"The statue of John Donne survived intact. He was a Dean of St Paul's, though many remember him best for his poetry. Some stonework is left from Inigo Jones's original choir." He had to shout to make himself heard above the yelling, banging, and construction noises on the other side of the wooden hoarding, as well as the hubbub of the street behind them filled with pedestrians, carriages and carters. "The lead roof of the old building melted, and ruined everything inside. They say there was molten lead running through the streets here." He gestured again with his cane.

"It must have been a terrible sight, the fire." Henry kept his face solemn, but he was eager for more details. "Did you see it, sir?"

Master Devereux stared into thin air. "I was a young man then. Alyce and I had an alehouse at the rear of Fleet Street." He glanced sideways at Henry with the ghost of a smile, "I was neither quite so respectable, nor as wealthy, in those days." A smile that he quickly suppressed hovered on his lips. "The old place burned to the ground and I had to begin again." He gave a deep sigh as he arranged his muff over one arm and held his cane in the other hand.

"Alyce and I had to flee to my father-in-law's house in Southwark. The bridge prevented the fire from spreading across the river."

"Did it take long to clear up the mess?" Henry asked, trying to imagine what rivers of molten lead must have looked like.

"Years, Henry, years. Master Wren, as he was then, had to engage a team of thirty laborers to operate a battering ram to demolish the ruins of the old cathedral."

"A battering ram?" Henry glanced over at the site, almost hoping it might still be there.

"Yes…of his own design. However, it was slow work. To speed things up, he enlisted the services of a gunner from the Tower, to explode gunpowder under the cathedral." Robert gave a throaty chuckle. "That worked too, although it frightened the residents hereabouts."

"How long have they been building?" Henry peered through the fencing, but he could not see much.

"Work began about three years after the fire, but the foundation stone wasn't laid until 'seventy-five. Work has been intermittent over the years, much to Wren's frustration."

"How so?"

Robert balanced both hands on top of his cane, his lips pursed as if considering. "Well, Compton, the Bishop of London, voted for the Exclusion Bill, so King Charles withdrew the funds."

Henry cocked his head, listening. "There's work going on now. I can hear it."

Robert nodded. "King James called his first Parliament this spring, and reinstated the coal tax revenues, which funds the building work. For the next fifteen years, at any rate."

"Shall it stay like this, sir?" Henry nodded at the building rising above the fence. "With a flat roof?"

Robert looked up at the towering edifice. "Indeed, no. Sir Christopher's plans include a magnificent dome, painted with ecclesiastical murals visible to the congregation from the cathedral floor. It will be the highest building I shall see in my lifetime."

"Is this to stop thieves?" Henry pointed to the hoardings on the opposite side of the road.

"Partly," Master Devereux nodded. "Many say Wren chooses to hide his masterpiece behind this." He tapped one of the panels with his cane. "To confound those who would criticize his design. The Commissioners say his plans for a dome is too Catholic for an Anglican cathedral." He leaned closer. "They are staunch Whigs, and anything that smacks of Papism sends them into paroxysms of criticism."

"I wish I could see it properly." Henry glared at the fence, willing it to vanish.

Robert tapped his nose with his cane. With a knowing smile, he said, "Well my boy. There's a gap in the boarding a little further on, from which you can see the workings. However, I advise you to stay in sight of my coachman, lest you become a target for footpads. I'll see you anon." He aimed a brief salute in Henry's direction, before he turned on his heel and strode across the cobbles of Paternoster Row.

Chapter 13

Henry picked his way across the cobbles at the bottom of Ludgate Hill, where the stench of the river was strong. A shout from his left made him jump backward, just in time to avoid a man pushing a loaded handcart down the incline. Congratulating himself for not sustaining an injury on the dirty road, he was almost run down by a laden pony coming from the other direction.

Unlike the streets of Exeter, where he might have received a sympathetic query as to whether he might be hurt, both men merely snarled and continued their journeys without further ado.

Finally, Henry reached the high wooden fence that ran around almost the length of the street. He followed it for a hundred paces or so until he found the gap in the boarding that Master Devereux had mentioned.

Henry craned his neck to see through the narrow gap, beyond which the glistening white building rose like a cliff face, the late autumn sky visible through the glassless windows and the fact the building was not roofed as yet.

Workmen and stone carvers clambered over a complex network of wooden scaffolding like insects on a piece of rotting fruit. Men in workmen's breeches hefted stones and carried planks of wood, tools, and leather buckets of water expertly over rubble. Young boys lugged mortar to the base of the stone façade to be hoisted up by baskets to stonemasons perched on platforms high above the ground. The stonemasons themselves were easy to identify, all of them covered with a fine white dust that made them look like ghostly apparitions.

"Stand aside, boy, for my master to pass." A harsh voice at Henry's shoulder made him jump.

Lost in the spectacle of the building site, he had not

heard a carriage pull up behind him. "Beg pardon, sir," Henry muttered, his back pressed against the fence.

The watchman hopped down from his box and with an obsequious salute, opened a door in the fence for a man who had alighted from the coach. Slightly stooped and not much taller than Henry, the man was immaculately dressed in an embroidered long-coat and voluminous white curly wig that fell halfway down his back. Penetrating brown eyes beneath thick brows in a lined but well-shaped face scanned the site possessively. His upright walk meant Henry could not discern his age very well; though he was not a young man, he could not describe him as elderly. Several workmen in leather aprons, their hands white from stone dust, hurried forward to engage the newcomer in urgent conversation. He addressed each one in turn, standing amongst the piles of rubble, discarded pieces of scaffolding, sheets of sacking and bits of stone, with as much aplomb as if he presided in a drawing room.

A male servant stood a few feet away, one hand resting on the shoulder of a small boy of around six or seven. The child wore a blue velvet long-coat and a brown curly wig on his narrow head, but something about him struck Henry as unusual. The child's eyes looked empty, as though unaware of his surroundings. He repeatedly tugged at the servant's sleeve, while making small mewling noises. The servant removed the boy's hand, only for the grasping fingers to return. The expression on the servant's face remained unchanged, as though this behavior was a common occurrence. Aware he was staring, Henry turned back toward the original object of his interest.

One by one, workmen bowed and backed away, dispersing into the crowded site. With a final glance and a nod at the industrious hive before him, the man turned and made his way back toward the carriage, his small entourage following.

Henry froze as the man's shrewd brown eyes raked him from his polished shoes to his face, the man's lips curling upwards into a benign smile. "Young man, you appear to have an uncommon interest in my cathedral. Tell me, then, what you think of it?"

"A wondrous structure, sir. I have never seen anything like it." Henry frowned, recalling what the man had said. "Did-did you say, *your* cathedral, sir?"

"I certainly feel it is mine." His voice was low and soft, his eyes taking on a faraway look. "For it is my design, and I have petitioned two kings to provide me with funds to make my dream a reality." He inclined his head. "My dear young sir, you are not from London, I can tell by your speech."

"Indeed not, sir, I am from Exeter."

"Ah! An historic city indeed, and with a fine cathedral of its own." He laid a finger against the side of his nose and gave an amused chuckle. "A proper Norman structure, at that."

Belatedly, Henry snatched off his hat and gave a bow. "Allow me to introduce myself, sir. My name is Henry Woulfe."

"I am honoured to make your acquaintance, Master Henry Woulfe." A bemused smile tugged at the man's mouth as he returned the bow. "I am Sir Christopher Wren."

The servant's face appeared round the side of the open carriage door, but Wren dismissed him with a backward wave. Henry had already guessed the stranger's identity, though hearing his name spoken aloud brought a wide smile to his face.

"I should have been disappointed had you not heard of me." His new acquaintance inclined his head so far to one side, Henry wondered how the heavy wig remained in place. "I have lately become the Member of Parliament for Plympton Erle, in your own county of Devon."

Having no idea of this fact, Henry stayed silent, storing the information to tell Master Devereux later. "Sir, my host and patron has told me much about this wonderful structure."

"And who might your host be, young Master Woulfe?"

"He is Robert Devereux, sir, of Lambtons Inn."

"Ah." Wren lifted his cane to his nose. "I know your

patron. I have often dined in his excellent establishment. He crossed his elegant hands over the silver-topped cane and leaned backwards. "And you, Master Woulfe, are you by any chance interested in architecture?"

Henry grinned. "Indeed, sir, though I had no notion of it before I arrived in London. However since coming across this magnificent cathedral today, I should like to know more about this white stone, sir, I find it somehow familiar."

"There is a reason for that, young sir." The architect held up a finger. "Exeter Cathedral is built of the same stone, which is why you find it familiar. Found on a small island off the Dorset coast, it is of a certain softness, ideal for carving, and weathers well after exposure to the elements."

The servant's face appeared in the window of the coach at intervals as they talked, each time with varying degrees of annoyance. Sir Christopher ignored him. Delighted to have such a famous man's undivided attention, Henry's heart swelled.

"However London air is full of dirt, soot and other impurities, which are not good for the stone," Wren said, dismayed. "See how dull this façade has become?" He indicated a pillar on the unfinished structure. "See the difference?" Beckoning Henry closer, he lifted a piece of sacking which revealed several slabs of untouched stone that shone with pristine whiteness. The stone almost sparkled, as if it had tiny shards of glass embedded within it. The half-constructed building seemed almost dull in comparison.

Dropping the sacking back in place, Wren slapped his hands together to remove the dust. "So, Master Woulfe, would you have a fancy to see inside my cathedral?"

"Tha-that would indeed be an honour, sir," Henry stammered, then paused, his enthusiasm vying with his duty to Master Devereux. "However, my patron will have finished his business for the day, and I have to return. Although I hope there will be other occasions. And if I have to use my two feet to get here from Holborn, I shall certainly do so for the privilege."

"Then I am happy to issue an invitation." Sir Christopher placed a hand on Henry's shoulder and guided him back through the wooden door in the hoarding.

Henry paused beside the carriage, where a footman stood rigid beside the open door.

The child Henry had spotted earlier leaned out of the carriage, his hand flapping in agitation. "Now, now, no need for alarm, I am returned." Sir Christopher sighed, his head inclined toward Henry. "This young man is my son, Billy."

Henry bowed and murmured, "Your servant."

Sir Christopher climbed into the carriage, calling to Henry through the open flap. "I will send my man to Lambtons to call for you. Shall we say, Friday at ten of the clock?"

Before Henry could give a response, the driver had cracked his whip and the carriage lurched away up Ludgate Hill.

On the short journey back to Holborn, Henry treated a bemused Robert Devereux to an animated account of his meeting with the acclaimed architect.

Henry chose not to mention the vacant-eyed boy. Not because the child discomforted him, but more from a desire to protect a weakness he saw in his new acquaintance's life, a weakness he did not yet understand.

* * *

When Alyce announced that Helena could not take her place in London society, or rather Lambtons' society, without suitable clothes, all three Devereux women threw themselves into the task with enthusiasm.

Heedless of Helena's insistence that she was of sufficient means to finance her own wardrobe, Alyce waved her aside, saying the honour was hers.

"My own girls have more than enough for this season, so there is no pleasure to be found there. But you my dear, are darker, a little taller." In a small aside so as not to let her daughters hear, she added, "…and far more striking, so I shall have a wonderful time dressing you."

A veritable army, including a seamstresses and her assistant, a milliner, a hosiery peddler, a wigmaker and a cosmetics merchant arrived within a day, crowding into Alyce's private salon next to the chamber she shared with her husband.

"That's Mistress Groves," Celia indicated a haughty looking woman in heavy face paint, accompanied by two frail-looking girls, their arms laden with parcels. "She's the Duchess of Somerset's dressmaker."

"I doubt you've ever seen her like in Exeter." Phebe said, superciliously.

Helena silently agreed, though she wasn't going to admit as much to Phebe.

During the protracted measuring session, where Helena submitted to having bolts of cloth draped over her shoulders and around her waist, Celia and Phebe pored over the items draped across chairs and covered the bed for inspection, while Helena was convinced they remained to see which items might be discretely acquired for themselves. There was so much to choose from, she found she was unable to make a decision about anything, but even that in itself was exciting.

* * *

Bundled up in an outdoor cloak with a heavy rug tucked around her knees, Helena occupied a corner seat in the Devereux carriage as it bowled through the open spaces of Holborn into noisier, busier thoroughfares toward the river and the New Exchange.

"Helena!" Celia chided as Helena hung out of the carriage window. "You'll lose your necklace or headdress ribbons to a scoundrel if you don't watch out."

Helena giggled, fascinated at the attention a fine coach attracted. "I cannot help myself, the City is still such a novelty to me."

When forced to halt, traders dodged in between the

traffic, trying to attract their attention; thin, dirty hands thrust through the windows, or clung dangerously onto running boards until a footmen dislodged them with a well-aimed whip.

Celia adopted her haughtiest pose and looked away in distaste, while Phebe smiled prettily and pretended interest in the trays of tawdry stuff placed under her nose.

Leaving the coach in a side street, Celia led the way into the pillared main hall of what she called the 'Change, with its vast concourse covering two floors lined with open shops under a canopied ceiling. Each one bore an impressive display of brightly-coloured trinkets, laces, hats, gloves, and fans, arranged on trays and boxes to attract the shopper.

"They marry well," Phebe whispered, indicating the well-dressed female stallholders with their painted faces. "They meet many fine gentlemen by working here."

Helena tore herself away with difficulty from each stall, only to be accosted by the occupant of the next; faced with so many gloves and fans, ribbons, muffs and petticoats, she found making a choice quite beyond her.

Determined to purchase something, she settled on a pair of silk hose from Philip Danbury's shop and a small ornamental japanned box. Celia and Phebe trailed behind with bored expressions, though Helena remained entranced, constantly uttering admiring phrases.

The maid — not Chloe on this occasion, but Alyce's — trailed behind with a sullen expression, her presence completely ineffective as a chaperone, for Phebe greeted almost every young man they encountered with fulsome compliments, ensuring the entire hall was aware that the younger Mistress Devereux was in the building.

One gallant sauntered away, having failed to elicit more from Celia than a cold stare.

"Why were you so curt with Master Gillingham just now?" Phebe admonished her. "He was simply being no more than amiable, not trying to rob you of your virtue!"

Helena stifled a shocked laugh, but Phebe was in full flow. "…and even if they were, he is unlikely to announce the fact in the 'Change. You're quite safe." She swung her muff from one hand to the other, her sharp eyes scanning the hall as she spoke. "Why, if I should emulate you and simper like a schoolgirl, I shall never be noticed."

"You are bold and indiscreet Phebe. What will poor Helena think of you?" Celia sniffed. "She cannot be used to such outrageous attention seeking."

Phebe pulled a face, bowing to mutter a polite, "Sir," to a slightly built young man in brown velvet who approached them. With a sweep of her arm, Phebe introduced him. "Master Jack Montague, allow me to present Mistress Helena Woulfe, who has lately come to town from Exeter. My sister Celia you know, of course."

Phebe inclined her head, adding, "Jack is cousin to Sir Charles Montague."

With no idea who the Montagues were but resolving to question Celia on the subject later, Helena's gaze fixed on the impossibly high periwig which almost overwhelmed his narrow face.

"Shall you attend my lord's soirée this evening, to celebrate His Majesty's birthday?" he asked in a high, almost feminine voice with a pronounced lisp, while he gazed at Phebe with an enraptured expression. "I assure you it will be a well-attended occasion."

"A shame, then, that we have conflicting plans for that evening." Celia imitated Alyce's haughtiest tone. "I shall be sorry not to see Master Evelyn, whom I am told shall be there."

"Oh…oh yes, he certainly shall. A remarkable old man is he not? So full of Court stories. I never tire of listening to him," he concluded, his tone intimating the opposite was true.

After a polite interval and much bowing, he moved off down the concourse.

"Huh!" Phebe flicked her fan back and forth. "When shall I be invited to a Court Ball, and not simply the parties held afterwards?"

"Never. You're not aristocracy, Phebe." She tucked her arm into her sister's and drew her in the opposite direction.

"Do you have a preference for that young man, Phebe?" Helena asked, glancing back at her new acquaintance.

"Not at all," Phebe smirked, earning her a hard glare from her sister. "He is very satisfying to practice on, don't you think?"

Helena felt instant admiration for Phebe, obviously a young lady determined to make the best of her opportunities.

When they returned to the coach, Phebe banished the maid to the outside seat, leaving them to gossip inside on their way back to Holborn, a heap of prettily wrapped parcels balanced on their knees.

Celia attempted yet again to warn her sister of the dangers of forward behavior in public, but Phebe waved away her criticism. "It's all very well for you to eschew flirting, Celia, but we don't all have a Master Maurice dancing attendance upon us."

"Who is Master Maurice?" Helena asked, watching a slow blush suffuse Celia's face. "He was that pale creature at dinner the other night," Phebe giggled. "The one with the dog eyes, who quivered each time Papa spoke to him."

"He did no such thing." Celia bridled. "Ralf is a goldsmith, too, which may explain why he spends so much time in Papa's company."

"Have you been acquainted with him long?" Helena asked, ignoring Phoebe's smirking face.

"Well," Celia hesitated, "actually I know him hardly at all. We have met but three times."

"He's Papa's choice," Phebe said. "Though my sister offered no objections to the match."

"I have a duty of obedience to Papa, Phebe, as have you." Celia glared at her. "The contract has been drawn up and there is only my portion to be settled."

"I offer my felicitations." Helena attempted a smile, although she felt a sudden pang at the prospect of losing her new friend so soon.

Phebe sighed and huddled into the corner.

“You disapprove, Phebe?” Helena asked.

“It would be inappropriate and irrelevant for her to approve or disapprove,” Celia retorted, “and if Papa decreed Master Maurice would be her husband instead of mine, she would still have no grounds on which to object.”

Helena fell silent, recalling that no one had asked her opinion on Martyn Blanden, either.

Phebe snuggled into her fur-lined cloak, her eyes narrowed. “No one shall sell me to the highest bidder, like some commodity. I’ll marry whomsoever I choose.”

“Can you not be happy I am to be the wife of a man who may one day be as rich as Papa?” Celia’s blue eyes moistened. “I am to have a house, servants, and a carriage every bit as grand as this one. Ralf will take me out into society far more than I am permitted to at present.”

The threatening sky opened and heavy rain began pounding the wooden roof of the carriage, so they had to raise their voices to be heard.

Phebe gave a contemptuous sniff, then appeared to soften. “If you are content, Celia, then I shall be happy for you. However my husband shall be my own choice. Then, if the marriage is not happy, no one will be to blame but myself.”

“Why would it not be happy?” Helena pulled the rug tighter around herself as water began to find its way through the leather flaps. She remembered the servant girl and the coachman getting drenched on the outside seat, but felt it inappropriate to mention it. “Your father would take every precaution that the man he found for you would be good-hearted and well-bred.”

Lifting her pert chin, Phebe held Helena’s gaze. “Perhaps you should ask Millie Bryant that same question, and see how she answers.”

“Phebe! You are not to talk about such things!” Celia’s eyes flashed.

“Millie Sanders, or Mistress Bryant, as she became,” Phebe said, defiant. “Married just such a young man, chosen for her by her father.” Phoebe’s brown eyes shimmered with emotion. “They were married less than a twelvemonth, during which he spent her entire portion and then he turned her out of the house, where he now lives with his mistress."

Celia gave an impatient tut.

"Please, go on, Phebe," Helena urged, fascinated.

"Millie is the sweetest, kindest girl who ever lived, yet she had to beg to be allowed her back into her family, as if the disgrace were her own." Phoebe's voice cracked. "Her family treat her like an upper servant, an investment that went wrong. She cannot find a better husband, as she is still tied to that brute Bryant, who cares not a fig for her and is still received into society, where poor Millie is not." She slumped back in her seat, breathless.

"You must be very fond of her, to champion her in this way." Helena said.

"I am forbidden to see her." Phebe blinked rapidly.

Impulsively, Helena leaned forward and grasped the younger girl's hand, at which Phebe gave a start of surprise, though she didn't pull away. "I am so sorry." Helena strained to make herself heard above the drumming rain. "That is not to say such a fate would be yours. Your family would never tie you to a husband who discards a good wife."

"They certainly will not, for I shall find my own."

"Perhaps he—"

"Leave her, Helena," Celia interrupted. "She will change her mind when she is reminded of her duty."

With a final glare in Celia's direction, Phebe threw back the leather flap covering the window, heedless of the cold rain lashing her face, where Helena heard her say firmly, "I shall never change my mind."

Chapter 14

During Helena's first hectic weeks in London, a constant stream of guests paraded through Lambtons, some to pay their respects to the orphans of the ill-fated rebellion, others, she felt sure, out of sheer curiosity.

When she had expressed bewilderment at so much attention, Alyce had tried to explain. "Your distracted grief gives you an enigmatic air, my dear, which will secure you a husband before you know it. Men adore mysterious women."

Helena had not known how to respond, but despite her forthrightness, she liked and admired Alyce Devereux; it was only willful Phoebe's occasional bouts of jealous resentment that soured her contentment in her new surroundings. However, of late Phebe was making an effort to be agreeable since their moment of mutual understanding in the carriage.

Helena found being surrounded by people at all times of the day stifling. Although she loved the teeming life that made up Holborn and its surrounding streets, the perpetual rumbling of carts and loud voices became too much for her to bear when she needed some time to think.

Samuel had delayed his return home by over a week, but when the weather changed for the worse, he had announced his need to set off before the roads became impassable. Saying goodbye to him had been harder than she imagined, though Helena had determined to be strong. He was her last link with her home. From now on, she and Henry would forge their own path in this strange but fascinating city. Would they rise up in society to a position of affluence, or disappear into the anonymity that engulfed so many?

She eased her way through the bustling kitchens, where cooks shrieked at the scullery maids, serving men exchanged bawdy jokes in loud voices, pans clattered, and meat sizzled.

Helena slipped through the rear door into the walled garden, her breath forming wispy clouds in the cold air. The walled space suffered from a lack of attention. The plants not been properly trimmed back for the winter, and the hedges were ragged and overgrown in places. Yet it was quiet, and offered some respite from the ever-constant clamour of the inn. Seats nestled in arbours in the walls, with ornamental hedges trimmed and trained to form a covered archway, which, Helena imagined, gave cool shelter on sunny days.

On her second tour of the pathways, she turned at the bang of the kitchen door. Henry was hurrying toward her. "Here you are!" he called brightly, pulling his cloak tighter with a dramatic shiver. "It's bitter cold out here."

"Walk with me. It will help you keep warm." Ignoring his cursing, she looped her arm through his. "Tell me, Henry, how do you like living in an alehouse?"

"I'm enjoying it, and besides," he placed a finger to his cheek in a gesture characteristic of Master Devereux, "Lambtons is no ordinary alehouse."

Helena's laugh rang across the dormant winter garden. "You don't think Father would disapprove of us being here?"

He frowned. "What makes you say that?"

She shrugged, suddenly overcome by sadness. "I would not care if he came back and dragged us away in a rage. But as each day passes, I doubt more and more it will happen."

"That he will drag us away?"

"That he will come back."

Henry stared off with a frown, making Helena sorry for being the cause of his melancholy. He had been so much happier lately, spending every moment he could with his new friend, Sir Christopher Wren. In an effort to lighten the mood, she asked the first question that came into her head. "Have you been at St Paul's again today?"

His face showed surprise. "How did you know?"

She raised both eyebrows in response.

Henry stamped his feet and blew on his hands. "I met Master Hawksmoor this morning."

"And who might he be?" Helena feigned enthusiasm.

"Sir Christopher engaged him as his pupil when he was not two years older than I am now."

Helena waited, suspecting there might be more.

"He's taking me to see the new chapel, the one the king has had built in Whitehall Palace."

"Do you think that's wise?" She halted on the pathway, everything she had learned about Papists rushing into her head. "Has he not filled the chapel with figures of saints and gold statues?"

Henry laughed at her expression. "Helena, I'm not going to attend Mass, I going there to study the building."

On their stroll back toward the kitchens, she looked down as Henry scuffed his feet on the gravel. She was about to reprimand him for damaging his shoes, but the words died on her lips. He was no longer her little brother. Circumstances had turned him into a man heartbreakingly too soon. He spoke with care these days and was no longer the enthusiastic boy who would say the first thing that came into his head.

"Are you listening to me, Helena?"

"Oh yes, yes, of course I am. Tell me, Henry. How serious is this interest of yours in architecture?"

His eyes shone. "In no other city in the world is there so much building going on. Everywhere you go there are builders, carpenters and stonemasons."

Helena refrained from pointing out that he was one of few who might feel this an advantage, instead saying, "Father always imagined you would go into the army."

"Which army?" he said, one brow raised.

Helena opened her mouth, and then closed it again. He had a point, and Master Devereux complained constantly of the large numbers of soldiers the king kept in barracks on

Hounslow Heath, soldiers who by rights should have been discharged after the rebellion.

"I am sixteen, Helena," he said firmly. "I have decided I want to be an architect." He halted beneath an arbor, its leafless branches twisted together above them in a high curve. "If you will agree, I want to ask Master Devereux to find a master to indenture me to an apprenticeship."

"Are you sure about this?" At his expectant nod, she felt the prick of tears behind her eyes. He was talking about a career, about leaving. She cleared her throat. "If-If that is what you want, Henry. But we shall have to tame this." She tugged at a thick strand of fair hair, which, being hatless, he had left to hang loose on his shoulders.

He jerked his head away, laughing in mock protest. "This is what I want, Helena. However I must be sure you are happy about this path I have chosen."

Helena slowed down her footsteps. "I love London. Lambtons is a wonderful place and the Devereuxs couldn't be kinder. But as to my future," she gave a bemused shrug, "I shall have to be married to obtain anything in life, as Celia is always reminding me."

"I would feel better about leaving, if you were."

She wondered if he meant happy, or married, but decided not to pursue the subject. She inhaled a deep breath, tucking her arm beneath his. "So tell me, how does one go about becoming an architect?"

Henry brightened, his enthusiasm palpable. "I need a Master willing to take me on for a liking, and—"

"Whatever is a liking?" She bit her lip to prevent herself laughing.

"This is serious, Helena." A sharpness entered his eyes, betraying hurt.

Chastened, she composed her face into an expression of studious enquiry. "Explain."

"I stay with the Master for a period of a month, to see if we get on well together, and to determine if I have aptitude for the work. If he is agreeable, I pay him a premium, that is, an agreed sum of money, for a seven-year apprenticeship."

"Then shall you build cathedrals?" Helena forced herself to sound cheerful, though the idea of Henry leaving her for so long made her chest hurt.

His chin lifted in mock disdain. "Eventually, I might. Most likely I shall be a journeyman to gain experience."

"What would a premium cost?"

He puffed up his cheeks and blew out a breath air that condensed into a stream of white in the chill air. "I have to study mathematics and drawing, so several hundred pounds would be needed for my tuition."

Helena turned her shocked gasp into a cough. The pleading look on his face told her that any reservation on her part would crush his dreams. "Th-that doesn't sound insurmountable. We'll speak to Master Devereux this evening." When he flushed she said, "I assume you have already spoken to Samuel?"

"The day before he left, yes. Oh don't look at me like that, Helena. I had approach him before he left for Devon, I—"

She halted on the gravel and turned to face him. "A whole week ago, Henry. Why did you not say anything to me?" He started to speak but she held up a hand, halting his excuses. The situation already felt out of her control. "What did he say?"

"That I would make a better architect than a wool man, at any rate."

"I can see you have thought of everything." She had not intended her voice to be so sharp, though he barely noticed.

"I knew you would be happy for me and not mind my going." He gripped her arm so hard she called out in protest as he dragged her toward the door. "Let's go in, Helena, I cannot feel my feet."

Mind? Of course she minded, though she allowed him to bundle her into the kitchen with its steamy warmth and enticing smells.

When Lubbock bore down on them with a tray of freshly baked pasties, Henry fell on them ravenously.

Helena nibbled at hers, unable to force it past the lump

in her throat.

* * *

Master Francis Newman, a city architect with several public buildings to his credit, had accepted an invitation to the Lambtons for supper and an audience with Robert Devereux. A younger man than either of them had anticipated, he had piercing light blue eyes and a pleasant manner. Over an excellent supper and a few glasses of wine, Master Newman agreed to take Henry on as his apprentice.

Samuel had agreed to send the premium required on completion of the "liking" and Henry was to reside at Master Newman's house in Charles Street, to learn the profession.

"What do you think of him?" Henry whispered, from their position at the back of the room where Robert Devereux drank wine with Mr Newman.

"He's amiable enough," Helena said, non-committal, trying not to glare at the man who was about to take her brother away from her. "You are the one who will have to work with him. For seven years," she added, with a tinge of bitterness.

"It will pass quickly, you'll see." Apparently nothing would dampen Henry's enthusiasm.

All too soon after their conversation in the garden, Helena stood with the Devereuxs on the road outside Lambtons, shivering from the chill, but unwilling to cut short her farewells to Henry.

In the cold morning air, which Alyce had declared was injurious to their health, Henry bounced on the soles of his feet as he thanked the senior Devereuxs for their hospitality, embracing Celia and Phebe with enthusiasm. Having disengaged himself from Alyce's suffocating clutches without giving offence, he gathered his sister's hands in his. "I will make Father proud of me, Helena."

Helena's prepared words of love and encouragement caught in her throat. "I know you shall," she croaked, her eyes swimming with tears.

The chair stood on the cobbles with its lid up and door open. Henry climbed inside, and the chairmen hoisted the poles between muscled arms, setting off at a trot over the cobbles, calling “make way, make way there”, as hawkers and streetwalkers leapt out of their path.

“Charles Street is a mere step away,” Phebe snapped in response to Helena’s heavy sigh. “You’ll hardly know he’s gone.”

Celia glared at her sister, who flounced away along the hallway, leaving the two girls alone in Helena’s room. Celia chattered happily and Helena stared moodily down at the sodden garden.

Despite her friend’s overt sympathy, Helena could not explain that she felt adrift in a world where she had no place. Lambtons felt like a stage where she played the part of a tragic heroine, the daughter of the rebel whose fate was unknown.

At night, Helena lay sleepless, listening to the watch calling each hour, her loneliness gnawing at her until the London dawn crept across the sky.

* * *

Lambtons came alive in the evenings, the ground floor a noisy, bustling, aroma-filled place where servers crashed through doors and ran from room to room in response to shouted orders from customers and cooks alike.

However, one particular evening, things weren’t quite the same. Henry had been gone only a day, and yet she missed his cheerful face peeking round doorframes and his laugher in the hallways.

Alyce looked up from her place beside the fire as Helena entered the salon. “Have you told her, Robert?”

“Er—not yet, woman. I have hardly had an opportunity.” He beckoned Helena closer, shifting sideways on the chaise lounge to make room for her. “Do sit with me, my dear.”

Helena frowned. He never called Alyce “woman”.

Then watching the flush suffuse his face, her stomach lurched in a familiar feeling of dread. What was wrong now? With Henry gone, had they decided her fate too must be organised before she became too much of a burden?

Robert gave a cough. "We thought you should hear it from us, instead of through gossip in the dining hall."

"Hear what, sir?" Helena kept her face calm.

"That Lord Grey has been given a pardon," Robert said, wincing as Alyce gave her throaty laugh.

"Hardly given, Rob," she snorted. "He paid forty thousand pounds for the privilege."

Helena closed her eyes and inhaled slowly. Her initial excitement at the word "pardon" diminishing by the second. "Even if Father came home tomorrow," she said sighing. "We could never raise such a sum to free him."

"There's more," Alyce said, ignoring Robert's frantic gestures to be quiet. "Oh Robert, just get the tiresome business over with. She must be told sometime." She turned an eager expression back toward Helena. "Edmund Prideaux and Nathanial Wade have also been freed."

Robert fiddled with his cravat, adding, "They too have had to pay exorbitant fines that may well ruin them."

"They won't be dead though, will they?" Helena offered a feeble smile. "I cannot blame those two for surviving in any way they can. But I still place my father's fate, whatever that may be, at Lord Gray's door. He was one of the chief instigators."

"It does seem very unfair." Alyce tossed her elaborately curled head, setting the woven ribbons on her headdress quivering. "When Lord Grey attends court balls as if nothing had happened."

"Perhaps…." Helena fingered the lace at her sleeve, then split a look between them as if the idea had that moment occurred to her, "I should find a husband with the qualities required to run my father's business." *Or what is left of it.*

"Not an unachievable ambition, my dear," Robert said carefully. "However, you should not overlook your personal happiness."

"Security and position are what I need. To expect anything else in my circumstances is somewhat self-indulgent, don't you think?"

"Oh, as for you being a social pariah, that will pass, my dear." Alyce waved her fan, though the fact she sat close enough to the fire for orange flames to be reflected in her face paint struck Helena as contradictory.

"Monmouth had many detractors during his lifetime," Alyce went on. "However it appears his scandalous death has given him the status of a martyr. Everyone I speak to regards you as someone worth cultivating."

Her attempt to tease a smile from Helena, if that was what it was, failed miserably. "I'm still the daughter of a fugitive rebel—alive or dead. I'm hardly good marriage material."

Before Robert could contradict her, she rose, gave a polite curtsey and made for the door.

Despite her dramatic exit, Helena paused outside the door, her back against the wall while she waited for her rapid heartbeat to slow. Had she been too impulsive in her decision to put practicality before happiness? A decision she had made with bravado, false pride, and, she admitted to herself, some bitterness. The only man she had met since her arrival in the capital who had made her heart beat faster was William Devereux.

Only a heavy curtain designed to stop draughts separated her from the room where Robert and Alyce's voices reminded her she had not closed the door.

"Having been fortunate enough to marry for love," Robert said. "I cannot help but advocate similar happiness for all my girls."

"Helena is not your girl, Rob," Alyce replied, though there was no resentment in her voice, merely pragmatism. "You're such a sentimental creature. I'm certain she'll see things differently when an attractive young man comes along."

"Perhaps," he replied. "Still, I am convinced such cold practicality can only bring her more suffering. I hope, in time, she will reconsider."

Helena pushed herself away from the wall and headed for the stairs. They would soon discover they had another Phebe on their hands. A woman with a mind of her own who made her own decisions.

If marriage was Helena's only path to security and respectability, she would take what came her way, with no thought for a personal happiness she had left behind in Exeter.

Chapter 15

The prospect of her first Yule spent without her family filled Helena with dread. However, she soon found herself caught up in the anticipation-charged days of Christmastide at the famous Lambtons Inn. Servants darted through corridors with laden arms, and balanced on ladders draping the hallways with boughs of fragrant laurel, holly and mistletoe.

Serving men, kitchen maids, cooks, servers and pot-men all worked together with the incomparable Carstairs, who organised the occasion like a military campaign.

Phebe stood in the entrance hall and wrinkled her nose. "It smells like a forest in here."

"I know," Helena sighed dreamily, taking deep breaths.

Alyce glided regally between the upper rooms and the kitchens, issuing orders and supervising the preparation of the vast amount of food required for the season. There were the traditional vast Christmas pies made with game, chicken, eggs, sugar, raisins, orange and lemon peel, mixed together with rich spices. A cauldron of plum "porridge" bubbled away on the fire, with generous portions of raisins steeped in wine and spice, its rich, fruity aroma permeating the air. Sides of beef, venison, pork and various screeching poultry arrived in the kitchens, until the cooks protested they had no more room to prepare it all.

A self-important Lubbock appeared at intervals, carrying the news that *Lord T* had arrived with his party for dinner, or that the *Earl of S* and his lady wished a private supper in an upper room.

Harassed kitchen girls scurried between the tables, and serving men bore laden trays at a run up the stairs to the small dining rooms.

"We have a system of signals," Phebe revealed to Helena in a rare moment of confidence. "We can alert others as to when a person of consequence is served *à deux* in one of the private chambers. Then we can hover nearby when they leave, and see who they are." She indicated a young man on the floor below who gestured with both hands to another server.

"I see," Helena said, not seeing at all.

"Who do you think it is?" Celia asked, throwing herself into the occasion.

"I know not, but if you wait long enough," Phebe declared confidently. "The entire court of St James will pass along this corridor."

Helena awoke on Christmas morning, determined to overcome the sadness that lay like a stone beneath her ribs. Consoling herself with the knowledge Henry would be arriving later to eat dinner with them, she threw herself into the festivities, distributing the fruits of her frequent shopping expeditions to the 'Change amongst her new friends.

When she went to her room in the afternoon to fetch a shawl, she found a tearful Chloe crouched by the fire. "What's wrong, Chloe?"

The maid looked up, her face tear-streaked. "Master Dev'ro is so kind, Mistress. He gave me this." She sniffed, holding up a gold chain at the end of which twirled a gold cross.

"It's very pretty, Chloe." Helena noted it was a thin, light trinket and not of the best quality.

The maid's open delight made Helena almost ashamed at the extravagance of her own gifts. A prayer book bound in white kidskin, given to her by Master Devereux. For all his flamboyance and emphasis on wealth and position, Robert was a genuine and devout Anglican.

Alyce had presented her with a turquoise silk shawl and a gold pin studded with jewels of green and blue, fashioned like a peacock. Phoebe's gift was a hand-painted fan, and several lengths of ribbon, exquisitely made by the Huguenot weavers in Spitalfields. Helena ensured she made a special point of displaying pleasure over these, for Phebe was still unpredictable, as capable of delivering a barbed retort as a kind word.

Celia gave Helena a pair of dancing shoes in gold-embroidered blue brocade with latchet ties. “For your first real ball in London,” she said, as Helena marveled at the paste jewels attached to the heels.

Henry arrived with his arms full of decorated pasteboard boxes filled with sugared fruit, spiced almonds, stationery, and new quills. Others held combs and hair ornaments, wig brushes and buttons; these he distributed with largesse.

He spent the entire day at Lambtons, eating, drinking and talking with the family and inn patrons, even flirting with Phebe, who at one point was convinced the Duke of Buckingham was in the dining hall, annoyed when no one would believe her.

“Oh, ignore her.” Alyce leaned forward provocatively and caressed Henry’s cheek. “Phebe is always searching for famous faces among the patrons.” In his mildly tipsy state, Henry tolerated Alyce’s attentions unembarrassed.

Helena studied her brother with new eyes. In the few weeks of their separation, he had grown apace with new clothes that made him more a gallant than a child. His features had lost the boyish enthusiasm that displayed every emotion, and replaced by a more considered maturity.

All enquires with reference to his apprenticeship he answered with forethought and intelligence that made Helena proud.

“This has been a wonderful Yule,” Helena said, at the end of the evening when everyone collected their candles, ready to light them to bed.

“It’s not over yet.” Celia handed her a candle from the box at the bottom of the stairs. “Don’t forget the Lambtons’ Twelfth Night party. Father invites the patron who submit subscriptions to cover the cost of their dinner.”

“Mummers perform plays in the main hall, and we have musicians and tumblers to entertain us.” Phebe touched the wick of Helena’s candle with a taper. “Then there is the Twelfth Night Cake, with a bean and pea concealed inside. Do you have such things in Devon, Helena?"

"Indeed we do, and whoever finds them rules as King and Queen of the festivities." Helena recalled her previous Christmas with a pang.

"Celia was Queen last year." Phebe gave her father a level stare as if he were wholly responsible for the oversight. "Therefore this year, I insist it shall be me."

"You are too old for petulance," Robert scolded, though the soft look in his eyes belied his words. "The fates will decide who shall rule Twelfth Night."

* * *

Helena dressed in a plum-colored gown that fell to the ground in silken folds, with a split skirt pulled back to reveal an ivory silk underskirt. The gilded oval of silvered glass on her bureau blurred Helena's features, giving her an ethereal look. Eschewing the paint and patches Alyce favored, she brushed a sheet of Spanish paper gently against each cheek, then rubbed it into her lips to deepen their natural colour.

Chloe fastened her square ruby pendant round her throat, then wound wine colored ribbons into her hair, teasing out the little "favorites" and "heartbreakers" onto her temple and neck. "Is something wrong, Chloe?" Helena smoothed cream into her hands to whiten them, while watching her maid's frequent glances toward the door.

"No, Mistress," Chloe began. "It's jus', they're giving a party in the kitchen today for the servants, and I thought…." Her voice trailed off.

For the first time Helena noticed that Chloe wore her best skirt and bodice, with her hair not hidden under her usual white cap but dressed in curls fastened with ribbon.

"You may go, Chloe." Helena took pity on her. "Make sure you are back in time to help me disrobe."

Chloe sketched a hasty bob and hurried to the door with as much grace as her damaged leg allowed, passing

Celia at the door, all pink and plump prettiness in a yellow-gold gown with a row of emeralds, a Christmas gift from her doting parents, at her throat.

"Is it time to go down?" Helena patted her hair and smoothed her bodice. Loud chattering and laughter drifted up the stairs, accompanied by haunting mandolin music.

"There's someone you must meet." Celia joined her at the mirror, their gazes locked in their reflections. "He's not a guest, but you don't know him, so I suppose that makes him a guest, in a way."

Helena placed her hands on either side of her waist, taking cautious breaths to see how much leeway her corset would allow. "Who is this guest who is not a guest?"

"Come and see." Celia darted to the door and back again, like a puppy asking to go out.

They descended the stairs to the sound of clinking glass and female laughter drifting up from the public rooms. Bemused, Helena's gaze rested on a tall young man at the bottom of the stairs, to whom Alyce gave full attention. One slender hand caressed his arm as she gazed adoringly into his face.

Phebe hung onto his other hand, and Robert stood to one side, smiling proudly.

As if sensing her presence, the newcomer turned and met her gaze. For a moment, he reminded Helena so vividly of the late Duke of Monmouth, she almost gasped, then shrugged the thought away as ridiculous. He wore a sapphire blue long-coat with deep turned-back cuffs in pale yellow, and heeled and buckled black shoes. White lace frothed at his wrists. A carefully knotted cambric cravat was around his throat, and the ensemble was completed with a full-bottomed black wig.

"What do you think of him?" Celia whispered, though she did not wait for Helena's response before rushing on. "My brother William, come home from his tour. It's a new fashion you know, for young men to see some of the continent before they embark on a career."

Helena smiled as realization dawned. Alyce frequently talked about her son in dreamy tones, regretting his absence and bemoaning the fact they did not possess a likeness of him to show Helena. Now here was the real thing, standing in the hallway. Alyce's motherly pride had not embellished her son's looks, at all.

Helena took mental stock of how she might appear to him, gratified that her fashionable gown flattered her figure, and that her hair had been washed that morning.

Robert looked up and caught her eye, beckoning her forward.

Although she tried to remain aloof, Helena found herself drawn into the newcomer's deep brown eyes, alight with obvious appreciation.

He bowed over her outstretched hand murmuring, "My pleasure, Mistress Woulfe." He lifted his gaze to her face, but retained a firm grip on her hand. Helena felt the entrance hall recede, her fingers resting comfortably in his palm. William's eyes flamed with silent laughter as if in challenge.

Helena refused to look away, hoping she didn't blush and betray how he affected her.

"Isn't Helena lovely, William?" Phebe slid her arm possessively through his, forcing him to drop Helena's hand. "You must tell us about Italy and France. We want to hear all your stories."

Alyce stepped briskly to his other side, and with Robert leading the way, they entered the throng of partygoers. At the door, William glanced backward, his gaze fixed on Helena as if an invisible thread ran between them.

Light-headed, Helena returned his steady appraisal, then Celia jerked her forward, breaking the magic. "Helena, you're blushing," she said, mischievously.

"Not at all. It is exceedingly warm in here." Helena lifted her chin and this time, she was the one dragging Celia along in her wake.

The party gathered momentum, with new arrivals crowding the hall being greeted exuberantly by those they knew. Men wore high periwigs in a variety of colors, piled high on their heads with rows of thick curls flowing over their shoulders. Some sported tiny black patches on their faces, to disguise scars and blemishes on their skin. Others wore as much face paint as the women, making them look like garish mannequins, with splashes of red dabbed beneath their eyes.

Wherever Helena found herself during the evening, William was never far away. Flattered, she encouraged his company. She introduced him to Henry, who had arrived with Master Newman, his pleasant, homely wife and their eldest daughter, who he introduced as Mary Ann.

"What a wonderful party," Mary Ann exclaimed in a musical voice, her hands clasped together in delight.

"How are you enjoying your "liking", Henry?" William's gaze drifted to Helena as if seeking approval for the pertinent knowledge he possessed of her brother.

Henry's mild expression altered to one of earnestness. "Master Newman took me to Stationers Hall this last week, to have my indentures stamped, so now I am officially an architectural apprentice."

William turned a laugh into a cough and beside him, Helena resisted the urge to ask Henry if this procedure had been as painful as it sounded. Instead, she observed how pretty the Newmans' daughter was. Henry blushed, refusing to look at the subject of his embarrassment.

"Well, do acquaint us with her, Henry," Celia urged, appearing in the middle of his embarrassed stammering.

Left with no choice but to present his patron's daughter to his employers, Henry acted with grace and dignity, but also a good deal of stammering.

While these niceties were being observed, Helena's gaze slid to an elderly gentleman, who appeared to be giving a lecture to a group of enthralled guests in the middle of the room. Clothed in black with a long ebony periwig on top of a narrow face, he spoke in a braying voice, his heavy-lidded eyes displaying tired cynicism.

"Who's that serious-looking man over there, Celia?" Helena tilted her fan toward him.

"That is Master John Evelyn, Commissioner of the Privy Seal," Celia whispered. "The short, plump person with spaniel eyes sitting beside him is Master Samuel Pepys, the Secretary to the Admiralty." With a sigh added, "They're both quite old, but have some fascinating stories of their youth at the court of the old king."

"My Uncle Edmund worked for Master Pepys, many years ago." Helena said, exchanging a look with William, who gave a slow nod, evidently impressed.

Celia's eyes flew open in surprise. "I had no idea, Helena, how interesting!"

"He looks very proud." Helena said in a stage whisper.

"Master Pepys?"

"No, Master Evelyn. He appears to be a well-respected man, judging by the crowd he has gathered round him."

"He was a close friend of the late king, and therefore has a lot of influence at Court." Celia took her arm and guided her closer. "Godfrey Kneller painted his portrait, which is something of a privilege, as that gentleman only deigns to paint people of consequence."

"A gentleman painter?" Helena smiled, knowing all about Master Kneller, but Celia's way of describing people was so entertaining.

"Simply, a gentleman who paints." William smirked at her from her other side. "That particular one will paint himself into a knighthood, if I am not mistaken."

"He would never paint me, William, I am far too lowly." Celia giggled. "I believe Master Evelyn is not overly fond of His Majesty, due to his favouring of Papists."

"Why is that?" Helena asked, liking Master Evelyn immediately.

"He was distressed to hear of King Charles's deathbed conversion to Catholicism, albeit it was only a rumour." Celia's voice dropped conspiratorially. "Though to be anti-Papist is hardly news. It applies to almost everyone in this room." She gave a derisive laugh. "As for his attire, he's in mourning for two daughters he lost this year from the smallpox."

"Two daughters? Oh, how sad for him." Helena felt immediate sympathy, his loss reminding her of her own.

Celia sighed. "Mary, the elder, was a lovely creature. She was to have been one of the queen's ladies."

Helena watched William hail some friends on the other side of the hall.

"Evelyn's a nice old soul," he whispered, his breath warm on her face, "though quite a dry stick. I'll offer the compliments of the season when I have consumed a deal more wine." he dropped a swift kiss on her hand, and she stared at the tiny creases in front of his ear. "I beg your indulgence, Mistress Woulfe." His wig brushed her cheek and sent a frisson down her back. She watched him walk away, her face flushing, and distracted enough that she had to ask Celia to repeat her question.

"…I asked, would you like me to introduce you?"

"To Master Evelyn?" Helena frowned, trying to recover her composure. "No, I don't think…."

However, at that moment, the man himself glanced in their direction. "Ah. The elder of Master Devereux's delightful daughters," he called out, beckoning with a feminine hand. "The pride of Lambtons. How are you, my dear?" He made an ostentatious flourish.

"I am well, sir. Do allow me to present Helena Woulfe, Master Evelyn. Helena, Master John Evelyn."

The elderly courtier bowed over Helena's hand. "My good friend Robert has spoken of you, my dear, but he skimped disgracefully on the details." His hooded eyes sparkled with amusement.

Helena's surprise must have shown on her face, for he added, "London is a village, Mistress Woulfe, everything is known here." Still moving languorously, he waved a hand in a small circle as if to include her in the conversation. "We were discussing the worsening plight of the Huguenots, since King Louis revoked the Edict of Nantes." He gazed around at the small crowd of enthralled onlookers. "Abhorring the fact that Protestant churches are being demolished all over France, and that whole families are being imprisoned, and libraries burnt."

"I, too, have heard of it, sir," Helena said, watching Alyce sidle up to Evelyn and flutter her eyelashes.

"The persecution is barbaric, but the *London Gazette* remains silent on the subject. All intelligence comes to me by my friends or through letters. Such a strange state of affairs, I find, for what is still a Protestant Country. Should we not all be up in arms on behalf of our French neighbours?" He held his slender hands palm upwards as if inviting her opinion.

Alyce spoke instead, her fan flapping. "Now we have a Catholic king and queen, do you anticipate such persecution will cross the Channel, Master Evelyn?"

Celia glared at her mother, and two elderly ladies gasped in horror, leaning on their companions for support, while the gentlemen murmured darkly.

"Protestantism in France is not the same as Anglicanism, my dear." Evelyn placed a finger to his cheek as he considered the question. "Huguenots follow the beliefs of John Calvin, who states God has willed the majority of men to eternal damnation."

"…which some of them richly deserve," Robert interjected, creating a ripple of nervous laughter through the small circle.

Helena glanced sideways to see William walk by, an attractive red-haired woman on his arm, but his gaze held Helena's. Embarrassed he had caught her looking at him, she turned away quickly.

"Master Calvin thought so, too." Evelyn gestured to a passing server to bring him a glass of wine. "However, they do not discover if they have lived righteous enough lives to become God's elect, until they die."

"What would be the purpose of living a virtuous life, if it avails us nothing?" Alyce sniffed. "A thankless religion, to my mind."

"Catholic doctrine states a priest can grant direct entry to Heaven, and has the ear of God." Helena said, summoning her courage. "Little wonder then the French king has made Calvinism illegal, when such doctrine strips his church of its power."

Master Evelyn's admiring stare joined several others, who seemed less than impressed that a woman had dared to venture an opinion. Aware of the close scrutiny of those around her, Helena dared not turn her head to see if William was among them.

The conversation was noisily broken by a group of performers who turned summersaults and threw painted wooden hoops into the air. Cries of delight replaced bemused stares when one held a flaming wand, and appeared to swallow it.

When the jugglers dispersed to entertain another group, Helena found herself isolated at the side of the room beside Mr Evelyn.

He inclined his head, one hand cupped beneath his chin. “I knew Monmouth quite well, you know, my dear. I thought him a lovely person, handsome, and of an easy nature. That he should be so debauched and greedy as to allow himself to be seduced by crafty knaves was his tragedy, when he had so much already.” With a final low bow, he moved off into the crowd.

Helena rose from her returning curtsey with her gaze on his retreating back, murmuring, “He was the craftiest knave of them all.”

Chapter 16

Dinner was served in the largest of the dining halls; it sparkled with light from a thousand candles. The Devereuxs and their guests listened attentively to William recount his tour of far-off countries, with their impressive architecture, bad roads, intractable foreigners, and unbearably hot weather.

When the time came, Henry was given the honour of making the first cut to the Christmas cake with a flourish amid loud clapping. He was so handsome in a new suit and with a flattering wig in his natural hair colour. Helena looked at the young girls who gathered round him to receive the first slices. She examined each face, but Mary Ann Newman's was not among them.

On discovering the pea in her slice, Helena's instinct was to remain silent. However, Celia spotted the damning item on her plate, and loudly declared her to be Queen of the Revels. The announcement was greeted with roaring applause.

Helena reluctantly took her place on the decorated chair, her throne, while William clapped with enthusiasm. When the "King" proved to be John Evelyn, he pleaded his age and constitution as being inadequate to the position, so William, amid loud catcalls and suggestive laughter, stepped forward and begged to be Helena's champion.

"I have never been Queen of Revels." Helena whispered. "What do I do?"

"Simply follow my lead." William's broad wink made Helena's cheeks flame even hotter.

The evening grew more raucous as time went on, with the performance of outrageous tasks meted out by the "King" and "Queen". Four serving men carried Helena round the room on a makeshift litter. Celia had to polish the buckles on Helena's shoes, then a simpering young woman, whom Phebe insisted was the mistress of someone important at Court, followed William around the room with his gloves on a silver tray.

As dawn light crept through windows rimed with a crisp frost, Lambtons emptied of revellers, who lurched out to waiting carriages and sedans into a street that echoed to drunken greetings and compliments of the Season.

Alyce surveyed with dismay the discarded wine glasses, ribbons, and food leftovers on every surface.

"Leave it for the servants to clear up in the morning," Robert said, dismissing the yawning serving staff to their beds. "It is no more than the mark of a successful Twelfth Night!" he announced happily.

Drooping with exhaustion, Helena was about to follow their example, when William appeared at her shoulder. "Allow me to escort you to your chamber, Mistress Woulfe." His words slurred into near incomprehension.

Inwardly thrilled, Helena doubted he could see her properly, with such unfocussed eyes.

"The bottom of the stairs would be quite adequate, sir," She replied, her hand held out toward him, palm downwards.

"Ah, too forward? Do forgive me." William took her hand in his and turned it over, planting a lingering, yet firm kiss on her palm.

The effort to remain upright became too much and he staggered to one side, caught by a hovering footman who twirled him around and supported him up the stairs. When they finally reached top, William waved an unsteady arm in farewell and blew her a dramatic kiss over his shoulder.

"William is so amusing." Celia laughed, tucking her arm through Helena's.

Helena didn't reply, bemused to discover she felt the warm imprint of his kiss on her hand all the way up to her room.

* * *

Leaden skies gave way to snow, which swirled into doorways and drifted down the wider chimneys. Venturing beyond the firesides was an unwelcome ordeal.

On a particularly frigid dark afternoon, Samuel Ffoyle's carriage rolled to a halt on the cobbles outside the inn.

Helena watched his arrival from the window in Celia's room. "I did not expect him until spring. Are not the roads treacherous at this time of year?"

Celia shrugged. "Maybe he has some important business requiring his attention."

"Perhaps." Frowning, Helena grabbed her shawl and hurried outside as Samuel alighted from the carriage. Tall and imposing as ever in his city peruke, he had the remains of a frown on his face, as if he had been berating some unfortunate commoner.

"And how many coachmen have you sent off with burning ears today, Master Ffoyle?" Helena teased, throwing her arms around him. Though it was still mid-afternoon, the sky hung low and dark over a street where the only light was from the yellow glow of the inn lamps through the leaded windows.

A second figure in a wide brimmed hat emerged from the coach.

"Elias!" Helena gasped. "I had no idea you were coming to London."

Tiny white flakes drifted from the black sky and settled onto Elias's bare head as he bowed over her hand. "It is good to see you, Mistress Woulfe." His voice sounded forced, his gaze shifting to his father, who seemed reluctant to look at him.

Helena frowned. *What was going on between these two*?

Elias reached back into the carriage, and as Helena blinked snowflakes from her lashes, long, feminine fingers grasped his outstretched hand, followed by the arm and then the head of girl with large light eyes and high delicate cheekbones in an oval face.

Her presence provoked very different reactions in the

two men. Elias solicitously helped her navigate the narrow step, while Samuel set his lips in a firm line and turned away.

Enveloped in a voluminous traveling cape, the girl's white cap beneath the turned-back hood lay askew. Strands of pale hair blew across her face in the cold wind, but she held her chin high, her light eyes glittering with defiance, and not a little fear.

"Th-this is my wife Amy." Elias stammered an introduction.

Amy inclined her head in shy acknowledgment, her gaze flickering to her father-in-law, who still avoided her eye.

"Your wife?" Helena asked, open-mouthed in shock.

Several unspoken questions invaded her head. Samuel gave a dismissive snort and stomped past them to where Robert waited at the inn door. After a brief exchange, in which Helena heard Samuel ask, "Is he here yet?" the pair disappeared inside.

"Father is…displeased with us." Elias addressed the closed door, his jaw set. "Our marriage was something of a surprise." He gave a tense half smile towards Amy, who stared at the ground.

"As it is to me, Elias." Helena took his arm and pulled him toward the inn. "Let us go in," she urged. "I am freezing out here."

Neither he nor Amy moved.

"Er…we shall not be staying here, Helena." Elias glanced self-consciously at the footman who held open the carriage door. "Father has insisted we go to the Red Lion in Holborn."

"Oh, I see," Helena mumbled, not at all sure she did. "Then we shall talk here." She clambered into the carriage and settled herself under the fur rug lying on the seat. Amy climbed in after her and with a last glance back at the inn, Elias followed, slamming the door on the surprised footman.

"I'm delighted to make your acquaintance, Mistress Woulfe. I've heard so much about you from Elias and my sisters-in-law."

"I wish I could express the same sentiments, Amy." Helena felt awkward. "However, I'm delighted to meet you too."

"Father does not approve of our marriage," Elias said, his voice dull with resentment. "As his firstborn, he thought to choose a wife for me who would bring the greatest benefit to himself."

"Elias!" Helena gasped. "That's unfair, your father—" she paused at the sight of his tense face, thrown into relief from the lights of the inn opposite. Bitterness clouded his eyes and his jaw clenched. "Yet you are married, Elias, so he must have given his consent."

"We gave him little choice." Elias's bark of laughter sounded hollow.

"Let *me* explain, Elias." Amy covered his hand with hers, silencing him. "I was betrothed to someone else. An arrangement I consented to at the time."

"Go on…." Helena nodded in understanding. Hadn't she faced a similar predicament with Martyn Blanden?

"Well." She licked her lips, revealing small even white teeth. "When I met Elias, I realised I could not in all honesty go through with the marriage. My heart would not have been with the other man, and I could never have made him happy."

"You do not need to convince me, Amy." Helena said, discomfited by the emotion in their shared glances, knowing she witnessed something too intimate to be shared.

When she looked back at Helena, Amy's eyes were soft. "Elias felt the same about me, so we approached my parents to have the betrothal dissolved."

"They refused." Elias's voice choked with remembered anger. "When we asked Father to intervene, he would not help us. He said a betrothal is as binding as a marriage."

"I don't understand. You must have persuaded him eventually? Or you wouldn't be here, and married." Helena studied each of their faces, confused.

"Not at first, no." Elias's voice held derision. "Father

decided Amy would be married as arranged, and I would accompany him here to manage his new warehouses. He planned to send me far enough away not to create…well…difficulties. So we did what was necessary to ensure we could be together."

"How?" Helena broke off as Amy performed a gesture universally understood, laying a hand gently on her stomach.

Helena closed her eyes briefly, sighing. "Oh, Elias."

His features partly in shadow, Helena could not see his expression, though his sharp exhalation spoke volumes. "What else could we do?"

"Samuel is a proud man, Elias." Helena said, aware nothing she could say would make any difference now. "He must have been deeply hurt."

"I know that." Elias's fist clenched beneath Amy's delicate hand. "I was angry with him for dismissing us. He treated me like a child."

"How can you say that? He did what he had to. Amy was betrothed."

"I didn't think how it would make us look. I could only think of Amy."

"Or…you didn't think of her." Helena instantly regretted her sharpness. This affair was none of her concern.

"I should have behaved better." Amy tucked her arm beneath his. "But the damage was done."

Hasty marriages and babies born without benefit of clergy were an accepted part of rural life, of any life. And yet Samuel was the Worshipful Master of Clothmakers, and there was bound to be scandal attached to this union.

Elias tenderly arranged the fur rug over Amy's knees, the gesture making Helena feel unaccountably lonely. "Thus, I am still to be banished from Ideswell," he said. "The consolation being that Amy is here with me as my wife."

"He won't forgive you easily, Elias," Helena said. "Or you, Amy."

Amy sighed. "Four days confined in a coach and

sharing lodgings has been more punishment than you can know." She closed her eyes, as if at remembered ignominies endured at the hands of her father-in-law. "No matter, it is over now, and when Master Ffoyle returns to Ideswell, we will be alone."

"You appear to view your banishment as a wonderful opportunity."

"How else should we view it?" Elias shrugged. "I'm to be in sole charge of Father's serge distribution, its storage and sales in the capital. Yours too, Helena." he added.

"Where shall you live?" His enthusiasm was infectious, and the notion of having a friend in London began to appeal.

"The warehouse is in Freemans Yard, where Father has also purchased a house for us." His involuntary grimace betrayed his disappointment.

"Isn't it a nice house?" Helena imagined he could show more gratitude. "Samuel could have made you live in cramped lodgings near the meat market instead."

Elias winced and Amy giggled.

"It's near Cornhill and the warehouse district." Elias went on. "Father made a point of informing me that it's convenient, but neither elegant nor fashionable. Merchants who deal in woollen goods, millinery, hosiery, and the like are located there. Drapers Hall has a garden where Amy can take exercise, which is good for her condition." He gave Amy another adoring gaze. "And Freemans Yard is almost wholly Dissenter." Elias laughed. "To plague Father, we could always threaten to attend the Presbyterian Church." He sniggered at his own joke while Amy flapped her hand.

"Elias, you know he is determined to shake off his Puritan origins."

"Exactly!" Elias said. "Give him some time. He'll accept us eventually." He dropped his voice. "He'll have to."

Helena hoped his optimism was not misplaced.

"Father is not a cruel man." Elias seemed to read her thoughts. "If I do well here in London, the whole family will benefit, and Mother will be working on him at home."

"Your mother approves?" Helena felt the first spark of hope.

"Oh yes." Amy's face lightened. "Mother Ffoyle has always liked me, but she dared not speak up for me."

Helena remembered the loaded looks Samuel and Meghan exchanged during her stay at Ideswell, which told of lively disagreements between them about offering shelter to the Woulfes after the rebellion. Helena suspected those heavy glances had been resurrected when they discovered what Elias and Amy had done.

"But you are married, and there is to be a child." Helena tried to sound encouraging.

Two enraptured faces greeted her words, but then Amy looked crestfallen again. "I have yet to buy childbirth linens in preparation. There was no time at Exeter. And of course I should have a winding sheet…."

Elias gripped both her hands in his. "You are young and strong Amy, do not speak of dying. This child will be born healthy and you shall be safe, I am sure of it."

Helena suppressed a shiver. Childbirth was a perilous business for both infant and mother. It was common for even the healthiest women to greet news of a new life with the chance it might end her own.

"I am well prepared," Amy said. "I have some saffron in my baggage."

"Saffron?" Helena frowned, confused.

"An infusion taken moderately during the pregnancy that facilitates birth." Amy smiled. "Mistress Hannah Woolley recommends it in her household manual. Her advice is invaluable."

Helena would have liked to question Amy more on the subject of Mistress Woolley, but at that moment the carriage door flew open and a flurry of icy snowflakes swirled into the cosy interior.

"What is going on out here?" Samuel stood glowering at them from under his black wig. Without waiting for a response, he grabbed Helena's hand, pulling her bodily onto the road. "Come inside, Helena. You'll catch a chill from this foul air."

Without a word to his son or daughter-in-law, he slammed the door shut again, ordering the coachman huddling on the box to drive off. "Be at the warehouse at eight tomorrow," he called.

Helena's last glimpse of Amy was a white face peering out from under the leather flap before the carriage turned the corner, the wheels cutting lines in the fresh snow.

* * *

Chilled to the bone in just her woolen day gown below a thin shawl, Helena offered no resistance as Samuel propelled her into the Devereux's private salon, where a fire crackled and hissed in the hearth. Helena hurried toward the welcoming flames, rubbing her stiff hands together to get the blood flowing.

Samuel had discarded his cloak in the hall and sat on the chaise, his feet splayed out in front of him, both elbows resting on his knees.

Tense seconds stretched, while Helena prayed he was not about to attempt to ally her against Elias. She turned and faced him, her chin lifted in defiance. "Elias told me what he has done, Master Ffoyle. However, I'm sure he intends to atone for his disobedience." His jaws clenched as he ground his teeth. A bad sign for him.

"Huh, I cannot help feeling he has taken this action to repay me for forbidding him from joining Monmouth."

"You were proved right about the rebellion, Samuel," she said, though it cost her to admit. "But for him to marry purely to spite you isn't in his character. From what I have seen he truly loves Amy, and…."

He silenced her with an upheld hand. "Helena, I will not discuss Elias with you. He is my problem, and I will deal with him. Nor is he the sole reason I am here." He paused and inhaled slowly. "There is someone else who wishes to see you." He rose, strode to the door and swung it open. "He arrived on the post coach this afternoon, but agreed to wait until my arrival before speaking with you."

Helena's breath caught in her throat, and for a fleeting second she thought he might be…then her stomach settled again as the familiar figure of Tobias Lumm stepped into the room.

Helena stared. "Lumm? Wh-what brings you to the City?" Strangely, in his expensive long coat and wide brimmed hat, he didn't look out of place any more than Samuel did.

Looking handsome and totally at ease with himself, Tobias appeared almost amused by her discomfort, then exchanged a loaded look with Samuel, who gave a slow nod.

The fact struck Helena then that these two were friends. It made no sense. When did such a thing happen? If there was news of her family, which was surely the only reason he would want to see her, Samuel alone could have brought it.

"This is quite an alehouse." Lumm removed his hat, tapping it gently against his thigh as he gazed around appreciatively. "The room Master Devereux gave me is a virtual palace."

"Lambtons is no ordinary alehouse." She gave the standard response without thinking. "Your visit is unexpected, Lumm, though you are welcome all the same."

He set his hat onto a side table, tugged off his gloves and flung them into it, each movement masculine and deliberate.

Samuel made to leave. "I will see you later, my dear."

Helena started after him, but Lumm called her back. "He has left us alone for a reason, Mistress."

She froze as the door clicked shut, halted by his tone.

Lumm sat down on the chaise Samuel had recently vacated, relaxing into the upholstery as if he belonged there. He indicated the empty space beside him. "Please, sit. There's something I need to say to you."

Helena was tempted to remind him a gentleman did not sit in a lady's presence, but the time for trivial niceties appeared to have passed. Still uneasy, she did as he asked, watching as he brought a small square packet from the pocket of his long coat and held it out.

The sight of familiar handwriting on the upper side set her heart racing. "It appears to be a letter…" she said, making no attempt to take it from him, "…that must have lost its way, judging by the condition it is in." At the same time her breath caught and a shiver ran through her veins. *It cannot be.*

He held her gaze. "Addressed to Lady Elizabeth. Had not the messenger the foresight to ask at *The Ship* for the location of Loxsbeare, it may have ended up in Lord Blandon's hands. As it was—" He shrugged, placing the letter in her hand.

"Y-you're living at your father's inn now?" Helena stared at the packet in her hand. He nodded. "I could never serve Blanden. Not after what he did to Sir Jonathan."

"I appreciate your loyalty," she whispered, blinking back tears at the sight of her mother's name in looping, brownish script. The writing blurred as she stared at it, an urge snatch the page and devour the contents was strong. Yet still she could not bring herself to take it.

"Read it, Mistress Helena." He said, his voice barely above a whisper.

She lifted the letter slowly, as if she expected the paper to burst into flames, weighing it in her hands. The parchment was hard, brittle and cracked in places along the folds, and slightly greasy to the touch, the clumsy seal broken.

She did not hear the click of the door, but sensing she was alone, the only sound in the room the crackle and hiss of the fire, Helena began to read.

Chapter 17

September 3rd 1685
The Hague

Dear Mother

This is the first occasion I have had both the resources and inclination to write of the events of these last weeks. I am impatient to assure you that I am alive and well, but would I had more welcome news, for surely everyone at home must know the fate of our expedition.

Our hopes were so high that day we left for Taunton, but before I venture into the worst of it, I must tell you there will always be one light, that shines through my darkest memories, and that is Monmouth. He was everything I remembered from my youth, and more. No one could have been prouder than myself on that day he was proclaimed King at Taunton's market cross, or surer that the course we had chosen was right.

All too soon did it turn to hopelessness and despair, although the early signs were there, when the squires of the West did not come as they had promised. Those who gathered under our banner were faithful and determined men, though there was barely a real soldier among them.

At first, it was a true adventure, a test of our spirit and resolve, when even the weather turned against us, for after the drought of early summer, we faced days of heavy rain, with mud to our knees and our clothes forever sodden. With no proper tents, we slept in the open, with diminishing supplies, so more often than not we went hungry.

Copies of King James' pardon were handed out amongst the men by kin and clergy, after which the desertions began. We cursed those for slipping away in the night, but I hold no bitterness in my heart for their wish of family and hearth. I longed for it every day myself.

The Royal Army closed in, and we were no longer welcome where we had marched in triumph just days before. Warned off by the town authorities, we dodged troopers through hedge and village, as they hunted us like rabbits.

I was assigned to Lord Gray's Horse under Captain Jones when Monmouth decided to launch a surprise attack on Feversham's men. A man named Godfrey was to guide us across the moor at night, but still we got lost in the mizzle.

We found the Langmoor, but as the first horses were crossing, a shot warned of our coming, so Captain Jones took us full tilt against Compton's troopers before the King's infantry could arrive. We put their Commander out of action straight away. Not bad for a cabinetmaker, wouldn't you say?

I could make out lights ahead, and thought they were of the town in the distance. Then an officer shouted they were the tapers for the matchlocks of the Dumbarton's Scots Brigade. Our infantry fired on them with musket and cannon, killing some of them. I heard later that Churchill made the rebels pay for that indignity.

A deafening volley of musket fire from Albemarle's militia terrified the horses. This proved our undoing, for they scattered and turned about, stampeding backwards into our own upcoming infantry. My own horse reared, then a musket shot caught him in the neck and he went down like a felled tree. Gentle Strider, companion of my boyhood, was never meant to be a soldier. I fell with him, injuring my shoulder as I hit the ground, rolling into the path of a dragoon who aimed his musket straight at my face.

I froze, certain I would be killed, but another horse crashed into his and he was crushed beneath both flailing mounts. I gained my feet again, though the Lord knows how. I scrabbled for my sword as our infantry surged toward the Royal troopers, caught in their forward charge.

I saw neither my father nor Uncle Ned during that frantic hour when the fighting was at its worst. Then the dawn came, and with it a massive charge by Feversham, through the mist, cutting through what was left of our men. Musket balls screamed past me in waves, shredding men and horses.

Wade's boys were driven back to the Langmoor Rhine, and the Taunton Blues fought like demons, though they must have known they stood little chance. Then Oglethorpe's horsemen thundered over the moor, howling and hacking at any rebels left standing, although there was little sport left for them.

The boom of the guns and hundreds of hooves battering the ground filled my head, so I could barely gather thought, much less fight. Rage burned in me at the sight of our boys' easy slaughter. Somehow I stopped cowering and ran at the troopers, swinging my sword through red cloth and flesh as they came at me. I carried blood that was not my own on my clothes for days afterwards.

I did not see the blow that struck me from behind, plunging me into a deep stream, where I lay stunned and soaked by muddy water with some poor drowned wretch beside me. When I came to my senses enough to crawl out, my clothes caked with mud and blood, it was into a field fallen eerily silent.

I breathed in the acrid stench of powder in the air. It seemed like every one of Monmouth's boys lay broken on the earth. Unrecognizable heaps of bloody, dirtied clothes, with pallid faces; the ground littered with discarded weapons, bloodied pikes and scythes, boots, coats and hats, all in a mass of corpses, and mangled horses.

I staggered from their accusing eyes, trying not to see the dead hands clutching wounds, convinced some of them reached for me. I know not how long I crouched beneath hedges up to my waist in stinking water, while King's men searched the nearby cornfields, shooting or hanging men where they found them.

It took me two days to reach Lymington, where a

fishing boat master bound for Cherbourg took me aboard.

I would like to think the man enough of a good Protestant to help a distressed rebel, but I fear the villain only sought to relive me of my gold. I let him think he robbed me, but am enough of Edmund Wolfe's nephew to have kept some back and well hidden. I have already discovered the life of a fugitive is very costly.

The voyage in heavy seas in such a tiny vessel convinced me it would surely be my last. I doubt I shall go to sea again without serious misgivings, but daily I remind myself I have life at least, when so many do not.

I am in a poor but Christian lodging here in The Hague, with another Rebel outlaw, an intelligent fellow whose name is Daniel Foe. A splendid companion, who is much saddened at having to leave his young wife in London. I suspect he will not stay here long.

I have scant news of my officers, although the plotter is here in our company. They say Matthews and Foulkes are still at large, and we heard Lord Grey is preparing to purchase his freedom in exchange for information; but best I don't dwell on that.

I have heard no news of Father or my Uncle, but they are without doubt the bravest and best men I know, so I pray God has preserved them.

When I have been presented to his Majesty of Orange, I shall write again, although how long it is before I can return home, I cannot tell. Tales of the savagery meted out to those captured has sickened us all. For York to have murdered his own nephew so callously, then to spread rumors that Monmouth offered to convert in exchange for his life, are beneath contempt.

Surely the Prince of Orange would not allow this travesty to go unpunished, with the Protestant Church in more danger than ever before? When I return, I hope to be among those of like mind, who would make the Devil of York account for his cruelty.

I pray you are kept safe, and Helena and Henry also. I long for the day we can be together again.

Your respectful and loving son

* * *

The comfortable sitting room at Lambtons faded and Helena was taken back to the courtyard at Loxsbeare, the morning after Sedgemoor. She could still hear Henry's anguished protest when dirty water spilled on his shoes.

Her throat burned as the words were forced from her. *Mother, Aaron's alive. He got away.* Then her elation clouded with bitter disappointment that she would never be able to tell her. This was compounded by the fact he had no idea where their father was.

Unnoticed, Tobias had slipped back into the room, circled the chaise, and sat beside her.

Helena kept her gaze on the page in her hand, her thumbnail picking at a small tear beside her brother's name.

"He doesn't know where Father is." She looked up into sympathetic eyes, so familiar she gave a choked sob. Then she mentally shook herself and swiped her wet cheek with the back of her hand. What an odd thing. Of course he was familiar. She had known Tobias Lumm for nearly two years now.

"I know. No one in Exeter has heard from him either, as far as I know."

"He wrote this months ago." She held the pages up between them. "He'll be wondering why no one has responded. I shall have to tell Aaron about Mother, and Uncle Edmund. He expects…."

"He expects nothing," Tobias cut her short. "He'll be more than grateful that you and Henry are safe and well."

"Why are you here, Tobias?" Helena let the pages fall into her lap. "Samuel could have brought this to me. You owe us nothing. You lost your livelihood when Loxsbeare was seized. Why would you want to come all this way for Henry and me?"

"On the contrary. I owe the Woulfes a great deal. And with your permission, I'm determined to carry it through, and go to The Hague to see Master Aaron on your behalf."

Every suspicious thought Helena ever had about Tobias rose in her throat, and threatened to choke her for its injustice. To think that he should demonstrate such devotion, when her actions toward him at Loxsbeare had been nothing less than spoiled petulance. Her shoulders slumped and with a silent nod, she gave way to quiet, heartbreaking sobs.

Tobias gathered her in his arms like a child, the cloth of his coat rubbing her cheek, the smell of damp wool overlaid with leather and warm skin filling her senses. Familiar, masculine smells, which brought with them the painful realization that no one had held her for a long time.

When her tears subsided, she pulled away, embarrassed at her lack of control in front of a servant—despite that he was no longer in her service.

He handed her a large kerchief. "If you will give your permission, I wish to go to Holland."

She took it gently, sensing their relationship had altered since his arrival. Never a subservient man, he had always treated her insolence towards him with humor and tolerance, an indulgence she didn't deserve. "Something tells me that you will go anyway." She gave him a watery smile, acknowledged by his wider one. "His letter only mentions the street and the town. How will you find him? And is it safe for you to go?"

Inexplicably, she did not want Tobias to walk into danger. Rumour said that the king had sent his agents into France and Holland in search of fugitive rebels, who were to be dragged back to England to face trial. Who was to say it wasn't true?

"Someone will know where he resides." As if he read her thoughts added, "I doubt His Majesty has men on the lookout for messages going back and forth to the continent. His scandalous promotion of Catholics into key positions has given him more than enough to cope with at home, without worrying about Aaron Woulfe."

"Or Sir Jonathan Woulfe?" She sighed, then brightened. "Maybe there are other rebels in Holland who do know what happened to Father. People Aaron hasn't yet encountered."

"One thing at a time, Helena. I believe Samuel has sent a messenger to fetch Henry, so he may be told."

"Henry! Yes of course he would want to know. I should have thought...." She noticed he did not say, "Master", but hardly cared. She rose to her feet, the letter still clutched in her hand. "Thank you, Tobias. You mentioned you had a room, so I assume you'll be staying here for a while?"

"A few days. Until I can book passage from Woolwich."

"So soon? You'll have to excuse me. I must find Celia and tell her the good news before Henry arrives. He's bound to be full of questions."

The sound of William's familiar laugh drew her steps towards the door of the taproom, anticipating his delight at her news. These last few weeks, William always wanted to hear her stories about her family, openly sympathetic where her father and brother were concerned.

Unlike other taprooms in local hostelries, the room was plain but stylish. There were benches and scrubbed tables set in booths. Shoulder-height glass panels afforded privacy from adjoining patrons who gathered to drink, take an ordinary meal, and talk. The room was always spotlessly clean and the staff disciplined, and what Carstairs called, "of high moral character".

Smiling, Helena retraced her steps, intending to go in, knowing he would be as delighted as she to know about Aaron. William occupied a booth opposite the door with an attractive woman, who on closer inspection was hardly in the first flushes of youth. William pressed his lips to her hand, while fixing her with his amorous gaze. From her delighted protestations, Helena could tell she was receiving the same flattery he always employed when he addressed her.

Helena stepped back into the shadows as a shaft of anger ran through her. A server with a tray narrowly avoided a collision, his expert arm guiding the tray over her head. He turned a grimace into a gracious smile, bowed and moved on into the dining room at the end of the hall.

Blood throbbed in Helena's temples as she ran up the stairs, though by the time she gained her room, her sharp disappointment had passed. Why should William not flirt with any woman he chose? Besides, the man had little to do other than hang around the dining rooms in search of female distraction. He lived on the generosity of his father and possessed no skills of his own with which he could begin to provide anything like the life she had lost. He reminded her of a cat, stretching and preening under whoever's hands he found himself at the time. Sometimes, Helena suspected boredom alone drove him to lay siege to her; so why had seeing him use his charm on another affect her so strongly?

If she could not attract a wealthy man who could give her what she needed, a reliable one with ambition and ability was her only alternative—not a vain, idle fop, with a roving eye.

Surprised at herself for allowing William's actions to disturb her so badly, she refused to allow him to spoil her special day. Helena returned downstairs, resolving never again to be susceptible to William's feline grace.

Chapter 18

Tobias wrapped his heavy long coat around his shoulders and huddled on the forecastle deck of *The Sirius*, shivering in the bitter cold, icy salt spray that whipped across his face. He bore the discomfort stoically, preferring to brave the prevailing wind, rather than suffer the nauseating yawing of below-deck.

The gale howled like an animal in pain, greeted cheerfully by the crew who declared it meant an earlier arrival at their destination. The ship had left Brewhouse Quay on the tide the previous day, and the coast of Holland formed an uneven gray mass on the horizon, partly obscured by horizontal rain.

The rain turned to drizzle as they pulled into The Hague, the vessel lashed down with ropes.

Tobias joined the small group of passengers who clumped down the rickety wooden gangplank. None of whom had uttered a word to him throughout the overnight voyage.

His leather bag tucked under one arm and one hand holding down his hat, Tobias glanced around the dockside, wondering which way to go. An old man approached him, narrowed eyes staring out of a wrinkled face. Tobias grasped his bag tighter, returning the man's stare in silence.

"Waar u bent die gaan?" the old man mumbled.

Tobias frowned, and shook his head

The man tried again. *"Kan ik u de heer helpen?"*

Dismissing the conversation as a waste of his time, Tobias turned to go, when an English voice behind him spoke, "He asks vere you are bound, and can he be off help."

A smiling blond man of about his own age sat perched on a cart pulled by a well-built, but elderly horse. "Thank you, sir, I'm looking for a street called—" He pulled a sheet of paper from his pocket and peered at it. "Grote Markt."

"The market." The carter pointed with a curt nod. "I go there. I gif you a ride."

Tobias slipped a coin to the old Dutchman, who nodded his thanks and shuffled away.

"Could you take me to an inn near the market? I need to make enquires."

At the carter's languid nod, Tobias climbed onto the cart, his bag beneath his arm and hand clamped firmly onto his hat. Distracted from his discomfort by the rows of neat, tightly packed brick built houses with ornamental gables, Tobias wondered whether he could have travelled by water instead. Everywhere he looked, the canal weaved along his route, jammed with conveyances piled high with goods and people.

One thing his foster-father had taught him was that good gratuities made for reliable service. Thus when the man dropped him in the main square, he rewarded him well.

"Take the door to the left. The landlord knows everyone who comes to The Hague since the summer. He will tell you vere the man is whom you seek." As if as an afterthought, added. "You don't vish him harm, I trust?"

Tobias grinned, hitching his bag beneath his arm. "No, I wish him no harm. He's a friend."

"Goot!" The carter clicked his tongue at his horse. "Prince Villiam is sympathetic to these men, ja?"

Pulling his collar up against the biting wind, Tobias entered the inn, a low-ceilinged room with roughly-made wooden benches, badly scarred and marked, but which looked clean. The landlord professed no knowledge of Aaron, but another man at a table in the corner of the room proved more forthcoming, in a clipped, disinterested sort of way.

"Back alley, black door, top floor, rear," was all he said, pocketing the silver coin Tobias proffered.

A tiny, wizened man, his black cap covering his head

down past his ears, opened the door, peering up at Tobias with myopic gooseberry eyes. Mention of Aaron's name brought smiles and nods, together with a pointing finger to an upper floor. He took Tobias to a narrow staircase at the back of the hall and pointed again, indicating he should climb to the top.

Tobias paused on the tiny landing, placed his bag on the floor and took a cleansing breath before he raised a fist to knock.

The door opened tentatively at first, then when the occupant saw who it was he flung it open.

"Lumm!" Aaron ushered him inside and closed the door on the tiny apartment, where he relieved Tobias of his hat and slapped him repeatedly on the back as if reassuring himself he was real.

"Pardon my hesitation in opening the door just now, but I thought you were a creditor." Aaron grinned as he guided his visitor to a rickety chair set at a tiny round table in a corner of the room, and bade him sit. "I gather my letter reached Mother at Loxsbeare?" He hastily removed a thin pile of linens from an equally fragile chair opposite and sat down. "I apologise for my Spartan lodgings, but they are all I could find."

Aaron's face looked too thin, his blue eyes wary under a vivid red scar that sliced through his left eyebrow, though the broad smile and twinkling blue eyes were unmistakably Aaron Wolfe's. He wore his fair hair shorter, held at the nape of his neck with a wide black band; most likely in tribute of his lost duke.

Tobias assessed his surroundings at a glance. Set beneath the eaves of the ancient building, the walls of the room were lime-washed, the floorboards bare and uneven. A small, square gable window looked onto clumps of contiguous rooftops of the city, washed of their colour under the winter sky. The window held no hangings to keep out the cold wind, and the furniture was old and decrepit. The door of the next room stood open and through it, Tobias spied a narrow bed with meagre coverings.

When his gaze came round to settle on Aaron's face

again, all his well-rehearsed speeches deserted him. "I've brought letters for you, Sir." Tobias, faltered on the "Sir", but Aaron appeared not to notice. "And money." He withdrew the bulky packet from his coat and set a square packet and a cloth bag on the table between them.

"I appreciate them all, Tobias. The money is particularly welcome. As you can see," he indicated his worn clothes, "I wear hand-me-down garments these days."

Aaron stared at the letters hungrily for a moment before turning back to Tobias. "How is everyone at home? I've been worried for them all since the Rebellion failed."

He leaned his forearms on his knees, his chin jutted forward, a stance so familiar it brought a lump to Tobias's throat, and he couldn't speak.

"Is it so bad?" Aaron whispered.

At one time, the arrogant Aaron Woulfe had possessed no insight to a man's feelings. Spoiled and indulged, he had seen no need to dig below the surface to a man's soul.

Tobias nodded, admiring of the change in his former master. *Where to begin*? "There has been no news at all of Sir Jonathan, Master Aaron."

"I feared as much." Aaron exhaled, nodding. "He could have been caught and sent for trial. Then there would be no hope." He leveled his gaze at Tobias's face, waiting.

Tobias swallowed. "Your Uncle Edmund is dead."

Aaron gave a small groan, then rubbed his hands over his face as if washing it. "May his soul be at peace," he murmured so Tobias barely heard him. He jerked his head up and met Tobias's gaze. "Was he hanged?"

"No. Killed at Sedgemoor." Tobias did not see how the manner of his death made a difference, but this detail appeared to matter to Aaron, who released another low, relieved breath.

In the heavy silence that followed, Tobias knew if he did not say the rest of it there and then, he might never be able to. He licked his lips and took a deep breath, summoning his courage. "Master Aaron. Your moth—Lady Elizabeth is also dead."

Aaron's eyes widened and his mouth worked silently.

He looked away, then back at Tobias, his expression darkening. He leapt to his feet, the wooden chair clattering onto the boards behind him. "You lie!"

Tobias did not react, merely held his gaze.

Understanding dawned, and Aaron relaxed his stiff shoulders. Finally, he found his voice. It was cold. "How did she die?"

Haltingly, Tobias told him about the day the militia came to Loxsbeare. He recounted the scene in the hall when the soldier snatched her necklace, her fall, and Henry's grief. The days so vivid in his head, his voice broke before he had finished.

Aaron's fists clenched as Tobias talked, his knuckles bloodless, the veins on his neck bulging, as his whole body tensed in suppressed fury.

When Tobias stopped speaking, he expected Aaron to crash his fist into the wall, or hurl the remainder of the scanty furniture around the room in a rage, or even scream accusations at Tobias.

Instead, a heavy silence stretched between them until Aaron crumpled to his knees on the bare floorboards, dropped his fair head forward and sobbed like a child.

Once again, Tobias found himself in the role of physical comforter to one of the Woulfes. This time the grief was so deep, so heart-wrenching in its intensity, Tobias found his own face wet with tears. He murmured repeatedly as they clung together, ironically like brothers, "I am sorry, I am so sorry. I beg your pardon."

They broke apart finally, without embarrassment, knowing neither of them would ever speak of the incident again.

Aaron pulled himself to his feet. "There is nothing to forgive." He strode to the corner of the room and splashed water on his face from a ewer on a lop-sided dresser. When he spoke again, he seemed chillingly calm, his hair wet at the hairline. "There is an unremarkable eating-house a few doors away. The food is a little unusual. Mostly cold, and consisting of cheese and some odd sort of fish. But it is economical and filling. I have funds, thanks to you. Would you dine with me?"

The brittle invitation tore at Tobias's heart. He accepted with a silent nod. Aaron collected a shabby brown coat from a hook behind the door, and they clattered in single file down the narrow stairs. There was no sign of the old man, as they let themselves out on a street where the biting wind from the North Sea funnelled between the buildings.

Tobias pulled up his collar and jammed his hat low, but Aaron seemed impervious to the chilly weather.

The inn was no more than adequate, the food as bland as Aaron had described, but at least their seats in an alcove by the fire gave them privacy. With orange flames reflected in Aaron's eyes, he listened as Tobias talked.

Aaron accepted the loss of Loxsbeare with naked, but silent grief, expressing his relief his brother and sister were safe, grateful his mother and uncle received Christian burials. He expressed incredulity at Helena's foray into Somerset. "She is an unusual girl, my sister." A tear slid down his cheek, which he wiped away.

Tobias told him about Henry becoming an apprentice architect, and Aaron's face suffused with genuine happiness. "You don't say!"

The door opened and a face appeared round the jamb. A pair of shrewd eyes scoured the room before alighting on Aaron. The man stepped inside, and as he approached their table, Tobias studied him. He was tall and lean with stringy brown hair and a large, Roman nose that sat uncomfortably on a thin-jawed face. His eyes were sharp and piercing, and he stooped.

Aaron beckoned the newcomer to their table. "Master Ferguson, do join us."

If Tobias hadn't known the man's nickname was The Plotter, he would have been able to tell it from his furtive attitude.

Aaron moved his stool to make room, but the newcomer declined with a hand gesture. "I came ta gie ye the news." His accent was so thickly Scottish, Tobias had to concentrate to make out his words. "The King has pardoned us, Aaron." He rolled the name over his tongue, already eyeing the door as if eager to be off to spread the news elsewhere.

"All rebels?" Aaron tensed.

"The messenger arrived on *The Sirius* this morning," Master Ferguson replied, nodding. "Tha news'll be posted in the market place later today."

Tobias frowned, wondering which of the men he had shared passage with had been the messenger.

Master Ferguson leaned both hands on the table and stared into his friend's face. "We cae' go haeme Aaron." He beamed.

Aaron rose to his feet. "We must tell the others." He followed Ferguson, to the door, and then turned back. "Tobias, will you wait here until I have consulted with my friends?"

Bewildered, Tobias nodded. "The next ship for England does not sail for three days." He glanced around the gloomy taproom. "Might I obtain a room here?"

Aaron nodded, and then without a backward look, both men were gone.

* * *

In the time it took for Tobias to negotiate with the Dutch innkeeper to secure a room, change the linen he had worn for the last two days and wash his face and hands, Aaron had returned.

A new nervous energy had invaded Aaron. He took his seat in the taproom they had vacated an hour before. From a burdened man, visibly reeling under the recent loss of half his family, Aaron's eyes had acquired a new determination. His self-possession restored, he reminded Tobias of the young man he knew at Loxsbeare: the arrogant young Crown Prince instructing a servant, with every expectation of unquestioning obedience.

"When shall I book our passages home, Master?" Tobias asked, keeping his voice low. For some reason, their presence appeared to be attracting attention from other patrons.

"You'll be returning alone, Lumm. I'm staying here, in The Hague."

"For what reason?" Tobias asked, open-mouthed in shock. "The king's pardon means you can return to England without fear of—"

Aaron held up a hand. "I have friends here. Friends who saw what I did at Sedgemoor and barely got away with their lives, as I did. We shall not go back to England to live under the tyranny of the Papist King James."

"What will you do?" Tobias dipped his nose to his tankard, judging it ill advised to mention life in England under any authoritarian monarch was much the same.

"I can afford to stay and establish my own household, thanks to our Master of Clothworkers, Samuel Ffoyle." Aaron grinned and tapped the money pouch inside his coat. "The Prince of Orange sympathizes with our situation. His wife was distraught at her most beloved cousin being murdered by her own father, so I feel sure he'll soon commit to our cause with troops."

Tobias's gaze swept the room nervously, wishing Aaron would lower his voice, but didn't like to ask.

"I can see you don't understand my reasons, Tobias. However the Protestant religion is in greater danger than ever while this king is on the throne. Can you not see?"

Tobias couldn't see. News of the Pardon would be all over England by now. Helena and Henry would be expecting their brother home. How could he return alone? He stared into Aaron's face in search of a chink in his resolve, but saw none.

"I have instructions for you, Lumm," Aaron went on, oblivious of Tobias's discomfort. "On your return to London, I wish you to call on a friend of mine. I'll give you a letter to take to Master Daniel Foe of Deptford. Accompany him to Samuel at Lambtons. He'll explain my reasons, if you feel you cannot."

The thought of Samuel Ffoyle waiting patiently at Lambtons for his protégé's return made the ale curdle in his stomach. At this rate, no one was going to welcome Tobias back, without their precious boy.

Unable to summon a convincing agreement, Tobias merely nodded just as Master Ferguson appeared at the door and made for their table.

The two men sat over a heartier supper than Tobias suspected either of them had eaten in a long time, making plans for the brave new society Prince William promised them.

Disillusioned and robbed of all energy after a stressful and disappointing day, Tobias rose wearily to his feet and stumbled to his room at the back of the inn, where he slept the clock round.

Three days later, Tobias stood in the stern of the ship taking him back to England, his inside pocket heavy with a bundle of letters for everyone at Lambtons. The wind had dropped, and the sea was calmer, forecasting a longer, but easier crossing. Among his fellow passengers were several exiles who, unlike Aaron, were eager to return home.

The sailors threw the mooring ropes over the side, and to a symphony of called orders and echoed responses, the ship eased away from the dock. Tobias leaned on the rail, watching the land slide away from him, and remembered: he had lacked both the courage and opportunity to broach the facts of his own paternity.

Chapter 19

Henry tucked into his second portion of cold beef and potatoes fried in bacon fat with a resigned sigh. Despite his protestations that he was quite replete, Mrs Newman had piled his plate, again.

After five daughters, having a young male to care for at last appeared to please her. Not that Henry minded, her attentions going some way to helping him miss his own mother less. He was looking forward to work more than usual on that particular morning. Master Newman had requested a meeting the evening before, where he expressed more than usual satisfaction with his work.

"You won't be spending all your time on building sites and in stone warehouses in the future, young Woulfe," he had said, a fatherly hand on Henry's shoulder. "It's time you began to learn the more aesthetic aspects of being an architect. Drawing, planning, ornamentation, and the like."

"I'll look forward to the new experiences, sir," Henry had responded with genuine enthusiasm, though he forbore to explain how much he enjoyed getting plaster dust on his hands. He liked nothing better than to run up ladders, hang precariously over drops, and scramble along buttresses to see how the masons were progressing.

On this particular morning, however, Henry's thoughts were not on stonemasons. Instead, he contemplated Mary Ann Newman's green eyes and rich, glossy hair. She was the most exquisite creature he had ever seen. Diminutive and fine-boned, she made Henry's lack of height seem dominant and manly beside her.

Her eyes had attracted him first. Wide and luminous, with tiny golden flecks within, they reminded him of Helena's. He hesitated to mention this, for fear of allotting Mary Ann a status equal to that of a relative. Thus, with a genuine compliment withheld, he was rendered tongue-tied in her company. Henry couldn't stop looking at her, drawn repeatedly to her delicate features and her perfect bowed lips that held a perpetual smile.

From her position further along the table, Mary Ann flicked frequent glances in his direction from under her long, sweeping lashes, an occurrence that Henry had at first assumed mocked him.

He quickly learned that Mary Ann was not only intelligent and quick-witted; she never grew bored with his talk of the characteristics of stone or how mortar was mixed, like Celia and Phebe Devereux did. Sometimes even Helena suppressed sighs and rolled her eyes when he grew particularly enthusiastic about a building, or a style of brickwork.

In contrast, Henry found the younger Newman daughters, though charming, somewhat irritating. All four vied for Henry's attention, performing small tasks to gain his notice, until he found himself bestowing constant gratitude for their efforts.

"I used the tiniest stitches on the tear in your coat, Henry," fourteen-year-old Joanna simpered, her attempt to look doe-eyed and appealing not sitting well on her plump frame. "Only a small tear on the hem at the back, but I thought best not to allow it to worsen. You must have caught it on a carriage door as you climbed down."

Henry nodded politely. "Thank you for the effort, Mistress. I had not been aware of the damage until you mentioned it."

"Do you like the feather I picked for you, Henry?" Margaret, the twelve-year-old smiled coyly, brandishing her gift. "The colour will suit your new hat perfectly."

As if she too had become weary of her sisters' girlish chatter, Mary Ann flicked Henry a knowing look and left the room.

The void she left felt like a chasm opening up, though Henry forced himself not to watch her retreating figure. "Thank you for a most satisfying meal, Mistress Newman," Henry dabbed his mouth with a napkin and rose. "I look forward to this evening's supper, which I know will be every bit as good."

"Would you not take more buttermilk, Henry?" ten-year-old Millicent beamed up at him from beside his shoulder, in imitation of her elder sisters' flirting. "I used my Dutch grandmother's special method."

"Perhaps I might have some, warmed, before bed." Henry said.

Before Jane, the six-year-old member of the family could request her doll repaired or a ribbon tied, Henry made his rapid escape along the long hall to where his coat, hat, and muff hung from the rail in the hall. Before reaching them, Mary Ann stepped out of a side room into his path, opened the front door and slammed it with a resounding bang. Pressing a finger to her lips, she drew him into the room behind her and silently closed the door.

Henry smiled. "I have to meet your father…."

She cut him off with a deep kiss, pressing him back against the door.

"I know," she said, her lips brushing his as she answered. "We haven't been alone for days." She leaned back, and smoothed down his shirt with both hands, sending ripples of pleasure across his skin.

He released a tiny groan and traced the line of her chin with one hand.

"Could you get away and meet me somewhere?" she wheedled, bringing the tips of his fingers to her mouth, nipping at them with her teeth.

Henry swallowed. "You are bold, Mistress Newman, you know that don't you?" He tried to look serious, but knew his enraptured expression gave him away.

"I know, but only with you." She jutted out her chin, pouting.

"Your father is waiting for me at Christ Church, Newgate. It's almost complete, and Sir Christopher will be there for the final inspection. I mustn't be late," Henry insisted, though made no effort to move from the circle of her arms.

"Later then," she breathed into his neck. "Think of

somewhere we can be alone."

"We are alone," he teased.

"You know what I mean." She giggled, leaning into him for another urgent kiss.

The door behind him creaked in protest and they sprang apart. "Mother might have heard that," Mary Ann whispered. "She'll be coming to see what I'm doing." His arms still encircled her waist and she caressed his neck with one hand.

"Perhaps you and your maid could pay a visit to St Bride's Church sometime around three of the clock?" Henry suggested.

Mary Ann gave the slightest of nods, then slid past him to open the door, checking the passage before signaling him to emerge. The footman standing in the hall saw everything, and nothing, his back ramrod straight as he stared at thin air.

Avoiding the man's eye, Henry slipped past him through the front door, turning to blow Mary Ann a kiss as she closed it behind him.

Outside, Henry's gaze alighted on two chairmen slouching against the wall of a building opposite. Henry liked sedans, which could ease through spaces a carriage could not, making his frequent journeys through the city more efficient. He beckoned with his chin, in a fair imitation of Robert Devereux. One chairman nudged his companion before hurrying toward him, the cumbersome conveyance slung between their broad shoulders.

Henry settled into the comfortable interior, wondering how the workmen on the building site were capable of even flexing their fingers in such weather. Wishing spring would come, he shoved his hands inside the fur muff, his hand closing on a small square of parchment.

Frowning, he brought the paper into the light to read. It was from Mary Ann. The words were overly-sentimental, but they meant everything to Henry, whose lips curved into a smile as he read. He re-read the note twice, then touched it to his lips before tucking it back inside the muff.

He and Mary Ann had skirted around each other for

weeks, with shy smiles and awkward exchanges. He still did not know quite when their attraction had intensified into stolen kisses and secret meetings, but he did not regret one moment of it at all.

Their mutual pleasure distracted Henry from the terrible dilemma neither could face discussing. He might have private means, but he was also an indentured apprentice to Mary Ann's father and therefore forbidden to marry. For him to become betrothed to his patron's daughter under the man's own roof in secret would be devastating for his future career, not to mention Mary Ann's reputation.

According to his indenture, Henry could not contemplate marriage for another six years, although the thought their union constantly occupied his thoughts. With such an obstacle hanging over him, Henry had not dared talk of the future; it was imprudent enough snatching private moments in the present. That Mary Ann would wait for him was something he knew instinctively. However, she too needed the approval of her parents and his guardian. Without them, what would become of Henry's grand schemes?

Since the wonderful news that his brother Aaron was still alive, news which Mary Ann had been as excited about as Henry himself, he had longed to see Aaron and place his future in his brother's hands.

He still could not bring himself to mention it to Helena; she and those Devereux girls teased him enough for blushing in Mary Ann's company. Aaron would clap him on the back and laugh at his gaucheness, but he was head of the family now, and would know what to do, even if Henry did not. Everything would be better once Aaron came home.

Henry gazed unseeing at the interior of the sedan as it rocked and bumped along in the heavy traffic. He kept the leather flap down, allowing the familiar sights of London to pass him by unnoticed, his thumbs gently stroking the square of parchment inside the muff.

They turned a sharp corner and the chair jolted,

causing the chairmen to shout a protest. Henry put out a hand to steady himself but was thrown hard against the padded backboard. He righted himself and threw up the flap, craning forward to scan the street.

They had almost collided with a large handcart, which lay on its side, its load spilled onto the cobbles. Henry joined in the abuse and yelled at the hapless carter gathering up his belongings from the filthy road, ordering the way be cleared so he could complete his journey. Henry was a busy man and could not tolerate delays.

* * *

Lambtons was busy, and in order to keep out of the way of running feet, Helena found a private corner in the kitchen parlor where to sit. The sounds of raised voices and the clashing of pots and clunk of cleavers on wood filled the background. A cook shouted at a maid for dropping a plate; a serving man relayed a customer's orders, while the door to the dining room swung open with a creak, then flapped back into place with a rhythmic whoosh.

The kitchen parlour was where Mistress Carstairs ruled her domain, a scrubbed wooden table on one side and a potbellied stove the other. A narrow shelf circled the room above head height, displaying a collection of blue and white Delph, sent to the housekeeper by her Dutch son-in-law.

Helena joined them on cold afternoons, warming her feet at the stove and chatting to Lubbock, who sipped tea like a gentleman and gossiped to Mrs Carstairs.

He reminded her of Benoit in some ways, the cook at Loxsbeare, whose fastidious nature and vanity about his appearance was the bane of the servants' hall.

Helena settled herself at the oak table, her journal and a bowl of coffee beside her. The doors on either side of the room stood open, the kitchen side revealing the cooks bullying the serving men, while the other gave onto the clamour of the dining areas. In a sudden flurry of movement, Lubbock scrambled to his feet, bowing respectfully.

"Mistress Woulfe, I thought I might find you here." William leaned against the doorframe, arms crossed over his chest, his black periwig arranged artistically over both shoulders.

"Indeed, you have found me, sir." She tucked a hand beneath her chin. "With my favorite gentleman at Lambtons." She nodded her head toward Lubbock, who hovered in the background.

William pressed both hands over his heart. "And I came hot-foot from Wills, leaving my coffee untouched in my haste to be the first to bring you the news."

"How thoughtful of you. And what news is this?"

"King James has issued a general pardon to all those who fought in the Western Rebellion."

"Everyone?" Helena sprang to her feet, all traces of the coquette gone. "All pardoned?"

William's eyes told her *no*. "Those who came over from Holland with him are excluded, as are a few of the more prominent rebels. Sir Jonathan Woulfe is still listed amongst the fugitives condemned to death. Aaron Woulfe, however, is a free man."

"Thank you, William. At least half your news is good." Helena's cheeks grew warm, which she told herself was for Aaron's sake, but the feel of William's eyes roving over her face and sliding down onto her bodice made her quiver. *Did Father know he could not come home? Where would he go now? For nothing would convince her he was dead.*

Lubbock made a mumbled excuse about having duties to perform and slipped away. Most likely, Helena imagined, to inform the rest of the kitchen staff. She smiled as Mistress Carstairs appeared at the door, only to be pushed back by the retreating Lubbock.

William flicked up the back of his coat and sat opposite her at the table. "Is this coffee still hot?" he asked a passing serving girl.

"This ten minutes, Master William." Her face scarlet, the girl bobbed an awkward curtsey and hurried away.

William's fingers brushed hers as he passed her the

cup. A sharp jolt ran through her, and, when she looked up, the sudden flare in his eyes showed he had felt it too.

She withdrew her hand with an inward sigh, wondering why he created such mixed feelings. During his kinder moments, William treated her with genuine affection, and it would be churlish to rebuff him. Then he would make a frivolous joke at someone else's expense, talk disparagingly of an enamored lady in Helena's company, or lose a vast amount of money he had not earned at a gaming table, and her heart would harden against him.

They were still staring into each other's eyes when Celia arrived with Phebe hot on her heels.

"Have you heard about the Amnesty?" Celia asked, waving a hand at Lubbock's retreating back.

"Yes." William and Helena replied simultaneously.

Celia clasped her hands together. "Isn't it wonderful? Aaron can come home."

"Why are you sitting here in this horrid little room?" Phebe's gaze flicked around the parlour with distaste. "Do come into the salon, both of you. There's a lovely fire in there."

"I cannot wait to meet your brother," Celia said as they traversed the hall and took their places on the settles, chaises, and chairs around the welcoming blaze.

"I am sure he will adore you, as I do," Helena said, appreciative of Celia's enthusiasm for someone she had not met.

"Do you think he could stay here, at Lambtons?" Phebe asked, positioning herself behind her brother's chair, her long fingers caressing his shoulders.

"I expect he would prefer his own establishment," William said, his gaze still on Helena.

Celia's hand flew to her mouth. "Oh, but suppose he insists you go and live with him?"

"That seems unlikely, at first at least." Helena said, laughing. "In any case I shall insist I remain…." she stopped short as the truth occurred to her. As head of the family, Aaron could command her to live where and how he wished and she would have no choice but to obey. She wondered why this idea held no appeal, then pushed the thought away.

"Will Aaron know about the pardon by now?" Helena asked.

William laughed. "No doubt all the rebels in The Hague will crowd every available ship out of the harbor as we speak." He was still looking at her, and she revelled in his appraising scrutiny, unable to tell if the thrill she felt was due to her brother's imminent return, or to William's smile.

Robert and Alyce arrived to join in the general celebration, speculating with their daughters as to where Aaron might live.

"I insist we have the blue guest room prepared for him," Alyce announced. "At least, for when he first arrives." She clasped her hands together just like Celia. "How wonderful to have a real Rebel in our midst. I shall be the toast of the district."

Helena listened distractedly, hearing only snippets of their conversation.

William observed Helena with a half-mocking smile, his high-backed chair positioned so close to hers that their toes almost touched. He had a habit of staring into her eyes as if she were the only person in a room, daring her to be the first to look away. When she could forget his sheer masculine physicality, he was excellent company; he often sought her out for fascinating discussions on any subject that came to her. Helena experienced a heady sense of her own feminine power during these sessions, exchanging banter in flirtatious verbal jousts.

"That's enough of the absent master Woulfe, or I shall become quite jealous," William commanded them with a glint in his eye. "I would prefer to discuss more entertaining subjects."

"Such as what, William?" Phebe enquired, one brow raised.

William paused, one ankle crossed over the other, swinging his foot gently. "Helena, I hope you'll allow me to escort you to the Pleasure Gardens at Fox Hall when the sun decides to shine. They are particularly pleasing in the springtime."

"Will we ever have a spring?" Phebe pulled her shawl tightly round her shoulders. "Master Evelyn told me the other evening that this winter had been unusually mild, but I disagree. I'm constantly freezing, no matter the fires are lit every day."

"You haven't answered me, Helena," William said gently.

"In regard to what, sir?" Helena feigned interest in a piece of embroidery. She hated needlework with a passion, but the activity gave her a focus. "Oh, the Gardens. That would be most agreeable. I shall have to seek permission from my brother first." She peered up at him through her lowered lashes, and so intent on being coy, she pricked her finger.

"Never mind mincing about the Gardens all day, William," Robert snorted. "What about I purchase a commission for you in the Navy? A respectable enough life for a man."

"Eh?" William tucked in his chin and rcgardcd his father with a mixture of surprise and horror. While Robert was busy calling in every favor he possessed to find gainful employment for his son, the object of all this industry had so far expressed nothing but ennui at the prospect of work.

"His Majesty was Lord High Admiral when he was a young man." Robert tried again. "You have to have some ambitions for your future." William wrinkled his nose and waved the suggestion away, not bothering to respond.

"The uniform would be so flattering, do you not think?" Alyce pointed out with mild regret.

"You are not enough of a gentleman, William," Robert jabbed the air with the stem of his pipe, "nor are you rich enough to be able to idle your life away." He snapped his newssheet and dipped his head to the printed page again, dismissing his son with a shake of his head.

Helena looked down at her sewing. From what she knew of his activities, William did exactly that. His days spent wherever young men went, to bet fortunes on the turn of a card or the progress of a louse up a wall hanging. Then there were the lengthy drinking sessions in the public rooms, or the nights he joined a group of affluent young fops in one of the private rooms upstairs, catcalling from the balconies to passersby below, until Robert called an outraged halt to their rowdiness.

William got to his feet with a sigh and wandered to the window, where he stood staring at the street, his hands held loosely behind his back. After a moment, he appeared to make up his mind, and turning on his heel, bowed to the ladies, saying he was off to visit a coffee house.

"Which one, Will?" Phebe asked, following him out.

Helena suspected she did so to retain his attention, but they were at the door before he answered, so his reply was inaudible.

When he had gone, Celia sidled up to Helena and perched on the edge of a chair. "I cannot understand you, Helena. How can you remain so unmoved, when every female who lays eyes on William, falls instantly in love with him?"

Helena smiled. She had seen those ladies he charmed, then immediately forgot, hanging on the fringes of his company at gatherings, hoping to rekindle his interest. If he noticed their existence at all, his eyes would skim over their earnest faces with a vacant smile, and they would forgive him, call him a rogue, and sigh after him.

"I like him very much." Helena shrugged, pretending to wrestle with an intricate stitch. "Though I beg you not to misunderstand his attentions. He is only flirting with me, there is no real attachment."

Pouting, Celia fiddled with the box of sewing threads at Helena's side. "You would settle him down," she whined in her petulant voice. "I know he spends too much time gaming, and drinking and…." Helena arched an eyebrow, and Celia whispered, "…yes, well, probably whoring too." Her light tone indicated it a minor fault. "However, if you and William were married…."

Helena whipped her head round to stare at her. "Married?" she said in a fierce whisper. "Whatever makes you think he would…I mean, that I would…?"

Celia wasn't to be distracted. "You would be perfect for him. Your practical sense would enable you to mould him into a stable and respectable husband."

Helena did not reply, one hand hovering in midair as images of a life as William's wife paraded through her head. A future filled with worry over paying the servants, keeping creditors at bay, and hiding the playing cards loomed into her head. Then the face of a vapid redhead she had seen in his company flashed in front of her eyes. She stabbed the linen viciously with her needle.

"It simply will not do, Celia." Helena's gaze went to Robert in the chimney corner, his head still bent studiously to his newssheet. In an opposite chaise sat Alyce, in black lace over scarlet silk, her brow creased in concentration over a novel.

"I suspect your matchmaking is the result of you having spent this morning in the company of your betrothed."

Celia's deep flush proved her right.

Master Ralf Maurice called at Lambtons almost daily, making it clear he could not wait for them to be married.

Helena observed them together with wry amusement, intrigued that a pleasant, but undistinguished and shy man had overnight become Celia's romantic dream. The bride-to-be tripped around the inn with a beatific smile, bestowing goodwill on everyone. Phebe, exasperated with her sister's cloying sentimentality, flounced out of the room whenever marriage was mentioned.

"William might very well offer for you, Helena, if you gave him sufficient encouragement," Celia suggested huffily.

Helena held up an imperious hand. "I don't want a husband. Well, certainly not yet, at any rate." *And not that one.*

Chapter 20

When Tobias returned to London with a companion, that the self-conscious stranger in the taproom was definitely not Aaron Woulfe.

"I have invited Master Foe to take a libation with us," Robert explained. "Phebe and Alyce will be down shortly, for had I failed to inform them, they would insist I repeat whatever Master Foe says over nuncheon."

By the time the ladies appeared, Tobias had confirmed what Helena had already guessed. Aaron was still in The Hague.

Helena took the empty seat, which happened to be beside William, who like the others, was putting the stranger under close scrutiny. Master Foe appeared to be in his mid-twenties, with a swarthy complexion on a long-jowled face that threatened to turn to fleshiness in later life. His chin and nose were both sharp, and there was a mole beside his full mouth. Definitely insignificant beside the handsome and colorful Tobias, his wool coat looked as if it had been made for someone broader. His linen, if frayed, looked laundered, although shadows of old stains remained.

"It was kind of you to attend us here, Master Foe." Robert said in an obvious attempt to put the man at ease, but this proved unnecessary when the newcomer returned his look with pride and not a little arrogance.

"Er…actually, sir." Foe gave a cough. "I returned to London from The Hague last year." His gaze darted round the room, as if the word itself might rouse Troopers from the corners. "I was eager to return to my wife. I also had some pressing family business requiring my attention. Master Woulfe, cognisant of my distress, gave me passage money he could barely spare."

"You were not afraid of the soldiers?" Helena asked.

Foe's eyes clouded. "I feared being brought to account for my involvement, certainly. In fact, my name is on the Petty Jury List for Cornhill Ward. I'm in the process of negotiating with a Master Penne to have it removed for a…a consideration." He blushed. "Which ah…Master Woulfe has provided, since his fortunes have altered of late."

Helena rolled her eyes, fixing the newcomer with her fiercest glare. "Why has my brother not come home?" She tried to appear calm, but her anger was well-nigh tangible.

Foe turned admiring eyes on her, then flinched. "I believe, Mistress, from the letter Master Lumm brought me, that Master Woulfe feels the loss of his mother and his uncle keenly. He will take time to recover from the dreadful news."

Helena clamped her lips together to stop the angry tirade that sprang onto her tongue. *Did Aaron think he was alone in his grief? What about her? And Henry?*

Foe rested his elbows on the table and steepled his fingers. Helena wondered for a moment if he was preparing a prayer for them all, but instead he said, "Master Woulfe feels the time is not yet right to return to England, not when our present monarch still occupies the throne."

"He's not coming back at all?" Helena regarded him with disbelief, though the truth was right in front of her. Aaron hadn't sent this man to prepare the way. He had sent him as his replacement.

"Has Master Woulfe been presented at the Prince of Orange's Court?" Alyce asked, revealing rather more décolleté than their guest seemed comfortable with.

Foe flushed and looked away. "I am reluctant to reveal Master Wolfe's specific plans at this stage. For security reasons, you understand. However I have been told the Prince of Orange keeps a close eye on the situation in England," he stammered. "Though it is widely believed he is not unsympathetic."

"And how does that concern my brother?" Helena demanded, her patience wearing thin.

Foe's eyes filled with righteous fervor. "As it should

concern every Anglican!" He scanned each face in turn. "The king's closeness to French Louis, a standing army in peacetime, his promotion of Papists into high office. All these events indicate he intends bringing the country back to Rome. By force, if necessary."

"I disagree," Robert said, indignant. "I know no one in London who has found life more difficult as an Anglican, since the succession."

"Perhaps, sir." Foe gave him a superior smirk. "Though Catholics seeking office in court and Parliament have found it considerably easier of late. One would think we didn't have such a thing as the Test Act."

"Actually, Father," William ignored his mother's warning glare, "Evelyn complains of seeing Popish pamphlets on the streets, yet no moves have been made to have them banned, or the publishers imprisoned."

Robert looked about to respond, but William had not finished yet. "The king is aware his preferment of Catholics is making him unpopular. His attempts to have that very act you mentioned repealed, sir, proves that." He turned to the circle of faces. "Master Foe may be right. King James may well be arming himself against his subjects in order to force his religion on the country."

William turned toward Helena with a slow wink she pretended not to see. Was his fanning of the political flames been to impress her, or to annoy his father?

"There is also the fact King James keeps over thirteen thousand soldiers in barracks." Foe held up a finger to emphasis his point. "Their regiments should have been disbanded after the rebellion. No, he retains them to put down any objection to his Papist schemes."

While the company absorbed this thought, Robert took the opportunity to whisper an instruction to a server at the door. The man scurried away to comply.

Helena bit her lip in frustration. It seemed Master Foe and Aaron had been closeted with their fellow fugitives for far too long, with time lying heavily on their hands. The only use they appeared to have made of it was to imagine plots and counter-plots coming out of Whitehall against the entire Protestant world.

With his wife to distract him, Foe would most likely adjust to normal life again in due course, she imagined. However, the longer Aaron remained in Holland, the more romantic a figure he would become in his own eyes, if not those of his fellow Protestants. In her view, Aaron should return to England as soon as possible to take up the ties of responsibility he still had left.

"And tell us, Master Foe, what does your future hold in London?" Robert asked, apparently determined to divert the conversation away from religion.

"I'm a hosiery merchant," Foe replied. "Although, in truth, I have had a great deal of time to think these last months."

"I should imagine you have, sir," Robert muttered under his breath, passing his guest another glass.

"Pamphleteering is rewarding, but can be somewhat dangerous." Foe took a gulp of Robert's best claret. "I also write for the *Review,* but I have a novel in mind."

Robert raised an eyebrow. *Political or religious rhetoric perhaps, but a novel*?

"And what shall this novel be about?" asked Alyce.

Helena smiled. Alyce spent a great deal of her free time devouring novelettes, the more racy the better.

"I have not yet a story in my head, Mistress Devereux." Foe's face softened at being the focus of Alyce's dazzling smile. "However, when I was hiding from Troopers after Sedgemoor, I found myself huddled beside a gravestone with a most unusual name inscribed upon it. I have never forgotten it, and since then I have had a notion to name my hero after that dead man."

"What was the name?" Tobias asked.

"The gravestone bore the inscription, *Here lies Robinson Crusoe*."

"Strange indeed," mused Robert. "I wonder what manner of story one could write around such a name."

* * *

"What does he say?" Celia asked Helena, referring to

the letter Aaron had sent through his messenger.

Master Foe had proved the hungriest man she had ever seen, and he had spent the entire day partaking of Lambtons' finest cuisine before Robert saw him off to Deptford in his coach. By evening, Helena's jaw ached from smiling at the man's accounts of how the entire country and everyone in it were doomed under the Papist King James.

Helena broke the seal with growing excitement, only for her chest to hollow out as she read her brother's much anticipated handwriting. "He says, he hopes I am well and happy and will continue to conduct myself respectfully in my Guardian's home."

"Oh dear." Celia swiveled on the stool next to Helena's dresser, her voice dull. "Does he have nothing more personal to say to a sister he has not seen for so long?"

"My sentiments exactly!" Helena snapped the page and read on, "'I must thank you for the service you have performed in bringing our dear Uncle Edmund's body back to Devon.'" She broke off with an angry sigh "He writes as if I were a stranger! Listen to this!... 'I have most graciously been received by His Highness Prince William, who discussed with me in a personal manner the most urgent need to protect the Protestant religion in England….'" She parodied the final words as she paced the room.

"That sounds dangerous for your brother," Celia murmured. "Should he have committed such intimate details to paper? I mean, mentioning the prince?"

"No, he should not - it's practically treasonous!" Helena crumpled the page in her hand as she continued to pace the room. "I cannot believe that after all he has been through, all *we* have been through, he takes such a risk!"

She could hardly believe her handsome, sunny brother had written to her in this way. All those nights she had lain awake after the rising, sending messages into the heavens for him to stay alive, keep safe, and come home to her. Then his first letter addressed to her contained inane instructions to behave, and a calm announcement he planned yet another armed rising against the king.

"Why do men who have bloodied themselves in battle, crawled away from the field of blood with their lives and little else, their names ruined and lost everything, why do they simply get up and do it all again?" Helena demanded.

Celia shrugged. "Perhaps their memories are poor."

Helena only half-listened, her thoughts on Aaron's last words. She read them again, running a finger beneath the line. "'...our father appears to have disappeared into the mud and mist of the battlefield.'" She slapped the offending page on her bureau, telling herself he was wrong. Their father still lived, somewhere.

* * *

"Would you care to break your fast with me, Mistress Helena?" Lumm strode forward and grasped her hands as she descended the stairs early the next morning. "If you have not yet dined, of course." His expression was guarded, as if he presumed too much.

He looked nothing like a steward, in an emerald green long-coat with strands of his peruke tied into knots with colored ribbon.

"I should be glad to." Helena accepted his proffered arm with genuine pleasure, glad of the opportunity to discuss Aaron with him alone.

Lubbock showed them to a table in a corner of the dining hall, the room almost deserted so early in the day. A serving man brought thin slices of buttered bread and hot chocolate for Helena, while her companion ordered new ale, fresh bread, cheese and cold meat.

"What do you think of Lambtons?" Helena asked, noticing he took no more than mild interest in his food.

Helena pulled her shawl tighter, wrapping her chilled fingers round her cup of chocolate in the cold room. Like the observant host he was, Lubbock set a brazier near their table without being asked.

"I wonder what my patrons at *The Ship* would think of

this." Lumm grinned as his gaze swept the elegant room. "When Samuel told me where you and your brother were going to live, I never imagined anything so grand."

Helena looked around her, trying to see what he saw. Lambtons surprised everyone on their first visit, but she was now accustomed to its unexpected luxury. "*The Ship Inn* must be very different from—from Loxsbeare." Simply speaking the name aloud brought a lump to her throat.

He glanced at her over the rim of his tankard, then set it down with a nod. "How could it not be? But I shan't talk about the past if it upsets you."

"No, I don't mind," she lied, forcing a smile. "Though I would rather hear about Aaron. How is he, really?"

He wiped his mouth on a linen napkin and leaned back in his chair as if giving himself time to consider. "He is changed. Still handsome and charming, but his personality is—darker, somehow."

Helena did not respond, having come to this conclusion herself.

"His hatred of the king colours his judgment, I feel. As it did for…"

"…f my uncle, Edmund Woulfe?" Helena finished for him.

He gave a slow nod. "Having to tell Aaron about your mother was the worst thing I have ever done." He turned from her to stare morosely into his morning draught.

"They were very close." Helena's hands trembled as she reached for the chocolate pot. The container came up light in her grasp and she indicated to a server to bring more. "Is what he is doing dangerous?"

"I cannot say, but Prince William of Orange strikes me as a man who will not act until certain of a favorable outcome." His voice held a cynical note.

"And there is still no news of my father?"

Lumm was prevented from speaking by the arrival of the server, who removed the empty plates and replenished the ale and chocolate. With a nod and a smile at them both, he slid a plate of tiny biscuits onto the table.

"They have been experimenting in the kitchen again."

Helena watched as he plucked an oval from the dish, examining it closely before taking a bite.

She frowned, the action sticking a chord in her head, his mannerism familiar. The tilt of his head, the way he held his hand—something that struck a memory she couldn't quite place. "I couldn't help but notice that you and my father appeared to enjoy an unusual relationship at Loxsbeare."

"What do you mean?" He stared at the biscuit he turned over in his fingers.

"You talked to him in a way that no servant talks to his master."

"My relationship with Sir Jonathan bothered you?"

Helena shrugged. "You were always in his company. Out on the estate and in the house. You went with him to Exeter and Plymouth, when before he always used to take…." She faltered, unwilling to admit the one he often took was herself. Her father's neglect had hurt her. "I distrusted you."

"I know." His gaze held hers with something like compassion, yet without resentment. He brushed crumbs from his breeches with the back of his hand. Watching him, Helena's eyes narrowed. How he reminded of someone. *But who*?

"Why did you want to bring me the letter, then go all the way to Holland to see Aaron?"

He ducked his head, and slanted a look at her from beneath lowered lashes that made her gasp at its familiarity. "Who are you, really, Tobias Lumm?"

He smiled, a slow, beautiful smile, bringing tenderness into his eyes. He leaned forward until their faces were inches apart. "Sir Jonathan met my mother about a year before he married Lady Elizabeth." The corners of his mouth crinkled and a dimple appeared.

Helena saw it, and everything became clear. "Go on," she whispered, her heart hammering in her chest.

"He was young, younger than I am now. He was handsome and wealthy, with a whole city paying him homage as Thomas Wolfe's son. There was some rivalry between him and his twin when they were younger, I believe, so…." He gave a shrug as if explanations were unnecessary. "My mother was pretty, flirtatious, and flattered when he paid her attention."

"Father told you all this?"

Tobias nodded. "When I first came to Loxsbeare."

"What happened?"

One arched brow slid upward. "When she discovered she carried me?" At Helena's nod, he went on, "What you would expect? Your grandfather, Thomas Woulfe put money into the inn on condition Jim Lumm made an offer for my mother. Your grandfather had already sought a betrothal for your father, and he wasn't going to let my mother ruin his plans."

"Yes I see. When did you discover you were not his?"

"Mother burdened me practically from birth with the knowledge Jim was not my father." His mouth twisted. "She would taunt him when he tried to discipline me, so he let me run wild, and saved his fathering for my four half-brothers." He saw her frown and hurried on. "He was a good father. I never had to suffer the beatings my brothers did. In some ways, that spoiled me." He indicated his embroidered burgundy vest beneath the long coat and breeches and the perfectly tied cravat and lace at his wrists. "She encouraged my vanity, as you see." He laughed a full, happy laugh, revealing even teeth.

"When you were young, did you know who your father was?"

"No, not until Sir Jonathan offered me the stewardship of Loxsbeare."

Helena sat back in her chair, her thoughts torn between resentment that she had never known any of this, and fascination at the fact her father had another child.

In a way she was pleased, because had their lives not been so dramatically altered, they would still be living at Loxsbeare, where Helena's distrust and jealousy would have rejected the truth, and spoiled any future relationship between them. Idly she wondered if her mother had been aware of the situation.

"Your mother knew," he said, as if reading her thoughts.

"She always treated you kindly." Her tone was defensive, forestalling any complaint.

"A true lady, she always behaved graciously toward me. Although she had every reason not to do so. When Samuel Ffoyle suggested Sir Jonathan employ me at Loxsbeare, she agreed willingly."

"Master Ffoyle knows?" Helena stared, then shook her head, laughing. "Of course he does, Samuel knows everything."

The tables began to fill as morning diners greeted Lubbock jocularly, calling for mulled wine and hot pies to keep out the cold.

Helena stared at the new arrivals without seeing them, too occupied with her own thoughts. Then something occurred to her. "Have you told Aaron all this?"

"I intended to." Lumm sighed. "When news of the Pardon came. I imagined I might bring him home, to you and Henry. However, my plans went somewhat awry, when he decided to use his inheritance on intrigue in Holland."

The word *inheritance* jogged Helena's brain. "Father managed to keep some of his estate back for us. Did you know that?"

He reached across the table to take her hand. Helena let him, even welcoming his touch. Huddled in a booth, they could have been lovers on a secret tryst. The look he gave her was certainly loving, but not lover-like. The more she looked at him, the more of herself she saw in his features.

"He left me the property your grandfather owned near Bedford House." His gaze searched hers, seeking approval.

"He was your grandfather too, Tobias." Saying his given name seemed the natural thing to do just then. "I'm glad he gave the house to you. I am delighted too that you are my half-brother."

His devastating smile reappeared. "Thank you, Helena. I thought you would be angry."

"I would have been, a year ago. But I have lost too much of my family to be in a position to reject someone who actually wants to be connected to me." Her happy laugh caused several gazes to swivel in their direction.

"I wanted to tell Aaron all this," Tobias relaxed back in his seat, "but seeing his grief for your mother, it did not seem appropriate, somehow."

She looked down at his hand, which rested on the table between them and felt a lump in her throat. He had Aaron's hands.

Aaron's selfishness clearly demonstrated he cared for her less than she had imagined. Then there was Henry, who had betrayed her in his own way, when he left to live with the Newman's. Neither brother had given a thought as to how she would find her way in a world where marriage was the only respectable choice for a woman. But then, who would marry her now? The daughter of a convicted traitor who faced certain death if he dared return?

She inhaled, making a decision. "I'll keep your secret, Tobias. When do you return to Exeter?" She sipped her third cup of chocolate of the morning, nursing her new knowledge.

"The coach leaves from *The Rose Inn* in under an hour." He nodded to Chloe, who stood with his bag at her feet beside the door, stood up, and gathered his Brandenburg coat from a nearby chair. "I hope you will allow me to write you. That is, if you do not feel it inappropriate for the landlord of a small inn to write Mistress Helena Woulfe of Lambtons?"

"This is not really my home, Tobias. I'm merely a guest here. Of course I want you to write to me." She rose with him and wandered outside into a street that teemed with life, noise, and less than savoury smells.

He dropped a swift kiss onto her hand, then turned and walked away, his duffle bag slung casually across his shoulder, his hat tipped back on his head.

"I al'ays told you he was a strange one," Chloe snorted at her shoulder.

Helena returned Tobias's backward wave. "Stranger than you could ever know," she murmured.

Chapter 21

Helena sat by the window overlooking the garden in her room, déshabillé in a loose, flowing gown tied over soft linen petticoats. The pastry she had dipped in her cup of chocolate halted mid-way to her mouth as she stared at Celia.

"You are to be married in a month? What precipitated such a speedy decision?"

"Sugar and spice and all things nice, I believe." Celia sneaked a slice of bread and butter from Helena's breakfast plate.

"You're making no sense." Helena placed her half-filled cup onto the tray between them. Was her friend being innocently spontaneous, or was she being deviously witty?

Celia rearranged her lace bertha round her voluptuous shoulders. "Ralf's great uncle died last spring…which is a tragedy of course…." she waved the bread in the air. "Although Ralf hasn't seen him since the age of five, or was it six…?" She trailed off and stared at the ceiling, a finger at her cheek.

"Celia!" Helena prompted.

"Oh, sorry. His uncle's will stated when his ship returned from the West Indies, the proceeds of the cargo were to go to Ralf." She nibbled delicately at the bread as she talked. "Everyone imagined it must have been lost in a storm, or to pirates, or something, but the *Emerald* came into port last week. The cargo went for auction and sold for four thousand pounds." She dragged the words out for effect. "Therefore, we have no need to wait and can marry immediately. Is that not wonderful news?"

"Did Ralf ask if you were willing to marry earlier than planned?"

"Should he have done?" Celia asked, reaching for

another slice of buttered bread.

Helena sighed and changed the subject. "Which church shall you be married in?"

"We shall marry here of course, in Lambtons." She licked butter from her fingers with a grimace. "No one of quality gets married in church."

"Why ever not?" Helena stared, the concept quite unknown to her.

"Because, the ceremony would have to take place during divine service, when everyone who cares to may come and watch. The notion of a charivari would simply mortify Mama."

"What is a charivari?" Helena asked.

"A charivari, my dear," Celia's mouth twisted in distaste, "is when a band of complete strangers gather outside the bride's window with drums, whistles, and bang sticks. They make as much noise as they can until they are paid to leave."

The image of Alyce Devereux confronted with such a spectacle made Helena smile.

"We are to have an evening wedding," Celia declared, this apparently being the height of sophistication. "As it is, Father will have to pay the clergyman twenty shillings for us to marry outside canonical hours." She rolled her eyes and sighed. "There seems to be a fee for everything one wishes to do these days." Barely pausing to draw breath, she gabbled on, "Ralf is taking me to see his house tomorrow."

"He has bought a house?" Helena said, envious.

Celia frowned. "Well no, the uncle left it to him. An old retainer lived there. According to the will, he could not have been dislodged. However, he died months ago, so now the property belongs in its entirety to Ralf. Is that not convenient?" Celia asked, her eyes shining with excitement.

Helena's thoughts went to the old servant, whose death appeared to have no effect on Celia. A year ago, Helena too would have been hard pressed to have given sympathetic thought to a servant. She wondered if this new aspect to her character was a good thing or not.

Pouring more chocolate for herself and Celia, she pondered on how complicated life had become, with so many things to feel sad about. She could hardly remember the days when all that concerned her was how her new gown looked, or if her father would take her riding. *How swiftly and with such randomness could fortunes be turned.*

The fact she lived comfortably with generous people reminded her there could have been a far worse alternative. In fact, had Master Devereux expected her to work as a serving girl in his inn, she would have been in no position to complain. The thought made her shiver.

"Why are you looking so melancholy, Helena?" Celia asked suddenly.

"Is that so? I apologise. What have I to feel melancholy about?"

* * *

On Celia's wedding day, Helena wandered through Lambtons' halls. The walls were hung with ribbons, branches, violet and yellow heartsease, and cream meadowsweet like an enchanted garden, while serving men and girls bustled around like insects in response to Alyce's shrill orders.

Despite several visits from the seamstress and hours of being measured, pinned and tucked in preparation for their wedding outfits, it was not the bride who declared her gown did not become her.

"I hate the colour. It makes me look pale," Phebe announced. Her complaints persisted most of the morning, and throughout Chloe's weaving of sprays of rosemary and bay dipped in scented water. However, when Phebe caught sight of herself in the long glass, her features softened. "I look like a wood nymph," she declared, smiling for the first time that day.

The invited guests thronged the main dining hall, while the taproom regulars peered in at the windows to wish the bride happiness.

Alyce made her grand entrance late, gliding into place beside Robert in a fuchsia silk gown, her face painted and patched like that of a courtier. Ralf wore nut-brown velvet, sumptuously embroidered with leaves and spring buds to match the season, which complemented the design picked out on Celia's cream bodice. He stood shuffling his feet beside the bride, in an ebony wig that did not suit his pale colouring, his responses made with much stammering and false starts, whereas Celia was word perfect. After the ceremony, the principal guests surged forward to shake hands with the newlyweds, some to show approval for an alliance well-forged, while others congratulated themselves for whatever part they played in this union.

Helena moved between acquaintances and strangers, chatting to guests who devoured the elaborately-prepared supper of roasted meats, savory pies and pasties, puddings and sallets, with cheeses, nuts and fruit, together with the excellent wines, ales and spirits Robert had bought especially for the occasion.

Close to midnight, the wedding party all trooped noisily upstairs to the newlywed couple's chamber in preparation for the bedding ceremony. Before the Groomsmen arrived, Alyce untied Celia's blue silk garters, destined to be worn on their hats for weeks afterward, insisting, "We cannot have young men hunting disrespectfully beneath your skirt."

Celia stood shyly in her negligee as a loud knocking came at the door and a male voice called, "Ho Madame, let us in, we have a groom to put to bed!" Without waiting for permission, the door flew open, and a group of young men crowded the bedchamber, pulling a blushing Ralf after them.

The Bridesmen removed Celia's garters and the riotous process of tying them to the men's hats followed, hindered somewhat by the copious amounts of wine everyone had consumed.

There followed loud and suggestive toasting, mostly at the groom's expense, before a blushing Celia and self-conscious Ralf clambered onto the canopied bed. Phebe and Helena took up their positions, with their backs to the bed and each holding one of Ralf's stockings.

"Why are we doing this again?" Helena asked Phebe in a whisper.

Phebe rolled her eyes, obviously scornful of the entire process. "Tradition states that if one of the stockings lands on one or both of them, the thrower will be married within the twelvemonth."

Giving the superstition no credence, but happy to join in the general hilarity, Helena acted on an indiscrete cue from Alyce and hurled the length of silk at the bed accompanied by loud and tipsy cheers.

"Now you turn round," Phebe urged, grabbing Helena's arm. "Look, yours draped itself across Celia's face, but mine fell short. What a shame."

"You did that on purpose," Helena accused her, rewarded with Phoebe's mock innocent shrug. "Now what happens?"

"It's the men's turn. Only they throw Celia's stockings. Watch out!" Phebe tugged her swiftly aside. "These gallants tend to be less than gentle when they are full of Papa's wine."

Repeated, the procedure proved a good deal noisier and far less skilled. The first stocking caught on the tester above, while Henry toppled over as he threw, drawing rowdy laughter as the stocking slid to the floor.

Handsome in navy blue silk, William led the group of inebriated young men to raucous teasing of the bride and lewd suggestions to the groom.

When Celia's blushes threatened to turn into tears, Ralf earned Helena's admiration by calling for silence and, nightshirt notwithstanding, firmly ordered everyone out.

More laughter followed the disorderly mob onto the landing.

"And you say this was better than a charivari?" Helena asked.

"Indeed, yes. Much more refined," Phebe countered, staring at her as if she were demented.

Helena stood to one side as the guests surged past her

down the stairs. She arched her neck to release tense muscles, easing her shoulders luxuriously, and at the same time taking care not to disturb her elaborate coiffure.

The chatter below receded. In the comparative silence that followed, Helena sensed she was being watched. She swiveled round at the same second a young man stepped from the shadows to her right. He leaned nonchalantly against the wall, an enigmatic smile on his lips, and his arms folded over his broad chest.

Helena's gaze roved his wine-colored suit worn with a loose white silk cravat, his brown hair tied back. He was not wearing a wig, and his air of unadorned masculinity made the rest of the male guests look overdressed. She placed her right hand on the rail, aware the pose showed her off to advantage. "I don't believe we have been introduced, sir."

Her admirer smiled, pushed himself away from the wall and joined her at the balustrade. Even though she was wearing heeled shoes, he was taller, an agreeable quality in any man. Handsome too, with a face that possessed a strong symmetry and penetrating brown eyes beneath well-shaped brows. The set of his shoulders and his steady gaze that scrutinised her with easy confidence gave the impression he did not hope for attention, but commanded it.

"Actually," he responded in a soft, measured voice that sent ripples of pleasure running along Helena's spine. "The bridegroom performed that ritual earlier." The gaze he fixed on hers held reproach.

"Sir, I do not recall…." she stammered. How could she have forgotten having met this attractive man? She studied his face, coming to halt on a tiny dimple in the centre of his clean-shaven chin.

His raised brows made her start, her face grew warm and she turned away.

"I have accepted the slight." He gave a mock sigh, "Which I'll have to learn to live with."

"Forgive my defective memory, sir, but I have had duties to perform today. However, as there is no one present to do so for a second time…." She glanced round at the deserted landing. "I am…."

"I know who you are. It is I who have been overlooked, remember? Guy Palmer, at your service." He made her a slow and elegant bow that would have done justice to any courtier. "I'm a goldsmith banker, like my friend Ralf, although he has the advantage of a late, great uncle to accelerate his way in the world. I'll have to work a little harder, in a less salubrious part of Hatton Garden, to catch up."

"Do you resent the circumstances that separate you and Master Maurice?" Helena asked, detecting a hard edge to his voice

"Not at all, one could never resent Ralf. He's a dear fellow."

"I'm sure you will do admirably," Helena said. "Even without the uncle."

"I intend to." His lips curved but there was no smile in his eyes. "And I do in fact have an uncle, but he is still very much alive."

Helena inclined her head and pretended to study the closed doors of the ground floor salon, from where muffled sounds of noisy revels drifted out.

"Ralf deserves happiness," Master Palmer went on. "The acquisition of a presentable wife and companion will, I am sure, enhance his life in every way."

"You know the bride well, sir?"

"Truthfully, I have spoken to the lady but once. However, today I have had the opportunity to observe her physical attributes for myself and like to count myself among the confirmed admirers of Mistress Maurice."

"You make her sound like a horse instead of an ideal wife." Helena laughed, throwing back her head.

"Both should be assessed carefully, and with an eye to the long term," he said, looking deep into her eyes.

"Indeed? Like a financial investment?"

"Ah, I see you understand me perfectly." He met Helena's indignant surprise with a broad smile. "Finance is a subject in which I am particularly adroit. Now," he cocked his arm and half bowed toward her. "Will you allow me to escort you back to the party?"

"Master Palmer," Helena began, "When you said before you knew who I was…."

"You are Mistress Helena Woulfe, the daughter of Sir Jonathan Woulfe, a fugitive Rebel wanted by the Crown." Helena turned a hard gaze on him, halting on the staircase so that he almost overbalanced on a step. "I know what it is to have embarrassing relatives," he added.

"Embarrassing?" Helena drew the word out in enquiry.

He winced. "A bad choice of words, do forgive me. I was trying to reassure you that we are none of us untouched by the precarious times in which we live."

"I appreciate your diplomacy, Master Palmer, if that was your intention." She bridled, unsure whether she was being insulted or seduced. "However, I have never regarded my family as an embarrassment. High principled, courageous, even misguided," she loosened her grip on his arm, "but never embarrassing."

"Your loyalty does you credit, Mistress Woulfe." He covered her hand on his forearm with his own, and held it there. "It is an admirable quality to disagree with someone's actions, and yet remain their champion."

"What makes you think I don't agree with their actions?" She tapped her fan against her lips.

The pupils of his eyes expanded into black circles as he appeared to search for the appropriate response, and failed.

As they reached the bottom of the stairs, their reflections in a floor-to-ceiling mirror on the wall opposite showed what an attractive couple they made. Helena slowed her steps to drag out the moment, just as something occurred to her. "Palmer. That name sounds familiar."

"Barbara Palmer is my aunt." At Helena's frown he went on, "The Countess of Southampton, Duchess of Cleveland, mistress of the late Charles II, and mother of six of his children," he recited. "It may have been less, due to there being considerable doubt about two of them."

"Are you—close?" Helena asked, intrigued.

He shrugged. "Hardly at all, I'm afraid. We are related

by marriage. Her husband, Roger Palmer is an uncle, but their marriage was not a success."

"How could it be?" Helena knew she sounded cynical, "With a King for a rival?"

He inclined his head in agreement. "Besides, the lady—and I use the term purely in respect of her title—lives in Paris, and has done for the last ten years, since the king sent her away."

"Was it true she converted to Catholicism to keep the king when his interest waned?"

"If that was her intent, it proved ineffective. King Charles used the Test Act as an excuse to have her removed from court."

"And you, sir? Are you are a Catholic, Master Palmer?" Helena asked, unaccountably relieved when he said he was not.

When they reached the door to the party, Helena found herself reluctant to cut short their conversation. "Lady Castlemaine was reputed to be very beautiful."

"She was. Once. However, her youth and beauty are both behind her now, and she has always had a vast appetite for money and a venal way of life."

Helena did not know whether to look shocked or impressed, so chose the latter; their bold conversation was an exhilarating change from the small talk to which she was usually subjected to by male acquaintances.

William's first instinct when he passed a looking glass was to stare at himself. During her entire talk with Mr Palmer, where Helena had sneaked quick glances in the hall mirror, her companion had been looking only at her.

They entered the dining hall amidst a wave of high-pitched female laughter, together with the oppressive heat and odours emanating from sixty warm, confined bodies. A group of young men clamoured around Master Palmer, while Phebe dragged Helena in the direction of the supper table.

When Helena scanned the faces around her a little later, he was nowhere in sight.

"He's quite attractive isn't he?" Phebe whispered.

Helena started. "Who is?"

"Master Palmer. I saw you talking to him in the hall."

"Do you know him?"

"Ralf has spoken of him on occasion. He's another goldsmith." She shrugged, as if dismissing them as a species. "Handsome enough, but rather serious." Then her eyes flashed. "He has a notorious aunt though. Try to guess who she is!"

"I couldn't possibly!" Helena pretended to be affronted, watching as Phoebe's smile slumped in disappointment. She smiled to herself, somehow confident theirs would not be an isolated encounter.

* * *

Helena tried not to feel the loss of Celia too much in the weeks after her wedding, and instead attempted to share in her friend's happiness as a new bride. Phebe also appeared to miss her sister and sought out Helena's company far more often than before. Helena also had Guy Palmer's visits to lighten her days, for that young man had lived up to all her expectations and called at Lambtons requesting to see her, at least three times a week.

One stifling evening, the family gathered in the summer salon that overlooked the walled garden. Despite Alyce's hatred of fresh air, the rear doors stood open to encourage a cool breeze into the room, bringing with it the scent of roses and honeysuckle overlaid with a tang of the city.

Robert looked set for a relaxed evening, resembling an eastern Pasha in his saffron silk banyan, his periwig replaced with a cotton cap. He found the city unbearable in summer, and looked forward to a quiet evening away from the stifling clatter of the public rooms. Alyce offered wine, but feeling the heat, Helena declined in favour of lemonade.

"It seems that due to the unseasonable cold and wet last month, the king's troops packed up their tents and retired to quarters." Robert flicked a finger at his copy of the London *Gazette*, muttering, “Standing army, indeed.”

He plucked a clay pipe and taper from the box on the hearth, then intercepted a disapproving glare from Alyce. Instead, he caressed the bowl in his hand, as if drawing comfort from its smooth feel.

On the other side of the room, William bent over the bureau, a quill in his hand.

When Phebe approached and stared over his shoulder, William shielded his writing with a well-placed arm, simultaneously taking a sip from a nearby wine glass.

“I declare, Will, why cannot I see?” Phebe demanded, sulkily. “I’ll wager you are composing poetry to some lady you saw across the ’Change and liked the look of.”

“Go away, wench. I’m busy.” William snarled, though at the same time a flush crept up his neck.

A stray fly droned lazily somewhere in the room, and as William swatted it away, his eyes swiveled to Helena, who pretended she did not notice.

Helena’s muslin clung stickily to her back, strands of hair escaped the pins and curled damply on her neck. The weather was too hot and heavy to read, and her hands too clammy for sewing. Restless, Helena crossed the room and perched on a stool beside Robert, wondering whether she could excuse herself and go to her room this early, without appearing rude.

“Ah, Helena, my dear. How opportune.” Robert removed the stem of the unlit pipe from his mouth. “I was wondering, my dear. With my elder daughter settled, and my youngest baulking me at every turn if I so much as mention the subject.” He shot Phebe a hard look across the room. “What, may I ask, are your feelings on taking a husband?”

Helena brought her fan up to her face to hide an impending blush. “Under certain circumstances I believe it to be an agreeable institution.”

“An oblique answer if ever I heard one.” Robert’s brow rose, and he inserted the pipe stem into the corner of his mouth. “Do you have a young man in mind?”

“Why, I had not thought of anyone, sir.” She smiled at

him.

"Nonsense. Young Guy Palmer has been hanging around for weeks now. Surely he has declared himself by now?"

Helena did not turn her head, keenly aware of William's hand having stilled on his quill as he stared at the wall. *Searching for inspiration or listening*? She couldn't be sure.

"My dear," Robert leaned in close to whisper, "despite Master Palmer's grasp of financial matters, which is admirable, he does not call to see me."

Helena stopped smiling, the time for evasiveness over. "I would value your opinion of him, sir."

"He's from a respectable family, and he has an excellent head for business."

"Respectable? Even his aunt by marriage?"

"Oh, my dear. Especially her."

Helena burst into spontaneous laughter, which Robert joined. William turned slowly from the desk, an elbow on the chair back behind him. Alyce and Phebe exhibited identical frowns, their expressions demanding explanation.

Robert waved them away with his pipe. "Guy has a thriving business of his own," Robert said, "which I am well positioned to promote. Although to his credit, he has given no hint to that effect during our association."

"It is almost as if you had chosen him for me yourself, sir." Helena said, though a tremor of apprehension made her voice shaky. Accepting the young man's attentions was one thing. Marrying him quite another.

Just then, William looked up and caught her eye, his intense look apparently not lost on Robert, who swiveled his head slowly toward her with a look of enquiry.

Helena looked away, aware that it would not do to let Robert believe she toyed with his son's affections while treating Guy as a serious suitor.

Robert leaned toward her conspiratorially. "Had I taken against Master Palmer, my dear, he would not still be calling. I thought to see how things were with you on the subject, so I may know how to respond when he offers for you."

"*When*? Not *if*?"

"Assuredly when, Helena, my dear. I do believe you've become quite the coquette."

"Master Devereux?" she began. "If—when—Master Palmer offers for me, would it be necessary for you to ask my brother's permission?"

"I take it you mean Aaron, for you surely do not refer to young Henry!" His laugh ceased in the face of her stony expression. "Um…well. I don't profess to understand your reasons, my dear, but it's quite unnecessary. I am your guardian until he returns to England."

"I would prefer it." She kept her voice low but firm.

He removed his pipe from his mouth, head tilted as if about to request she explain herself.

"Thank you, Master Devereux." Helena said, forestalling him, and returned to her seat on the chaise next to Alyce.

"Henry called this morning," Alyce said, breaking the silence that had fallen between them. "He is still upset about Compton's suspension. He thinks it will hold up the building of the cathedral again if Compton is punished."

Helena smiled, aware her brother's focus was on the new St Paul's and not any religious question.

"I hear Compton refused to discipline one of his clergy for preaching anti-papist sermons. This had so enraged the king, he suspended him."

"That won't make King James any more popular," William said, his head bent to his correspondence.

"Compton will be back in favor again soon." Alyce sounded confident. "The king himself wants the cathedral finished."

Helena accepted a glass of the cold lemonade from Alyce, her gaze on William, who slid his writing into a drawer of the bureau and locked it, taking the key out of the lock. He rose from his chair and strolled around the room, his hands held loosely behind his back. "He wants to allow Catholics as dons and undergraduates at Oxford and Cambridge."

“Where did you hear that, Will?” Alyce’s tone held scepticism.

“At The Grecian.” William picked fluff from his sleeve. “He argues that the colleges were founded when England was a Catholic country and should therefore be available to them.”

“Sir Edward Hales has been acquitted for holding office in the army.” Robert pointed his pipe stem at his *Gazette*. “Blasted man’s a Papist!”

William smiled. “What did you expect when the king packed the court with his tame judges? The verdict was a foregone conclusion.”

“Have you read this news-sheet before me?” Robert glared at his son, accusing. “The king is making Parliament irrelevant.”

He clamped his teeth down on his pipe so hard, the stem broke off in his mouth. He spat the pieces out and hurled them into the hearth.

“I think you’ll find Parliament will hold out against the king’s attempts to repeal the Test Act.” Alyce said, revealing an intellect as a rule she kept well hidden.

“What? Oh yes, I suppose you are right,” Robert mumbled, though Helena doubted he was convinced.

Helena allowed their chatter to pass over her head, her thoughts still on Robert’s endorsement of Guy Palmer as a potential husband.

Guy had become such a familiar face at Lambtons, Helena discovered that to avoid him successfully would have meant her virtual exile from her own home. Yet strangely, when he did not call, she missed him.

Respectful and engaging, he had the ability to correctly judge her mood; so when she felt uncommunicative, he happily chatted to others, bestowing gentle smiles on her from a distance. She had to acknowledge Robert was right; he would make an excellent life companion.

William had resumed his seat and was twisting one hand back and forth, studying the way the light caught his emerald ring. With a sigh, Helena consigned him to the back of her mind. A pity he was such a fop.

"Have you heard from your brother lately, Helena?" Robert asked.

"Yes, Master Devereux. I fear he is still plotting with the Prince of Orange, although he appears to be living well in The Hague."

"He does? Do tell us." Phebe slid along the settle toward her, her face eager.

"He has purchased a house which he has thrown open to other fugitives, so they may spend their days in scheming and leisure."

"I almost envy him." William laughed.

Helena stayed silent on the subject of Aaron's decisions. The fact both her brothers had left her to fend for herself in a world where men made all the decisions still aroused her anger.

That her future would depend on the good nature of whomever she married remained a truth she found difficult to reconcile. That she was fond of Guy, enjoyed his company and looked forward to his visits, was a reason to view an offer of marriage with favour.

Guy was not rich, but he was capable, ambitious and, according to Robert, extremely hardworking. Therefore, if marriage was the only way she could regain her status in life, then marry she would.

If Robert's prediction came true, when Guy declared himself, she would accept him and put herself out of the influence of both Aaron and Henry. Even if her father should return, he could not overrule the wishes of a husband. As time passed, everyone told her Sir Jonathan Woulfe must surely be dead. She refused to believe it. *Not yet.*

She glanced at William, who had resumed his seat at the bureau and his writing. Let him write all the silly verses he wants; he would regret it when she was married.

Chapter 22

Henry accepted an invitation from Master Newman to take a glass of claret in his private sanctum in Charles Street: a small room at the front of the house strewn with maps, pens, tools and miscellaneous cartons piled up in one corner.

"Is this a special occasion, if I may ask?" Henry accepted the full glass. He hadn't been asked to sit, so he leaned against the desk where he studied a plan of a church.

"Ask away, my boy, ask away." Francis Newman grinned as he poured ruby liquid his own glass. "Mistress Newman and I are celebrating a forthcoming marriage."

Henry took a mouthful of his wine, not anticipating Newman's next words. "My beautiful daughter is to become a bride."

A knot of dread descended onto Henry's chest, hovered there, and slowly expanded. He swallowed. "You…er…have five beautiful daughters," Henry stammered, the drawing forgotten. "To which of them do you refer?"

Master Newman guffawed. "Well, two of them are well below marriageable age, one is still in the schoolroom, and the other not prepossessing enough to attract any young man's fancy." He paused at Henry's startled look. "Not that I would disparage my sweet Joanna to her face. However, I'm sure you can guess who the fortunate daughter is."

Henry set his glass aside, eliciting an enquiring look from his host.

"Not to your taste?" Newman asked, surprised.

"It is excellent, sir, but I have a headache I am reluctant to worsen." A lump formed in his throat. "All-allow me to congratulate you on your news." Aware his hopes were about to be cruelly dashed, still a contrariness rooted him to the spot, as he waited for the damning words to be spoken.

Newman frowned. "I'm sorry, Henry, I had no idea. You must retire and get some sleep." He patted Henry on the back. "Before you go, I must tell you that Sir Joshua Holt has offered for my Mary Ann. They are to be married in two months. Is that not excellent news?"

The blood in Henry's ears roared, and his mouth opened and closed like a fish. Was it possible his employer did not see how this news affected him? Or perhaps he knew how Henry felt about Mary Ann, and this was his way of ensuring his apprentice never declared himself?

"I-I don't believe I know the gentleman."

"He is extremely wealthy." Newman's eyes glowed in appreciation. "There is an estate in Hertfordshire that runs to three thousand acres, not to mention a fine townhouse with at least fifty servants. He has a nephew." This was said almost regretfully. "He will inherit, as the estate is entailed, but the portion he has agreed to settle upon Mary Ann is…oh well, perhaps I shouldn't dwell on it." He gave a sheepish grin. "Suffice it to say, he is a fine match for my girl."

A dense fog wrapped itself around Henry's senses, but Newman ploughed on. "He's somewhat older than she is." He looked momentarily uncertain, then a smile twitched at the corner of his mouth. "The truth of the matter is he's thirty years older, but what does that matter, if he gives my daughter a place in society?"

Thirty years! Henry fought to keep his face impassive. The man was older than Newman himself. How could he give his beautiful Mary Ann to an ageing lecher, no matter how wealthy and respected he might be? He shook the thought away, realising how ridiculous that was; were not wealth and society what mattered to everyone?

To discover he was not penniless and alone had changed everything for Henry. Having some of his father's wealth at his disposal was what enabled him to be in Master Newman's drawing room, dressed in gentleman's clothes and drinking a gentleman's wine. It was wealth and society that would allow him to fulfill his dream and become an architect, visit rich men's homes as an equal and enjoy their society.

For Mary Ann, the question was far simpler. She belonged to her father to be given in marriage by him, to a man who could provide for her and offer her a secure home, a future, and respectability.

"And Mistress M-Mary Ann, does she consent to this match, sir?" Henry hardly recognised the sound of his own voice as he stumbled over her name.

"Eh?" Newman asked distracted, apparently oblivious to Henry's discomfort. "Oh, I have not yet informed her of her good fortune, but I don't expect anything but submissive gratitude from that quarter."

Newman paused in thought, the wine pitcher still clutched in his hand. "I admit I've heard disturbing tales from other fathers whose daughters have given them all manner of difficulties over the subject of marriage. Praise be, I have a dutiful child, who would never go against me or her mother."

Newman raised the pitcher as an invitation for a refill, which Henry declined. Instead, he left his on the table, fearing he would choke.

Pleading his worsening headache as an excuse to cut short the conversation, Henry stoically offered his congratulations and withdrew.

"You'll raise a glass at the wedding, though, won't you Henry?" Newman's cheeks glowed with wine and good humour. "You are my best apprentice after all, and I would have you present at the ceremony."

Henry inclined his head in assent, his aim to get out of the room before his feelings showed on his face.

His host was right; she was a dutiful daughter, who adored both her parents and would offer no objections. Mary Ann was lost to him, forever.

The hour was late, and apart from his host, the rest of the household slept. He lit a candle at the bottom of the stairs and dragged himself up to the second floor. As he rounded the corner leading to his room, he felt rather than saw her.

"Henry?"

He could tell by that one, choked word she had been crying. Mary Ann detached herself from the shadows, the yellow glow of his candle throwing her face into sharp relief. Her eyes were red-rimmed and she gave a sad sniff, yet she was still the loveliest thing he had ever seen.

"Henry," she sobbed. "The most horrible thing has happened."

He sighed. "Your father said you had not yet been told."

"You know?" At Henry's nod, she gave a tiny moan. "Mother told me." She wiped her eyes with a kerchief. "She imagined I would be overjoyed and swore me to secrecy." She took a step toward him and burst into fresh tears.

The floor creaked under their combined weight and with a furtive glance along the darkened corridor, Henry ushered her into his room, closing the door firmly behind them.

Mary Ann leaned against the door, slumping as if her knees were giving way. "What are we to do?" Her eyes were pleading.

He placed the guttering candle on the low windowsill, where it stilled, and glowed brighter. His reflected face in the pane looked drawn, his eyes large, as he stared at the shadowy rooftops reaching away into the darkness.

Mary Ann grasped his arm with both hands. "I don't want to marry him. I won't marry him, I…."

"Yes, Mary Ann, you will," Henry's voice was almost cold. He didn't move, nor could he look at her. He felt he would break into a thousand pieces if he tried.

She gasped, the kerchief pressed against her mouth. "You want me to?"

"No!" He burst out in a harsh growl as he turned toward her, her distraught face like a knife twisting in his stomach. He reached out his arms toward her, and with a ragged sob, Mary Ann collapsed against him.

"I could refuse." She lifted her face to his, her eyes full

of unshed tears.

"And tell your parents you wish to marry me? The consequences would be devastating." She opened her mouth to speak, but he pressed the tips of his fingers against her lips. "Not just for us, but for our families too."

She stared at him, horrified, large tears spilling onto her cheeks.

"Your Father would discharge me from my apprenticeship, and no architect would agree to continue my training." The truth of his own words tore at him. "Aaron would cut me off from my allowance and might not even allow me back into my father's business. Helena may accept us, but she is in no position to offer practical help. We would have nothing."

He held her away from him, his hands gripping her upper arms, willing her to understand. "Do you have any idea what it would be like, to be penniless and with no friends?" She shook her head, the wispy curls at her temple bobbing. "Well, I saw what my future would hold without those things. Even if I could stand such a life for myself, I could never do that to you. Eventually, you would hate me for it."

"I could never hate you, Henry."

"We would be shunned, Mary Ann. And how could you bear never to see your mother, or any of your sisters again? Apart from you, Helena and Aaron are all I have. I cannot lose them." He bit his lip, his throat almost closed with pain as she collapsed again into his arms, defeated. His eyes stung with hot tears as he realised his words had penetrated her despair.

"How stupid of me to think we could…." she broke off. "Oh, Henry what are we going to do?"

"There is nothing we *can* do," he whispered into her hair.

They clung together in the gloom of Henry's attic room, making oaths and promises to help each other through the future they would spend apart. As the night deepened and their loss became real, they separated, painfully, with fresh tears on both sides.

Henry spent the rest of that night in wakeful misery, imagining Mary Ann crying herself to sleep in the room below his. For the first time since his apprenticeship began, he did not look forward to the morning.

* * *

Viewed through a crack in the door to the kitchens, Helena watched Robert and Guy Palmer emerge from the salon, the older man's arm encircled Guy's shoulder. His look was one of guarded nervousness that told her the interview Guy had requested on his arrival had been a success.

She backed away, and returned to her place at the parlour table, flicked open her journal and pretended to study the last entry. Her gaze fell upon Guy's name in large letters on the page, and she slapped her hand over the words she had penned, saying she expected his proposal, just as the man himself appeared.

"I met Phebe in the hall just now," Guy said. "She told me you would be in here."

"Phebe knows everyone's movements at Lambtons. Do take a seat, Master Palmer."

"Were you aware..." Guy perched on a chair opposite, "...that you always greet me with mild surprise, as if you have no expectation of seeing me? Surely you must know by now that I am your most devoted admirer?"

William's face flashed into her head, but she dismissed him instantly. "I am flattered, though to prove I have been paying attention, there are some things I have learnt about you."

"Which are?" He laid his arm on the tabletop, his fingers hair's breadth from her journal.

"That you were orphaned at the age of ten, and brought up by your father's much younger brother. He is a kindly man, but a confirmed bachelor with a penchant for exotic travel."

"You have been paying attention, I—"

Helena held up her hand. "There is more. Your Uncle

Arthur left you in the care of a string of semi-neglectful tutors and housekeepers."

"...which made me realise at a young age that acquiring success lay entirely in my own hands," He finished for her.

"Exactly." She adopted an expression of rapt attention, at the same time closing the journal and moving it away from his reach. If she had miscalculated, what he would have read there could be embarrassing.

"I have something to ask you, Helena, which I am not finding easy. May I ask you to remove your attention from that book for a moment?"

Startled, she released the journal that slipped to the floor with a small thump. "No, leave it," she said as he bent to retrieve it, suddenly nervous.

"What was it you wished to ask?"

"Helena," he said slowly, as if savouring her name on his tongue. "Would you do me the honour of marrying me?"

There, he had said it. Was this where she was required to exhibit breathless excitement? Surprise? Even a little fear? If only she could blush on command, it might make the situation easier. As it was, she had no idea at all how to react, even though she had expected this. "Master Palmer, why do you wish to be married to me?" It was the only thing she could think of to say.

"Why would any young man not want you for a wife?"

"A pretty compliment, sir and I am flattered." She inclined her head. "I simply ask, why do *you* wish it?"

"I feel we would make a good marriage, as we have a great deal in common."

"Such as?"

"I-I have no living parents, yet I am financially sound." He swallowed, as if it struck him that was the wrong thing to say, but it was too late to retract.

"I'm not actually an orphan. At least I hope not. I ask, because I am curious to know if there is any emotional attachment to your offer."

He blinked, opened his mouth, and then closed it

again.

"Oh, no matter." This time she was certain she blushed. "I'm not making myself clear."

"Do you imagine I would seek a marriage with someone I did not feel affection for?" His voice rose sharply.

Helena lifted her chin. "I don't know you well enough to make such a judgment."

"Has it occurred to you," he said, his forearms on his splayed knees and chin jutted forward, "I have no idea what your feelings are either?" At her hesitation, he went on. "I'm no courtier, and you are not a duchess. Perhaps we are expecting too much of one another."

Helena blinked, surprised the meeting did not appear to be going as she expected. What did she expect? A besotted young man who would worship at her feet because she had agreed to be his wife? She did not realize she was frowning until he reached forward and smoothed a finger across her forehead.

"Helena." Her calm acceptance of his touch appeared to give him courage. "I would not have called upon you so diligently these last weeks, had there been no emotion on my part."

"You've indeed been most attentive, Master Palmer, but you have never—" She left the sentence hanging.

"Professed my undying devotion?" He inclined his head, arching one eyebrow. "Is that what you want of me?"

"You could have professed a little," she wheedled. Perhaps Robert was right and she was indeed a coquette? Yet wasn't this exactly what she wanted? Then why was she urging for more?

He propped his chin on an elbow, a warm smile on his lips. "I love you Mistress Woulfe, and you will never have reason to doubt my devotion.

"When I first saw you at Ralf and Celia's wedding I was certain then that we would marry." He laughed self-consciously as he absently massaged her thumb. "I even toyed with the idea of asking you that night."

"I might have refused you, then," she teased.

“Does that mean you are not refusing me now?”

“I have forgotten the question.” Impulsively, she reached across the table and took his hand, her fingers resting lightly in his as if they belonged there.

His gaze slid sideways, then back at her face. “Are those serving girls still watching from the kitchen?” he asked without turning his head.

Helena shifted looked past his shoulder and nodded, a smile tugging at her mouth. Guy gave a slow, thoughtful nod, then without lowering his voice, he repeated his proposal. “I asked, Mistress Woulfe, for your hand in marriage.” A ripple of sighs and giggles erupted from behind them.

“I accept your offer, Master Palmer.” She held his gaze, surprising herself at how delighted she felt.

Guy released a slow breath, and pulled her hand up to his lips. A tiny flame of anger lit his eyes and his grip on her hand tightened. “Helena, I hope that having laid bare my feelings has proved more than simply a source of amusement to you.”

“There are very few times in a woman’s life,” Helena began, aware she had teased him too far and he was now angry with her, “when she has the advantage of a handsome gentleman. Surely you would not condemn me for making the most of mine?”

“In that case, you are forgiven for teasing me.” He snatched his hand away and rose. “Now. May I inform your guardian we are formally engaged?”

She hesitated. “Yes…you may. If that is what is expected.” His eyes darkened for a second, then he turned and strode across the hall.

Helena stared after him for a moment, mildly bewildered before she reached and retrieved her journal. She continued to sit, listening to the familiar kitchen noises in the background. What was she was supposed to do now? She idly fingered the fastening on the leather book, toying with the idea of recording the fact she was going to become Mistress Palmer. Like Lady Castlemaine. What would Aaron have to say about that?

Guy's discomfort was something she had intended to exploit a little before accepting him, but at some point in their exchange, the balance of power had shifted, and Guy had taken control. Perhaps that's as it should be; what woman wants a husband she can bully?

A small knot settled beneath her breastbone at the thought of Aaron, whose letters had lately taken the form of political rants and religious tracts, with appended instructions as to how she and Henry were to conduct themselves in his absence. Would he be angry and disapprove of her decision, or would he be glad to have her off his hands? She had taken a while to admit to herself that she had been disappointed when Henry had chosen his own path without discussing his plans with her. He had spoken to Samuel first, and simply presented her with his decision. Though she was happy for him now seeing how happy he was, and he would welcome another fireside to visit, and a table to eat at during his free evenings.

The prospect of having her own household was a heady one; no matter it would not be grand, like the Saffron Hill property Ralf had provided for Celia. She glanced round the snug room where she sat, wondering if she too might have Dutch delft arranged in a rack on the wall, like the housekeeper.

"Helena. Whatever are you doing sitting here all alone?" Helena jumped at the sound of Phoebe's voice. "You must join the family and let us all fuss over you, now that you are a betrothed woman."

"Did Guy already tell you?" Helena rose slowly from her chair. "Or did your father?"

Phebe smirked. "It was Lubbock. He's been hovering at doors all morning hoping to be the first to spread the good news."

"Ah! A far more reliable source." Helena smoothed down her skirt and tucked her journal into a pocket.

Phebe linked their arms as they crossed the hallway, accepting Lubbock's low bow at the door of the salon. "Have you seen my brother, Lubbock?" Phebe asked, drawing Helena to a halt. "He should be here to join in the festivities." She leaned closer to Helena, whispering, "…and to kick himself for having missed his chance with you."

"Phebe, really!" Helena snapped, though an uncomfortable heat flood into her face.

"I saw the young master a little while ago, Mistress Phebe," Lubbock regarded her down his long nose. "I informed him of Mistress Helena's recent news, but he seemed somewhat, well, disconcerted."

"He wasn't drunk again, was he?" Phebe sighed. "I swear he's getting worse of late. He almost started a fight with Guy Palmer the other day when—" she broke off and patted Helena's arm. "Listen to me, I'm as bad as Mama."

Lubbock coughed into a fist before answering. "No, Mistress he was not. However, he did say something about going to the coffee house, and that the prospect of His Majesty's Navy had begun to appeal."

"He was jesting with you, Lubbock. Can you see my brother on board ship?" Phebe erupted into high-pitched giggles.

Suddenly numb, Helena trailed at Phoebe's elbow, the prospect of never seeing William again engulfed her in a cold, almost panicked sweat.

"Are you happy, Helena?" Phebe asked suddenly, pausing in the doorway.

"What a strange question." Helena looked at her askance. "I am to be married. Is that not a cause for any woman's happiness?"

Images of William in uniform filled her head, followed by visions of vast, empty oceans with dangers, threats, storms, and pirates. Her stomach hurt. Even if nothing awful happened to him and he came home, it would not be for years.

"Not so strange." Phoebe's penetrating stare reminded her of Alyce. "It depends on whether it was a rehearsal, or the real thing."

"You are an odd one, Phebe." Helena's laugh sounded unconvincing even to herself.

Chapter 23

Preparing for bed that night, Helena gave an annoyed groan when she saw her last remaining candle had guttered to a stub. She had already dismissed a yawning Chloe but did not wish to finish her toilette to an accompaniment of scratching from the rats behind the skirting. With only a loose manteau over her nightgown, and her hair falling loose over her shoulders, she managed to reach the deserted hall unseen. She knew fresh candles were kept in a box beneath the hall table.

With a supply safe in her pocket, she had gained the first landing on her way back upstairs, when she heard footsteps descending from the flight above.

A low male voice murmured something, and a woman giggled in response, their voices growing louder as they drew nearer.

Helena smiled. Someone had been entertaining a lady in one of the upper rooms. Aware suddenly that they were bound to pass her, and with no time to cross the landing before they reached her, she ducked back into an alcove and waited for them to pass.

A man and a woman swayed into view, his arm encircling her waist as they giggled together and half-staggered down each step. They reached the landing window, through which moonlight shone onto the woman's face, her chin tilted to her companion's while she laughed throatily into his eyes with a look of total infatuation.

The couple turned the corner about to descend the last flight of stairs, when the man must have heard something and swiveled his head toward the alcove where Helena stood.

Helena froze as her gaze met William's, and held it.

Surprise lit his eyes, followed by embarrassment.

Helena stared him out, nursing a small triumph that he was far more uncomfortable than she.

In response to the woman's whispered enquiry as to what he was looking at, he merely turned and swept her down the steps in front of her.

Once he was out of sight, Helena eased out from her hiding place and fled back to her room. Clicking the door shut as firmly as she could without slamming it, she hurled the candles across the room and launched herself onto the bed.

"I was right about him all along," she muttered, punching her pillows into submission. "He's a shallow, dissolute rake, with no thought for anyone but himself and his own pleasures."

The idea she might have considered William, for even the briefest of moments, as a prospective husband, made her burn with shame. She stared at the canopy above her bed until well after the watch called two of the clock, her bed uncomfortably rumpled, before she finally fell asleep.

* * *

One particular sultry day, Helena visited the New Exchange, taking Chloe with her. Helena enjoyed wandering the stalls at her own pace, without having to listen to Phoebe's constant prattle, or having to wait for her when she stopped to chat to acquaintances every few yards.

With no parents on either side to make the arrangements on their behalf, Robert insisted their winter wedding would be held at Lambtons. Even with such a small celebration, there was still plenty of shopping to do. Helena located the shoemaker Alyce had recommended on the upper concourse, whose proprietor became particularly attentive when the name of Devereux was mentioned. A thin man, who looked as fragile as if he might snap in the middle at the slightest pressure.

His peruke was the colour of dirty ash, and he kept dipping his head whenever he spoke. Having spotted several pairs of heeled shoes with decorated lappets, she strode to the far side of the shop to examine his work more closely.

"Are they for a special occasion, Mistress?" he asked, bobbing forward.

"My Mistress is to be married," Chloe answered for her, blushing guiltily at Helena's annoyed frown.

"In that case, I insist I make you bespoke ones myself." His ferrety eyes sparkled and he measured her feet with spidery fingers, scratching figures on a page.

Once the process was complete, he bowed her to the door again with repeated assurances. "I will have them delivered to Lambtons in a little over a sen'night, Mistress Woulfe."

Helena emerged from the shop onto the balcony on the upper concourse, from where she caught sight of a man in a brocade long coat and curly brown periwig at a stall a little way along. He twisted a polished cane in one hand as he bent over a tray of men's gloves on the stall.

Helena froze as recognition slammed into her like a blow. She halted mid-stride, causing Chloe to collide into her back, the parcels she carried littering the floor at Helena's feet.

"Oh, Mistress, I do beg your pardon," Chloe dipped and collected the parcels as she spoke. "Are you quite well?" she asked righting herself. "You've gone quite pale, whatever is...?"

Helena lifted her finger to her lips. She hauled a ragged breath into her chest, staring fixedly at the man's back. Hatred welled up inside her in a hot rush, and she ground her teeth, mentally reciting every insulting name she could summon.

He had yet to notice her, but just then his head swiveled in her direction and he gave a start.

Raising himself slowly to his full height, he lightly swung his cane in one hand as he closed the gap between them, ignoring the protests of patrons forced to move aside.

"Mistress Helena Woulfe," he drawled, offering her an inadequate bow that bordered on the insulting.

"Lord Blanden," Helena replied in a voice calmer than

she thought possible.

Lifting her chin, she returned his arrogant stare. His expression was not soft or ingratiating, as it had been when she was his future daughter-in-law. This man was self-satisfied—leering even—and his thin lips formed a sneer as his gaze flicked insolently over her.

The noise and bustle of the 'Change went on around her, but Helena's ears were filled with a roaring sound as she stared back at the hard face of the man she had hoped never to meet again.

* * *

"How opportune that fate has decreed we should meet thus, Mistress." Blanden arched an eyebrow, his wry smile transforming into a disparaging smirk. "I came to the city with the express purpose of seeking you out."

"Me, Lord Blanden? What could you possible want from me?" She schooled her expression into an aloofness Phebe would have applauded, though the sight of man's face made her nauseous.

He stared around at the bustling 'Change as if he had not heard her. "I have business at the Court of St James. Did you not hear I have been made one of his Majesty's Commissioners?"

"I did not, sir." She inclined her head. Nor did she care.

Her apparent disinterest seemed to anger him, and he stepped forward, bringing the cane up in front of her face. "I know what Ffoyle did for you and that whelp brother of yours." His voice was laden with menace.

"I see my father's assessment was correct. You are no gentleman," Helena replied, refusing to show him weakness, though she could barely breathe.

Chloe uttered a small cry beside her, but Blanden ignored her.

A party of well-dressed women brushed past them like ships in full sail, their laughter ringing round the hall. Blanden didn't move out of their way, forcing them to circumnavigate him.

"Those houses in the Magdalen Road should be mine, as well as the warehouses on the quay," he spat the words as if he had waited a long time for this confrontation. "And don't think I don't know Samuel Ffoyle's flock of sheep trebled last summer, too."

Helena swallowed. "Wasn't my father's house and his lands enough payment for your treachery, Lord Blanden?" She dragged out his name as insolently as she dared.

"I'm not answerable to you, Mistress." His low growl brought curious stares their way, but no one intervened. "I have nothing to feel guilty for. I did my duty by our Sovereign and my reward," he lifted his fleshy chin in defiance, "will be to attend the king's birthday ball this autumn."

Helena's grip on her fan snapped one of the bone spars between her fingers, the sharp edge cutting into her skin.

"I hear you are living in Lambtons alehouse." Blanden gave a cruel laugh. "More than a traitor's brat should expect, in my view." His rodent eyes slid over her again. "Although I have to admit you look exceedingly prosperous for it." He sounded almost disappointed.

His eye caught the diamond pendant at her throat, and his eyes widened. He tapped her neck lightly with the cane. "Was that your mother's?" he sniggered. "It's part of the estate, I think, as are all her jewels." He lowered his voice to a whisper, which made her skin crawl. "I'll have those, too."

His taunt acted on Helena like cold water, her fury replaced her fear, and a retort sprang to her lips. She bit back her boast of Henry's career and her forthcoming marriage. Why give the man more ammunition? Instead, she expelled a steady breath. "I'm sure it will not surprise you if I express no delight at this encounter, Lord Blanden. So I'll bid you good day."

She stepped past him, but he caught her arm in a vice-like grip. Helena tried to look away but she was enthralled by a tiny bead of spittle on his lower lip. "I will ruin Ffoyle, as I ruined your father, and he will wish, instead of your mother, it was he whom you sealed in that vault in St Mary Arches."

"Do not imagine there will be no reckoning with the Woulfes, Lord Blanden." Helena dragged the last two words out in insult, her cheeks blazing. Her fingers itched to slap him hard across his face with all the pent up anger of the last months. "My brothers are young yet, but they will make you pay for your cowardice."

Raw shock crossed his face which told her that despite Aaron's letter having done the rounds at *The Ship Inn*, Blanden did not know her brother still lived. Blandon's hold on her arm loosened, increasing her confidence. "I would be grateful, My Lord, if you would oblige me by not dying too soon, and thus deprive them of their revenge."

She rolled her shoulder out of his grasp and marched away, Chloe bustling behind her.

Half way along the concourse, Helena's legs weakened. A tiny cry emerged from her lips, but she gathered her courage and pushed on. Not daring to look behind her to see if Blanden followed, she concentrated on the summer sun that flooded through the multi-paned window at the end of the concourse, drawing her forward.

Chloe caught up with her as she gained the walkway outside. "Mistress, oh, Mistress," she gabbled breathlessly. "I never thought you could…I mean, the way you…."

Helena steadied herself against the wall with one hand. "Go and tell our driver where I am, Chloe. Now!" The maid clamped her mouth shut and scurried away.

Helena stood alone amongst the crowds entering and leaving the 'Change, some so close she could smell their sweat and the powder on their faces. Her heart hammered, and she felt the tell-tale prick of tears.

Long minutes passed, during which she expected Lord Blanden to appear and renew his taunts, then the coach rolled to a halt besidc her and with sobbing relief, she clambered inside.

Helena stared unseeing out of the window. How dare Blanden insult her after all he had done! And why would he want to hurt Samuel? He got what he wanted, although by his threats it seemed he was not satisfied. How he must have hated the Woulfes. But why? He and Father were friends once, before King Charles died.

Her stomach lurched, and she chewed the base of her thumb, relieved Chloe had finally stopped her chattering.

Helena had been going to marry his son. Could Lord Blanden do what he threatened, and claim the remainder of the estate? If he succeeded, she and Henry would have no income whatsoever. How would Henry continue with his training as an architect, or Aaron remain in The Hague, if Samuel was unable to send him money? Would Guy Palmer still want to marry her if she had nothing?

A tiny groan escaped her and inwardly she cursed Miles Blanden. The summer's day was ruined; her pretty parcels and the shoes she had ordered for her wedding were engulfed into a world where evil men instilled their insidious dread.

Helena's first instinct had been to pour out her distress to Robert and rely on him for an immediate solution, but when the coach pulled up outside Lambtons, she had changed her mind.

She couldn't spend her life relying on others. This was something she had to sort out for herself. She was determined that Blanden would never hurt her or her brothers again.

* * *

Helena had heard no further word from Lord Blanden with regard to his threat, though in some ways, his silence was worse. If the man took some sort of action, she could devise a strategy to fight him. Was he simply bluffing in order to frighten her? Or was he serious about seeking the rest of the Woulfe estate? There was no way of telling. Whatever his intentions, she wished he would simply get on with it.

One afternoon, Helena found herself alone at home. Robert had taken Alyce and Phebe to visit Celia at Saffron Hill, an outing Helena had declined, having pleaded a headache. This wasn't a complete lie, for she was in no mood for Celia's chatter or Phoebe's barbed remarks about her forthcoming wedding.

The shoes had finally arrived that morning with apologies from the shoemaker for their lateness, despite Helena having sent the first pair back because they did not fit well enough. On her way up the stairs to her room, she heard a hard voice growling at Lubbock.

Helena turned to where Lord Miles Blanden stood below her in the entrance hall. It was too late to retreat. All she could do was stand perfectly still, watching him shrug off Lubbock's offer to take his sword and gloves. Appraising him when he had not yet registered her presence was a strange feeling. If she did not hate the man so much and her flesh didn't crawl when he was near, she could even say he was handsome. A little taller than herself, and though stickily built, he was all muscle, with a little extra weight. His heavily lashed brown eyes showed intelligence, and his skin was unblemished, with the light tan of a born countryman. His jaw sagged, but only slightly, and certainly less than expected of a man in his late forties.

He glanced up and caught her gaze, then smirked. "Good day to you, Mistress Woulfe," he drawled, instilling more insult into his voice than propriety. He took in his surroundings, raising thick eyebrows in surprise, as if he did not expect such opulence.

Helena's knees buckled. She fumbled for the balustrade and gripped it hard, then raised her chin, determined not to stumble.

He extended a hand, but she remained three steps above him, her arms at her sides so he was forced to drop his. Nor did she reply to his greeting, but waited, her heart hammering with terror. At the same time she was furious he had dared to come to her home like this, unannounced and uninvited.

Three serving men traversed the hall bearing laden trays. A group of patrons who had recently arrived were clustered at the entrance, darting looks at them and muttering. Lubbock also hovered close by, a look of suspicion mixed with concern on his face. When she gave him the tiniest of nods, he backed away, but she knew he would remain within earshot and felt slightly reassured.

"I was not aware you patronised Lambtons, Lord Blanden," Helena said, forcing the words through clenched teeth.

He gave a short bark of a laugh. "I dine at Pontacks, Mistress Woulfe." His second sweep of the room displayed contempt. "However, I have gone out of my way on this occasion. I wished to inform you that I have lodged my petition for the rest of Sir Jonathan's estate. I expect a favourable answer directly."

With difficulty, Helena remained calm, her voice light with unconcern. "You can lodge as many petitions as you wish, sir, but you can prove nothing."

His reaction was no more than a flash of his eyes as he took a step forward, switching his ubiquitous cane from one hand to the other. His calm demeanour struck her as more threatening than if had he blustered and shouted. He was far too sure of himself.

"I have proof," he said, his voice almost a whisper. "Ffoyle paid virtually nothing for those houses and the warehouse. Nor is there any bill of sale for the sheep, or your mother's jewels."

Helena had to stop her hand from instinctively touching her mother's pearl necklace.

"I do have a solution for you, my dear," he went on, his unctuous voice repulsing her even more.

"What sort of solution?"

"How else does a young woman get herself out of financial straits? Why by marrying, of course."

"Which, in your case, is out of the question." Helena almost laughed. "If my memory serves, Lady Maude is very much alive. As for me, I'm…." she broke off, Guy's name on the tip of her tongue, but bit it back in time.

"There is of course that obstacle." He pressed a finger to his cheek as if considering. "However, there is nothing to prevent me taking a mistress."

"You cannot be suggesting…." Her voice failed in both disbelief and anger. One look in his eyes showed he was indeed serious.

She gave the hallway a frantic look, but they were virtually alone, apart from Lubbock, whom she knew lurked in the shadows. But could he hear their conversation? She doubted he could hear the conversation above the hubbub of the dining rooms. Even so, he would only intervene if she was physically in danger. Or if she screamed.

Blanden shrugged. "Why ever not? You could even return to Exeter. I could install you in a house in the city." He waved his cane in the air. "Not at Loxsbeare, which would be quite impossible, of course. The situation is not without merit, if you consider you would benefit again from all the things you once enjoyed."

"Except my soul," Helena murmured, clenching her fists.

"I think you'll find your soul will survive, my dear." He leaned closer, his warm breath on her cheek. "In return, I might be prevailed upon to withdraw my petition. You may keep the warehouses and the other property. Your charms would adequately compensate me for those."

Helena closed her eyes, fighting an urge to claw her fingernails down his cheeks. She even conjured the lines of ragged skin and blood welling into the scratches, accompanied by colourful insults that would have shocked her father. Her tongue thickened in her mouth and she couldn't speak. After all this man had done to her family, now he insulted her in the worst way any man could offend a woman.

"Hmm." He tapped her cheek lightly with his cane. "Think about it, my dear. I'll return in due course for your answer. Though I feel we both know what it will be. After all, you wouldn't want to impoverish your brothers, not to mention remain destitute for the rest of your life, would you? Or perhaps Devereux would let you be a serving wench in his tavern."

He wheeled round and strode for the door, pausing on

the threshold with that now familiar smirk. "Good day to you, Mistress Woulfe. I have so enjoyed my visit, which I shall repeat quite soon."

At the click of the lock, Helena's knees gave way in earnest, and she collapsed onto the stair, her blood throbbing in her head while bile rose in her throat.

Chapter 24

Helena retreated to her room, and paced the floor, shifting from fury to repugnance and then back to hatred. She dwelled for a while on revenge too, but knew she would not achieve that unless she foiled Blanden's disgusting scheme. Though how she could do so, and keep possession of whatever she and her brothers had left, was beyond her.

There must be a way. If only her father would come back. He would never have allowed her to be so treated so. He would have killed Blanden first. But then, Father had no idea that he would be betrayed by someone he had considered a friend.

She had barely finished cursing the man, let alone worked out a solution, when Lubbock knocked discreetly at her door to tell her that Guy Palmer had arrived.

"I'll be down in a moment, thank you, Lubbock." She groaned inwardly, wondering how she could possibly act normally in his presence, when their very future together could be threatened.

She tidied her hair and slapped her cheeks lightly to give them colour. Her lips were red and slightly swollen, the result of her having constantly bitten them in the interval since Blanden's departure.

"I didn't expect you to call today," was Helena's unenthusiastic greeting when she met Guy in the hall, only reaching to give him a peck on the cheek as an afterthought.

"I have news which I simply couldn't wait to bring you." He brandished a sheet of stained parchment that looked as if it had travelled a long way. "My Uncle Arthur has written, congratulating us on our marriage."

"That's kind of him." Helena tucked her arm through

his, and drew him into the Devereux's private parlour. "Is he coming back from wherever he is for the wedding?" She took a seat on the chaise, patting the space beside her in invitation.

"What?" Guy frowned, as if caught in mid-thought, then quickly recovered himself. "Ah, no, that's not something I anticipate. He's somewhere near the Cape of Good Hope as we speak. However, he writes to say he has given us his house as a wedding gift."

"House? What house?" Helena sat up straighter. Guy had always lamented his Lincolns Inn lodgings inadequate for a married man, but he had never mentioned a house.

"He bought it from his cousin Roger, with profits from his Africa Holdings." Guy slid onto the seat beside her. "The goldmines there are something he once had in common with the house of Stuart."

"The King has goldmines in Africa? How interesting."

"Not any more, my dear," Guy said with an indulgent laugh.

Helena pursed her lips and narrowed her nostrils. She wished he wouldn't address her like a schoolmaster. He was only a few years older than she. "You mentioned a house," she said with barely restrained impatience.

"I did. It's in King Street, near the Palace Gate."

"King—Barbara Palmer's House?" She gaped. "Lady Castlemaine?"

"Indeed." He read aloud from the page in his hand. Uncle says, "…although the lady has not lived there for over twenty five years, the property still retains a certain reputation, and perhaps some of its former energy, also." His throaty laugh conveyed his avid excitement at this unexpected gift.

"Th-that is indeed very kind." She chewed her thumbnail absently. "You must add my gratitude when you next write."

"It's a most comfortable house." Guy folded the page and stuffed it into an inside pocket, then peered intently into her face. "Not large, but well appointed." He sighed. "My dear, you do seem distracted today. There is nothing wrong, I hope?"

"What?" Helena dragged her thoughts away from her problems and concentrated on his face. "I'm sorry, do go on. You were telling me about the house."

He was such a kind man. Handsome too, and so considerate of her feelings. She liked him a great deal, and fervently hoped her feelings would grow after they were married and got to know one another properly.

"Indeed yes. King Street leads directly into the White Hall palace yard, though the road is only wide enough for a single carriage, so it isn't too noisy. The *Blue Boar Inn* stands at one end, the *Kings Head* at the other, so we are well served with hostelries."

Helena could not decide whether this was an advantage or not. At least she would be able or order an "ordinary dinner" delivered at short notice should her housewifely skills not be up to scratch.

"You seem uncertain, Helena," Guy frowned, peering at her.

"Of course I am. I simply…." Unsure whether she should feel thrilled or disappointed, Helena decided not to appear either. "Guy," she began carefully. "Is your uncle aware of my family—er—circumstances?"

"My dear Helena, Uncle Arthur is as anti-Papist as anyone. Besides, he would never hold a man's politics against his daughter." The implication he might do so if she had been a son went unspoken.

She bridled slightly. "We do not know my father's fate. Should he return to England, I intend to welcome him into my…forgive me…our home, unreservedly."

"Well y-yes, of course, my dear, that goes without saying," Guy stammered, apparently taken aback at her vehemence.

Was his agreement so prompt because Guy did not expect Sir Jonathan Woulfe to ever appear at his door? Did she even have any hope of it herself anymore?

Guy brought the visit to an abrupt close, possibly because she had had to ask him to repeat himself more than once. "May I flatter myself it is our forthcoming nuptials that occupy you?"

Helena looked up. "Um—yes. Yes, that must be why I cannot concentrate. There is so much still to organise."

"Then I shall not keep you. I heard Robert's voice out in a hall a moment ago, so I assume he has returned. I shan't stay, but do give him my compliments."

The door finally closed on him, and Helena released a heavy sigh, then jumped at the sound of Robert's voice. "You decided not to tell him then, my dear."

"I didn't hear you come in." Helena summoned a smile. "Tell him what?"

"About Lord Blanden's visit this afternoon." He strolled further into the room and hovered beside the fireplace.

"How did you know?"

"Lubbock may not always be evident in his person, but he has remarkable ears."

"Did-did he hear everything?"

"He said he was interrupted, but he said something about a petition."

Her breath left her in a rush. Hopefully she could keep the worst of Blanden's threat from him until she devised her strategy.

"I see. And no, I didn't tell Guy. If the petition is successful, I will tell him then."

"I cannot imagine Guy would abandon you purely for not bringing him a dowry, Helena. I believe that young man truly loves you."

His voice held no censure, only understanding, for which she was grateful.

"How could I ask him to support not only me, but my two brothers as well? That wasn't part of our bargain."

"Perhaps not, but—"

"And you, Master Devereux," she interrupted, rising. "Do you relish having a penniless, unmarriageable ward on your hands indefinitely? No, don't answer." She swept out of the room calling over her shoulder, "I don't want to think about the possibility either."

She had reached the hallway when Lubbock stepped in

front of her. He paused, coughed and flapped his hands.

"What is it?" Already irritated, Helena was about to brush past him when he coughed again.

"I'm sorry, Mistress, but Master Henry is here."

Helena gave the empty hallway a swift glance, frowning. "Why sorry, Lubbock. Show him into the salon, I'll be there in a minute."

"He's in the kitchens, Mistress." Lubbock shuffled his feet. "I'm afraid he is somewhat, well…er…in his cups. He can barely stand and has been sick in the scullery."

She closed her eyes briefly, sighing. "Oh dear, not again." She wiped a hand across her brow. "Can you get him up to my bedchamber?"

"Of course, Mistress. I'll get a couple of the serving lads to help."

Helena thanked him and turned for the stairs. What was wrong with Henry lately? Of the two of them, he had been the more pragmatic. He had put the horrors of the rebellion behind him and was making a good life for himself as a capable architect. She had put down the incident at Elias Ffoyle's as an isolated occasion brought on by too much celebrating. Now it seemed his drinking was becoming a habit.

* * *

Samuel and Meghan Ffoyle arrived from Devon with their youngest daughter Deborah, in anticipation of the arrival of their first grandchild.

"Such good fortune they arrived when they did," Amy said to Helena on her first day of her up-sitting at the house in Freeman's Yard. "Because that same night, I barely slept for the dull pull in my abdomen. I didn't understand the import at first, so sent Elias to fetch his mother."

Amy's fair curls bobbed beneath her cap, her eyes alight with excitement as she talked. "Naturally poor Elias was frantic, what with the house filled with my gossips. Then the Dutch midwife had to endure Father Samuel's questioning as to her qualifications," she broke off with a breathless laugh. “Ah, but it is all over now, thank the Lord, and our little Jenet is here at last. The nurse removed the childbed linens this morning, and I am now allowed natural light into the chamber for the first time.”

Helena perched gingerly on the bed. “And how are *you*, Amy?”

“I am perfectly well.” Her stiff tone indicated she had repeated this phrase, often. “Not that anyone will listen. I was permitted a hip bath today, and cannot tell you what a luxury it felt after the poultices and herbal washes the dry nurse brings me. That woman behaves like a constable. Elias has to beg permission to see me, and he pays her wages!”

Helena sniffed, determined not to endure what she saw as barbaric practices when her turn came. The idea of lying in a darkened room on soiled bed-linens for two weeks after childbirth filled her with dread.

“And Mother Ffoyle,” Amy went on with mild resentment, “is too occupied with the baby. Her own and mine.” Amy sniffed. Then her face softened. “Have you seen my baby today?”

“Yours or Mistrcss Ffoylc’s?”

“Mine.” Amy’s hand brushed against her breast, and she winced. “Mother and Father Ffoyle have been wonderfully kind, but I’m counting the days when they return to Ideswell.”

“They mentioned downstairs just now they’re leaving Deborah behind,” Helena warned.

Amy nodded, the arrangement evidently suited her. “Have you seen my Katherine?” she asked again.

“I have, and she is lovely.” Helena lied, sending up a silent wish the pink blob with puffy slits for eyes in the cradle would grow prettier as she grew.

Apparently satisfied, Amy rested back on her pillows with a sigh. Then her nose wrinkled at the sight of the formidable figure of the dry nurse in the doorframe. “One visitor is quite sufficient on your first day, Mistress.”

“Fiddlesticks!” Amy sniffed. “I thought I would die of loneliness up here. And there is a wonderful party going on downstairs that I am allowed no part of." Her eyes welled with tears.

Helena rose and backed away. "I mustn't tire you."

Leaving Amy to the woman's ministrations, she descended the stairs into the hall just as the front door was flung wide, revealing Henry. Doffing his hat, he made Meghan a gallant bow, at the same time pausing to tip the link-boy who had stood between the dirty coach wheels and Henry's new suit.

"My dear boy!" Meghan almost knocked him off balance as she pulled him inside. "You cannot imagine how happy I am to see you. Samuel! Henry is here. See how fine he looks."

"I could not miss the baptism of my first godchild." Henry adjusted his coat with a wide grin.

"I swear sure you have grown a hand span since I saw you last," Meghan cooed, while Henry endured having his cravat rearranged and a tendril of wayward hair tweaked behind his ear.

Helena debated whether or not she should tell her brother about Miles Blanden, but decided not to burden him. She would handle the situation alone.

They joined the rest of the family and neighbours who had come to welcome the new baby in the small but cosy salon of Elias's and Amy's home.

"I hear you were not best pleased about Amy having a Dutch midwife, Samuel," Helena said.

"Licenses!" Samuel scorned. "Granted by the diocesan Bishop, not a doctor at all. And testimonies arc sought not from medical practitioners as to the woman's expertise, but from six honest women who can vouch for their character and moral standing."

Helena looked up to where Meghan approached from the kitchens, a harassed look on her face.

"I hope you aren't upsetting Helena with talk of the king's recent visit to Somerset," she snapped, accusing.

"I've said not a word, Meg," Samuel scorned. "Though I wonder at the purpose of such a gruesome pilgrimage," he murmured "The villagers of Westonzoyland laid planks over the Bussex Rhine, so he could examine the battlefield."

"I didn't know he had gone there." Helena frowned, summoning the faces of Jane and Gil Fellowes and their comfortable house near Weston church, certain they would not have been a part of such a spectacle, at least not willingly.

"His Majesty brought Major Wade with him." Meghan gave a derisive sniff. "He was pardoned in exchange for information, although what that could be…." she broke off as Henry joined them.

"Wade?" His slightly unfocussed eyes raked them all. "He was Father's commanding officer." He drained his glass of wine in one gulp and reached for the nearest jug and poured more.

"I heard an interesting adjunct to the Rebellion story," Samuel began, ignoring Helena's eyebrow gestures in Henry's direction. "That man who murdered Heywood Dare. What was his name?"

"Andrew Fletcher," Henry said loudly, his eyes unnaturally bright.

"That's the man." Samuel held up a finger. "Monmouth sent him back to the ship *Helderenburg* for his crime. Fletcher forced the pilot to steer for Spain." He paused to take a cold pasty from a passing server, studying it before lifting it to his lips.

"You were saying?" Henry said, slurring his words slightly.

"Eh?" Samuel looked up, confronted by faces waiting for him to continue. "I'm sorry, what was I saying? Ah yes, the ship wasn't supposed to go to Spain at all, you know. *The Helderenburgh* was on his way to Carrickfergus to urge a second rising among the Irish Protestants, and to call for Monmouth against the king."

"So the Irish never had a chance to join the rising?" Henry reddened, swaying slightly. "That was three weeks before Sedgemoor. If the ship had reached Ireland as planned…."

Helena placed a restraining hand on his arm. "There's

no point to this, Henry. It's over and done with."

"There might have been a different outcome, but for Fletcher," Henry snarled.

"Would you excuse me?" Helena threw Samuel a hard look, surprised at his insensitivity, and drew Henry away to a quiet corner of the room. He was so volatile lately, and now he had evidently consumed more than his customary amount of wine. Where had this strange anger come from? Since they arrived in London, Henry had been the first to put aside his animosity for what had happened.

"And if Argyll hadn't been captured, and if Lord Delamere had acted as he promised." She lowered her voice to what she hoped was a soothing tone. "And if Gray's cavalry had been better schooled." She stroked a strand of hair away from his forehead. "It's over Henry. We have to get on with our lives."

Henry turned cold eyes on her. "Unless the Prince of Orange invades England, and brings our brother with him."

"Hush, that's Rebel talk!" She shook his arm but he shrugged her off and, with a low groan, made his way toward the table where the jugs of wine were laid out.

"What's wrong with Henry?" Deborah asked, replacing her parents at Helena's side.

Helena shook her head. Whatever it was, she didn't think it was the fate of Fletcher.

"How are you liking London, Deb?" Helena appraised her green silk gown with its yellow échelles that complimented her red-brown hair, and made an effort to stop worrying about Henry, and Blanden, and enjoy the gathering.

"I wanted to talk about the wedding," Deborah said.

"It's not until early November," Helena replied, her gaze still on Henry, who was now flirting with a neighbor's daughter, making her blush.

Deborah frowned. "Oh no, I did not mean your wedding, Helena." Catching herself, she flushed. "Although, I offer my congratulations, of course. No, I was referring to Susannah's. Has Father not told you?" Her face took on a look of mock innocence.

"Has Father not told her what?" Samuel said, returning.

"Susannah is to marry?" Helena looked at Debs, and then back at Samuel, who nodded. "Why, did no one tell me? Do I know the fortunate young man?"

"You do, my dear, and he is not such a young man either," Samuel chuckled. "It is Nathan Bayle."

Helena opened her mouth in a silent "o". The Ffoyles had been in London nearly a month, yet no one, not even gossipy Debs, had mentioned one word about it.

"I think it's a perfect match," Henry interjected, staggering back into the circle, the blushing girl at his side. He gave a loud hiccough, then sniggered, as if his bad manners were a huge joke.

Helena turned on him. "You knew?"

Henry shrugged. "As our family's former servant, Bayle wrote to me out of respect."

"Yet you saw no reason to mention it to me?" Her voice trembled a little.

Henry frowned, as if confused. "It was not my news to give, but as Samuel has made it public, or rather Debs has, I can freely offer my congratulations."

Suppressing a sharp remark, Helena turned to Samuel. "I'm delighted for Susannah. Do give her, and Bayle, my congratulations."

Samuel's steady gaze told Helena he was not fooled by her feigned poise. "I knew her heart had been inclined that way for some time, did not you?"

Helena was about to reply she had had no idea, when an image swam into her head of Nathan and Samuel poring over a pile of ledgers.

"He is somewhat older than her." Samuel twirled a glass by its stem. "Which gave me cause for concern at the outset." He glanced pointedly at his son, who looked away. "However, Nathan Bayle is a fine man and an excellent agent, so the situation suits everyone."

Helena listened to the Ffoyle trio's excited chatter without really listening. On the one hand she was happy for Bayle and Susannah, yet at the same time resentful she had been overlooked. Then another feeling, closer to guilt, that after his devotion all her life and during those days in Weston in particular, she had consigned Nathan Bayle to a time and place she tried not to visit too often. Henry had kept secrets from her too, but then had she not kept the truth of Tobias Lumm from him as well? She still had not come to a decision about Lord Blanden. Days had passed and she had heard no word from him, but knew it was only a respite. She would have to make a decision soon. Feeling sorry for herself, she subjected Henry to her bad temper in the carriage all the way back to Lambtons. He mostly ignored her, as he dozed tipsily in a corner.

* * *

A sharp wind blew between the buildings as Helena stepped onto the street outside Lambtons. Passersby barely paused to acknowledge acquaintances, who hurried between carriages and houses, grimly hanging on to flapping cloaks and lifting hats. The food peddlers and hawkers had left early, most likely searching for warmer alleys and more sheltered squares.

The guard to whom Helena presented herself at the Palace Gate had given her pass no more than a cursory glance. "This way, Mistress," he indicated the path that ran alongside a wall. "I was instructed to show you into the Privy Garden."

He halted beside a wooden door, indicating she must go through. He did not follow but let the door close behind her with a thump. Helena allowed her hood to fall back on her shoulders as she was enveloped in the relative peace and still quiet of the garden, where rows of classical statues draped in Roman robes occupied individual plinths in a patchwork of lawn. She wandered the pathways between them, examining the blank, serene faces of mythical gods and goddesses, imagining their blind eyes gazing into the distance to a place where grapes and olives grew beneath a burning sun.

Fat pigeons strutted across the roofs above her, the air

heavy with the scent of late summer flowers. She imagined the royal family walking in the rooms behind the windows above her.

"Good day, Mistress Woulfe," a voice drawled from behind her.

Helena swung round, her face relaxing into a smile as she bobbed a curtsey. "Thank you for agreeing to see me."

John Evelyn, Keeper of the Privy Seal, immaculate in unrelieved black smiled down at her. Still slender and upright for a man in his sixties, he held a japanned cane in one delicate, almost feminine hand.

"I was intrigued by your note," he said, stepping closer. "I hope you do not mind the location of our meeting. I assumed you might appreciate privacy."

Helena relaxed. "Thank you for your understanding, sir."

"Shall we walk?" He extended an arm and, with her hand on his sleeve, he guided her along a gravel pathway. "I confess I'm not entirely ignorant of the reason for your visit."

Helena stiffened, her gaze on her feet. If he knew about Blanden already, maybe it was too late?

"I presume you wish to discuss the petition, which a certain person has lodged with his Majesty."

"Are—are you familiar with my situation, sir?"

"I am, Mistress Woulfe. Sir Christopher Wren is a close friend, and has a great fondness for your brother, Henry isn't he?"

Helena nodded, relieved.

"This—person seeks to obtain the remainder of your father's possessions in Exeter. Specifically, the property and business interests signed over to Master Ffoyle before the Rebellion." He studied a late flowering rosebush as if fascinated before murmuring, "Have I summarized his expectations correctly?"

"You have, sir. Is there any possibility his Majesty might refuse his demand?" Helena risked a quick glance at his averted face, expecting ridicule. Why would the king refuse to grant one of his own Royal Commissioners what amounted to a traitor's possessions?

A gust of wind swept through the garden, swirling the leaves into a colourful whirlwind. A louvre banged shut on an upper floor.

"Tell me, how is that other brother of yours, Master Aaron Woulfe?"

She whipped her head round and met his gaze, suddenly fearful. Relieved to see he was smiling. "London is a village, my dear. Secrets don't thrive here."

"It was stupid of me to imagine otherwise." Helena relaxed a little. "He's in The Hague, sir, with…." she trailed off as a man in a black cloak, a wicked looking sword at his waist, approached.

Evelyn paused beside a sundial as the man drew near, and tapped the podium with his cane. "This was King Charles's favorite item in the garden, you know."

"I-It's very beautiful." The plain marble column struck her as quite unremarkable. Her eyes followed the figure, who nodded to Evelyn but strode on without stopping.

"Lord Rochester knocked it over once with a somewhat colourful expletive." Evelyn gave a light laugh. "He was drunk, of course. That fellow was always drunk. His Majesty was incensed, as I recall." He lowered his voice. "I believe Aaron Woulfe has plans in respect of the Prince of Orange?" His gaze held hers for long seconds before he gave a slow nod. "Ah! Don't answer that. I can see by your countenance that my source was accurate."

Bile rose in Helena's throat, and the question she did not want to ask burst from her. "Is Aaron putting himself in danger, sir?"

He spread his delicate hands outwards, but did not reply, the answer in his heavy-lidded eyes as they held hers.

Helena pushed herself away from the sundial with a small cry. As if she didn't have enough to worry about.

"You look unwell, my dear." Evelyn took her elbow. "Come, sit. I cannot have you falling into a faint. I'm far too old and frail to catch you." He gave a brittle laugh and guided her to a bench.

Helena fought dizziness, while her companion

occupied the seat beside her, allowing her time to recover.

Her breathing slowed, and she recalled that during his lifetime, this man had seen a king beheaded outside the Banqueting Hall, not far from where they sat. He had endured the Commonwealth, was befriended by Charles the Second, remained in the city by choice during the terrible plague of 'sixty-five, and even witnessed the conflagration that had destroyed so much of it the year after.

Evelyn was known to abhor the religion of the current king, yet remained a loyal servant. Had Helena's own family been as wise as this man and put aside their prejudices, how different their lives would have been. Feeling more in control, Helena twisted on the bench so she could see Evelyn's face. "What should I do to protect my brother?"

Evelyn stroked his chin. "I admit His Majesty's favoritism of Catholics is a cause for concern. My position here, and indeed that of many Anglicans, is at risk."

"I understand, sir." She folded trembling hands in her lap and stared off angrily. Why did Aaron have to be such a principled fool?

"I knew Monmouth, you know, Mistress Woulfe."

"Yes. You told me at the Twelfth Night party at Lambtons." Helena watched as courtiers wandered the paths and talked together, an occasional high-pitched laugh floating across the garden.

He turned to her in surprise. "I did?"

She nodded. "Master Evelyn, who are those people?" The group listened intently to a gesticulating man in a pale brown wig and elaborate suit, as if what he said was of paramount importance. Two footmen stood a little way off, while another liveried man held two small dogs on leads.

Evelyn followed her gaze. "Ah, that, my dear, is King James. Our second Sovereign of that name."

The king. The man whose army had killed her uncle, the reason her father could not come home, and an indirect cause of her mother's death. He was why Aaron was still abroad and not here, safe.

Her jaw tightened, and she forced herself not to grind

her teeth, remembering with a wry smile her father's warning that she didn't want to end up with a wooden set.

"The lady beside him is Queen Mary Beatrice." Evelyn whispered "Do you think her beautiful?"

Helena looked at the tall, dark woman, evidently a foreigner, whose hand rested possessively on her husband's arm. "Indeed, although her silks, furs and jewels make a significant contribution to that beauty."

Evelyn gave a gentle laugh.

"Who is that man beside his Majesty? The handsome one on the left, in the black peruke?"

Evelyn's gaze rested on the man. "That is the Chief Chancellor, Lord Jeffreys."

An involuntary shiver went down Helena's back, and gathering her skirts, she rose from the bench. "I must go, sir." She hesitated, regretting her impulse. He had still not told her what might happen with Lord Blanden's petition.

Evelyn held up a restraining hand. "I doubt they have an inkling of who you might be, Mistress."

The party wandered off through a doorway, and Helena sank back onto the seat again. The footman with the dogs lingered while the spaniels sniffed around the path, though in seconds, they left too.

"Am I a threat to them, Master Evelyn?" The thought gave her a modicum of satisfaction.

"Your brother might be, although the king has far more weighty personages to worry about." Catching her expression, he went on quickly. "I suggest you write to Aaron and advise caution."

"About taking action against the king?"

"About whom he tells that he is taking action against the king."

Helena almost laughed. There was no judgment in his advice. In fact, he appeared almost sympathetic. "I doubt he would listen to me in any case. My brother is foolish, impetuous, and headstrong. He has not given a thought to how this may affect me, my brother Henry, or…." She held her hands up in a helpless gesture. "However there is a more urgent matter."

"Lord Blanden, yes I am aware of him," he said slowly, staring off, his eyes narrowed.

Helena's eyes swam with unshed tears. Was she asking for too much?

He exhaled noisily, his hands braced on his thighs as he pushed himself to his feet, his extended arm toward her. "Now, let me escort you to the street and summon a hackney."

All the way back to Lambtons, Helena could not fathom out whether he had agreed to help her or not.

Chapter 25

"Thank you, Lubbock," Helena said, trying to stop herself shaking as Lord Blanden was shown into the small salon. "We shan't require any refreshment. His Lordship won't be staying long."

"A pity." Blanden's irritating smirk appeared. "I was hoping you might at least offer me some of Devereux's wine. He keeps a good cellar, I'm told." He neither bowed, nor did he accept her silent invitation to sit. Instead he toured the room, his cane held to his bottom lip while he examined the furniture and pictures on the walls.

"An excellent one, sir," Helena said, silently promising herself he would never enjoy anything at Lambtons. Least of all the wine.

"Business has kept me busy in the city this last week or so." He continued his slow tour of the room, passing close to the chaise where Helena sat, her fists clenched on the upholstery. "Or I would have come sooner. In face I've an appointment with the Chancellor Jeffreys this afternoon to discuss a certain petition." He circled the chaise and paused beside her.

Not daring to look at him, Helena closed her eyes and swallowed, fighting to keep her breathing even. He gave off a fusty odour of badly-stored clothes, combined with an earthy smell of male sweat and ale.

"I take it you have had sufficient time to consider my proposal?"

"I have, sir." Her stomach lurched, and she pressed a hand to her abdomen in an effort to control the roiling inside, convinced he must hear it. "I don't think we would suit." She glanced at the clock while at the same time fingered the note in her pocket. He said he would be here. Where was he?

"Come now, Helena," Blanden's use of her given name set her to grinding her teeth. "I think you are teasing me. But then women like to be persuaded, I find. After all, what choice do you have? He reached out a hand and traced the line of her jaw, then his fingers slid down her neck and onto the bertha tucked into her bodice, tugging it gently.

Helena froze, unable to protest or even slap his hand away, enraged at his presumption. The fact that he took his time and actually chuckled, evidently relishing her discomfort, made her want to thrust him away and scream that he was a monster. Her bravery deserted her and she could only swallow and will him away.

When she didn't respond, he laid the cane on the floor and took the seat beside her, his chin lowered to just above her shoulder. "I did not take you for a cold woman, my dear. And the prospect cannot be so unwelcome. After all, I am a lusty, full grown man, knowledgeable in the ways of women." He gave another chuckle, this one low and menacing. "A better one than my mealy-mouthed son would have made, that I can promise you."

Her shock overruled her horror. "How could you talk of your own dead son in such a manner?" Blanden went to take her hand in his, but she snatched it away. "A boy he may have been, but he was a good soul. Kind and gentle."

"He was a disappointment," he sniffed. "I, however, will not be."

Helena held her breath, wondering how long this farce would have to continue. Then the corner of the curtain twitched and she smiled. Gathering her courage she turned her head and stared into his eyes. "You already are, My Lord."

"You disrespectful wench!" His mouth curled into a sneer as he grasped her upper arms in both hands and swivelled her roughly towards him. "For that, I'll make sure I ruin your brothers and I'll have you anyway. Then I'll—"

He broke off as the curtain over the door was swept aside and Robert advanced into the room, John Evelyn and Alyce behind him. They still wore their outdoor clothes, which told Helena Lubbock must have warned them at the door that Lord Blanden was already here.

"I see you wasted no time, sir." Robert removed his gloves slowly, looking meaningfully at his own hands.

Helena squirmed and rolled her shoulders out of Blanden's hold and rose, backing away from the chaise, and stood next to Robert.

"I-I was merely paying Mistress Woulfe a call." Blanden stood, tripped over the cane he had placed on the floor, and staggered slightly.

"As what, sir?" John Evelyn asked. "An old family friend?" The Devereux husband and wife advanced on Lord Blanden like wolves circling their prey. "I think not."

Blanden bent to retrieve his cane. On the upwards movement his gaze flicked to Evelyn, and froze in recognition.

"Not leaving so soon, My Lord?" Alyce asked, striking Blanden's cheek with her fan so hard, it left a red mark, but he seemed too astonished to react. "Did you imagine Helena to be alone and friendless in London, sir?"

"I-I have an interview with the Lord Chancellor." Flustered, Blanden attempted to circumvent Robert, who sidestepped him, bringing him up short.

Blanden turned to his other side, only to be halted again by Evelyn. "I believe, My Lord, you have been busy lodging petitions?"

It's perfectly valid," Blanden almost whined. "The property is rightfully mine, and…."

"Stop blustering, man." Robert took a step toward him. "You're a liar and a villain, and you will get no more of Sir Jonathan's possessions."

Robert and Evelyn had deliberately positioned themselves far apart, which meant he had to constantly shift position as they took turns to talk in order to face his questioner.

Evelyn stepped away and behind Robert's back he directed a slow, knowing wink at her, which sent a ripple of warmth through Helena's veins, like brandy on a cold day. Her ragged nerves settled, and she breathed normally again.

Helena realised she had been foolish to be so frightened of Lord Blanden. He was no threat to her. He was simply a greedy malcontent who took pleasure in browbeating women. He could not even be true to his own faith. Robert had discovered that, to ingratiate himself with the king, he had publicly converted to Catholicism. She wondered what his associates in Exeter would think of that.

"I've perused the document, My Lord." Evelyn's tone made the last two words an insult. "In my position as Privy Seal, I decree it holds no merit. Therefore I have refused it."

"But—His Majesty…." Lord Blanden spluttered.

"The King will not even see it, sir." Evelyn's voice was like a whip, slicing through the man's protests. "It is over, My Lord."

Narrowing his eyes, Blanden gave a guttural snarl, his black cane tapping rhythmically into the palm of his hand as he glared at each of them in turn.

Lubbock was either listening at the door, or his reputed psychic powers were not fantasy after all, as he chose that moment to fling open the door. He immediately stepped to one side and bowed an invitation for Blanden to leave.

Left with no choice, Blanden strode to the door, turning back on the threshold. "I'll be lodging the petition again in Exeter," he growled as he swung on his heel, waving the cane at them. "I'm an important man. The Magistrates dare not ignore me."

"You would be advised to look to what you have already acquired by treachery, Lord Blanden." Robert called after him. "Your ill-gained wealth can be lost just as easily."

The door swung shut with a resounding bang, and a smirking Lubbock retreated in the direction of the kitchen.

"Are you quite well, my dear?" Robert asked.

"I thought you were never going to get here," she said, weak with relief. Then louder. "Thank you, Master Evelyn."

Evelyn flicked a thick lock of his peruke over one shoulder, his thin lips curling in a mischievous smile.

"You're quite welcome, Mistress Woulfe. I have to say I quite enjoyed that."

"We couldn't locate that damned petition at first." Robert's eyes beseeched her to excuse the expletive.

"I had my entire office turned upside down, but we found it in the end," Evelyn said. "Don't worry, my dear," he continued when Helena took in a quick breath. "I ensured the thing was destroyed, and no record of it remains."

"I had no idea you were aware of Blanden's threat." Helena blinked back tears. "I had decided to solve the problem alone, or rather with Master Evelyn's help."

"Couldn't leave things as they were," Robert slapped his gloves against the palm of his hand. "Not when you were so distressed the other day. Evelyn told me you had gone to see him. I insisted he tell me what it was about. Damned blackguard." At Evelyn's start he rushed on. "No, not you, sir. That Blanden fellow. Though I was a trifle disappointed he did not put up more of a fight."

"Even so, I'm grateful to all of you. Especially you, Master Evelyn."

"You are most welcome, my dear." Evelyn made a courtier's leg in acknowledgement.

Helena smiled, but she was still uneasy. Lord Blanden hadn't been all bluster when he informed on her father, nor was he a coward when he demanded Judge Jeffreys hand him Loxsbeare. She shivered, telling herself it was simply a reaction to seeing him again. "What if he does present his petition to Exeter?" She broke off, unable to voice her worst fears.

"Oh, I doubt he will receive a sympathetic hearing," Evelyn said airily, offering Alyce his arm. "Not when it has already been rejected here. I shall send word to the City Magistrates to inform them of the fact."

"That is settled then." Alyce tucked Helena's arm beneath her elbow. "Let us go in to a well-earned dinner and forget all about Lord Blanden. I simply do not wish to hear the man's name mentioned again."

"Neither do I," Helena whispered.

Robert halted her with a hand on her elbow. "Helena, when I came into the room, did I misinterpret what I saw?"

For a long moment as she stared into his sympathetic eyes, tempted to tell him about Blanden's proposition.

She summoned a bright smile. "He won't bother either of us again." She tucked her arm through his, hoping she was right. "Let's go into dinner. I'm quite ravenous."

* * *

Helena leaned her hands on the wooden sill, breathing the sharp night air through the open window. In only her linen shift and underskirt, she waited for Chloe to arrive and help her dress. The cold had dampened the worst of the coal smoke, and she didn't mind the winter wind that tugged her unbound hair away from her face.

From downstairs came the bustle and clattering of the cooks and serving men as they prepared her wedding dinner. Since morning, daylight had strained through a layer of yellowish cloud drifting northward from the industrial city fires south of the river, the cobbles slick with ice that clung treacherously, thawing during the day to freeze again as the temperature dropped near dusk.

The inn lamps had been lit, throwing a welcoming glow onto the darkening street.

Pitch torches flanked the door in preparation for the guests, who would have to pick their way through a layer of grimy water between their carriages and the main door. The larger dining hall was shut off from the curious public for the nuptials, and, by evening, the intense cold had dampened down the worst smells of the city.

Helena looked at a small canvas propped up on her bureau depicting a scene of Exeter's North Gate with the road leading up to the Weare Cliffs, a view Helena knew intimately. The letter that came with it sat at her right hand, and she read the most interesting part again.

Dear Helena

I hope you will accept this gift to remember me and

your home city.

I relate here a strange tale of your former home, which may interest you. Lord Blanden has complained for months about disturbances in the property at night, which have increased in frequency since he returned in such sour spirits from London.

His lady's screams brought him running in the middle of the night, armed with a loaded musket. He fired at what he describes to anyone who will listen as a white apparition.

When the house was roused and the candles lit, there was nothing there, not even bloodstains.

More rational citizens suggest that Blanden's frantic shot went wild and the intruder fled, but his lordship swears he aimed true. Blanden claims it was a demon; one that couldn't die and would be returning to kill them all.

Now everyone talks of Blanden's ghost with a wry smile and sage nod.

He isn't seen much in the city now and even his servants have deserted him, which is no more than he deserves for the way he treated the Woulfes. His Catholicism is a particular cause for censure, as is the sad-looking old priest living at Loxsbeare.

Go into your marriage with an easy mind, dear sister, and be happy.

Your loving brother, Tobias.

Be happy. Could she dare expect such a blessing? Wasn't it enough to have the chance of a secure home with a man who gave every indication he cared for her and would be kind? Did being happy simply mean not being miserable? Or was there more to it? She shivered, wrapping her arms around her upper body, but it was not the night air that turned her blood cold. *I wish Mother was here.*

A sigh of disapproval and the distinctive scent of bruised roses reached her, announcing the arrival of Alyce. "What have I told you about unhealthy practices, my dear? The night air is most injurious to your lungs." She sailed across the room and slammed the window shut, muttering darkly.

A smile tugged at Helena's mouth; she had never been able to explain to a city dweller like Alyce that sometimes, she longed for the clean air of Devon and would dream about filling her lungs with the scent of cut grass and damp leaves.

Alyce turned from the window, her wired fontange tilted forward from her crown with ribbon bows and lace, a new fashion she carried off beautifully.

"There is something I need to discuss with you, Helena," she said, arranging herself on the chaise at the end of the Helena's bed. "I regard you as my own daughter, and as such feel I owe you a certain courtesy."

"How kind," Helena murmured, surprised. Alyce had never sought her out this way before. Her gaze drifted to a brown, leather-covered book in Alyce's hands. Oh no, not Mistress Hannah Woolley? Amy Ffoyle dragged her copy out at every opportunity, regaling Helena with the woman's wisdom for young housewives.

"I know what you are thinking." Alyce smirked. "And no, this is not the scribbling of that jumped-up lady's maid with literary ambitions. My dear, this is a far more interesting work. It is called Aristotle's Masterpiece."

"I don't think I am familiar with it." Helena frowned.

Alyce's eyebrows rose. "I would be most surprised if you were. This book…" She patted the leather with affection, "…contains all a woman should know when they become wives. Or mistresses," she added mischievously.

Helena's cheeks flamed. "I-I appreciate your sentiments, Mistress Devereux, but—"

Alyce interrupted her. "I don't deal in sentiments, as well you know. This," she slapped the cover affectionately, "is a font of knowledge for an inexperienced woman." She paused to fix Helena with a hard stare. "I presume you have no knowledge of men?"

Helena gasped, horrified. "Never!"

"Not even with that young man, Blanden, was it?"

"We were no more than children."

"That is no safeguard in my experience." Alyce sniffed, flipping the pages. "This part here will be of especial interest to you as a maiden."

Helena caught a glimpse of something she never imagined to see on a printed page, and certainly not on her wedding day. "There are—drawings." She sucked in a shocked breath.

"My dear," Alyce gave a long-suffering sigh. "Later tonight, you will be expected to know something of what is laid out here. You should at least be forewarned."

Helena opened her mouth to protest, but Alyce held up a hand. "There's nothing more disconcerting to a red-blooded man than a shrinking virgin. His pleasure will be quite spoiled if he has to make explanations and calm ragged feelings."

Helena swallowed. "Er—I feel sure Guy will make my duties in that direction clear when we…."

"Huh! Then you will be more fortunate than many women. Oh, don't glare at me with such an injured expression, Helena. It will not harm you one whit to read what Aristotle has to say."

Helena's curiosity battled with her embarrassment, but before she could decide how to react, Alyce slammed the book shut, and rose. "Well, no one can say I did not try, but if you choose to walk into marriage with the ignorance of a lamb, I refuse to take the blame for any anguish that might be caused."

"Don't go, Alyce. Maybe I was a little hasty. May I at least see?" What was it she was asking to see?

Alyce inclined her head, sniffed and resumed her seat. "I can spot Guy's ilk at a glance," she gave a musical laugh. "He'll need encouragement."

"What sort of encouragement? "Helena asked nervously.

"He needs to know you aren't hostile to the physical side of your duties."

"I-I have made it clear I shall be his true companion," Helena stammered, hurt.

Alyce regarded her with sympathy. "He doesn't want a companion, my dear, he wants a lover."

"But I am to be his wife, not some tavern girl!"

"Ah, that is where so many young women misjudge the nature of marriage. You should be civil and respectful towards him in the public eye and a saucy, forward wench in the bedchamber."

"Are you sure?"

"I know what I know. Now…" she softened her tone, "as a gentleman, Guy would not expect you to have the proclivities of a courtesan."

"Would I knew what those were, I might anticipate married life with a little less apprehension." Helena surprised herself at her sharpness. She had never admitted, even privately, that the prospect of married life sometimes filled her with stomach-wrenching dread.

"Then, my dear, I and my friend Aristotle will show you."

Together, they leafed through the pages Alyce enthusiastically, Helena with shaking fingers. "See here, for instance." Alyce ran a finger along a line of text. "*A wife must never be sorrowful or despairing when she lays with her husband as should she conceive, the child would have a malevolent temper.*"

Helena frowned. "Could that be true?"

"It would certainly explain the disagreeable character of some of my acquaintances." Alyce's laugh came again. "The knowledge that their parents conceived them in sorrow makes me less inclined to dislike them so much." Her exuberant mood was so infectious, that Helena found herself laughing with her.

"And what of this, Mistress Devereux?" Helena asked, *"That man derives much more satisfaction in the embraces of a loving wife, than in the wanton dalliances of a deceitful harlot."*

"As to that," Alyce gave a knowing smile. "I would not place all my faith in Aristotle's wisdom."

Helena suppressed the smile that tugged at her mouth and turned the page slowly. "It appears most of this advice is aimed at those seeking to begin and keep a pregnancy, as if that were the only purpose of marriage."

"It is the reason for life after all," Alyce's face lapsed

into seriousness. "Apart from one's duty to God, of course."

"Oh, yes of course I didn't…." Alyce's gaze met Helena's, her lips twitched and as one, they both burst into spontaneous, raucous laughter.

The heady excitement of being part of the world of married women and their secrets banished all traces of Helena's embarrassment. Being Guy's wife was in reality far more than playing housekeeper in his house and the preparation of his meals, stuff of girlish fantasies compared with what Alyce was showing her.

"And this is all quite necessary?" Helena asked, their reading finished.

"More to be aspired to, rather than necessary. Such devices will contribute much to his pleasure, and to yours."

"Mine?" Helena lifted her eyebrows in surprise.

"Of course." Alyce's eyes sparkled mischievously. "If you imagined physical pleasure is solely a man's domain, then you've been sorely deceived."

"Not so much deceived as kept ignorant," Helena said, halted by the appearance of Chloe, her pale eyes fixed nervously on the chatelaine of Lambtons.

"Ah, here is your maid, come to dress you for the ceremony." Rising, she hefted the volume into her arms, her eyes dancing with mischief as she delivered her parting shot. "I shall see you later, my dear, but remember, Aristotle and I will be waiting should you ever need us again."

* * *

Helena woke the morning after her wedding in her husband's arms, lying within the warm darkness of the closed bed hangings, not daring to move in case she woke him. Through a chink in the fabric, she saw it was not quite light outside. She teased the hanging closed again with a bare foot shutting out the frigid cold of the room.

Guy moved in his sleep, his rough chin rubbing against her forehead. She smiled, recalling the power that had been hers mere hours before.

Fortified by some of Robert's excellent wine, and using phrases she had never used before, she had submitted to his embrace with uninhibited delight and curiosity.

Disjointed images replayed in her head of pale skin glowing red from the firelight, their combined taut, urgent hands pulling and kneading, his broad, naked shoulders and the swish of sheets combined with the low creak of the bedframe beneath her.

She had observed his responses in an almost detached way, marvelling as his eyes grew smoky and his breathing quickened to an urgent moan in response to her fingers exploring his bare skin.

She gazed at the prone figure beside her, his arm heavy across her hip, and tried to identify what is was she felt for this man, who was to be her companion *tell death did them part.*

No desperate longing tugged at her heart, nor did the prospect of his absence fill her with dread, but there was safety and warmth in his presence. Revelling in their new-found intimacy, she ran her hand across his naked shoulders, stroking the soft hair at the nape of his neck.

Recollections of their first night together sent ripples of warmth into parts of her body she had barely been aware of before. She hoped it would all be repeated, and often. She stretched luxuriously under the coverlet, whispering to herself, *thanks to Alyce and the wisdom of Aristotle, I am truly his wife now.*

"Is something amiss?" Guy groaned sleepily into her shoulder.

Helena smiled. "Nothing at all, husband. Everything is as it should be."

The End

Also available from Books We Love

Book 2 The Goldsmith's Wife

As a Londoner constantly drawn back to the city, Anita connected with its history at a young age. When the rest of the school trip were busy throwing the contents of their lunch boxes across the school coach, Anita daydreamed about men in high white wigs, long coats and petticoat breeches climbing into sedan chairs on the cobbles of Paternoster Row, where the sight of Christopher Wren being lowered down the outside of the half built St Pauls Cathedral in a basket was a daily occurrence.

Author's Note

As part of my research for this book, I visited the Blake Museum in Bridgwater, which contains memorabilia of the Duke of Monmouth and the Battle of Sedgemoor.

A guide sat in a corner of the room, dressed in the uniform of Monmouth's army and when I identified, correctly, a uniform of one of "Kirk's Lambs" on display, the guide stared at me levelly and said,

"We don't talk 'bout him round 'ere."

They have long memories in Somerset.

 # Salute to Thomas Rainborough, a popular Leveller leader and sailor, murdered in 1648

** 1675 the Duke of Monmouth, an excellent rider and sportsman, had carried off the international plate at the St Germain horse race.*

The Woulfes of Loxsbeare continues with Helena Woulfe's story in London, where life alters for everyone after the Glorious Revolution.

EMAIL: akdvsn@yahoo.co.uk
BLOG: http//thedisorganisedauthor.blogspot.com
FACEBOOK: http//www.facebook.com/anita.davison?
GOODREADS: http//www.goodreads.com/AnitaDavison
TWITTER: @AnitaSDavison

bookswelove.com

23170500R00164

Printed in Great Britain
by Amazon